A LITTLE SECRET

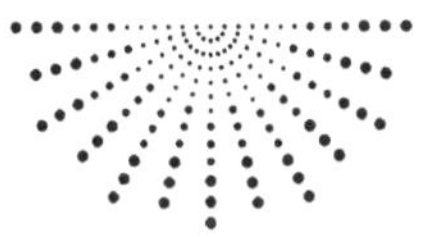

KELSIE RAE

TWISTY PINES PUBLISHING, LLC

DISCLAIMER

DISCLAIMER CONTAINS SPOILERS

A Little Secret involves a character with epilepsy. Her seizures are described in detail and may be triggering for some people. A Little Secret also includes a miscarriage which is described in detail and may be triggering for some people.

A Little Secret
Cover Art by Cover My Wagon Dragon Art
Editing by Wickedcoolflight Editing Services
Proofreading by Marjorie Lord
Published by Twisty Pines Publishing, LLC
September 2024 Edition
Published in the United States of America

To all the girls who love a good secret...

Family Connections

Colt & Ashlyn
(Don't Let Me Fall)
Jaxon
Griffin
Dylan

Biological Siblings
Colt & Blakely
Theo & Macklin

Theo & Blakely
(Don't Let Me Go)
Ophelia
Tatum

Macklin & Kate
(Don't Let Me Break)
Everett
Finley

Henry & Mia
(Don't Let Me Down)
Archer & Maverick (twins)
Rory

PROLOGUE

GRIFFIN

A few years ago...

"Well, would you look at that." I pull Finley into a hug, realizing the girl barely reaches my armpit. "You shrunk."

My best friend's little sister has always been short. Or maybe the age gap has always been too big, and now that I'm officially a senior in high school and have hit a few growth spurts, she'll never catch up.

This doesn't mean she hasn't changed since I last saw her, though. The baby fat from her face is missing, making her look older and more mature. Her mascara makes her gray eyes pop even more than I remember, too. And, thanks to her braces being removed since the last time I saw the girl, her smile is whiter and brighter than ever. Simply put? My best friend's little sister is fucking gorgeous.

Craning her neck up at me, Finley arches her brow. "I grew two inches since the last time you saw me, thank you

"

very much. You just happened to grow a foot. That's a *you* problem, not a *me* problem."

My mouth twitches. "Like everything else in the world. Right, Fin?"

She grins. "Exactly."

And just like that, my childhood crush flares to full force. I've always had a thing for Finley Taylor. I won't ever do anything about it, especially after my half-assed comment in the car with Ev earlier. He's my best friend *and* Finley's older brother. I'm not gonna lie. I was curious if time and distance would affect my attraction to her. All it took was two seconds to debunk the theory, leaving it dead in the water.

"Hey, man, I'm gonna shower, then we can go out," Everett announces beside me. He had to pick me up at the airport straight from hockey practice, thanks to my flight's early arrival. After I jokingly asked if he'd be cool if I took Fin on a date while I was visiting, he shot me down flat. I figured he'd watch me like a hawk while I'm here, so the fact he's willing to leave me alone with her while he showers must prove he bought it. That I was lying. That I didn't mean it. And maybe I didn't. Maybe I shouldn't. I shake off the thought and tuck my hands into my jean's pockets.

"I'm sorry. Did you say you want to go out?" Finley interjects. "You two are gonna ditch me? Rude."

"We could always stay in," I offer. "Play a game or something, then go out tomorrow night?" I turn to Ev. "Not gonna lie. I'm pretty wiped."

Like the Fourth of July, Finley's stormy, almond-shaped eyes light up. "I am a hundred and ten percent on board with this idea. I'll get the cards."

As she darts away, Everett squeezes the back of his neck and watches her go, calling out, "I didn't say yes!" She doesn't even bother acknowledging him. Shaking his head, he turns to me. "I'll be back in ten. You good?"

"Yeah, man. I'll hang out down here."

"Not gonna hit on my sister, right?"

I lift my hands in defense. "It was a joke."

"A bad joke." He shoots me a glare, but it soon turns into a smirk. "I'll be down in a few."

The stairs creak beneath his weight as he strides up them, leaving me alone in the family room. I've been here a few times. The place is nice. It reminds me of their cabin back in Lockwood Heights. Same massive fireplace in the family room. Same epic kitchen. The only real difference between the cabin and this place is the location of the bedrooms. At the cabin, they're on the same floor. Here? I glance at the staircase where Everett disappeared when Finley appears a few seconds later.

Flashing the red deck of cards in her hand, she asks, "Wanna play BS?"

I nod. "Yeah, sure."

She motions for me to sit on the leather couch as she kneels at the coffee table and begins splitting the deck in two, leaving five cards in a separate pile. BS, er, Bullshit, is a simple card game. The goal is to get rid of your cards as quickly as possible by playing one or more cards face down in the center of the table and stating which cards you played. The player can either tell the truth or lie through their ass about which cards they play. It's the opposing player's job to decide whether or not the person is lying. If they decide you're full of shit, they call it out. If Bullshit is called, the cards are shown and one of the players winds up taking the cards. First person to get rid of all their cards wins.

"So...I heard about the Tornadoes contract," Fin says,

mentioning the NHL team I signed with last week as she deals the cards. "Congratulations."

"Thanks."

"Are you sad you're gonna have to play against Ev's team? I heard the Rockets are pretty badass."

I shrug. "Not too worried about the Rockets, since I have a few years until I'll have to think about it. For now, I'm gonna focus on college and LAU, where I get to play with Ev, so…"

Ev and I have both been accepted to Lockwood Ames University, along with the rest of our friends, and damn if I'm not excited to play hockey and share a place with everyone. Me, Ev, Mav, Archer. It's gonna be amazing. As for our NHL contracts? Well. We'll get there when we get there.

"Good point," Finley offers. "Can I tell you how jealous I am that he gets to move back to Lockwood Heights while I have to stay here in Boringville?"

With a low laugh, I reach for my half of the cards and begin sorting them by number. "Come on, this place can't be that bad, can it?"

"Debatable," she humphs when a phone buzzes. I check my cell to see if it's mine, and Fin does the same. Taking her cell from her back pocket, she nibbles the edge of her bottom lip, fighting a shy smile as she looks at her notification. The sight pulls in my gut, and my brows dip.

"Who are you texting?" I ask.

She glances up from her phone, but her attention falls right back to the screen. "Hmm?"

"I said, who are you texting?"

"Oh, a guy from school."

"A guy from school, huh?" I scoot off the couch and onto the floor beside her. As if she has something to hide, she pulls her phone closer to her chest, her thumbs flying across the screen. Curiosity piqued, I tilt my head. "I thought this place was Boringville."

Her lips purse. "Okay, maybe there's a perk or two around here."

Dylan, my little sister and Finley's best friend, mentioned Finley found a guy friend at school. I assumed he was gay, but all it takes is one look at the girl in front of me to piece the truth together.

She's interested in him. Really interested.

"You sure you're old enough to be dating?" I ask.

She shoots me a look. "I'm sorry, are you my father or my brother's best friend?"

"Hey," I protest. "Give me a little more credit. I thought we were friends, too."

Her gaze narrows, and she studies me carefully.

"What, we're not friends?" I challenge. Fuck, it shouldn't hurt, but, uh, what the hell?

"I mean, you're more like a pain in the butt," she offers dryly, "but I guess I'll let you claim the title."

"Gee, thanks."

I almost forgot how sassy she is. The girl has had no filter since before she could walk. I should know. We've known each other our entire lives. Everett's my best friend, but with him a little older than me and Finley being Dylan's age, I always considered myself her friend, too. Only seeing them a few times a year since their mom took a new job far away from everyone else caused more than physical distance. They say absence makes the heart grow fonder, but where this girl's concerned, it only leaves me on edge.

With a wry grin, she bumps her shoulder with mine. "I'm teasing. You know you're my favorite, Griff." Phone buzzing, she looks back at the screen, distracted again.

Favorite, my ass.

"So, has Ev kicked the shit out of your little friend?" I prod.

"No." She rolls her eyes, hits send on whatever response she'd typed, then sets her phone face down in her lap. "Not yet, anyway."

I chuckle softly. "Does that mean I get to do the honors?"

"Pretty sure it's never been your job, either."

"Oh, it isn't?"

"Nope. Besides, you're too nice to beat up some guy all because he thinks I'm pretty."

My heart thumps faster. "He thinks you're pretty?"

"I mean, all guys think I'm pretty." She tosses her long dark hair over her shoulder and tacks on a pointed look. "Right?"

I don't know how she does it. How she rides the line of being annoying and arrogant and sassy and cute as a fucking button.

"Yes, you're very pretty, Fin." My attention falls to her pouty lips for a split second, but I quickly pull my head out of my ass, reminding myself where the hell I am and who the hell I'm talking to, adding, "And humble."

She laughs. "You know me too well. But even if you didn't, my point stands. Friends don't beat up other friends' boyfriends." Hesitating, she glances at the cards lying on the white oak coffee table. "Friends *also* don't get mad at other friends when the first friend ditches the second friend to hang out with a guy…"

My eyes bulge. "You're ditching me for this guy?"

"I mean, ditching is probably a strong word."

"It was your word, not mine," I counter.

"Okay, you make a good point, but regardless, I'm not ditching you. I'm…thinking about taking a rain check on the game."

"Thinking about it, huh?"

She grimaces, her nose scrunching. "Maybe?"

Maybe.

Maybe means yes. The realization shouldn't be a hit to my ego, but it is. I know I'm only her brother's best friend, but I haven't seen this girl in months, and she's ditching me for a guy she could see every other day of the week? What am I? Chopped liver?

"What's his name anyway?" I ask.

"Drew."

"Drew," I repeat.

"Yes. Drew," she volleys. "What, did I stutter?"

No, she didn't. The girl doesn't stumble over anything. Nah, she charges in full force with zero hesitation, wearing her confidence like a second skin and doing nothing half-assed. Including dating, apparently. The idea shouldn't bother me, but it does. And I don't exactly care to witness it firsthand.

"And this...Drew"—my expression sours, and I lean into it, hoping she buys the response as over-the-top sarcasm or some shit—"is better company than me?"

"I mean, I get to kiss Drew without the guise of a bet, so I'm gonna go with...yeah." She winks. "He's a lot better company than you." Her smile stretches. "He's also a better kisser." My jaw drops, pulling a laugh from her until she waves me off. "Okay, okay. If it makes you feel any better, I was his first kiss, so I basically taught him all he knows. And in a weird way, I have you to thank for it."

"That doesn't make me feel any better at all," I counter, remembering the last time we played Truth or Dare and wound up kissing. It wasn't much—barely a peck. But I could've sworn she lingered, and damn, if the memory hasn't been taunting me for months.

"Why?" Finley asks. "Because I passed along all the

knowledge I gained from our kisses during Truth or Dare to the guy who sits by me in English?"

"You saying I was your first?" I ask.

"Technically, Chad Godfrey in kindergarten was my first, but sure." She squeezes my forearm and bats her long lashes up at me. "I'll let you claim the title."

"Friend and first kiss," I muse, cocking my head. "Yet here you are, ditching me."

The girl has the decency to look contrite as her teeth dig into the inside of her bottom lip. "Like I said, ditching's a strong word."

"Still doesn't make me feel any better," I grumble.

"Of course it doesn't. Didn't make Ev feel better, either," she adds with a laugh. "Don't worry, though. Between Ev, you, and the rest of the guys, my expectations on how I deserve to be treated are through the roof, and I think you'd approve of him."

Seriously. What the hell happened while I was away? I stare at the cards, forcing my grip to loosen so I don't crumple the shit out of them as I clear my throat.

"Him," I repeat.

"Yeah. Drew." She rolls her eyes again. "Keep up, Griff."

"Sorry, I guess I didn't picture you as someone who'd be interested in dating and shit."

"I mean, maybe not the shit part yet, but yeah. I guess I am interested." She scoots closer. "Anyway,"—her lips brush against my cheek—"it's good seeing you again. I've missed you."

The feel of her mouth against my skin fucks with my head, making my jaw tighten. I shouldn't crave it. Hell, there's nothing to crave. She's a friend. Only a friend. Not even a friend, apparently. Just Everett's little sister. Turning my head, I take in how close she is. How easy it would be to capture her mouth with mine. To make her stay. "Missed you, too, Fin."

"I'll see you later, okay?"

"Yeah, for sure." She stands, and I watch her walk toward the front door. "Keep it PG, all right?"

"Yeah, okay, *Dad*." Wiggling her fingers back and forth as she walks out the door, she adds, "Toodle-oo!"

CHAPTER ONE

FINLEY

A few years later...

It shouldn't bother me.

It. Shouldn't. Bother. Me.

For the thousandth time today, I open my phone and look at the random girl's Instagram post with Drew. My boyfriend. Long-term boyfriend, actually. We've been together for almost four years. She tagged him in it. That's how I found the photo. And I hate it because the stupid picture is *just* incriminating enough to mess with my head but innocent enough to pass off as an overreaction if I decide to freak out about it.

Which is exactly what I did thirty minutes ago.

To be fair, Drew and I have been having a lot of overreactions and freakouts lately, so I'm pretty impressed with my current restraint. I could've called him and ripped his head off personally. Instead, I punched my pillow a dozen times, screamed until my lungs ached, and seriously considered cutting bangs.

I didn't, but the day's still young.

I tap the edge of my cell against my chin.

To call or not to call. That is the question.

Part of me believes overreactions and freakouts are inevitable when it comes to long-distance relationships. The other part? Well, I can't help but wonder if it'll always be like this. Fight and make up. Fight and make up. Except the fights are becoming more frequent, and the making up is more difficult thanks to the thousands of miles separating us.

It wasn't always this way.

Drew was my safe space. My best friend.

Well, other than Ophelia and Dylan. But those two are more like my sisters. We were raised together, becoming three peas in a pod, thanks to our parents. They all went to the same college we attend, Lockwood Ames University, and they weren't kidding when they promised to be friends forever. Most of my childhood memories involve Aunt Mia, Aunt Ashlyn, and Aunt Blakely in one way or another. The sentiment extends to their husbands and kids. We aren't all technically related by blood, but I still call them my family.

My mom and dad moved us away from everyone else because of my mom's job when I was a teen. It was easy to feel lonely when they uprooted me and my brother, Everett. I was convinced I'd never forgive them for taking me away from Lia and Dylan.

Then I met Drew.

I touch the screen again, and my phone lights up, showcasing my boyfriend next to someone who most definitely isn't me. They're at a bar. Her arms are looped around his neck, and his hand is on her waist as they smile at the camera. It's enough to make a person pause, especially a girlfriend who's across the country from her boyfriend starring in said picture. AKA *me.*

My nostrils flare, and I hit Drew's name, dialing his number.

It rings three times, then goes to voicemail.

Throttling my phone, I push his name again and bring my phone to my ear.

Ring. Ring.

"Hello?" Drew croaks.

"I'm sorry. Did I wake you?" I snap.

A groan echoes through the speaker, followed by the sound of rustling sheets. "What did I do now?"

I squeeze my eyes shut and let out a slow breath. "Who's @mollie69?"

Another groan follows my question. "Fuck, Fin. It's too early for this."

"It's almost noon," I remind him.

"Yeah, well I was out until almost four in the morning, so you'll have to cut me some slack."

A bitter laugh escapes me. "You're not helping your case."

His sigh is weighted and borders on annoyed. I don't blame him. I'm annoyed with both of us.

"Mollie's just a friend, Fin."

"Just a friend," I repeat. "Why'd she tag you?"

"Because we're *friends*," he emphasizes. The word grates on me, and so does his tone. Like I'm the one in the wrong. The one walking on thin ice.

"Is this the same Mollie you drove home a couple weeks ago?" I ask. "The one giggling in the background?"

"Fin," he mutters. Damn, I can almost taste his annoyance. "Can you please…not give me shit for once?"

I hate how he does this. How it's always my fault. Then again, he clearly thinks I do the same thing to him. Maybe I am. If the roles were reversed, would I respond differently?

Would I expect him to respond differently? I don't even know at this point.

Closing my eyes again, I try to cool down. To get ahold of my frustration. To wrangle my acid tongue and all the damage I know it's capable of if I let loose. If I speak my mind. If I abandon the filter I've worked so hard to cultivate. But Drew? He's making it…difficult.

"Listen, I'm not trying to give you shit, Drew—"

"I'm allowed to have friends," he grits out.

Friends. Is that what the kids are calling it these days?

Pinching the bridge of my nose, I bite my tongue, forcing myself to choose my next words carefully. "I know you're allowed to have friends, but…"

"But what? She's attractive, so I can't hang out with her?"

My chest squeezes, and I rub at the ache. "So, you find her attractive—"

"Fuck, Fin," he snaps. "I'm hungover. I'm tired. You woke me up—"

"Did you kiss her?"

"No, I didn't kiss her, all right? Where's the fuckin' trust, huh?"

I lean my head back and suck my lips between my teeth. I want to trust him. I do. And I probably should. He's never cheated. I know he hasn't. But this is hard. It's hard being this far away from him when we spent years together. Years. Going to the same high school. Sharing most of the same classes. He was my first. He's my only. Sometimes, I miss the way things were. Before college. Before the distance. Before the snippy conversations and the fighting and the awkward pauses and the…life we've both built over the last few months. Without each other. While attempting to cling to the high school daydreams we wove together on late nights and early mornings.

It's confusing and overwhelming and exhausting.

So. Damn. Exhausting.

"Drew…"

Another tired sigh greets me. "What, Fin?"

"Do you think we should…" I gulp past the lump in my throat. "Do you think we should take a break?"

"Are you kidding me?" he demands. "No, I don't want to take a break. Fuck, Fin." A long pause follows his curse. "You're not allowed to be mad at me. Not when you post pictures of Griffin every fuckin' day!"

"What are you talking about?"

"You and Griffin," he spits, mentioning my older brother's best friend and my current roommate, thanks to our living situation.

Yeah, I didn't exactly plan for my kitchen to catch fire when I first moved here, but here I am, living with my brother, his friends, and Dylan until the renovations are finished. But I don't really see how Griffin and my living arrangement has anything to do with Drew and his so-called *friend.*

With a huff, I ask, "You're seriously bringing Griffin up right now?"

"Yeah. Yeah, I am," he seethes. "You're not allowed to be mad at me for hanging out with a group of people, one of which is Mollie when we both know you share a fucking wall with Griffin."

He's right. I do share a wall with Griffin. Well, technically, I share a floor slash ceiling with him since I'm currently staying on the second floor of the same house, but toe-mae-toe, toe-mah-toe.

It's not like I chose to be here, and even if I had, Griffin and I are a different story compared to Drew and @mollie69. We were raised together. We're friends. We were friends long before I even knew Drew existed.

Nothing has ever happened between us other than a few silly Truth or Dare encounters, yet it's always Drew's go-to whenever he's in attack mode, which, apparently, is right now.

"We've already had this conversation," I remind him.

"Yeah, well, you called me, so…"

"Why do you care about Griffin so much?" I say, exasperation tainting my words. "He's just a friend."

"So is Mollie."

"Mollie's different," I argue.

"How?" he demands. "How is she different?"

"Because you've met Griffin!" I shove my long, dark hair away from my face. "You know him! Hell, you took me to homecoming this year and shared a freaking limousine with him and his date!"

"Yeah, which means I know how he looks at you—"

My irritated laugh cuts him off. "He doesn't look at me!"

"Yes, he does," Drew yells. "He looks at you like he wants to fuck you, Finley, and then you go and post pictures of you and him together. How do you think it makes me feel, huh?"

Is he serious right now?

My nostrils flare, and I take a deep breath. "I post pictures of me with *all* my friends," I point out. "Mollie *only* posted a picture of you and her!"

"Seriously, Finley?" he spits. "We're gonna argue semantics right now? Do you have any idea how infuriating you are?"

I grind my teeth and push to my feet, pacing my room like a caged bull. "By the sound of your voice, I'm going to say *very*."

"Yeah," he grunts. "Very. But my point stands. If I can't be mad at you for being best fuckin' friends with your hockey boy, then you can't be pissed at me for going out with Mollie as friends."

"So, what?" I toss back at him. "You're saying I can't be friends with Griffin?"

"Yeah, you know what? That's exactly what I'm saying," he rushes out.

My lips part on a gasp, and my spine straightens.

Is he serious?

Damn you, mouth!

My heels dig into the plush carpet, and I take another deep breath. "Drew." My tone is softer now as I try to steady my breathing. I feel…blindsided. Off-kilter. Sucker punched.

We've had this conversation too many times to count. I know it. He knows it. But cutting someone out? Someone like Griff? Someone I've known my entire life?

His silence hangs in the air while my lungs struggle to work.

"Drew, you can't be serious," I force out.

"You know what?" He pauses. "Yeah. Yeah, I'm fuckin' serious. I don't want you living with him. I don't want you talking to him. I don't want you being friends with him." The words are spoken like a lash, whipping against my skin, making me flinch.

"Drew, I can't…I can't cut him out of my life."

"Why not?"

"Because he's Everett's best friend," I remind him. "His little sister is my best friend and roommate once the renovations are finished. It's not like Griff and I have a class together, and I can simply…sit somewhere else." I hesitate, attempting to even fathom how I would go about Drew's ridiculous proposition before remembering how impossible it really is. "Drew, our entire lives are literally entwined. Like, what do you want me to do?"

"I want you to tell him you can't be friends with him anymore."

"You're joking." I squeeze the bridge of my nose again and fight off my pending headache. "Tell me you're joking."

"What's there to joke about?" he asks. "If you're gonna call me up and be pissed about Mollie, then—"

"Fine," I snap. "Fine, you can hang out with Mollie."

"Oh, so you're saying you don't care about Mollie anymore?" he challenges.

"I'm saying I can't cut Griffin off, and if you're going to compare the two, then fine. You can hang out with Mollie."

"No," he decides. "No, you don't get to do this. You don't get to twist shit around and decide you're fine with me hanging out with Mollie all because your precious friendship with Griffin—which is fucked up, by the way— is on the line."

"So, what are you saying?" I ask. And I hate how I can feel it. The familiar weight. The heaviness. The charge of this conversation. The question is…is this it? The moment he ends things, and we're over? I've thought about it. I'm not going to lie. I even suggested it two minutes ago. Long-distance relationships suck. But it's Drew. My Drew. Mine.

"I'm saying I love you," he murmurs, "and your friend-ship with Griffin bothers me. Just like how my friendship with Mollie bothers you." His tone is softer now, but it doesn't ease the rigidity in my muscles or the way I want to cry and scream and throw something.

"Did you cheat on me?" I whisper.

"I would never cheat on you, Fin." He's so resolute. So matter of fact. "I'm not just saying it, either. I promise I would *never* cheat on you. You're my forever, baby."

I close my eyes again, letting his words wash over me.

We've said them a thousand times. Made promises we both had every intention of keeping.

We *still* have every intention of keeping.

"I love you, too," I whisper. "And I would never cheat on you, either."

"I know you wouldn't," he answers. "But I'm still not comfortable with your friendship with Griffin. I know you think he only looks at you like you're his friend, and maybe it's true, but it's still torture for me. Knowing he's close to you. Knowing I'm not."

I hate this, too. That I get it. I understand why my friendship with Griffin would bother him. He's Griffin. He's the captain of LAU's hockey team and looks hella good without a shirt on. He's also thoughtful and friendly and sweet and dedicated and…my brother's best friend.

"I don't know what you want me to do," I murmur.

"I know you can't avoid him entirely," Drew admits. "I know you live together until the renovations are finished, but…if you could at least set some boundaries," he offers.

"I've set boundaries," I remind him.

"Yeah, well, maybe you could set some more."

Defeat settles in my bones like a bag of bricks, and I press my fingers to my lips, staring out my bedroom window without seeing anything at all. Not really. Nothing but the future I've built, the one I've dreamt about, with someone asking me to do the impossible.

"What would you like me to do?" I ask.

"Tell him you can't be friends with him anymore. As far as you're concerned, he's friends with Everett, not you. It's what you've been insisting with me anyway, right?"

Yes. It's what I've insisted for years, even if it isn't entirely true. Sure, there's nothing but platonic love between me and Griffin, but…I do care about him. He's one of my best friends. The idea of hurting him to protect my relationship with Drew feels…wrong. Especially when Drew's being a controlling dick about the whole thing in the first place. There are boundaries in every relationship, and he's dangerously close to crossing one of mine. I don't like being controlled, and I sure as shit don't like being told what to do. But it also feels wrong ending things with Drew over a stupid Instagram post.

When did this get so hard?

"And your friendship with Mollie?" I push.

"Dead in the water. Promise."

My teeth dig into the inside of my cheek, and I clear my throat. "I'll think about it."

"Finley—"

"Take it or leave it, Drew. You're on thin ice as it is."

He sighs. "Fine. Take some time to think about it."

"I will."

"Good," he grumbles.

"Good."

"Good."

With nothing left to say, I end the call.

CHAPTER TWO

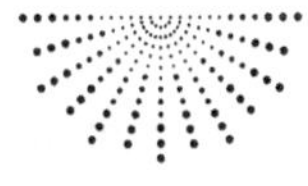

FINLEY

I send a text to my friends' group chat, telling them I need a girls' night, and because they're amazing, they get the ball moving. Ophelia's already waiting with our drinks when we head inside SeaBird. It's an amazing bar close to LAU and one of my favorite places to hang out. It has well-priced drinks, good food, awesome music, and just enough notoriety to bring in fresh faces every time we come. It doesn't hurt they got rid of the flashing lights a few years after my mom graduated, so I don't have to worry about my epilepsy being triggered, either. Reeves got all of us fake IDs after I mentioned how impressed I was with the one he'd given Dylan when they first started seeing each other. And even though I don't drink and only use the thing to gain entrance to bars, it's come in handy more times than I can count, and tonight is no different. Ophelia, on the other hand, has no issue using hers to get alcoholic beverages, though she's never had an issue keeping things in check. She has a fruity drink in front of her, along with two more matching beverages and what looks like a Diet Coke beside them. Yes, the girl knows me well.

When she sees us, she stands from her barstool and waves. "Hey!" Ophelia passes around hugs like they're confetti, then offers each of us a drink, mine being the Diet Coke with zero alcohol. "PS—Maverick says he should get a free shot to Drew's balls since we're ditching him tonight."

I laugh at the mention of her boyfriend's name and his lack of invitation, answering, "Nope. Drew's balls are mine to squeeze or caress, thank you very much."

"Caress?" Dylan snorts. "Ew."

"Hey, no kink-shaming," Ophelia quips. "Whatever floats your boat. Right, Fin?"

"Mm-hmm," I hum as I take a long sip of Diet Coke. "Though there will be no caressing anytime soon, I'll tell you that much."

"Are you gonna tell us what happened?" Raine prods. She's the newest member of the group. The only girl I haven't known for years. I like her, though. She's good for my brother even if they aren't official...yet. No, instead, they're pretending to be dating in hopes of keeping her abusive ex away from her. By some miracle, it's working. If it wasn't, there's no way I would've brought her here without my brother or any of his friends for backup. I might be brash, but I'm not stupid.

Even so, her question makes me roll my eyes. Part of me wants to pretend my fight with Drew never happened. That everything is great, grand, and wonderful when it couldn't be further from it.

I could use their advice, though. Even if the entire situation makes me feel...stupid. Her question rings in my mind again as I weigh the pros and cons. Am I gonna tell them what happened?

"Not until everyone's had at least three drinks so they don't judge me too harshly," I decide.

"You sure you'll even remember the story at that point?" Raine teases.

It's funny. How an off-hand joke can be such a stark reminder of our lack of history and how little she really knows about me. I smile around my straw. "I don't drink, so I think I'll be fine."

Her brows jump. "You don't drink?"

"Nope."

"Good for you."

"Meh. Don't be too impressed." I lift my glass and head toward one of the open booths as the rest of the group trails behind. Once we're all settled, I add, "I have epilepsy, and alcohol can be a trigger, so…yay me."

Tilting her head, Raine looks at me again with newfound curiosity. I guess I understand why she's so confused. Most people don't talk about neurological diseases as openly as I do. And maybe I wouldn't either if my mom hadn't been such an amazing example. She also has epilepsy and taught me to embrace it instead of sticking my head in the sand like she did for years until she met my dad and he helped her understand it's okay. It's okay to have epilepsy. To know your limits and accept them instead of pushing yourself to do more than you're capable of or to pretend it doesn't exist in hopes of making those around you more comfortable. Yeah, I have my dad to thank, too. Want to talk about a fantastic support system? Those two have mastered the craft. And so, even though epilepsy has an ugly side, I've accepted its part in my life. The good. The bad. And the downright ugly.

"You have epilepsy?" Raine asks.

With a syrupy sweet smile, I confirm, "Yup."

"I had no idea."

"Most people don't." I shrug and take another sip of my Diet Coke. "Usually, it's not a big deal, but if I decide to drop to the ground and start convulsing, maybe call my brother."

A surprised laugh slips out of her, and she shakes her head. "I'll keep it in mind."

I grin back at her. "You're a peach."

Looking at Ophelia, Raine hooks her thumb toward me. "Does she always talk this candidly?"

Ophelia leans closer and drops her voice as if we're discussing conspiracy theories. "You have no idea. Speaking of which,"—she clears her throat and palms her glass, giving me a pointed look—"I'm ready for all the reasons why we hate Drew."

And just like that, my amusement dissipates, and I stare at the caramel-colored liquid in my glass.

"Only I'm allowed to hate Drew," I defend. "Because on the off-chance I don't rip his balls off and decide to marry him, I still need you ladies to be my bridesmaids one day."

"We'll be your bridesmaids regardless of who the groom is," Dylan chimes in. "Now, what happened?"

Digging through my purse, I take my phone out, unlock the screen, then slap it on the table. "A girl tagged him on Instagram."

They all lean closer to look at the photo, but I don't. I only stare at my glass, well aware of what they see.

Ophelia and Dylan share a grimace as Ophelia pushes the phone back to me.

"Did you ask him about it?" Dylan questions.

"Yes," I huff. "He swears they're only friends, and maybe they are, but…"

"But something feels wrong," Raine finishes for me.

Swirling the straw in my drink, I nod slowly. "Yeah. And I don't know if it's in my head or if it's real, but when I asked if he wanted to take a break, he got pissed at me for even mentioning it, promising he loves me and only me, and he's been nothing but loyal the entire time we've been together, and it would be nice if I could show some trust instead of freaking out over nothing."

Ophelia gasps. "He said all that?"

"Yup." I bring the straw to my lips and steal another long drink of Diet Coke.

Lia's lips bunch as she watches me from across the table while Raine asks, "Do you believe him?"

It's a good question. One I've asked myself a thousand times since hanging up the phone this morning, er, afternoon.

"I *want* to believe him," I murmur, hating how much truth and vulnerability lie in the simple sentence. "I mean, he's been busy, but I've been busy, too, you know? I'm not stupid. I know a relationship goes both ways." I hesitate, and my face scrunches. "God, and then he accused me of having feelings for Griffin. Can you believe it? He said if I can post pictures of me and Griff, he should be able to post pictures of him and his"—I lift my hands and do air quotes—"*friend* without feeling like I'll jump down his throat. And then, I'm like...yeah. He's got a point, you know? I hate when he gets all weird and jealous whenever I talk about me and Griff, but we've been friends for forever, so it's not like I can just...cut him out."

"Is Drew asking you to cut my brother out of your life?" Dylan demands.

My expression falls, and I twirl the straw in my glass again, unable to meet Dylan's gaze. I don't want to disappoint her. I don't want her to lose respect for me or Drew. I don't want to deal with any of this, if I'm being honest. Griffin is her brother. Of course she's going to be pissed at me for even considering Drew's request. If Reeves, Dylan's boyfriend, asked her to cut Everett off, I'd backhand him for being a controlling asshole. Yet, here I am, allowing Drew to do the exact same thing. "Maybe."

"You can't do that," Dylan pushes. "You guys live together, he's like family—"

"I know." I sigh, pick my phone up again, and check the screen despite my best intentions. Yup. There he is. Looking right as rain next to a girl who isn't me. I set my phone back on the table, my stomach churning. "And I also know I'm done thinking about all of this. Someone take my phone. Actually, someone take all the phones."

I push my cell into the center of the table, and the rest of the girls follow suit.

With a smile, Ophelia opens her clutch, confirms the phones are on silent, slips them inside, and closes it up. "There."

"Thank you." I smile at Ophelia and take a deep breath. "Now…what do you say we dance?"

I'M NOT SURE HOW LONG IT'S BEEN SINCE WE WALKED ONTO the dance floor, but Ophelia and Dylan are bombed, and Raine looks pretty buzzed as well. Tipping her head back, she belts out the lyrics to the song blaring from the speakers, and I join in, singing at the top of my lungs. The words probably shouldn't resonate as well as they do, but hey. At the moment, I hate guys as much as the next girl, so sue me. Clutching her stomach, Raine cackles at my dance moves when someone slips in behind her.

"Hey, pretty girl," the stranger says.

"Yo," I snap. "We're having a girls' night, can't you tell? Now, get outta here!"

"Aw, come on," he replies. "We're only here to dance. Promise."

Gag.

Boys and their promises.

"Uh-huh, and I'm the queen of England, now, if you'll excuse us." I reach for Raine's arm, then grab a stumbling Dylan with my opposite hand, leading us to a different spot as Ophelia trails behind. The song changes to something less I hate men and more love is great, yadda, yadda, yadda.

Baloney.

Shaking it off, I sway my hips, grateful the guy didn't follow us as I get back in my groove.

Groove?

Blah. I sound like my mom.

"Hey, pretty lady," someone says behind me.

A pair of hands find my hips, and I peek over my shoulder. Tall. Broad shoulders. Round face. Gages. I'd give him a solid four out of ten on the attractive scale. Not that it matters. I couldn't be less interested in the opposite sex if I tried, and the fact that he's touching me? That he thinks he's allowed to touch me? I should knee him in the balls right here. Right now. Add to the fact he used the same hey pretty something as the guy from five minutes ago, and it makes the whole situation even less genuine and more cringy.

"Seriously?" My nose scrunches. "Is that like a new pickup line or something?"

The guy's brows furrow. "Huh?"

"Never mind. Now, if you could skedaddle so I can have my girls' night, that would be great."

"Aw, come on. My buddies and I just wanna dance."

"Buddies?" I challenge.

He tilts his head toward the same guys from two

minutes ago who have somehow managed to create a half-circle around us, their eyes eager and their mouths practically salivating at the prospect of letting them dance with us.

"I'm sorry. Do you not speak English?" I twist in the stranger's grasp and jab my finger against his chest. "I'm. Not. Interested."

His mouth lifts. "You're feisty. I like it."

"You know what else you're gonna like?" I ask. "My knee to your balls if you don't take your hands—"

"Hey, Pickles!" someone calls.

I glance across the dance floor, finding Reeves, Dylan's boyfriend, flanked by Everett, Griffin, and Maverick.

Well, what do you know?

If Dylan's surprised to see her boyfriend here, she doesn't show it. With a smile, she returns, "Hey, Ollie. Perfect timing." She turns to the guys bugging us. "Have you met my boyfriend, Ollie?"

"Nah, I don't think we've had the pleasure yet," Reeves states as he moves in even closer.

"Lucky man," one of the strangers offers to Reeves, perusing the rest of the girls like he can have his pick.

Ha! Not a chance, dipshit.

When his gaze lands on Ophelia, Mav steps around Reeves, and Lia darts toward him like a bunny on crack, wrapping her legs around his waist and kissing him. "You've been here the whole time, haven't you?"

"Looks like I've been caught red-handed," he confirms.

Butthead.

I asked for one girls' night, yet here he is, stalking his other half like a lovesick puppy.

Pathetic.

Adorable but pathetic.

Oh, who am I kidding? Why does everyone have such a cute relationship except me?

"I knew that was your bike in the parking lot!" Ophelia adds with a squeal.

Mav chuckles dryly. "You really thought I'd let you come here by yourself without me?"

"Mm-hmm."

She kisses him again as the stranger turns back to Raine. "Now, where were we?"

"You were just leaving," she reminds him sweetly.

"You sure?" he challenges.

Her eyes lock with my brother's over her shoulder. "Pretty positive, actually. Right, *babe*?"

Babe?

Interesting.

Everett steps closer, hooks his fingers through the belt loop on her pants, and tugs Raine into him, bringing her back to his chest as he gives the stranger a death glare. "I think it's exactly what he was doing."

It'd be cute if he wasn't my brother.

To be fair, I always knew he'd be an awesome boyfriend. Even if the title is fake for the time being.

"Another one bites the dust," the last dumbass taunts, but he doesn't give me an inch. If anything in his grip on my waist tightens. "And then there was one."

"Wrong again, buddy," Griffin says. "This one's taken, too."

I stare at Griff, my tongue growing a bajillion times its size as I take in his lopsided grin and easy stance. Like he couldn't be less intimidated even if he tried. The red fabric of his shirt stretches around his biceps and chest. White-washed jeans hang low on his hips. He looks like the boy next door. Effortlessly sexy with all the time in the world. When I realize I'm most definitely checking him out, my cheeks heat, and I tug my long, black hair over one shoulder. I mean, I'm a red-blooded human with eyeballs. How can I *not* notice he's sexy as hell? Especially when he goes into fix-it mode with a side of cocky. Like, hello. He's talented. Respectful. Easy-going. And we've played this game so many times. Where he swoops in to play the heroic boyfriend anytime a guy is too handsy or direct. It's never meant anything. Only an easy out. But it feels wrong this time. Like I'm betraying Drew by playing along.

Am I betraying Drew by playing along?

I don't...I don't know. And I hate how I don't know.

Why'd you have to get in my head, Drew? Why'd you have to make me do this?

Even though it kills me, I shift away from the stranger but keep my distance from Griffin, too.

"Griffin's right," I announce. "My boyfriend might not be at LAU, but he *would* care if he knew anyone here was trying to dance with me."

"It's only a dance," the stranger argues.

"Then I'm sure you can find a different partner." I tuck my hair behind my ear and avoid Griffin's astute stare on the side of my face. "Now, if you'll excuse me."

Then, I get the hell out of there.

CHAPTER THREE

GRIFFIN

What the hell?

I rush after Finley as she darts through the crowded bar. To where? I have no clue, and I'm not sure Finley knows where she's going, either. Just…away. From me.

When we reach the hallway leading to the bathroom, I manage to catch up and ask, "Hey, you good?"

Finley freezes and looks down at my hand wrapped around her bicep. Fuck, I didn't even notice I grabbed her. Not roughly, mind you, but still. Forcing my fingers to relax, I lift them one at a time from forefinger to pinky, ignoring how soft her skin is, and let her go as the crowd moves around us.

It isn't the first time I've offered a helping hand to Finley when it comes to the opposite sex. Nah, screw that. It isn't even the hundredth time. At this point, it might be the thousandth. And even though I've never crossed the line with her, Fin's never been one to shy away from flirting or pretending we're together if the situation called for it.

So why the hell did she run tonight?

She looked like she wanted nothing to do with me. Like I was a fucking pariah or some shit. Hell, if my friends weren't here to step in, I would've played the doting boyfriend for any of the girls tonight, so what's Fin's problem?

"You good?" I repeat.

Eyebrow twitching, Finley whispers, "Yeah, I'm good."

It's a lie. We both know it. Or maybe we don't. Maybe I can read her better than she can even read herself. It's not surprising, considering the girl in front of me.

"Fin," I warn, then glance toward the crowded dance floor. "What the fuck was that out there?"

"It was nothing."

"I was only messing around," I argue.

"I know."

"Then why are you lookin' at me like this?"

"I'm not looking at you like anything," she whispers.

"You're right. You're not looking at me at all," I growl, moving closer until she's practically pinned between me and the rough brick wall as the bar continues filling with people. "What's going on? Did Drew do something again?"

She rolls her eyes. "Griff—"

"What did he do, Fin?" I demand.

"He did nothing, all right?"

"Then what's wrong?"

"Nothing," she repeats. But her exasperation does me in. It taints her words, giving me way more information than she's probably comfortable with. It's always been this way with Fin and me, though. And maybe it's normal. Inevitable, even. To know someone so wholly after being raised together. To be able to read their thoughts as easily as your own after spending so much time together. And right now, something is off. Yeah, she might not admit it, but something is very wrong. I just don't know what.

Regret floods through me as I squeeze the back of my neck, hating how uncomfortable she looks. Like she wants to be anywhere but here. With me.

"Did I cross a line?" I ask. My tone is softer but just as weighted.

Her gaze flicks to mine, and the pain in them? The fucking indecision? It shoots straight to my chest.

Fuck. She's hurting.

Why are you hurting?

I replay what went down a few minutes ago but come up empty. Again.

"What's goin' on, Fin?" I push.

"I, uh,"—she stares at the ground—"I don't want to do this here."

Ignoring the warning bells going off in my head, I step closer until her back hits the wall. "Do *what* here?"

"Griff—"

"Say it, Fin."

Her gaze darts up to mine. "I can't be friends with you anymore."

The words hit like a sucker punch, and I jerk back. I expected…something, but I never expected this. Not after everything we've been through. "What?"

"I said,"—she takes a deep breath—"I can't be friends with you anymore."

"Why the hell not?"

Her tongue darts out between her pretty pink lips as she squares her shoulders. It'd be comical if her words weren't a knife to the ribcage. "Drew and I, we both think—"

A bark of laughter escapes me. "Are you serious right now?"

Mother. Fucker.

I knew he had something to do with this. I fucking knew it. That controlling asshole has been the bane of my existence since the moment Finley gave him her number all those years ago. How does she not see it? How does she not realize how fucking toxic he is for her? The guy has made her cry more times than I can count, yet she still bends over backward at every. Fucking. Whim. Which honestly, considering the backbone on this girl, makes zero sense at all.

Is she really this stubborn?

"Griff." She touches my arm, but I shift away from her.

"Of course, he has something to do with this." I scrub my hand over my face. "Of course he does."

"Look, you have to understand where he's coming from," she begs. "If you had a girlfriend who was really close with a guy—"

"We've been friends forever," I remind her. And I mean it. Literally. Since the day her brother and I were born, we were inseparable. Then Finley, Ophelia, and my little sister came into the picture, and the saga continued. Some families are tight. Ours? Ours is steel. Not just woven together but hammered into one. One family. One unit. Unbreakable. Unwavering.

Her attention falls to her feet, and a glint of hope ignites inside me.

Maybe.

Maybe I can get to her.

Maybe I can help her see how shitty he is for her. Now, he's asking her to give up relationships for him? It's bullshit. She has to see this.

Doesn't she?

Nostrils flaring, I exhale slowly, trying to keep my frustration in check as I repeat, "We've been friends *forever*, Fin."

"I know," she whispers. But she doesn't look at me.

Why won't you look at me?

"You think we can just…shut it off?" I squeeze my hand into a fist at my side. "We live under the same roof, Fin. We attend the same family functions. My best friend is your older brother, and your best friend is my little sister." I lean back on my heels, giving her space and taking in her profile as she stares blankly in front of her like I'm not even here, and fuck if it doesn't sting. "You really think you can avoid me?" I ask. "Write me off like I'm nothing? Like our relationship is nothing?"

"We can…we can keep our distance for a little while, you know? Nothing crazy—"

My scoff cuts her off. I drop my head back and stare at the ceiling, attempting to get a handle on shit, but the girl's making it difficult.

"I love him, Griff," she whispers.

The words scrape against my skin like sandpaper, and my head falls forward. How does she not. Fucking. See it?

"Have a good night, Fin." I push away from her, then head toward the exit, knowing she won't even bother to watch me walk away. Why would she? Her boyfriend forbade it.

Bullshit.

CHAPTER FOUR

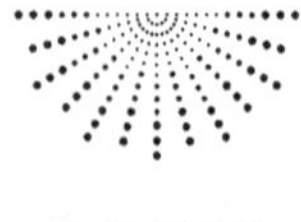

FINLEY

"Don't freak out, don't freak out, don't freak out," I whisper. The test wobbles against the edge of the porcelain sink as I set it down and push my hair away from my face.

I'm late.

It isn't entirely out of the ordinary, thanks to my medication, but I can still feel it. Like some weird sixth sense. I feel…different. And maybe it's some strange mother's intuition or something, but I feel like I already know… I already know the truth. It makes me want to puke.

"Don't freak out, don't freak out, don't freak," I repeat. It's been my mantra since I realized my period was late, but I haven't had the ovaries to buy a test until today. After my friendship breakup…*thing* with Griffin, I bought a ticket and flew out to see Drew. I wanted to reconnect, and I'd say it was great if I wasn't currently hiding in my bathroom, trying not to have a nervous breakdown.

I can't be pregnant.

I can't be.

Bouncing on the balls of my feet, I lift my head toward

the ceiling and shake my hands in front of me, trying not to have an absolute meltdown in the middle of my bathroom. Er, my brother's bathroom. Hell, it's not even his. Technically, I'm pretty sure this is Reeves' bathroom since he's the one who lives across the hall with Dylan, but who needs labels anyway?

My kitchen caught fire a few months ago. It practically burned the entire main area to a crisp, forcing me and my roommates to find a new place to stay until renovations are finished. My roommates are Dylan and Ophelia. Well, kind of. Initially, they were my roommates. Then Ophelia fell in love with Mav, and Dylan fell in love with Reeves, and blah, blah, blah. One thing led to another, and I'm pretty sure they still would've moved next door to be with their boyfriends even if our kitchen hadn't burned to a crisp.

Now here we are, all scrunched on one side of the duplex. Dylan and Ophelia don't mind, though. Not when they can sleep in their boyfriend's rooms and practice making babies like a bunch of jackrabbits. It doesn't make me feel like the fifth wheel at all, especially when my own boyfriend is thousands of miles away.

Yeah. Not gonna lie. Even if things are pretty good on the boyfriend front lately, long-distance relationships suck. Even the term "sucks" doesn't carry enough weight, but I'm too anxious to think of a better metaphor. I wipe beneath my eyes and let out a slow breath.

Especially now.

Now, my long-distance relationship *really* sucks.

As I reach for the pregnancy test, a loud knock on the door makes me jump, and the stupid thing clatters into the sink.

"Shit."

"Ev?" someone calls. Griffin, I think.

"It's Finley," I correct him. "I'll be right out!"

He doesn't answer, but I hear his fading footsteps as he leaves me alone.

We haven't talked since that night at the bar, and to say things are strained would be a massive understatement.

He hates me.

I can't even blame him for hating me.

A small part of me hates me too.

Another knock shakes the wooden door. "Fin?" Dylan calls.

Without looking at the result, I shove the test into my back pocket and cover the stick with my thick gray sweater. "Be right out!"

"Hurry! I want to say goodbye before we leave."

They're flying to Cancun. All of them are. Everyone but me. It's lame and disheartening, but I've tried not to dwell on it as I rinse my hands under the faucet, wipe them on the towel, and open the door.

Dylan's blonde hair is pulled into a high ponytail, her glasses propped on her cute little nose, as she grins back at me. "That was fast."

"I don't want you to miss your flight." Pulling her in for a hug, I squeeze her tight. "Don't have too much fun without me, okay?"

"On one condition," she replies. "Promise you won't kill Frankie."

My shoulders hunch, and I let her go.

Frankie, AKA my nemesis.

I know what you're thinking. Finley, you're so delightful. How can you have a nemesis? Honestly, it's pretty easy when the said culprit is covered in mucus, has green skin, a long, sticky tongue, and is *just* unpredictable enough to make any sane person queasy. Emphasis on the *sane*.

Crossing my arms, I pop out a hip and counter, "I make no guarantees."

"Finley," Dylan warns.

My badass facade crumbles, and I press my hands in a prayer gesture. "Please, please, please don't make me watch Frankie. I'll do anything, I swear!"

"I'll bring you the best souvenir, I promise." She squeezes my hands and lowers them. "But you can't kill him."

"What if he gets loose?" I ask. "What if he jumps on me or licks me with his sticky tongue?" A shiver runs down my spine.

"He's not going to lick you," she argues then hesitates. "Okay, he actually might, but only if he thinks you're his food—"

"Dylan!" I screech.

"You'll be fine. And remember, frogs are friends."

"Frogs are disgusting."

"Disgustingly adorable," she corrects me with a grin.

Seriously. I love Dylan. I do. But I still can't believe she let her boyfriend gift her a frog this Christmas when we both know I'm absolutely terrified of them. Actually, now that I think about it, he likely got her the frog because I'm terrified of them.

Bastard.

Not that I don't like Reeves. I do, actually. He's pretty perfect for Dylan, and I'd even venture to say he had my full support in dating my best friend until he purchased the green-skinned devil.

Jerkface.

"Pickles!" Reeves calls from the main floor. It's his nickname for Dylan. Poor girl. "We gotta get going! Come on!"

"Coming!" Dylan returns. She turns back to me. "I

already put Frankie's terrarium in your room on the nightstand, and his food is in the freezer."

I blanch. The thought alone is enough to give me the heebie jeebies. "Tell me you're joking."

"We've been through this a hundred times."

Throwing my hands into the air, I whine, "Well, you'll have to forgive my brain for dealing with trauma by blocking it from my memory!"

"Finley," she whines.

My bottom lip juts out, and I sigh, resigning myself to the inevitable. "Fine. I'll watch your stupid frog."

"And?" she prods.

"*And* I'll make sure he survives."

She heaves a relieved breath and squeezes my bicep. "Thank you."

"But I make no guarantees about my own safety, and if he kills me in the middle of the night,"—I wiggle my finger an inch from her button nose—"I will haunt you until your dying breath."

Her grin grows. "Deal. Come on." We pass the room she shares with Reeves as she tugs me to the stairs and down to the main floor, where the rest of our friends wait. Packed bags are scattered in the family room, and I nearly choke on my loneliness as I take it all in. They're leaving. They're all leaving. I thought I wanted the house to myself so I could make a plan and have a full-blown meltdown without any witnesses, but now that it's here, and I really am going to be all by myself for a week, it feels…hollow almost.

My eyes well with unshed tears, and I race toward Everett. He's standing next to Raine, his official and very *not* fake girlfriend. They really are cute together, and I'm not going to lie. I like her. I really do. But right now, I need a hug from my big brother. Throwing my arms around his waist, I squeeze Everett as tight as I can without giving a shit how it may or may not make me look like a wackadoodle. I need him, though. I need his strength if I'm going to get through this.

How am I going to get through this?

Not the week without anyone. I'm not that much of a baby. No, I mean the actual baby. The one I have a hunch is growing inside of me. *That* baby. How am I going to get through being a mom? I'm too young for this. I'm too young and too busy and too...*young*. Yes, I know I said it twice, but it's kind of a big factor here. Everett's arms hang limply at his sides for a solid two seconds until he wraps them around me, returning my hug.

"Hey, you okay?" he murmurs against the top of my head.

Oh, the things I could say.

"Yes, you big butthead," I voice aloud. "I'm going to miss you, is all."

His chuckle is warm and throaty as he squeezes me one more time. "You could've come."

"Yeah, yeah. I know I shouldn't have used up all my travel points on visiting Drew, okay?" *Boy, do I regret it now,* I silently add as the pregnancy test burns a hole in my back pocket. I don't want to be alone. I don't want to be anything. I only want to curl into a ball and cry.

"The good news is you won't be alone anymore," Everett offers, cutting through my spiraling thoughts.

I pull away from my brother, my brows wrinkling. "I'm sorry, what?"

"Griffin's staying here."

Frowning, I search the room for my brother's best friend. The man who has caused so many issues in my relationship with Drew it isn't even funny, and he has no idea. Okay, maybe he has a teeny tiny idea since I told him we can't be friends anymore, but I digress. He's the man who, for all intents and purposes, hates me. The man who's currently staring at my back pocket like it's a snake's head. I tug at the hem of my sweater, covering my jean-clad ass and the pregnancy test still most definitely burning a hole in my back pocket.

"You're staying?" I ask.

Dragging his attention from my backside, he folds his arms and leans his shoulder against the wall. "Appears so."

"Why?"

"Lost a bet."

Reeves chuckles, and my glare cuts to him before I turn back to Griffin. "Are you serious?"

"Is it a problem for you, Fin?" he challenges. His gaze sweeps along my body in a half-bored gesture. "Or maybe it's a problem for Drew."

My nostrils flare, and I open my mouth to bite the guy's head off when Everett butts in.

"Finley, relax. He didn't lose a bet, all right? Something came up, and he doesn't want to jinx shit. Sometimes, things just work out."

My molars grind, and I face my brother again. "Did you pay Griffin to stay home and babysit?"

Everett scoffs. "You really think I'd pay someone to babysit you?"

I cock my head.

"Okay, you're right," he concedes. "I would definitely do that, but no. I had nothing to do with Griffin's change of plans."

He lifts his hands in defense, but I bat them back down. "Then why'd he change them?"

"Like I said, something came up."

"That isn't an answer."

"If you want specifics, you'll have to ask him, but I gotta

go so I don't miss the flight. I'll text when we land." Shifting around me, he heads toward the door with the rest of our friends following, each of them stealing one final hug as they head outside.

With a quiet click, the front door closes behind Maverick, leaving me alone with the one person I want nothing to do with.

Marching toward him, I demand, "Why'd your plans change?"

His brows lift. "I'm sorry. Are you mad at me?"

"Why did your plans change?" I repeat, not bothering to hide my aggression. So, sue me.

"What's in your back pocket?"

My body freezes, and I reach for the stupid test, pressing my hand to it as if it'll make the damn thing disappear. "Nothing."

"I saw it, Fin," Griffin counters. Pushing himself away from the wall, his eyes narrow in suspicion. "What is it?"

"A thermometer," I blurt out. "I haven't been feeling one hundred percent, and I figured if Everett knew, he'd call my parents, and they'd freak out, or better yet, he'd insist on staying home and making sure I'm okay, and I didn't want him to worry, which is also why I was suspicious of you deciding to stay home out of the blue."

Damn, I'm a good liar.

Sometimes, I even impress myself.

"Speaking of which," I fold my arms, "why'd you decide to stay if it wasn't to nurse me back to health? Everyone's been gushing about this trip of a lifetime for weeks, that, by some miracle, you were able to squeeze in between games."

Ignoring my question, he asks one of his own. "How are you feeling? Dizzy or anything?"

"I'm not going to have a seizure, if that's what you're asking."

"That's exactly what I'm asking," he counters. "And are you sure?"

Sometimes, I hate my diagnosis. Epilepsy isn't for the faint of heart, and even though my mom has the same neurological disease and held my hand through all the ups and downs, it doesn't make it easier. The looks of pity. Concern. The kid gloves people use with me. Like right now. With the look in Griffin's eyes, you'd think I told him I might puke all over the floor.

"You know, if you get to dodge my questions, I don't see why I can't dodge yours," I argue. "Why'd you decide to skip the trip?"

"Not sure I owe you anything after your boyfriend's little ultimatum," he counters.

My lips press into a thin line as I stare up at him. Yeah, I'm short. Like can-I-put-her-in-my-pocket short. But even if I wasn't, Griffin would still tower over me. All the guys do. Then again, I'm pretty sure being built like a brick wall is a prerequisite for being a hockey player, so it's not like he's anything special, but what do I know?

That's right. Way too much, thanks to growing up with uncles who played in the NHL professionally and passed along their obsession with the sport to all their kids. Well, except for Tatum and me. Tatum is Ophelia's little sister and one of my younger cousins. But I digress.

"You still letting Drew call all the shots, Fin?" Griffin demands.

"You really think I let anyone call the shots?"

"The old Finley wouldn't have. This one, though?" His stone-cold gaze flicks over my body. "You tell me."

This is the most we've spoken since SeaBird. And considering his chilly yet white-hot expression, I'm gonna say, even though I've missed him, I think I prefer the silence over this. I want to call him out. I want to tell him he's wrong, and I'm still the strong, independent woman who doesn't let anyone push her around, but lately? Lately, I'm not so sure. And that's…that's a problem for another day. I dig my teeth into the inside of my cheek and squeeze the pregnancy test in my grasp. It's still hidden in my back pocket. Still nauseatingly light considering how heavy its result might be. You'd think the weight of my future would be heavier, but nope. The thing is flimsy and plastic.

Reading my silence as stubbornness, Griffin rocks back on his heels. "That's what I thought. Don't have a seizure," he warns. "And if you start to feel shittier, I'll be in my room."

His gait is familiar as he walks away. Like this is simply another day in the life of Griffin Thorne. And maybe it is. Maybe he's used to putting up with me and my stubbornness. Especially lately. But watching him leave? It'll never get easier, even if it's something I should be used to by now.

I hate it.

CHAPTER FIVE

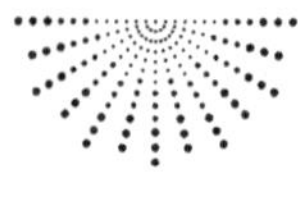

FINLEY

I still haven't looked at the pregnancy test results. Stupid? Yes. Cowardly? Also, yes. Justified? Not in the least, but hey. You win some, and you lose some. The test is tucked in my underwear drawer. After my shift at Rowdy's, a restaurant where I waitress, I came home, changed into sweats, and started a murder documentary because, honestly? There's nothing like a good, old-fashioned serial killer documentary and some popcorn to soothe a girl's soul. I'll also take Ben & Jerry's in a pinch, but right now? I want some salty, buttery popcorn more than my left boob, which is weirdly sore, now that I think about it.

Reaching onto my tiptoes, I blindly dig in the cabinet for some kernels of the gods but come up empty. Of course, I do. With a huff, I climb onto the counter and stand up on it so I can actually see the top shelf.

Reeses' peanut butter cups.

Nope.

Sweet Tarts.

No, thank you.

The granite is cold against my bare feet, so I shift from one foot to the other as I continue rummaging through the cabinet when a low voice asks, "What are you doing?"

Nearly jumping out of my skin, I turn around, clutching my chest. "Griffin!"

"What'd I do now?"

"You're not supposed to sneak up on girls like that!"

He lifts a shoulder, which only makes the bastard look even more effortlessly sexy in his T-shirt and jeans. "What? The murder documentaries going to your head?"

I scowl down at him.

"All right, I'll fold." He tucks his hands into his pockets, looking every bit the boy next door I've always pegged him for. "I'm sorry I scared you."

"Sure you are." I turn back to the junk cabinet and move a bag of cinnamon bears to the side, ignoring the pit in my stomach. It's hunger pains, is all. Not my never-ending guilt for writing off one of my best friends all because my boyfriend told me to.

"What are you looking for?" Griffin prods.

"Popcorn."

"It's all gone."

The stupid organ in my chest cracks at the prospect, and I face Griffin again but am unable to look him in the eye. Not really. "What?"

"Isn't it your week to do the shopping?" he counters.

My shoulders slump. To be fair, he isn't wrong. But I've also been a little preoccupied, thank you very much.

"Fantastic," I grumble under my breath.

It takes everything inside of me to not stomp my foot like an offended toddler as I jump to the ground in defeat. On impact, my ankle rolls, and I yelp in pain, bouncing on my good leg as I try not to bawl my eyes out. "Ouch, ouch, ouch, ouch, ouch, ouch, ouch."

Rushing forward, Griffin catches me before my ass hits the ground and pulls me into him. "Whoa, there, you good?"

"I rolled my ankle," I say through gritted teeth.

"Shit." He grabs my bicep carefully, helps me hobble to the table, and pulls out a chair. "Here, let me look."

"Griffin, I'm fine—"

"You're not fine—"

"Yes, I am. It's just a stupid injury."

He tears his attention from my foot and shakes his head. "Will you stop pushing me away for two goddamn seconds?"

My bottom lip trembles, so I suck it between my teeth and look down at my bare foot. Well, shit. He doesn't have to be such a jerk about it. I can feel Griffin's cold stare on the side of my face, but I ignore it, too emotionally charged to do anything at all except fight back tears. The problem is, I can't decide if it's because of my stupid foot, or my even more stupid decision to push away the man in front of me. Slowly, Griffin kneels at my feet, gently lifts my leg, and examines my ankle for any swelling. His touch is gentle. Soft. But I can still feel the calluses on his fingertips as they drag along the inside of my heel. It tickles. Not enough for me to pull away, but my foot twitches in his grasp as I steal a peek at him. And it's strange. How I haven't really looked at him since the bar. Like, if I did, I'd be breaking my promise to Drew or something. And now, with Griffin distracted with my bum leg, I can finally steal a peek—even if it's only for me—without dealing with the fallout.

His soft brown hair is a little darker than normal. The gold highlights from summer have faded, but he's as beautiful as ever. Griffin's always been pretty. Okay, handsome is probably a better word. He'd kill me if I ever described him as pretty. Even so, his eyes are a bright blue color, bordering on aquamarine. I've always been fascinated by them. Mine are gray. Don't get me wrong. They're pretty, too, I guess, but I've always been jealous of Griffin's eyes, not to mention his long dark lashes. Seriously, why does every guy have incredible lashes? It isn't fair.

I haven't really seen his eyes since our fight at SeaBird.

It's silly but true.

It's also easier than I would've thought. Looking at someone without actually *looking* at someone. I've been too afraid of seeing the hurt in his eyes. And the last thing I want—the last thing I need—is the added guilt of hurting someone I care about while trying to keep my world from unraveling around me.

"It looks okay," he mutters. "Let me grab an ice pack."

He stands and heads to the freezer, searching through the shelves when I remember Frankie's food is somewhere inside.

"Don't spill the insect guts!" I yell.

"What?"

"Frankie's"—I gulp—"food is in there."

"Okay?"

"Don't spill it," I repeat. "If you do, I'll have to buy everyone a new fridge."

He chuckles but doesn't give me shit as he pulls some frozen peas out and wraps the bag in a dishtowel. Handing it to me, he squeezes the back of his neck like he doesn't know what to do now that we're here and we're actually kind of, sort of talking.

Fun fact, Griffin. I don't know what to do, either.

"Thanks," I finally say.

"You're welcome." Scratching the scruff along his jaw, he adds, "Have you fed him yet?"

"The devil?"

"The frog," he clarifies dryly.

"Same thing," I point out. "And not yet. It's on tomorrow's to-do list."

He nods. "You're nice for helping out."

"They didn't exactly give me a choice," I grumble.

"True," he concedes. "So…"

I peek up at him. "Yes?"

"Am I allowed to carry you to the couch so you can be comfortable, or will Drew bitch about that, too?"

My lips press into a thin line. He's acting like an ass. A justified ass, but an ass nonetheless.

"I'm fine, thanks," I murmur.

"You're really this stubborn?"

"I think we both know the answer to that."

Stepping back, he waves his arm in front of him. "Be my guest.'"

"Seriously?"

"You said you don't need my help, right?" he counters.

My eyes thin as I fight the urge to take the bait. He wants to see me crawl my way to the family room? He should know me better than this by now. Let's be honest. Looking like a fool is one thing. Looking like a fool in front of witnesses is an entirely different situation.

Shifting in my seat, I give him a cheeky grin. "I'll, uh, I'll just sit here for a little while. Thanks, though."

"And miss the part where they say what the killer did to the body?" He hooks his thumb toward the family room where the murder documentary is still most definitely playing on the screen.

Damn.

He knows me too well.

"You could always pause it for me," I point out.

"Sorry." Tucking his hands into his front pockets, he

lifts his shoulders and looks boyishly adorable. "I only pause shows for friends."

Friends.

I'm seriously starting to hate that word.

My gaze narrows. "Were you always an ass or…?"

His mouth lifts. "You gonna miss your favorite part, or are you gonna let me help you?"

"I already asked for your help, and you said you only pause shows for—"

I squeal as he hooks his arm beneath my knees, then wraps his opposite one around my back, cradling me to his chest. He smells good. He looks good, too.

Grudgingly, I loop my hands around his neck and stare at the tiny dimple etched into his cheek. This is awkward. So awkward. "So."

Don't look him in the eye. Don't look him in the eye.

"So?" he mimics.

"How are you and…Brittany?"

It's a stupid question. I know they aren't exclusive. I know he hasn't really been exclusive with anyone in…ever.

Huh. Interesting. I'll have to unpack that little tidbit later.

Regardless, Brittany was his date for homecoming. That's it. His date to a dance. Yet, I threw her name out like a jealous lover or something.

Where the hell did that come from?

"She's fine," Griff answers. "Dating some guy from her gym. How are you and Drew?" A flash of the stupid pregnancy test hidden in my room flickers through my mind as a rumble of amusement seeps from his chest. "What am I thinking? It's not like it matters, right? You'll still do anything he tells you to because you're too stubborn to admit he's a dick."

"Speaking of dicks," I counter, giving him a pointed look.

Aaaand, so much for not looking him in the eye.

My breath stalls as I stare at him. He really is handsome. A true dashing, debonair man, even when he's being a bit of a butthead. I should be nicer, but I can't help it. If I let my walls down, we'll slip right back into friendship territory, and considering my current circumstances, it isn't really an option right now. Not anymore.

Despite the harshness of his words, Griffin sets me on the couch carefully, making sure not to jostle my sore ankle as he wraps his long fingers around it and lifts my leg into the air. After setting a pillow on the coffee table, he places my injured foot gently on top of it. My chest pangs at the sweet gesture, but I ignore it. Instead, I ask, "Why'd you stay home from the vacation?"

"Why do you think?" Standing to his full height, he rolls his broad shoulders, glances at the television, and shakes his head. "Still can't understand why you watch this stuff." Then, he saunters out of the room.

Thirty minutes later, the doorbell rings, and he returns to answer it, though I'm too engrossed in the show to care who's on the other side, or at least that's what I tell myself. Truth is, if it was anyone else's familiar gait, I'd probably strike up a conversation and ask why they haven't joined me on the couch, but I know better than to invite Griff if I don't want to deal with the can of worms I know will follow.

Nope. No, thank you.

Why are you so easy to miss, Griff?

I grab the remote and turn the volume up when the scents of butter and salt waft from the front door. Within seconds, a tub of movie theater popcorn is placed in my lap. I look over my shoulder in time to see Griffin pop a kernel into his mouth as he disappears back to his room.

Gone. Like a mirage.

A pang of regret and longing hit me as I watch him walk away. He bought me popcorn. Really yummy movie theater popcorn. Not even what I was craving. Nope. The guy went above and beyond, even when he's mad at me. I shouldn't be surprised, and in a way, I guess I'm not. Griffin's nothing if not thoughtful. He's a doer. A fixer. A quiet worker with a heart of gold and zero desire for recognition. It's why he's captain. Why his teammates rely on him. Why his friends rely on him. Why his family relies on him. A good ol' boy next door who will do anything to help, even sacrificing his ego to order a late-night snack for a girl who insists she wants nothing to do with him.

I wonder if it kills Griff. To see me go along with Drew's ridiculous ultimatum, knowing there isn't anything he can do to change my mind. I wonder if he wants to fix this, too. Our relationship. The one I screwed up.

Before Drew's ultimatum, I would've invited him to stay. Hell, I would've begged him to. Now? Well, I guess a small part of me knows I deserve the silence. The cold shoulder. The disappointment.

If only he knew.

CHAPTER SIX

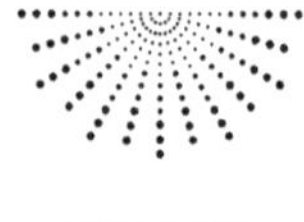

FINLEY

I can't sleep. It's stupid, but it's true. And it's weird. Feeling so damn bone tired but unable to turn my brain off. I blame the frog on my nightstand. I threw a towel over its terrarium as soon as Dylan and Reeves left, hoping the whole out of sight, out of mind phenomenon would kick in, but it hasn't done shit.

Deep breaths, Fin.

It's more than the devil's presence, though. I don't know how I know, but I do. Flipping onto my back, I stare at the ceiling. It's late. It's dark. I've already washed my face, brushed my teeth, and taken my medicine. So, why can't I sleep?

Go. To. Sleep.

My blood boils for no reason at all. Well, I guess that isn't entirely true. I'm pissed. At my foot. At Drew. At Griffin. At myself. At fate. It's annoying and frustrating and irritating and irrational and...I really, *really* wish I could sleeeep.

Slapping my arms against the covers, I squeeze every

muscle in my body as tight as I can, then force them to relax.

It doesn't do shit.

A soft groan echoes from the vent, and my attention snaps to the sound. Seriously? Am I so horny I'm hallucinating?

Another low groan rumbles through the vent. My eyes pop wide, and I sit up in bed. Yup. Yup, I most definitely just heard Griffin doing...something.

I bite the inside of my cheek, attempting to remember whether or not I heard him invite anyone over before I hobbled up to my room.

I don't think so, though.

He never brings girls here. Or at least, not since Dylan, Ophelia, and I moved in.

Another muffled groan slips from the vents, and I press my thighs together.

Well, damn, Griff. Sounds like you're enjoying yourself.

I smirk and shift toward the vent in the floor, holding my breath as my ears strain to listen.

Heavy breathing greets me, and my grin widens.

Yeah, he's definitely rubbing one out.

Although, now that I think about it, I could always...

I don't even let myself finish the thought. Why? Because my spank bank material is unusually saturated with a certain someone I'm not supposed to think about, and now, with the additional soundtrack, I'm almost positive this is as close to cheating as possible without technically crossing the line.

Honestly, though? Griffin is one of *those* guys. He's so... untouchable it doesn't even really feel like I would be fantasizing about a friend, and I'm not the only one. I'm pretty sure Griffin Thorne stars in more girls' fantasies than he'll ever fully understand. There's something about him. Lopsided grin. Blue-green eyes. Easy-going personality. And *just* enough emotional distance to have a girl's imagination running wild.

Wondering if she can fix him. If she can convince him to settle down. If she can be the one to steal his attention from the real love of his life: hockey. It's silly but true.

Griffin's a mirage. A temptation. A glimpse of what you want most but are never able to reach.

Tonight isn't any different.

I wonder what he looks like right now. Is he video chatting with someone? Is he watching porn? Is he using his imagination? If he is, what's he thinking about? *Who* is he thinking about?

His panting echoes through the vent, and I gulp.

Pour me a tall glass of water because this guy sounds… hot.

This much I know.

I shouldn't be thinking about Griffin or eavesdropping, but, uh…damn.

"Fuuuuck…" The word is low and throaty and raspy and…

I press my thighs together.

This is bad. This is really bad. Before I started dating Drew, Griffin was an easy guy to fantasize about. I blamed it on my teenage hormones and a lazy imagination because he was always there. And it's not like I thought anything would actually happen between us. I'd never put our friendship—or Griffin's friendship with Everett—on the line. But, uh, call me a sucker for being a girl who wants what she can't have because I have a feeling this is a solid album for an easy orgasm tonight if I'm stupid enough to take advantage.

Me and Griff.

On the couch.

In the car.

At the rink.

It doesn't matter. It never mattered. I'd think of him and…*hello there, orgasm.*

But that was before. Before Drew and I started dating. Before Drew threw down the gauntlet.

Don't. Even. Think about it.

I could use an orgasm, though.

Especially when masculine grunting is filtering through the vents, and I'm stuck with my own lonely thoughts as company.

Nibbling on the edge of my lip, I weigh the pros and cons, deciding sleep is more important than mental cheating, thanks to our relationship already feeling like a bumpy car ride lately. But if I only use the orgasm-inducing sounds and pin them with fantasies of Drew, then it's fine, right?

Yeah. Hello, loophole. Besides, doctors in the early 1900s would get their patients off all the time under the guise of mental health. Who's to say I'm not doing the same thing? A little…self-treating female hysteria. See? Perfectly rational and totally acceptable.

I almost choke on my snort as I slip my hand under the thick white comforter and into my underwear.

Drew, I remind myself. *Picture Drew.*

I'll just…use the little groans as fuel on an already smoldering ember.

Totally. Completely. Fine.

Closing my eyes, I imagine Drew on top of me. His hand sliding into my underwear. His…I sigh, annoyed by my own annoyance. Seriously, what is wrong with me?

With an annoyed huff, I try to focus.

Sleep. You're doing this for sleep.

My mouth twitches, and I glance at the closed door,

imagining what I would do if someone walked in right now. If they caught me…listening. I slip my hand further into my underwear. Yup. I'm soaked. Gently, I dip my finger inside and circle my clit, creating a…different and completely out-of-reach scenario.

"Hey, Fin?" a low voice growls from the hallway.

My breath hitches. "Yes?"

The door squeaks as it's pushed open.

Resting his shoulder against the doorjamb, Griffin crosses his arms. "What are you doing?"

"Nothing," I lie.

His gaze falls to the sheets draped over me. "You sure?"

I nod, slipping my finger deeper inside of me.

"Looks to me like you're playing with yourself."

I gasp and use my opposite hand to squeeze my boob. Shit, they're so sensitive lately.

"Your cheeks are red," Griffin whispers. "You're pretty when you blush."

"Who says I'm blushing?"

He pushes himself away from the doorjamb and strides closer to my bed. Grasping the sheets, he pulls them off the bed, exposing my spread legs as I play with my center.

I want to stop. I should stop. But…

His gaze darkens, and he cocks his head. "What are you thinking about, Fin?"

My mouth curves up. "Wouldn't you like to know. Now go away. I'm a little busy."

"Looks that way." The bed dips as he sits on the edge of the mattress, watching the white cotton sheets rustle near my crotch. His hand finds my knee, the heat burning the inside of my thigh as his attention slides to my face. "Need any help?"

"Maybe," I breathe out.

"You want my mouth or my cock?"

I press my fingers harder against my clit and rock my hips.

"Mouth," I whisper, squeezing my eyes shut as my imagination runs wild. "I want your mouth, Griff."

His lips quirk, and he climbs onto the bed. My legs fall open even more as he reaches for my underwear and shifts it to the side, blowing on my exposed skin and dragging the tip of his tongue along my slit.

My fingers move faster as I imagine it. His eyes pinning me in place as he tastes me.

Fuck.

I push my fingers deeper inside me, crooking them and moaning quietly, grateful Griffin's too distracted by his own entertainment for the evening to pay attention to lil' ol' me on the top floor.

Pumping my fingers, I rub my clit with the heel of my hand, imagining what Griff sounds like when he eats a girl out. If he's quiet. If he likes it. If he watches or closes his eyes as he licks and sucks and—

"Fuck, Griff," I moan. "Fuck."

I fall apart, unraveling against my hand as my back arches off the mattress, and my eyes fall back in my head.

When I finally come back to earth, my chest heaves, and I slowly catch my breath, savoring the tingles in my limbs and the aftershocks from my core as they spread along my body.

Seriously.

Why is masturbation so fucking good compared to most of my sexual encounters? I sigh and slip my hand from my underwear, throw off my covers, and head to the bathroom across the hall to use the restroom and wash my hands. Once I'm finished, I climb back into bed and fall asleep within minutes.

CHAPTER SEVEN

GRIFFIN

The girl has to know. She has to. There's no other reason she'd say my name and fuck with my head like this.

Right?

Or maybe it's why she said my name. Because she honestly believes I can't hear her through the vents.

Then again, why would she know? I don't bring girls home, and Everett's been staying at the cabin instead of sharing the room with me until the girls' side of the duplex is finished, so it's not like I talk to anyone when I'm in my room. And yeah, I shouldn't have jacked off last night knowing we're the only two home, but I thought she was asleep. I thought…

Fuck, did she hear me, too?

The door swings both ways. It was late, and I was quiet, but…it's possible. Shit, it's possible. Reaching for a glass from the cabinet, I fill it under the sink when a familiar creak comes from the hallway.

I turn toward the sound, and Finley stops short.

"Oh. Hi," she announces.

I lift my chin in greeting, then turn off the faucet and take a drink, watching her over the rim of the glass.

What are you gonna do, Finley?

"So." She swings her arms behind her and clasps her fingers at the base of her spine. "How'd you sleep?"

"Fine," I offer. "You?"

"Fine." She hesitates, and I swear we're in a standoff. A game of chicken. Hell, I feel like I've been transported to an old Western movie and am waiting for her to yell, "Draw!"

"There a problem, Finley?" I prod.

"No problem." She runs her tongue along her teeth, staring at me. "Did you...invite anyone over last night?"

She heard me. It's all she needs to say for me to know the truth. She heard me, and she thinks I had company. The question is, if she heard me, why the hell did she touch herself afterward?

I quirk my brow. "Is this your sleuthing face?"

"What?" she asks.

"Nothing, I just... Don't get me wrong. I know it's been a while since you've even looked me in the eye, but I figured you'd have a better sleuthing face than this. Honestly, it needs some work."

She rolls her eyes. "I don't know what you're talking about."

"Did I invite anyone over last night?" I repeat, tossing her own words back at her. "I don't know. How 'bout you, Fin?"

"Why would I have company over?" she volleys back at me.

"So, it was only you, huh?"

Her throat tightens on a swallow. "Okay, so the vents go both ways. Noted. Now, if you'll excuse me." She hobbles closer on her bum ankle with her shoulders back and her head held high, moving to the coffee pot beside me.

I grab her a mug from the cabinet, set it beside the coffee pot, and wait, refusing to back down or give her more room than necessary. Hell, if anything, I give her less. Call me a dick, but I'm curious. We've been dancing around each other for weeks now, masturbated a floor away from each other, and she's gonna...what? Pretend like nothing happened?

Her lips purse as she sidles up next to me, waiting for the coffee to finish brewing as I stare down at her and silently call her bluff.

Clicking her nails against the countertop, she stares straight ahead, like she can't feel my presence, until she finally blurts out, "There's nothing wrong with a little self-care."

"Not at all," I agree.

"Although, you should probably stick to the shower," she adds, craning her head up to look at me. "You know, so I don't have to be scarred and all."

I chuckle dryly. "You didn't sound very scarred."

"Maybe I was on the phone with Drew."

Liar.

My fingertips turn white against my glass. I steal another sip, ignoring the sizzle in my veins from his name alone. "Trust me. I know when you're talking to Drew."

"Oh, you do, do you?"

"You said so yourself. The vent goes both ways. And you weren't cursing or crying, so..." I hesitate and cock my head, taking her in. "I take it back. You did curse...right before you said my name."

Her gaze narrows, but a blush hits her cheeks. "You need to have your hearing checked."

"I could hear you just fine, and you obviously heard me, or else you wouldn't have done your self-care. Am I right?"

She scoffs. "Don't flatter yourself." Pouring the coffee into her mug, she turns around and faces me fully. "And I'm serious about using the shower instead. I don't want to hear…any of that."

"Why? Does it make you curious?" I challenge.

Another laugh escapes her. "Hardly."

My mouth twitches. "To be fair, I didn't know you were still awake. And I didn't say your name, but you sure as shit said mine." I shift closer, crowding her against the counter. "Pretty sure Drew would love that, wouldn't he?" My attention falls to her mouth. Fuck. She looks so…touchable like this. High, messy ponytail. No make up. Only a baggy t-shirt swallowing her curvy frame. My hand itches to reach out and grab her waist, but I fist it at my side instead. Bending closer, I breathe out, "Don't worry, Fin. It's our little secret."

Avoiding my gaze, she huffs, "Look, it's not my fault I've been particularly…amped up lately. And you might be able to hook up with any girl you want, but my boyfriend is across the country, so you'll have to forgive me for taking things into my own…hands."

I scoff. "Trust me. I don't mind at all. But next time, all you have to do is call me, and I'll lend a helping hand. Or was it my mouth you wanted?" I click my tongue against the roof of my mouth. "Honestly, I should thank you."

She glares up at me. "Why?"

"I get it now. Why Drew feels threatened."

"He doesn't—"

"He does. And he should. Because if the girl I was dating imagined someone else while fingering herself, I'd feel pretty fuckin' threatened, too."

Her eyes pop. "Excuse me?"

"Why haven't you broken up with him yet, Finley?" I demand.

"And what were you thinking about, Mr. High and Mighty?"

"It doesn't matter because I'm single."

"So you weren't imagining a girl who's in a relationship?" she challenges, bringing the coffee to her lips and taking a sip.

This girl drives me nuts. I fight the urge to throttle her pretty little throat and reach for the mug in her grasp instead. She gives it up without a fight as I steal some of her coffee, holding her gray eyes over the rim of the cup, and set it on the counter next to her hip.

"Guess that's our little secret, too. Right, Fin?" I push away from her. "I'm going to the gym. I'll be back in an hour. You good until then?"

"Why, of course." She bats her lashes. "I have my fingers for company." Lifting her hand, she wiggles them back and forth. "Toodle-oo."

Smartass.

CHAPTER EIGHT

FINLEY

There isn't much waitressing one can do with a bum foot. The good news is my dad shares ownership of the restaurant with his friend, Rowdy, so he barely batted an eye when I told him about my little accident and promised he'd find a replacement for me for the foreseeable future until I felt better. Seriously, the man's a saint. It also doesn't hurt that I know a few of the other waitresses have been begging him for more hours, though, so really, they should be thanking me.

My nose scrunches as I grab Frankie's food from the freezer with two fingers and hobble up the stairs to my bedroom. To be fair, I'm being dramatic. My foot's fine, but I called in sick anyway. Who wouldn't milk an injury if they had one? The frozen peas from last night helped a lot with the pain and swelling, which is kind of annoying, considering the culprit behind the idea. Still, I'm trying to be the bigger person and not be a bitch about it...to Griffin's face, anyway.

Carefully, I sit on the edge of my bed and stare at the covered terrarium on my nightstand. With a deep breath, I pinch the edge of the towel and lift it up, tossing it on the ground on the opposite side of the room as a shiver races down my spine.

Puffing out my cheeks, I mutter, "Come on, Finley. You can do this. It's only a frog. A measly. Slimey. Little frog." I almost gag but swallow it back. "You got this. You can do it."

Yes, I know I'm talking to myself, but at this point? I really don't care. Clicking my tongue against the roof of my mouth, I untwist the cap on the mealworms and peek inside, gagging as the stench hits my nose.

"Okay, I'm gonna puke."

I twist the cap back on and take another slow, cleansing breath through my mouth until I realize if I breathe through my mouth, I'll be letting the tiny mealworm particles touch my tastebuds, which, in a way, is like I'm eating the mealworms firsthand, and—

I grab the lined trash can beside my bed and puke, my stomach heaving what little I've eaten into the plastic barrier until there's nothing left inside of me.

Once I'm finished, I wipe my mouth with the inside of my shirt, make a mental note to shower as soon as I'm finished feeding the monster, and take a deep breath. Holding the oxygen in my lungs, I untwist the cap again, lift the lid off the cage, and dump a few dead mealworms into the terrarium before rushing into the bathroom across the hall like I'm being chased by the demon himself.

After scrubbing every inch of my skin with my hot pink loofah and body wash that smells like apples, I shampoo and condition my hair, then stand in the scalding hot water for another ten minutes, hoping it'll sanitize my skin and pulverize every molecule of mealworm potentially clinging to my body. Fifteen minutes later, the water starts to cool, and I shut it off, wrap a towel around me, knot the terry cloth by my cleavage, and brush my teeth. Twice. Satisfied, I stare at my reflection and, after a brief pep talk, head back to my bedroom for some new clothes when my heels dig into the ground.

The lid.

The lid is off the terrarium. I forgot to put the lid back on the terrarium, and the slimy devil is…shit. Where is he? I rise onto my tiptoes, attempting to steal a better look at the glass cage, but either the stupid thing is blending in with the plants inside or…

My lungs seize.

Squeezing my eyes shut, I count to ten and breathe out, "It's only your imagination. It's only your imagination. It's only your…" I peek one eye open and scream. The pounding of footsteps follows until my door is thrust open.

"What? What is it?" Griffin demands.

"Right there! It's right there!" I blindly point at my bed while hopping on my one good leg, trying not to pee my freaking pants, er, towel.

"What the hell are you—"

I grab his face and twist his head toward the devil on my comforter. "Right. There."

The stupid thing croaks, and I wrap myself around Griffin, tucking my face into the crook of his neck as if he has the power to save me from the big-eyed demon itself. "I'm gonna die, I'm gonna die, I'm gonna die!"

"You're not gonna die," Griffin murmurs. "But if you're worried about Drew being jealous of us talking, he's not gonna like you wrapped around me naked."

The name cuts through my frazzled brain, and I blink. Twice. "I-I'm sorry, what?" I look down, finding my towel barely hanging on my frame. The front of the terry cloth is open and dangles by my calves, proving that I am very much wrapped around my brother's best friend in my birthday suit.

Shit.

The demon croaks again, and I squeal, wrapping my bad leg around Griffin's waist and attempting to crawl up his body like my life depends on it. And who knows? Thanks to the green monster three feet away from me, it just might.

"Kill it, kill it, kill it!" I chant.

"I'm not gonna—"

It jumps off the bed and lands on the ground by my good foot. Screaming, I leap off the floor and wrap my body around Griffin like a frazzled monkey. My heart pounds so loud in my ears I swear he can hear it. And when I say he, I mean my nemesis. Franklin the Frog Thorne. Cursed be thy name. The towel is officially forgotten as Griffin's hands find my waist, and he pulls me closer to keep both of us from falling on our asses.

"Finley—"

"It's gonna get me!" I cry. Tears stream down my face, and I squeeze my eyes shut, losing my ever-loving mind.

"Wait. Are you…?" Griffin tries to pull me away from him, but I only cling tighter. "Finley, are you crying?"

"It's gonna get me, it's gonna get me, it's gonna get me!"

"It's not gonna get you."

"You don't know that!" I yell. "It knows where I sleep, Griff! It knows!"

"Finley, breathe." Keeping one hand wrapped around my waist, he leans back on his heels to center our combined weight and touches the side of my face, urging me to look at him. "Finley…"

It's a request. A very patient request.

I shake my head. "Is it still there?"

He hesitates. "I can't put him back in his cage—"

"Terrarium," I correct him.

"I can't put him back in his terrarium while holding you."

"Yeah, but if you put me down, he'll get me!"

"He won't—"

"He will," I argue, breaking out into a cold sweat as the reality of the situation crashes into me.

A low laugh escapes Griffin as he tries to convince me to look at him again, the pressure of his hand gentle but firm as he silently encourages me to lift my head.

Slowly, I do.

When he sees my face, his eyes practically pop out of his stupidly handsome head. "Holy shit, Fin. You're seriously crying?"

"Don't make fun of me," I pout.

The corner of his mouth lifts as his thumb brushes away the tears streaming down my face. "Don't get me wrong. I knew you had a thing against frogs, but *this*?"

He laughs, and I smack his chest. "I said, don't make fun of me!" His grip loosens, and I squeeze him even tighter. "And don't put me down!"

"I'm not gonna put you down in here, okay?" He steps into the hallway, and I force my muscles to relax, slowly sliding down his body. When my toes hit the cold ground, he adds, "You good?"

I nod, and his hand on my waist disappears as he takes a small step away from me. Cool air hits my body, and my nipples pebble, reminding me I'm still very much naked. And, apparently, Griffin is realizing the same thing. His eyes trail down my body as if they have a mind of their own, causing the frog fog—*ha!*—to finally clear from my brain.

I'm naked. In front of my brother's best friend. I'm naked in front of Griffin. *The* Griffin. Heat licks every inch his gaze touches, and I press my thighs together until I remember this guy most definitely should not be seeing me naked.

Folding my arms and twisting my hips to keep my lady bits from view, I clear my throat and say, "So…about that towel."

He tears his attention from my cleavage and disappears into my bedroom only to return with my discarded towel. "Here."

"What about the frog?"

His brows furrow. "What about the frog?"

I wag my hand at the towel. "What if he contaminated it?"

"Bloody hell, Finley." Dropping the towel, he grabs the edge of his shirt, yanks it over his head, and offers it to me. "Here."

My eyes trail down his bare torso, making my mouth water as I take in every rippling inch of warm, golden skin. "Speaking of bloody hell." I grab his shirt and pull it over my head, grateful it's long enough to cover my ass. "Damn, Griff. You're looking sharp."

He scoffs. "That isn't something you're supposed to say to someone who isn't your boyfriend."

"There's nothing wrong with having an objective opinion," I point out. "I would say the same thing to Mav or Reeves."

"Yeah, but Mav and Reeves aren't on your boyfriend's shit list, are they?" Griffin counters.

He makes a good point, but because I'm stubborn, I refuse to give in. "It's like acknowledging that Sydney Sweeny is gorgeous and Jenna Ortega has kissable lips."

"You think Jenna Ortega has kissable lips?"

"You think Jenna Ortega doesn't have kissable lips?" I counter. "And you're missing the point. All I'm saying is, objectively speaking, you're looking good, Griff. Keep up the good work." I pat his chest before realizing I'm patting his very naked chest.

Oops.

Clearing my throat, I lift my hand, adding, "And speaking of good work, there's a demon in my room who needs trapping." I snap my fingers. "Chop, chop, Griffin."

Grumbling under his breath, he steps into the bedroom, and I slam the door behind him, blocking the slimy monster's escape plan.

"I'll pray for you!" I call through the door. Then I wait. And wait. And wait.

Pressing my ear to the solid wood, I listen for screaming or croaking or cursing, but there isn't a sound. Not. One. It doesn't make me feel any better. Leaning closer, I close my eyes, like if I somehow shut off my eyesight, my other senses will steal its strength, and I'll be able to hear what's going on inside the room.

When the door swings open, I fall face-first into a very hard, very warm chest.

Whoops.

A pair of strong hands envelop my biceps, wrenching me away from Griffin's chest as I crane my neck up at him. "Oops."

"You good?"

I nod, and he lets me go.

"Did you catch it?" I ask.

"He's back in the cage."

"Terrarium."

"Terrarium," he corrects.

"Perfect." I clear my throat and fold my arms. "Uh, thank you."

"You're welcome."

"And thank you two times," I add, pinching the edge of the shirt I'd stolen as if to say, "Exhibit B."

"You're welcome two times."

I nod.

"You know, this is the most we've talked since SeaBird without being dicks to each other."

"You're a dick. I'm a bitch," I clarify. "But, yeah, you're right."

"It's nice," he adds.

My head bobs up and down. "Yeah. Yeah, it is."

"Maybe don't tell Drew I saw you naked, though."

I snort. "Probably a good idea."

"And maybe don't tell your brother, either."

I smile. "Our little secret."

He squeezes the back of his neck and rocks back on his heels. "If you need anything, let me know."

"I will," I murmur. As he slips past me, heading for the stairs, I call, "Hey, Griff?"

Glancing over his shoulder at me, he says, "Yeah?"

"It isn't…personal. Okay?"

His head falls to his chest, and my stupid heart splinters.

"Not sure what other label fits, but whatever you say, Fin. As long as you're happy, I guess."

Then he takes the stairs two at a time, leaving me alone in the hallway in nothing but his T-shirt.

Tiptoeing back to my room, I peek around the corner and squint my eyes, searching the terrarium for a trapped little green monster. When I spot it, my body sags and I step over the threshold, closing the door behind me with a quiet click. I should shower again since Griffin touched me with his hands after catching the demon spawn. But I'm too anxious. The look in his eyes… The way his low voice sounded so…detached. It hurt.

As long as you're happy, I guess.

Am I happy?

With a deep breath, I reach for my phone and dial Drew's number. It rings and goes to voicemail.

As long as you're happy, I guess.

The words haunt me as I tap the edge of my cell against my chin. My gaze trails to my dresser and what I know is hidden inside. It's Schrodinger's Cat. Two potential futures. And I have no idea which one's mine.

Would I be mad? Happy? How would I tell people? I see cute pregnancy announcements all the time on social media. The idea of posting something—anything—kind of makes me want to puke. The thought alone makes my stomach churn, and the feeling messes with my head. Is it morning sickness? Do you have morning sickness outside of the early morning? I don't even know.

My head feels fuzzy, but I march toward my dresser and open the top drawer, blindly searching for the plastic pregnancy test before I can talk myself out of it. When I find it, I force myself to read the stupid thing even if it kills me.

And there it is. Two lines.

I'm…

The pregnancy test slips from my shaking fingers as the world goes black.

CHAPTER NINE

GRIFFIN

As I pull on a fresh T-shirt from my closet, I try to erase the image of Finley's naked body pressed against me. Her warmth. The way her long black hair hung in ropes down her back. The way her lips parted as she begged for my help. And then, the sight of her in nothing but my T-shirt? Fuck. Kill me now. My cock stirs at the reminder, and I squeeze it angrily through my jeans. That was…a mistake. And the last thing I needed if I want to keep my head on straight. I need to calm the hell down, but being alone in a house with her isn't exactly a walk in the park. I swear, the woman drives me insane.

A loud thud echoes from the ceiling. My head snaps up toward the second floor, and my body surges with adrenaline. "Fin?"

Silence.

Striding down the hall, I call out, "Fin?"

The same eerie silence greets me. I grab the railing and pull myself up the stairs as fear licks up my spine. "Fin!" I yell.

My heavy footsteps thud against the floor as I dash

toward the room at the end of the hall. When I round the corner, my throat clogs and my fingertips turn white against the doorjamb, gripping the surface until my hands ache while my mind short-circuits at the sight.

Finley. On the ground.

Fuck, Finley's on the ground. She's—

Move!

I race closer, falling to my knees. Finley's convulsing. Her body wracking with uncontrollable and violent shakes. Being friends with Finley means receiving a lecture about what to do if she seizes. I search my memory for Uncle Mack's instructions, but my mind is a fucking mess.

Shit. Shit. Shit.

I rub my hand over my head, feeling so fucking helpless, I could vomit as I watch her helplessly.

Focus, asshole!

Make sure there isn't anything she can bump into. That's the first rule. I look around the room, but she isn't close to any chairs or anything. The dresser is far enough from her, too. Satisfied, I pull my phone out and start timing the seizure. My hand shakes as I push the start button. I set it on the ground and run my hands through my hair again, watching her body flop and jolt on the carpet. Her muscles tighten and spasm, pulling her in awkward directions.

Was it the frog? Is that what triggered her? Maybe it was me. I never should've been an ass like I was to her. So what if she wants Drew instead of a friendship with me? As long as she's safe and healthy, and—

I check the time on the phone again. It's been four minutes. I try to calm my breathing while dialing Finley's dad's number.

"Hello?" he answers.

"We're at four minutes," I rush out. "Fin's having a seizure."

"Have you called an ambulance?"

I shake my head until I remember he can't see me. "N-no."

"Four minutes?" he questions.

"Y-yeah. Four and a half—"

"Call an ambulance. We'll meet you at the hospital."

I hang up the phone without saying goodbye and dial nine-one-one.

As it rings, I look down at Finley. Her eyes are rolled back, only the whites are visible, and her long dark hair is a web of black across her face. The imagery shakes me to my core, and I blink back the tears in my eyes.

Fuck!

Please let her be okay.

I HAD TO LIE TO THE PARAMEDICS ABOUT MY RELATIONSHIP with Fin so they would let me ride with her in the ambulance. Not that I cared about technicalities. We might not be seeing each other romantically, but I do love her, and seeing her like that? Shit. She seized for over six minutes. Longest damn minutes of my life. She's asleep now. Resting my elbows on my knees, I lace my fingers together and stare at the white tile, waiting for the doctor to arrive. They already took her blood. Now, they're letting her rest. Uncle Mack and Aunt Kate should be here any minute. We've been texting back and forth since the ambulance.

"Knock, knock," someone calls, and a man in a white lab coat appears. "Hey, I'm Dr. Nordick."

"I'm Griffin. Nice to meet you."

"You, too." He glances at the hospital bed. "How's our patient doing?"

I follow his gaze, taking in the sleeping girl with cords strapped to her chest. "You tell me."

"Well, the tests all look good. I'd love to do a quick ultrasound to make sure the baby's okay, though."

Buzzing hits my ears, and I tear my focus from Finley to the doctor again. "What?"

"I said, the tests look good, and Finley's hormones look like they're where they need to be, as well, but I'd love to do a quick ultrasound to make sure the baby's okay. Congratulations, by the way. You must be excited."

"Yeah. Yeah, uh, I—"

"She didn't tell you yet?" Dr. Nordick questions.

I shake my head. "Uh, no."

"I apologize," he rushes out. "I assumed—"

"No worries. I'm, uh, I'm really excited." I clear my throat, wipe my sweaty palms against my jeans, and stand up. "Let me just…can you give me a minute so I can wake her up for the ultrasound?"

"Yes, of course. Also, I think her seizure was most likely triggered by her rapidly changing hormones. Once she's awake, I'd like to get her permission to consult with her neurologist regarding any medication adjustments."

"Whatever Finley thinks."

He nods. "Perfect. We'll be back in a few minutes with the ultrasound machine."

I force a smile, then turn to Finley and scrub my hand over my face.

What. The actual. Fuck?

She's pregnant? How could she be—why would she—fuck!

My mind races, my thoughts blurring together, one after another, until it's almost impossible to form a single coherent thought without it getting swept away by the next. Pregnant? How far along is she? Does she know? Is that why she's staying with the dipshit? Does he know? Does her family? Shit, when Everett finds out, he's gonna kill Drew. Fuck, I might do it myself.

I glance at Finley's still body again. The steady rise and fall of her chest. Her stomach. The urge to press my hand against it hits out of nowhere, and I squeeze my hands into fists, caught between awe and disappointment. I just can't figure out why.

At least she's okay. At least she's safe. The reminder spurs me on and quiets my racing thoughts. One hurdle at a time. The chair legs scrape against the linoleum floor as I drag it closer to the bed. Her arms lie limply on the mattress. Her skin looks like silk. Feels like silk, too. I should know. I felt it firsthand this afternoon.

She needs to wake up. She needs to have a fucking ultrasound.

Gently, I drag my fingertip against the outside of her wrist and murmur, "Fin? Hey, Fin, wake up."

Her eyelids flicker, and her dazed eyes blink slowly before focusing. When they land on me, relief fills them, and she lifts her hand, touching her temple. "Hey."

"Hey," I rasp.

"What happened?"

"You had a seizure."

Her expression pinches, and she nods. "Makes sense."

I smile at her easy acceptance. "How are you feeling?"

"Headache." She swallows. "Dry mouth."

I reach for a styrofoam cup one of the nurses delivered a little while ago and offer it to her. She takes it and steals a sip, her dry lips wrapping around the straw as silence fills the room.

"Thanks," she whispers.

"The doctor wants to do an ultrasound."

"A what?" She stares into her water, her brows stitched in confusion, and I can't tell if it's because she doesn't know about the baby or if the aftereffects from the seizure are still messing with her memory. They say it's normal. To be disoriented. To feel like your brain and your thoughts are as shaken as your body.

"The baby's fine, but they want to do an ultrasound to make sure."

Her eyes cut to me, and whatever fog of confusion had been present vanishes. Panic. That's what replaces it. Sheer. Fucking. Panic.

"Did you know?" I ask.

"Griff…"

"Does *he* know?" I push.

Her bottom lip wobbles, and she pulls it into her mouth, shaking her head. Honestly, I'm surprised. Not that Drew's in the dark, but that she's on the verge of tears.

I get it. Having a baby is a pretty big deal and shit, but Fin? The girl's an anchor. Well, unless frogs are involved. And I can't help but want to protect her from the impending tornado headed her way. Especially when I'm given a glimpse of the girl behind the impenetrable walls. The girl who's scared. The girl who's lying in a hospital bed, her skin practically matching the white sheets lying across her lap and an IV hooked into the inside of her elbow. The girl who isn't quite as put together as she'd like the world to believe.

And a fucking kid? Yeah, I'd say it's a doozy.

"Knock, knock." The sound grates on me as my attention snaps to the doorway. There's a woman in dark purple scrubs with light brown hair and a kind smile. "I'm Allie," she adds. "I'll be performing the ultrasound."

"H-hi," Finley offers.

"Do you have any idea when your last period was?" Allie asks as she steps into the room, dragging an ultrasound machine with her and, apparently, getting right down to business.

Finley shakes her head again. "I'm, uh, I'm not super consistent on the period front thanks to my medication, so…"

"Got it." The ultrasound tech gives her a reassuring smile. "No worries at all. We might need to do the ultrasound vaginally, depending on how early you are. Is that okay with you?"

"Uh…I mean, who wouldn't want a vaginal ultrasound?" She forces an awkward smile. "Sounds like quite the experience to me."

Allie laughs. "You're gonna be a fun patient. I can tell." Fiddling with the machine, she adds, "We'll start with the external ultrasound and see what we get. Sound good?"

"Sure, why not?"

"If you'll lift your gown for me but keep your lower half under the sheets, we'll get started."

"Perfect." Finley shifts the fabric around her waist, grabbing the edge of the gown and situating the white sheet to cover her lower half while exposing her stomach to the ultrasound technician.

Tearing my attention from the sliver of skin, I clear my throat.

I shouldn't be here. Drew should. The reminder fucks with my head. Or maybe it's the truth bomb in general. Fin's pregnant? Finley's fucking pregnant. And here I am, nothing but an observer. An observer who has no right to be here. So, why am I here?

"I'll, uh, I'll wait outside." I stand and head to the door so Fin can have some privacy and I can have a minute to wrap my head around shit. I always knew it would never work between us. I even said as much to Raine when she asked about my feelings for Finley a while ago. And I wasn't lying, either. Not really. But I guess I thought…or at least a small piece of me thought…maybe…someday, if the stars aligned, and we were in the same place, and Drew was out of the picture, and Everett didn't have a stick up his ass…maybe…fuck, I don't know.

Finley's pregnant.

"Griff?" she calls.

I pause by the door and face her. "Yeah?"

"Are my parents on their way?"

I nod.

"Don't…don't tell them, okay? Please?"

The request guts me, twisting like a knife in my stomach, but I nod anyway. "Our little secret, right?"

Relief shines in her gray eyes, and she dips her chin. "Add it to the list. And thank you."

"I'll be outside."

When I start to step over the threshold, she stops me once more. "Hey, Griff?"

"Yeah, Fin?" I face her again, my body caught between fight or flight. Part of me wants to shake her for not telling me. For not telling *anyone*. The other wants to pull her into a hug and promise everything's going to be okay and remind her she doesn't need to put on a brave face. Not for me. But I won't do either because neither is my place. Especially when she pushed me away and chose Drew over me.

Then again, now that the cat's out of the bag, I get it. Of course, she would. She *should*. Shouldn't she? Not that there was anything to choose in the first place. All I'll ever be to Finley Taylor is her brother's best friend. And Fin? All she'll ever be is the one who got away.

"Can you…" Finley lifts one of her shoulders in a half-assed shrug. "Can you be a peach and stay with me?"

My chest constricts, but I step back into the room and take a seat where I was as the ultrasound tech sets up her machine.

I shouldn't be here. I shouldn't fucking be here. Pulling out my phone, I send a quick text to Finley's parents, telling them to wait in the waiting room. They respond almost instantly and promise to do exactly that without bothering to ask any follow-up questions.

I know Uncle Mack and Aunt Kate well enough to know there will be an onslaught of questions once we're face to face, though. I make a mental note to come up with a solid reason why they can't come into the room for later. We'll need it.

As I start to tuck my phone back into my pocket, Finley reaches for me and grabs my wrist, surprising the shit out of me. Because this girl doesn't have a weak bone in her body. Fuck, I saw her convulsing on the floor an hour ago, and when she came to, she didn't even bat an eye, taking the situation on the chin like a seasoned pro. Yet, here she is, holding my hand, clinging to me, showing the tiniest hint of unease about what's unfolding in front of us.

A thousand questions sit on the tip of my tongue, but I can't ask any of them. Not yet. Not until we're alone.

Acid coats my throat as I stare at our entwined hands. The way she's holding onto me. The way her hand looks wrapped in mine. In a different world, I could've been excited for this moment.

Now? Now, I feel like I might vomit.

CHAPTER TEN

FINLEY

My parents left an hour ago after solidifying their decision to move back to Lockwood Heights. Apparently my little episode was the final push they needed. Yay me. To be fair, they've been teetering on the idea since I received my acceptance letter to LAU, but after spending the majority of their time at the cabin, or bouncing from one friend's house to another, then visiting me in the hospital tonight, I'm pretty sure the deal is sealed. I didn't bother pushing back, well-aware that once they find out about the baby, it'll be a moot point anyway. I'm going to need them. Me and Drew and… I close my eyes, trying not to get too overwhelmed.

Now I'm alone in my family room with the one and only Griffin Thorne as my parole officer. By some miracle, he kept his word and didn't blurt out the not-so-little secret I'm trying to keep on the down-low from my mom and dad as soon as they stepped into the hospital. Even so, he's not very good at hiding his emotions, especially since we're alone now. I bite the inside of my cheek to keep my sardonic smile in check as he stares at me from across the room, his emotions on lockdown. Well, at least *his* version of lockdown.

Yeah, I'm in the dog house for sure.

He hasn't said a word to me since the baby's heartbeat echoed through the hospital room.

It was so fast. Faster than I expected. It kind of scared the shit out of me because now that I've heard the sound, it's made my entire situation…real. All of it.

I should be mad Griffin knows. I should be pissed at the doctor for blurting out my not-so-little secret to him while I was recovering from my seizure, but I can't find the energy to be angry, even if he hasn't taken his eyes off me since.

I shift on the couch, my body aching. I feel like I was hit by a truck. It's a familiar feeling. Doesn't make it easier, though.

"How are you feeling?" Griffin asks, breaking the silence.

"Like a million bucks."

"I'm serious, Fin."

I paste on a fake smile and lean my back against the couch. "I'm fine, Griff."

His eyes narrow. "You're not fine."

"Yes, I am," I argue. "I'm fine. The baby's fine. Everything is…fine."

"That's bullshit, and you know it."

"Then why did you ask?" I toss back at him. "If you're so sure of how I feel, why even bother asking me?"

"Because you're not fucking fine, and I want you to admit it." He leans forward in the armchair across from me and threads his fingers together. "I want you to talk to me."

"Well, what else would you like me to say, Griff? That I'm pregnant with a baby I don't even know if I want right now, and I'm connected to a man I'm seriously questioning whether or not I want to be tied to, and I feel young and stupid and alone and scared and every other negative emotion a girl like me could have, not to mention the whole epilepsy side of things and whether or not my anti-seizure medication is working any more thanks to the hormones flooding my body, let alone whether or not said medication is affecting my baby's development. Yup, that makes me even more overwhelmed and frustrated and fucking terrified, all right? So, yeah. You're right. I'm not fine, but if I have to assess my actual feelings instead of hiding behind rainbows and butterflies, I just might lose my shit, and that isn't an option right now, either, so how am I, Griffin Thorne? I'm. Fucking. Fine," I snap.

"Okay, you're fine," he grunts, settling back in his chair.

"Thank you."

Silence envelops us, but it barely lasts a minute as he continues his intense stare.

I know what he's doing. Baiting me. Trying to convince me that opening up is the better option, when I'm so over-whelmed I don't even know where to start. Or maybe it's my stubbornness keeping my lips sealed. Yeah, I'm well aware I can be a bit hardheaded on occasion, but he has no right to come in here and demand I let him in. Not when he's so far removed from the situation he can judge me from afar.

Folding my arms, I hold his gaze and turn the tables. "Is this another game of Chicken?" I ask.

"Sticking your head in the sand won't get you anywhere."

"Thank you, Captain Obvious," I volley back at him.

"Says the girl who sucks at acknowledging reality."

"I don't suck at—"

"You have a baby in your stomach!"

"Uterus," I correct him. "And, yes. I. Fucking. Know!"

"Does anyone else?" he challenges, refusing to back down. "If the doctor hadn't mistaken me for the dad, would you have bothered to tell anyone, or would you have kept pretending like none of this is real until you delivered the kid?"

"I don't need a lecture from you."

"Yeah, well, you're getting one," he snaps. "Because I care about you and this?" His attention falls to my stomach. "This isn't some failed test you forgot to study for but can make up in the future. This is..." He sighs. "This is a lot, Fin."

"Again, I'm well aware, but thank you."

"Not gonna acknowledge the whole I care about you bit, huh?"

My nostrils flare, but I stay quiet.

"So what are you gonna do?" he prods. "Are you gonna tell him?"

"Him?" My voice cracks, and I chew on the edge of my thumb. "As in..."

"The father," he finishes for me.

"I haven't exactly had the chance."

"That isn't an answer," he points out.

"Yeah, well, it's not exactly something I want to tell Drew over the phone, and since I barely confirmed my assumption right before I started seizing, you'll have to cut me some slack for not having a game plan quite yet."

"So, what? You'll just wait until spring break when you can reveal the gender? Or hell, maybe you should wait until summer, and Drew can skip right ahead to meeting his kid firsthand during the long break. How does that sound?"

"Oo, you're annoying today," I huff, fisting my hands in my lap.

"I'd say the feeling's mutual, but I'm too stressed out

about everything that happened today to care." He scrubs his hand over his face. "You scared me today, Fin. You scared the shit out of me."

Well, damn.

The tension in my hands eases as I study Griffin across from me. The worry lines framing his blue-green eyes. The strain in his jaw. The concern radiating off him in waves. Hell, it's so thick I can almost taste it.

He cares. I know this, but even so, sometimes it's nice to see the reminder. That his frustration isn't because he's actually pissed at me. It's because he's scared for me. And yes, there's a difference. One I've failed to recognize until this moment.

"I scared you, huh?" I whisper.

He nods.

"You know, that's almost as bad as the *I care about you* bit," I mutter, causing his mouth to twitch. "And I'm sorry," I add.

"You don't need to apologize."

"I mean, I did kind of give you a heart attack this morning. How dare I drop to the floor and—"

"Not even gonna let you finish that sentence," he interrupts. "Sometimes your humor is way too twisted, you know that, right?"

I give him a cheeky smile. "It's one of my best features."

"Sure it is," he murmurs. The concern in his eyes doesn't disappear, though. If anything, it's only amplified as he holds my attention hostage. "I know I've seen you have a couple seizures, but today? It was all on me, and… shit, Fin."

"I'm okay, Griff," I remind him.

"I know you are. And I know I shouldn't yell at you—"

"You haven't yelled." I hesitate. "Okay, you haven't

yelled by most people's standards. For you, you've been a total monster."

He rolls his eyes. "Smartass. I guess I'm a little…overwhelmed. And concerned," he clarifies. "Because I know you want to say we're not friends and shit, but like I said, I care about you, Fin. I care about you, and today was a reminder that I could've lost you. We all could've lost you."

"I'm fine." I lick my lips. "And thank you, by the way. For calling an ambulance and staying with me and pretending to be the doting boyfriend and keeping my parents out of the loop for now."

He studies me carefully before tossing my own words back at me. "For now."

"Yeah." I tuck my hair behind my ear. "I'm not stupid. I know I need to tell them. I just…I can't get myself to say the words to myself, let alone the people I care about."

"Denial isn't going to get you anywhere," he reminds me gently.

"Yeah, but it's so much more palatable," I quip.

His chuckle is raspy and forced as he tugs at the collar of his shirt. "Are you…gonna keep the baby?"

"I was on the fence until the ultrasound," I admit. "Hearing the heartbeat, man." I puff out my cheeks and blow out all the air from my lungs. "Whew. That was a doozy."

"Yeah." His nod is slow. "Yeah, it was. How long have you known?"

"For sure? About five seconds before my seizure started."

"Shit."

"Yeah."

"And how long have you had a feeling?" he prods.

"A while," I answer vaguely.

"Can I do anything?" he asks.

"If I say I don't know again, will you yell at me?" I counter.

"Not gonna yell at you. Only trying to figure out how I can help when my hands are tied, you know?"

"Well, I have a few suggestions."

"Yeah?"

"Mm-hmm." I pat the couch cushion beside me. "You can start by sitting by me instead of staring at me from across the room like some creeper."

"Some creeper, huh?"

"I mean, a pretty good-looking creeper, but yeah." I grin.

His chuckle is low and dry, but he stands and strides closer, stopping once he's towering over me. "You sure Drew would like me sitting by you?"

"Probably not, but after the shit day I had, I could really use my friend."

He takes the open seat—leaving a solid six inches between us—spreads his legs and settles into the couch. "Here I am, Fin. Now, what?"

"I want to watch a show."

Bending forward, Griffin grabs the remote. He moves to hand it to me but changes his mind and points it toward the television on the opposite side of the room. Without any prodding, he turns on a documentary about Jeffrey Dahmer and settles back into the cushions again, making himself comfortable.

"You hate murder documentaries," I remind him.

"Every sane person hates murder documentaries," he tosses back at me.

My mouth lifts. "So, why'd you pick it?"

"Because you've had a shit day."

"You are a good friend, Griffin," I murmur. "The best, actually."

"Yeah, yeah." He grabs my feet and twists me around, letting me use the armrest as a makeshift pillow. "How's your ankle?"

Slowly, he digs his thumbs into my arch, and I practically moan at the contact.

"I'll take that as better," he quips.

"If you keep doing that, it will be."

"Your wish is my command."

Bringing my foot into his lap, Griffin massages it for the rest of the episode. It's the first time I've felt peace since I missed my period. Honestly, it might even be since before then. Since SeaBird. Since I put a wall between us. And yeah. I thought it was the right thing to do, but now? I peek up at him again. Now, I'm not so sure.

I WAKE UP TO BUZZING ON MY LAP. PEELING MY EYES OPEN, I find my phone resting on my stomach. Drew's name flashes across the screen, and I catch Griffin staring at it. I have no idea what time it is, but the light outside the windows is absent, and the "Are you still watching" disclaimer glares at me from the television.

It's been hours. Hours of binge-watching and napping and—

"You gonna answer?" Griffin asks.

"Nope."

His attention shoots to me. "Are you serious?"

"Look, it's not my fault that if I answer the phone, I'll feel obligated to tell him—"

"As you should," he interjects.

My gaze narrows. "What are you? The honesty police?"

"Something like it," he counters. "Look, you know I hate the guy, but he deserves to know."

"And he deserves to find out face-to-face, and since I'm still babysitting the demon frog in my room, it's not like I can simply jump on a plane and see him. And even if I wasn't watching the stupid amphibian, I still wouldn't be able to fly, thanks to my seizure earlier today, so…" I give him a smartass grin as if to say, case in point.

"Fine, we'll drive."

My eyes widen. "I'm sorry, what?"

"If you can't tell him over the phone, and you can't fly because of Frankie, I'll drive you."

Sitting up, I pull my feet from his lap and bring my knees to my chest, leaning my shoulder against the couch cushion. "It's a twenty-two-hour drive."

"So?"

"So, it's a long drive—"

"So?" he repeats. "If I was going to be a dad, I'd want to know."

I cock my head, surprised by the onslaught of imagery of that. Griffin as a dad. Swaddling a baby. Buying a mini jersey to match his own. The way his nose would wrinkle when he'd change the baby's diaper or how mussed his hair would be after a sleepless night. He'd be a good dad. He will be a good dad. Not anytime soon—fate likes him more than me—but still. The idea is…nice. Bittersweet, almost. And I don't know why.

Shaking off the thought, I murmur, "And you're so sure Drew's going to have the same sentiment?"

"Are you saying he won't?"

My lips press into a thin line, and I set my phone next to my hip on the couch cushion.

"You're nervous to tell him," he concludes.

"Well, duh." I laugh. "If a random girl told you she was pregnant, how would you handle it?"

His attention flicks around my face, and I hate how much it makes me feel...seen.

"You're not a random girl." My breath hitches. "Not to Drew."

Drew.

Right.

I tuck my hair behind my ear and quirk my brow. "So because we've been dating long term he'll automatically be ecstatic?"

"Ecstatic might be a bit of a stretch, but you two will figure it out."

"I'm glad someone's sure," I mutter.

"You love him," he offers. "He loves you. You'll figure it out because you have to. It's what people do when they love each other. They figure shit out."

I shouldn't find his confidence annoying, but I kind of do. It's like he's saying two plus one equals three. And sure, it does, but only if it's two plus one. What if I'm the only one who shows up? What if it's two plus zero? Then the answer is two, and what if two isn't enough? What if I'm not enough to hold this relationship—this family— together?

"I must've really knocked you on your ass," he notes. "Breathe."

"It's just...You make it sound so simple."

"Nothing in life is simple, Fin. And loving someone who's a pain in the ass is tough as shit, but you'll get through it."

I smirk. "And here I thought you were referring to me being the pain in the ass, not Drew."

"Depends on the day." He bumps his shoulder against my bent knees still pressed to my chest. "But first, you have to tell him."

Tell him. I have to...tell him. The idea alone makes me

feel like an elephant is sitting on my chest, but I hate it because I know Griffin's right. I know there's only so much procrastination to be had, and I've already used it all up. Now it's time to…pull on my big girl panties and face the music.

"Fine," I murmur.

"Fine?" Griffin challenges, not even trying to hide his surprise at my compliance.

"Yes. Fine," I grumble with a mock glare. "I'll let you drive me to see Drew."

"And Frankie?"

My nose bunches. "I mean, we might not be gone long. He could totally survive—"

"Fin."

"Fine, he can come, too, but only because my motherly instinct is starting to kick in, and it feels wrong to abandon him."

He chuckles. "Well, all right, then." He slaps his hands against his knees and shifts forward. "You should get some rest. We'll leave early tomorrow."

"What kind of early?"

"Four."

"In the morning?" I screech.

"It's a twenty-two-hour drive, Fin," he reminds me as if I wasn't the one to point it out minutes ago.

"Well, yeah, but…" My bottom lip juts out. "I really like my sleep."

"Pretty sure Drew finding out he's gonna be a dad is more important than your beauty sleep."

"First of all, sir, I think that's debatable," I hmph. "But fine. I'll just sleep in the car."

He snorts. "What am I? Your chauffeur?"

With a grin, I say, "Apparently." My smile falls. "There's only one minor flaw in our plan."

"Only one?" he quips.

I smack his chest. "Drew won't like the idea of you driving me to his place."

"I'll keep my distance," he offers. "He'll never have to know I'm there."

"You'd do that for me?" I bat my lashes for good measure, and he snorts.

"What's one more secret, right? Come on, smartass. Let's get some rest."

CHAPTER ELEVEN

I've known Finley her entire life, and I'm pretty sure this is the first time I've seen her this tired. Her long dark hair is piled on top of her head in a bright pink scrunchie. It's lopsided and looks like it might fall out any second. One of Everett's LAU hoodies swallows her whole, and hot pink sweats with the word PINK is painted across her ass. As soon as we pull away from the house, she slips out of her Birkenstock sandals and sets her feet on the dashboard, not bothering to open her eyes as I flick on the blinker and merge onto the main road.

"Feet down," I order.

With a yawn, she covers her mouth. "What?"

"Feet. Down," I repeat, reaching for her polka dot-covered feet.

She scoots away from me, her jaw unhinged. "Wait, why?"

"Do you want to break your pelvis?"

"What? Are you offering?" she quips with a wink.

I rest my elbow on the driver's side window and pinch

the bridge of my nose, praying for patience. "I meant if we're in a car accident."

"Well, then drive safely," she counters.

I tap the brakes, and she lurches forward, her seatbelt getting lost in her cleavage as her eyes pop open and she glares at me.

"Are you kidding me right now?"

"Just tryin' to keep you safe."

Thankfully, the streets are empty at this time of day, so I'm not actually too worried, but still. Better to be safe than sorry.

I can feel her glare on the side of my face, and honestly, I shouldn't expect anything less. The girl's more stubborn than an ox.

Giving her the side eye, I try a different tactic. "What about the baby?"

She doesn't budge and folds her arms over her chest, a grumbled "Well played" echoing from the passenger side. Setting her feet back on the rubber floor mat, she reaches for my phone in the cupholder.

As she shamelessly types in my password, I ask. "Can I help you?"

I shouldn't be surprised she knows it. The girl's a sneaky pain in the ass. Honestly, *I'm* an ass for not assuming she knew my password in the first place. She probably knows my social security number and poop schedule, too.

Without bothering to look at me, she opens my music app. "If I'm gonna be awake in the middle of the night, I'm gonna listen to some good music."

"It's almost five in the morning," I point out.

"Which is five hours before anyone should be awake, thank you very much. Now let's see..." She clicks her tongue against the roof of her mouth and continues searching my music streaming app, finally settling on… something. Her mouth stretches into a Cheshire grin.

I brace myself for nails on a chalkboard, and when the song starts playing, I realize I'm not far off. "Really?"

"I'm sorry, is there a problem with *The Descendants*?"

Other than it being a glorified, off-broadway musical the girls weaponized to torture me and the guys as soon as Maverick and Archer's little sister, Rory, became obsessed with it? Yeah, I could say there's a problem or two with the good ol' Descendants movie.

Instead, I turn the volume up and start belting the lyrics. "Rotten to the core, core, rotten to the core…"

Her laugh mingles with the chorus, and she joins in, twerking in the passenger seat. It's refreshing, though. Considering our vulnerable chat last night, it's nice to see her like this. The same Finley I've grown up with. The carefree Finley. The sassy, impulsive Finley. The one who isn't afraid to get under my skin and piss me off all because she has a twisted sense of humor. Seeing her broken in the hospital bed made me wonder if I'd ever see this side of her again. I should've known better, though. This girl's stronger than anyone gives her credit. She'll get through this, too. Even if it's without me.

Her eyes crinkle in the corners as she grins back at me, and I turn up the volume a few more clicks.

CHAPTER TWELVE

GRIFFIN

It's weird. Barely saying a few sentences to each other for weeks on end, then being crammed in a car with a person. I'd almost forgotten how much she makes me laugh, even when she isn't trying. Part of me wants to hold it against her. The fact that she cut me off. That she threw away our friendship, all because a guy told her to. The other part? I get it. I don't like that I get it, but I do. I care about Fin, even when I shouldn't, and today was a reminder of all the thoughts I've shoved aside for years, all because she was dating someone else. Knowing they'll have to stay locked up for the rest of my life is a bitch.

Then again, maybe it's for the best. I'm leaving, and if the Tornadoes reaching out is any indication of a timeline, it'll probably be sooner rather than later. That is, if I didn't already fuck up my opportunity with them by bailing on our meeting we had scheduled.

Fuck, I can't believe I bailed on them.

They're going to be pissed. I'm still not sure if I made the right call. I mean nothing to Finley, yet my future might be on the line for this little...road trip.

What the hell am I doing here?

Finley's always had me wrapped around her little finger, but this? This is a low point, even for me. We make it seventeen hours until my ass can't take it anymore, and we find a hotel. I debated making reservations last night when I suggested this insane plan but decided against it because I didn't know how far we'd make it on the first day. On the one hand, I'm glad we made it as far as we did. On the other, thanks to the ten bathroom breaks that convinced me Finley has a bladder the size of a pea, it's late, and this is one of the only hotels in town with an empty room.

To say the place isn't a five-star hotel would be a massive understatement, but considering the circumstances, I'm not too picky. Thankfully, Finley isn't, either.

Musk fills my nostrils as I juggle our bags down the hall and toward our room, grateful Finley at least had the courage to hold the terrarium so I wouldn't have to go back to the SUV. I'm exhausted. The last forty-eight hours have been a bitch to wrap my head around, and the idea of a bed and pillow sounds almost as good as a solid orgasm.

Almost.

Balancing the bags, I wave the electronic key in front of the lock and twist the handle. The door opens with a loud creak, and our bags hit the floor as I flick on the light. "Well, shit."

Finley peeks around me, her arms still wrapped around Frankie's terrarium after we played Rock, Paper, Scissors to see who would carry it to the room, and since my arms were already full of our bags, she only threatened to cut off my balls twice before giving in and taking it with us.

"There's only one bed," she notes.

"I'm aware there's one bed. That's why I said *shit*."

"Rude." She smacks my back, steps around me, and sets

the glass cage on the dresser next to the television, shivering in disgust. Once a healthy distance is between her and the terrarium, she turns back to me and crosses her arms. "First of all, I'm a delight to sleep with. And secondly, we're both adults. I think we can share a bed."

"And what would Drew say if he knew?" I counter.

"Fuck Drew. Oh, wait," she winks, "I already have."

"Yeah, and look where it got you." My attention drops to her flat stomach.

Sticking her tongue out at me, she snaps, "I think it's a little too soon for that kind of humor."

"Yet, you make it so easy," I return.

"Har, har. Now, enough chatting. I'm exhausted." She covers her yawn with her hand, takes off her sandals, and slips beneath the covers.

As I stare at her, dumbfounded, she rolls toward me. "I'm sorry. Is there a problem?"

"You're not gonna brush your teeth or pee or…?"

"Excuse me, sir, but I believe neither of those things is any of your business."

Folding my arms, I challenge, "Oh, so your bladder is finally empty after the last ten pit stops?"

She grins back at me. "Maybe."

"What about your meds?"

"What about them?"

"Did you take them yet? Prenatals, anti-seizure—"

"Yes, Dr. Thorne. I'm aware of which meds you're referring to."

"And?"

"And I took them when we stopped for those burritos. Now." She pats both sides of the bed. "Do you prefer one side of the bed to the other? Or…?"

Seriously, is the girl trying to kill me?

She's sitting in the center of the bed with the sheets already pooled around her waist and her eyes glazed with drowsiness as she peers up at me.

"I'll be sleeping on the floor," I announce.

"Why? 'Cause I'm so scary?"

"No, because Dylan says you move around a lot when you sleep, and I don't feel like getting kicked in the balls at two in the morning all because I'm sharing a twin bed with you. But thanks."

"Whatever. One, this isn't a twin bed, it's a…wait, what's the size bigger than a twin but smaller than a queen?"

Rubbing at my tired eyes, I grumble, "I have no idea."

"You're right. All that matters is you're wrong, and it's bigger than a twin."

"Get to your second point, Finley."

"And twoooo," she drags out, "Potentially being kicked is still better than attempting to sleep on the hard ground covered in stained carpet, don't you think?"

I glance down at the carpet in question, noticing a large brown spot. Yeah, this is not my night. My expression pinches, and I look back at Fin, lying, "You make it sound like an easy decision, but they're closer to a tie than you think."

"Exactly," she preens. "Although you do make a good point about Drew not being a fan of…" she wiggles her fingers between us. "*This.* So, let's do toes to nose," she decides.

I snort.

"Is that a problem?"

"Even if we're toes to nose, our genitals are still—"

"Ew." Her nose wrinkles. "Did you really just say genitals?"

"Would you prefer I call it my cock and your puss—"

She lifts her hand into the air and squeezes her eyes shut. "Nope, that's worse."

With a dry laugh, I scratch along my jaw, eyeing the opposite side of the bed warily. "Call it what you want, but they're still lined up no matter how we sleep." I lift my chin toward the bed. "Go to bed. I'll sleep on the floor."

"Griff—"

"Sleep," I push.

She shifts onto her back and stares at the ceiling as I flick off the lights, grab a free pillow from the bed, and crouch, preparing to set the pillow on the ground. I hesitate at the last second. She isn't kidding. There's definitely a stain on the carpet, and I sure as shit don't have to see it to know it's there. Does brown have a smell? Honestly, I think it might.

My face sours as I contemplate my shitty life choices that led me here. If I want any actual rest tonight, sharing a bed with Fin isn't a bad idea. The question is whether or not I have enough willpower to keep my hands to myself. Then again, I've done it for years, so…

My phone buzzes. Pulling it out, I find a message from Tina. She's a junior. Gorgeous brown skin. Wide smile. Caramel eyes. We've known each other for a while now, and even hooked up a few times in the past, though not recently. Not since Finley moved in. I told myself I was distracted by hockey, and my abstinence had nothing to do with my best friend's little sister living under my roof. Hell, I'm still telling myself that, but it's getting harder and harder to believe the lie. Especially now. When I'm stuck sleeping on the floor of a run-down hotel.

TINA

Hey, you. You up?

"Hey, Griff?" Fin murmurs.

I turn off my cell and set it down on the rock-hard ground, my face scrunching. What is that? Guilt? Shame? The feeling spreads in my gut as I set my pillow down and stare at the ceiling.

"Yeah?" I answer.

"Thanks for today."

I sigh. "Anytime, Fin. You know that."

"I do," she replies. "Which is why you're my favorite."

"Sure, I am." I laugh. "Smartass."

"Mm-hmm." She hums. "And, uh, Griff?"

"What, Fin?"

"You ready to give in and sleep next to me?"

"Not sure it's a good idea."

"Yeah, but really, it is. And I'm talking from a selfish standpoint."

"How do you figure?"

"Well, since you're driving me and my unborn baby all day tomorrow, I need you to get a good night's rest."

With a low laugh, I stand up, tug off my shirt, and lay down on top of the covers. Toes to nose, no matter how ridiculous her suggestion is. "Fine. You win." I shove my hands behind my head and stare at the popcorn ceiling. "Get some sleep, Fin."

"One more thing," she rushes out.

With a groan, I mutter, "What is it?"

"If, uh, if it wasn't for the baby…" Her words hang in the air, and my body turns to steel. Fuck, I could finish her sentence in a million ways, and so could she. The question is…how does she want to?

"What is it?" I push.

"I'd never choose to have you out of my life. Seriously. You mean a lot to me, Griff."

My eyes close, heavy with defeat. There are so many things I could say, but they're too late. I'm too late.

"You, too," I murmur, turning onto my side and giving her my back. "Get some rest."

CHAPTER THIRTEEN

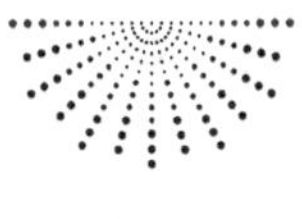

FINLEY

It shouldn't be this daunting. It's only a freshman dormitory. Four floors. Boring red brick. A few bushes along the front and stairs leading to the entrance. Nothing crazy. Drew shares this space with two roommates. I've only met them once. Patrick and Charles. They're nice in a hoity-toity kind of way. All pocket protectors and trust funds. I shouldn't expect anything less, thanks to the stereotypes Drew's been drowning in ever since he accepted his invitation to the Ivy League university. It was his favorite excuse. Why he could never step away to see me. Why he was too busy to take my calls. Classes are hard. Professors are unfair. Schedules are rigorous.

We already parked Griffin's SUV, and when I climbed out, he joined me without a word. Now, here I am, staring up at a building like it might open up and swallow me whole.

"You good?" Griffin asks.

I snap myself out of my funk and slip my well-practiced fake smile into place. "Yeah, why wouldn't I be?"

His gaze slides up and down my frozen frame. "Because you haven't moved from the first step in a solid thirty seconds."

"I mean, who wouldn't want to show up on their boyfriend's door unannounced to tell them they're pregnant?" I wave my fisted hands into the air like a lottery winner. "Yay me."

The guy doesn't buy it for a second. "You want me to come in with you?"

It's a good question. I should say no. The unpregnant version of me would've without hesitation. Now? Now, I could use a little support, and whether or not I want to admit it, Griffin's given me more than I could ever ask for. I should decline his offer, though. If Griff comes in with me, Drew will lose his shit. But I'm tired of putting Drew's needs above my own. I've done it for so long I've almost forgotten what it feels like to voice what I want. What I need. My little impromptu road trip with Griffin has reminded me of the opposite. That I'm allowed to have wants and needs and a person who supports—and delivers —said wants and needs in spades. Without bitching. Without grumbling. Without guilt-tripping.

Griff's a fixer. He's always been a fixer. And right now, he wants to help me fix my situation with Drew, even to his own detriment. If only fixing this was easy.

"Maybe just…" I wave my hand toward the front area of the building. "Stay close? I'll call you if I need you."

Tucking his hands into the front pockets of his jeans, he rocks back on his heels, his wary gaze never leaving mine. "Sure thing."

"Thanks." I offer him another smile—though it's as forced as before—and arch my shoulders back, preparing for the inevitable. It's going to be fine. It's going to be one hundred percent, totally and completely fine. I mean, let's be honest, my mom and dad got pregnant with my big brother when they were still dating. Yeah, she'd just graduated from LAU, and my dad most definitely had a stable job, but look how they turned out? Totally and completely fine. They also never fought and already lived together, but...poe-tae-toe, poe-tah-toe. *Poe-tah-toe.* Who says potato like that, anyway? No one, that's who.

"You goin'?" Griffin prods.

"Right." Clearing my throat, I unclench my fists, keep my head held high, and make my way toward the front of the building, one slow step at a time.

There are thirteen. Steps, that is. If that isn't a bad omen, I don't know what is. I skip the last stair just in case, then shake out my hands. I can do this. Easy peasy, lemon squeezy. Praying the punch code to enter the building is the same as when I last visited, I type it in and wait for the familiar unclicking of the lock.

Click.

With a deep breath, I grab the handle and open the main doors. Did it smell this stuffy the last time I was here? I search my memory but come up empty. Maybe it's my super human pregnancy nose or something. Maybe my rose-colored glasses have cracked. Or maybe I'm saying my rose-colored glasses have faded because I'm afraid that as soon as I tell Drew I'm pregnant, his rose-colored glasses will be shattered forever, and this whole thing will blow up in my face irrevocably.

Yeah, that's not a nauseating rabbit hole of negativity to fall down at all, Finley.

Focus.

Drew's room is on the first floor. Second door on the right. I lift my hand, preparing to knock, but the door's already cracked. Curious, I peek inside. The rooms are laid out into tiny apartments. The main area has a small gathering space and kitchenette with two doors leading to the bedrooms. Drew's parents shelled out a lot of money for the big room he has all to himself while Charles and Patrick share the second space. A horror movie is playing on the television in the main area. Honestly, I'm impressed. Drew hates horror movies. The back of his dark, shaggy head comes into view, along with long blonde hair pulled into a ponytail.

I wait for the gut punch to fully sink in, but it doesn't. Instead, numbness spreads through me. He isn't cheating. He isn't even technically snuggling, or maybe he is and the angle is more forgiving than it should be. They do look... close. And comfortable. Comfortable in a way I've never seen Drew. Not with anyone but me. Doesn't make it easier. The reminder of how different our lives are now that we've built them a few states away from each other. Honestly, should I really have expected anything less?

My gut's been telling me this for months. If only I'd listened. Now, it's too late. I need to get this over with.

Wiping my sweaty palms against my pants, I lift my hand to push the door open when a warm body hits my back.

"Can I help you?" a high yet *almost* masculine voice asks.

I peek over my shoulder and find one of Drew's roommates. Okay, so Drew's not on an *actual* date. That's something, isn't it? Or hell, maybe he's into orgies now. Wouldn't that be a fun turn of events?

Remembering my manners, I step aside and give the guy a small wave while my brain scrambles to figure out how the hell I should handle this situation. "Oh. Hi, Charles."

"Frita, right?" he asks.

"Finley," I correct. "But close. B- for effort." My gaze

drops to the orange bowl of popcorn cradled in his arms. Yup. He's definitely included in the little movie afternoon they've got going for them. Interesting. "I, uh, I see you *popped* out of your room for a snack? Get it? 'Cause it's popcorn?"

"Yes, I'm familiar with puns." He scoots his glasses up on the bridge of his nose. "Hello again."

"Hello to you, too. Here, let me." I push the door to his room open, then follow him inside without waiting for an invitation.

"Hey, what took you so—" Drew's jaw drops, making him look like a pathetic goldfish at the pet store as the girl beside him follows his gaze.

Well, would you look at that. If it isn't the infamous @mollie69.

Recognizing me, she scoots away, her head snapping back toward the television. She reaches for the remote, pauses the show, then turns into a freaking mannequin.

Sorry, girl. I'm not a dinosaur. I can still see you, even if you aren't moving.

With one hand on my hip, I put on the same fake-ass smile I'm all too familiar with and give Drew my full attention. "Hello, boyfriend."

"Finley!" He rushes toward me, pulling me into a full-bodied hug that makes my body recoil. Seriously. Is he this dense? As my feet lift from the ground, he spins me around and squeezes me tighter than a boa constrictor, making it hard for me to breathe. Or maybe it's the entire situation making me feel like I'm suffocating. Regardless, the over-the-top hug is almost enough to make me believe Drew's happy I'm here if I hadn't seen how wide his eyes were when I walked in on him ten seconds ago.

Yeah, you're not fooling anyone, buddy, even if your roommate's joining you in your little movie marathon.

I know what a guilty man looks like, and Drew? Drew looks like he's two seconds from crapping his pants.

I pat his back slowly, though it's more of an *okay, let me down* motion than a genuine touch. Once my feet are on solid ground, I step back, my attention sliding from Drew to @mollie69 and back again. "I hope I didn't interrupt anything."

"Not at all," Drew says. "We were all watching a movie as friends."

As friends.

The only people who waste their breath on a clarification like that are the opposite of friends. Don't they know the less a person says, the less evidence the other person can collect? Seriously, considering how many murder documentaries I've made this man sit through, you'd think a thing or two would sink in by now.

"Exactly!" @mollie69 chirps. "Hi. I'm Mollie, by the way. Drew's told me so much about you."

"I'm sure he has. He's great at filling people in so no one's left in the dark. Right, Drew?" I smirk up at him and pat his chest, noting the way his heart pounds against his rib cage like a freaking jackhammer.

Yeah, this is a wrench in both our days, that's for sure.

"So, what are you doing here?" Drew asks. "Don't get me wrong. I'm so happy to see you, and I love a good surprise, but how'd you get here? When did you get here? God, I'm so happy to—"

I lift my finger, cutting him off. "Mind if we go to your room and chat for a minute?"

Mollie starts to stand, her focus glued to the ground. "I should go."

"No. Stay. Seriously," I reply. "Your movie isn't even over, and the popcorn's been popped. We'll be five minutes tops. Then, he's all yours."

"Fin," Drew murmurs. I can hear the desperation in his voice. It only pisses me off more.

My attention slices to his. "Room. Now. I think you owe me that much."

His head bobs with his Adam's apple as he follows me into his room. It's gray and square and absolutely boring. No posters. No artwork. Just a desk. A closed closet. A small window. And a mattress. My lips purse as I take in his perfectly made bed. And to think the bun in my oven was likely conceived in this very room.

Perfect.

He closes the door behind him with a quiet click. "She's just a friend."

"Yeah, she, uh, she really looks like she's just a friend, but I'm gonna stick a pin in that for later," I decide. I feel like I'm about to explode. Like with the tiniest of sparks, I might literally combust. I'm mad. Confused. Nauseated. What do I do now? What do I say? Do I try to fix this? Do I knee him in the balls and promise to never see him again? I feel like I'm fraying at the seams. Like, with the tiniest of pulls, I'll unravel completely. I'm stronger than this. I know I am. But I'm also pregnant, which makes this the stickiest of situations, and I honestly don't know what to do.

"Fin, I'm serious," Drew murmurs. "There is nothing—"

"I don't want to hear it."

He steps toward me, his arms stretched out like he honestly thinks I'll let him touch me. When I give him a warning look, he stops in his tracks and runs his hand over his head before squeezing the back of his neck. "I'm serious, Fin. We were all sitting on the couch together so no one had to crane their neck to watch the movie. It was completely innocent."

"I don't give a shit about Mollie," I mutter, shifting my weight from one foot to the other as I battle my fight or flight instincts for the first time in my life. I've never been a flighty girl. That's Dylan's job. I'm a *grab-it-by-the-reins-and-hold-on-tight* kind of girl. So, what the hell is wrong with me?

"Then what is it?" he prods. "What's wrong?"

"I came to tell you…" My tongue quadruples in size, refusing to work properly, let alone air out all my dirty laundry for the one guy who deserves to hear it.

"Baby, tell me," he begs.

Baby.

I cover my laugh with my hand.

His brows pull. "What is it?"

"It's just…you said baby, and, uh, well, surprise." I laugh a little harder while fighting back tears. "I'm pregnant."

His eyes bulge, and his jaw goes slack. Like I've sucker punched him. Like I've blindsided him.

Welcome to the club, buddy.

Sobering, I tuck my hair behind my ear and take a slow step toward him to cut the distance between us. "I was surprised, too. Shocked, actually. Especially because I don't have any morning sickness or anything. I mean, it's technically still kind of early for those symptoms, but…" I shake my head and try to focus. "Honestly, I wouldn't have even known if…if I couldn't like, feel it."

"Feel it?"

"Not like, literally. I'm not that far along." I pinch the bridge of my nose and try to rein in my crazy. "I don't know how to explain it, and I know I sound like a crazy person, but, I could just…tell."

Collapsing onto the edge of the bed, he cradles his forehead in his hands. "Tell me you're joking."

"Don't get me wrong. I know I have a wicked sense of humor, and my sarcasm is always on point, but I'm telling the truth." I sit beside him, wipe my hands against my jeans, and tuck them under my thighs. "I'm pregnant, Drew. *We're* pregnant."

Dropping his hands back to his lap, he sits up straighter and scowls at me, making me pull away. I haven't completely lost my mind. I played out the possibility of him *not* jumping for joy, but the animosity wafting off of him is the last response I expect, especially after I just walked in on him being all cozy with a girl he promised he'd stop hanging out with.

"What are you going to do?" he demands.

"Well, for starters, I'm going to tell you to stop looking at me like I shit on your welcome mat, thank you very much."

"You can't just show up here and tell me you're pregnant—"

"What would you have preferred?" I ask. "That I tell you over text?"

The blood drains from his face, and he shakes his head back and forth. "You can't be pregnant."

"Oh, I most definitely can," I toss back at him. "I'm not sure if you remember or not, but it all went down in this very room if the math's right." I look around the bare walls and pat the center of his mattress like it's a dog. "Right. Here."

"Not possible."

"Oh, it's very possible—"

"You shouldn't have come."

"Why?" I demand. "So you could keep lying about cheating on me with your little *friend*?"

"Says the girl who's pregnant." He jumps to his feet. "How do we even know if it's mine?"

Throwing my head back, I release an unhinged laugh and stand up, too. "First of all, fuck you. I held up my end of the deal. The only reason Griffin's here—"

"Griffin's here?" he balks.

"That's what you're clinging to?" Another enraged laugh escapes me. Seriously, I am *this* close to losing my last marble. "Yeah. Griffin drove me here because I had a seizure when I found out I was pregnant with your baby, and now I can't drive for three months. I'm also babysitting Dylan's devil child, and it's not like they'll let you fly with those, but that's beside the point."

Breathe, Finley. You can do this.

"Drew," I murmur, "I came because I figured you have a right to know I'm pregnant. I came because I wanted us to…talk. Okay? That's why I'm here."

He stays quiet, staring at me like I'm nothing more than a stranger until, finally, his head shifts back and forth again, and he gives me a tight shrug. "Not sure what you want me to say."

My eyes bulge. "Are you serious?"

"Fuck yeah, I am. What do you want me to say?"

"Well, for starters, you could say we're going to get through this together and—"

"What's there to get through, Fin?" he demands. "Look, I think we both know things have been"—he scrubs his hand over his face—"kind of fucked lately."

"You're right," I agree. "And after what I walked in on, I think we can drop the kind of, don't you?" My throat constricts, but I swallow past it and step closer. "But this isn't about us, Drew. Now there's a baby involved, and—"

"You should get rid of it."

I jerk back, convinced that if he would've slapped me, it would've hurt less. His calloused words. The sharp indifference. Hell, indifference is too kind of a description. No, this guy isn't indifferent. He's making his stance very clear, but even then, I'm so blindsided I can't fathom it. Can't grasp his words and how much weight is in them.

"W-what?"

"I said you should get rid of it," he pushes. "I'm not ready to be a dad. You're clearly not someone who should have a kid—"

"What's that supposed to mean?" I reach for the desk, steadying myself as my legs threaten to give out.

"You said so yourself," he pushes. "You had a seizure because of the pregnancy. This could be dangerous."

"I'll be fine."

"What if the baby gets it?" he argues. "It's genetic, right?"

It.

I blink slowly in hopes of staving off the waves of dizziness threatening to take me under. "I'm sorry. Are we talking about my epilepsy?"

"Yeah. Yeah, I am." He shakes his head and waves his hands around the room like a crazy person. "You got it from your mom."

"So?"

"So, what if the baby gets it?"

"Gets it?" I scoff. "It's not like an illness you can contract, okay? Besides, just because it can be genetic doesn't mean anything. Everett doesn't have epilepsy."

"Yeah, but you do!" He stops in his tracks and faces me, his expression twisting with resentment and fear and... disgust. "What if it has it, too?" He waves his hand toward my stomach. "Do you have any idea how expensive it could be?"

My hands find my belly on their own. Like, subconsciously, I'm trying to protect their feelings. Their well-being in general, now that I think about it. But the strangest part of all of this? It's the fact that I'm speechless. I've never been speechless. But now that I'm here, standing in front of a person I thought I loved, thought I could build my life with, and he has the audacity to think something so vile, let alone say it out loud? To me? Someone he's supposed to love and cherish and fucking worship? I'm so blindsided I don't even know how to respond.

Shaking off my stupor, I ask, "I, uh, I'm sorry, but are you seriously thinking about money right now?"

"Of course, I'm thinking about the money!" he yells. "Kids are expensive, Finley! Add in one with your fucked-up genes, and, and I'm out. You need to get rid of—"

Burning hits my palm, and Drew's face snaps to the side before I register what just happened. I look down at my shaking hand, then back at the palm-shaped red mark on his face. I've slapped a person or two in my life, but it's never been so…instinctual. Like an out of body experience, and instead of the familiar shred of guilt accompanying the action, all I feel is…more rage as I stare at the sniveling man in front of me.

"In case it isn't clear, we're through," I announce. "I will not be getting rid of the baby, but trust me when I say they will never know your name, and they will never owe you anything. Not a single Father's Day card. Not a single moment. Not a single thought." I step closer, looking down on Drew's sorry ass as he cradles his flaming cheekbone. "Goodbye, Drew."

Turning on my heel, I leave his room, ignore his friends' curious stares, and race out of the dorm. My heart thrums in my chest so hard I swear I can hear it as I cling to the railing, forcing my breathing to steady so I don't pass out from lack of oxygen. I can't believe he said those things to me. That he blamed my genes? That he told me to get rid of our child? God, he's so disgusting. Bile claws up my throat as if my body's rejecting the idea of ever being touched by that selfish sonofabitch. My fingers dig into the cold, metal railing, and I close my eyes. How could he say those things? How could he think those things let alone say them? The world feels like it's spinning faster than a top. I mean, it is, but normally, I'm used to it. Right now? Right now, I seriously want to puke. I wobble on my feet, my legs mimicking Jell-O, when a strong arm wraps around my waist and tugs me into a warm side.

It's Griffin. I smell him before I see him. Sandalwood and the ocean and a warm summer breeze.

Peeking up at him, I open my mouth to tell him I'm fine, but he only shakes his head. "Are you okay?"

I look down at my shaking hands. "I, uh, I hit him."

"I heard." My gaze snaps to his, and he explains, "Window was open. If I knew the code to get into the building, I would've decked him myself. Fuck, Fin." He rubs his hand along my arm. "He had no right to say any of that shit to anyone, let alone someone he's supposed to love."

The familiar burn behind my eyes hits with full force as I bite the inside of my cheek to keep the tears from falling. "You know, I was thinking the exact same thing." Epilepsy is a bitch in more ways than I'll ever be able to actually articulate. The medicine. The unknowns. The recoveries. The way it affects even the smallest of decisions. But knowing someone who was supposed to love me unconditionally would have the audacity to throw it in my face and make me feel like an unfit parent is the lowest of blows.

Fighting the urge to collapse and cry, I swallow the lump in my throat and stare at the maple tree on the opposite side of the street. Its bare branches sway in the gentle breeze. I need to get out of here. I need to get away from… everything.

"He's an ass, Fin."

"It doesn't matter."

"It does," Griff growls. "That sonofabitch would be lucky to share a fucking Uber with you, let alone a kid."

I squeeze my eyes shut, hating the single tear managing to slip past my defenses and down my cheek. "Sure he would."

"Fin…"

"Let's get going." I wipe my cheek and look up at him, my gaze like fucking ice.

Concern brands his blue eyes as he stares down at me. And I know he wants to push the subject. I know he wants to reiterate how much of an ass Drew is. But it doesn't matter. Because nothing will take away the things he said to me. Not a single fucking thing in the world. And yeah, I know he's a jerk and I shouldn't care what he thinks, but the truth is…we both know I'll be replaying them for the rest of my life, and there isn't anything either one of us can do about it.

"Whatever you want, Fin," Griffin finally murmurs.

With a slow nod, I lean into his side and accept his help, too drained to even make it to the car by myself, let alone walk down thirteen cursed steps. Find a place to sleep. Check on Frankie. Drive home. Tell my family. Have a baby. Raise a baby. Alone.

I let out a slow breath. My to-do list is piling up faster than I can even compute.

What if the baby gets it?

My legs give out as my greatest fear slices through my mind, debilitating me, but before I can fall into a heap of anxiety and fear on the cold concrete steps, Griffin tightens his hold around my waist.

"I got you, Fin."

CHAPTER FOURTEEN

GRIFFIN

After Finley's settled in the passenger seat, I close the SUV's door and round the front, glancing at the building one more time. Drew's watching from the bedroom window, his expression unreadable. I give him the bird as I climb behind the steering wheel and crank the engine.

Motherfucker.

I can't believe he'd say shit like that. To anyone, let alone someone he's supposed to love. They've been together for years, and this is how he feels about her? I flex my hands against the steering wheel. I should've broken down the door and beat the shit out of him until he couldn't walk.

"How's your hand?" I ask.

"Stings."

The word is so...hollow. So unlike Finley that if I had a gun pressed to my temple, I'd say it didn't belong to her. But it does. It's all Finley. Just not...the girl I was raised with. No, this one's broken. Dejected. Fucked, if I'm being brutally honest. We all know the statistics. The possibility of slipping one past the goalie. Of winding up pregnant or knocking someone up. I never would've thought it would be Finley, though. The girl plans everything out. Every outfit. Every assignment. Every fucking thing to the smallest of details. What's she going to do now?

Unable to help myself, I steal a glance at her. She's staring at her lap, her hands pressed against her stomach. Her hair has fallen forward and shields most of her face from view. I don't miss the quiet sniffle, though. This girl doesn't cry. Not unless frogs are involved. The organ in my chest squeezes.

"I, uh, I'm sorry he didn't take the news like we'd hoped."

"We." A quiet scoff escapes her, and she wipes at her face.

"Yeah." I shift closer, reach around her still body, and grab her seatbelt, slowly clicking into place beside her hip. The sound reverberates through the silent cab, and she peeks at me, proving just how close we really are, dragging me back to all those years ago in her family room when she ditched me to hang out with Drew. I should've kissed her then. Maybe it would've saved her from the path she's on. Or maybe she'd still be here, but I wouldn't be. Different shades of gray and smoke and navy swirl in her glassy eyes, making them almost glow as she stares up at me...helpless. I was right. She's crying.

"*We*," I emphasize.

"There is no we," she reminds me. "There is no me and anyone." Her eyes fall to her lap again, and she sniffs quietly, her focus on the conversation hazy at best. She's giving in. Drowning in Drew's words. Letting them take her over.

A knife twists inside of me as I take her in. Beautiful. Broken. I should give her space. I should sit back in my seat instead of crowding her. I should stop letting her red-rimmed gaze tug at my sternum. I should do a lot of things.

She's Everett's little sister.

Everett's. Little. Sister.

And right now, this isn't about my feelings for her. This is about Finley and her baby. They're all that matter. All that will ever matter. Nudging her chin with my knuckle, I force her to look at me. "You're not alone. What about your family? And Dylan? And Ophelia? And Raine?"

Her bottom lip trembles.

"And me?" I push. "What about me, Fin?"

Her eyes fall to my mouth before flicking back to my gaze, and she pulls away from my touch, gutting me in the process.

"We should start driving," she whispers. "It's a long way back."

THE CLICKING OF THE BLINKER FINALLY DOES ME IN. IT'S been four hours. Four fucking hours of silence. By now, it's burrowed under my skin, leaving me raw and itchy and uncomfortable and frustrated. So fucking frustrated. Part of me wants to turn the car around. To barge into Drew's place, drag him out by his polo, and beat the ever loving shit out of him. Honestly, imagining it has been the best way to pass the time since drowning in Finley's silence wasn't flying. After the shit he said to Fin, he'd deserve every single hit. He's lucky he's still breathing. I fist the steering wheel, imagining all the ways I could kill him if we lived in a world without consequences.

"How do you get rid of a body?" I ask.

Her glassy eyes shoot to me. "What?"

"I said, how do you get rid of a body?" My eyes shoot to hers for a quick second then return to the crowded freeway. "You're the criminal mastermind, not me."

Her lips twitch. "Are you offering to kill Drew for me?"

I nod. "Happily. Do you think limb by limb is too gruesome, or should I just hit him with my car?"

A pathetic laugh slips out of her, and she wipes beneath her eyes. "I think limb by limb sounds pretty good right about now, actually."

"I can do that." I give her a smile. "Although, you'll have to help me get rid of the evidence."

"Another pro to ripping him into pieces," she offers. "You know, since he won't be so heavy, and I'll actually be able to contribute physically."

With a rumble of laughter, I reach across the center console and squeeze her knee. "I like your thinking."

Staring at my hand on her knee, she whispers, "Can I ask you something?"

I nod. "Anything."

"Who was your first?"

My brows stitch. "My first?"

"Yeah, your, uh, your first...taco."

"Taco?" I hesitate until her meaning sinks in, and my eyes widen. "You mean who's the first girl I had sex with?"

She nods.

I laugh a little louder and let her knee go. We've talked about sexual stuff in the past. I mean, what else would you expect after a few beers and games like Truth or Dare and Never Have I Ever. But like this? Without our friends around and no one to buffer the situation? It's new, and I'm not sure what to make of it.

Scrubbing my hand over my face, I'm caught between

my own curiosity and the line we've drawn in the sand when it comes to all things sexual long before this road trip. "You really want to know?"

She shrugs but stays quiet.

"Seriously?"

"You're right. It's a stupid question."

"Not a stupid question," I argue. "Just a...surprising one." I give her the side-eye and find her stormy gaze focused solely on me. Like she's hanging on to my every word. The silence drives me crazy. Part of me wants to pry. To ask the why behind her off-the-wall question. The other part? I guess I'm just grateful she's not still consumed by her conversation with Drew.

With a smirk, I answer, "My first was Jenna...Ortega."

She smacks my shoulder. "I'm being serious!"

"Hey, you're the one who said she had kissable lips. No need to be jealous."

Rolling her still-watery eyes, she mutters, "Whatever. Forget I asked."

"All right, all right," I concede, determined to keep her talking instead of silently losing her shit in my passenger seat. "My first really was named Jenna, though."

Her lips purse like she doesn't believe me. "You're joking."

"I'm not," I say with a laugh. "Her name was Jenna Galinski. Junior year. You?"

"Drew." She shifts in her seat. "Junior year."

I nod, unsure what to say. I guess I always assumed Drew was her first and only, but hearing it out loud? The reminder that he owns a piece of her she'll never get back, especially after the shit he put her through today? It's sobering and makes me want to turn the SUV around all over again.

Staring out the windshield, Fin whispers, "Did you love her?"

"Jenna?" I pause, then shake my head. "Not sure I've ever been in love, Fin."

"Did you *think* you were in love with her?" she prods.

Lifting my shoulder, I admit, "Honestly? Not really. I know it makes me sound like a dick, but…there it is."

She gives me a slow nod and tucks her hair behind her ear. "Hmm."

"Hmm?" I repeat, casting her another quick glance.

"I guess it makes sense," she murmurs. "Considering the fact that you've never really had a girlfriend."

She's right. I haven't. My parents have even asked once or twice over the years. Why I haven't seriously dated anyone. Why I haven't given anyone a chance. Don't get me wrong. I've spent plenty of time hooking up with girls and shit, but actual dating? I don't know. I always told myself—and anyone who bothered to ask—that I was focusing on my career in the NHL, and I'd take dating seriously down the road, but the truth is, hockey's always been the priority. The focus. I'd resent it if I didn't love it so much. The game. The adrenaline. The high.

Besides, finding a girl who's okay with all the traveling and the possibility of uprooting their life at the drop of a hat to move from one city to the next because of a trade is slim to none. I should know. I was raised in this life, thanks to my dad. Saw how much it affected my mom, and me, and my siblings. And we were the lucky ones. The ones who got to stay in Lockwood Heights. But even then, I remember the away games. The missed parent-teacher conferences. The empty seats at my own hockey games, all because my dad was traveling. It isn't easy. Expecting someone to sign up for that kind of life. Add to the fact that I'm aware of where my priorities lie, and…I guess I've never seen the point of it all.

"Why settle down when you know they aren't the one?" I finally offer.

She nods again. "How many…since Jenna Galinski?"

I pull back, surprised. "Are you asking for my body count?"

"You're right. It's weird." She shakes her head. "Forget I asked."

Forget she asked? Not a fucking chance.

"Why so curious?" I prod.

"It's just…" She tucks her feet under her ass and sits cross-legged in the passenger seat, facing me. "I've only ever been with Drew, and now that I'm going to be a single mom, my body's going to change, and I'm going to be super busy, and…"

Giving her the side-eye, I ask, "Are you afraid you'll never get laid again, Finley Taylor?"

A light blush hits her cheeks as she fiddles with her earring. "That's not what I meant…"

"You sure?" My dick twitches in my jeans, and I shift in my seat, squeezing the steering wheel until my knuckles are white. I never thought I'd have a conversation with Finley about shit like this. Up until I heard her masturbate a few days ago, I was convinced we'd never broach this subject.

The funny thing about Finley is she's never been shy. Never been humble, even. The girl's confident in everything she does. Seeing her vulnerable like this? Seeing the cogs in her Pandora's box of a brain is…refreshing, almost. And fuck, if I don't want to open it and see what's inside.

"I just don't know what to expect, that's all," she finally argues. "I've only ever been with Drew, and then when you add in everything else my future holds, you can't blame me for feeling like I can kiss any kind of physical relationship goodbye for the foreseeable future. So, sue me."

"Trust me, Fin," I rasp. "Any guy would be lucky to make your coffee, let alone hold your hand and…all the other stuff." My mouth lifts. "You're gonna be okay."

She gulps and looks down at her stomach again. "Sure, we will."

CHAPTER FIFTEEN

GRIFFIN

The bags fall with a heavy thud as deja vu washes over me. There are two beds this time, and my tired body sags with relief. Finley's eyes are bloodshot. The skin surrounding them is puffy and red from crying.

Despite her meltdown when Frankie escaped into her room, I've only seen the girl cry a handful of times. One time, when Dylan accidentally lit Finley's favorite Barbie on fire, and once when she woke up from a bad seizure. Oh, and let's not forget about the time Aunt Mia convinced us to watch *Marley and Me* on a projector screen in their backyard. Yeah, that movie was a bitch, and Fin wasn't the only one misty-eyed on the grass. Then there was the night we found out about Archer's accident, and I watched help- lessly as Everett held her in his arms while she sobbed until her voice was gone. The memory is enough to make my throat tighten, but I push it aside.

As I look over at her, my hands itch to hold her now. To promise everything's going to be okay, even though I have no idea whether or not it's true.

After our conversation in the car, she went back to being a mime. I get it, though. She has a lot to think about. A lot to process. A lot to consider.

She doesn't climb into bed like I expect. Instead, she silently digs through her bag for her toothbrush and medicine, then closes the bathroom door behind her. Situating Frankie on the credenza, I pull the covers back, put on a pair of basketball shorts, and change places with Finley. Once my teeth are brushed, I open the bathroom door, finding a lump on the nearest mattress.

"Did you take your medicine?" I ask.

"Yes."

Not a "Yes, Dad" or "Did *you* take *your* medicine?" or any other snarky response. Just…yes.

Flicking off the lights, I climb into the opposite bed, ignoring the worry settling in my stomach as I reach for the covers and pull the itchy cotton fabric on top of me. I need to sleep. I need to stop thinking about what Finley said in the car. I need to get out of my own head and make a game plan for the future. Finley's future.

Her quiet voice cuts through the silence and my ears perk. "Hey, Griff?"

"Yeah?"

"Can you… Man, I sound so pathetic," she mutters under her breath, but it's laced with a sad amusement, too. Melancholy almost.

"Tell me," I push.

"Can you…hold me?"

My chest squeezes, and I shift toward her, but she's already out of her bed, slipping beneath the white comforter on my own without waiting for my response. I've always liked that about her. The way she takes what she wants without remorse. Even when we were kids, and she didn't feel like watching Ophelia play hockey with the rest of the guys, she would hide everyone's gear and wouldn't tell us where it was until we'd give in and do what she wanted for an hour. It used to drive me nuts. Now, I envy it. Admire it, even.

The irony isn't lost on me. I'm miles away from where I'm supposed to be, all because I gave in to a pretty girl's request. I should be preparing for a very important meeting with the General Manager of the Tornadoes. Instead, I'm here. Sharing a bed with my best friend's little sister, and I can't scrounge up the remorse to regret it.

When Finley's bare toes brush against my calves, my muscles bunch, but I don't pull away, letting her steal my warmth as she tucks her icy toes against my flesh. If only she knew how much more I'd be willing to give her if she asked for it.

"I'm sorry," she whispers.

The scent of lavender clings to her dark hair and tickles my nostrils as I try to keep myself in check. "You have nothing to apologize for."

"Yes, I do." She twists in my arms and faces me, bringing us nose to nose. Reaching up, she drags her fingertips against my temple. "There's always been a we, hasn't there?"

My heart ratchets, and I wet my bottom lip but stay quiet.

"I'm sorry for taking it for granted," she murmurs. "For taking *you* for granted."

Fuck. If she'd stabbed me in the chest, I would've felt less. Because it shouldn't hurt. The reminder of how she chose Drew over our friendship, but it does. If she never became pregnant, would she be here? In my bed? Looking at me like this? Telling me these things?

"You do know you're kind of perfect, right?" she adds.

Her fingers skate across my scruff, branding me in a

way I doubt she'll ever even know. It takes everything inside of me to not close my eyes. Not to lose myself in this moment. In her touch. In her vulnerability.

"Hardly perfect, Fin," I mutter.

"Look at that. He's humble, too." She tacks on a fake-as-shit smile. "Can I tell you a secret?"

"Always."

Her fingers tremble against my jaw. "I'm terrified out of my mind, Griff."

My chest caves with the weight of her words. "It's going to be all right."

"You don't know that. No one knows that," she clarifies. And I hate how, even without any light, I can still feel her fear. Her insecurities. Her doubts. They cling to her silky skin. Tainting her words. This moment. Everything.

I want to take it all away. I want to bring back the confident, sassy, sarcastic-as-shit Finley. The one I know is hiding, thanks to Drew's comments from earlier.

"Our families have dealt with surprise pregnancies before, Fin," I remind her.

"You mean when my parents got pregnant with Ev?" She chuckles, but there isn't any humor in it. "Not sure the situation's the same. Especially not anymore. My mom had my dad's support, and—"

"And you have your family's. And your friends'. And mine."

"You." She touches the side of my face again, dragging her fingertips from my forehead, along my temple, down my jaw, then brushes them against the edge of my lip. It's like a feather. Light. Almost non-existent. But I can feel it everywhere. Every. Fucking. Inch of me is like a livewire. And I'm living, eating, breathing for her to do it again. To touch me again. To keep looking at me like this. Like she's curious. Like she could want me the same way I've always wanted her.

"Am I…am I wrong for wanting to keep the baby?" she whispers. "Even though Drew wants nothing to do with it?"

Drew.

I fight the urge to curse his name, forcing my body to relax.

"Drew's a jackass," I remind her.

"Drew's looking at the big picture."

"Fuck the big picture," I argue. "Do you want to have this baby?"

Her bottom lip quivers, but her head bobs against the pillow, confirming what I've known all along. "Yes. Yes, I want to have this baby."

"Then you're gonna have this baby," I promise. "And they're gonna be spoiled by everyone around them. Everyone." My mouth lifts. "Trust me. You might think you're alone in this, but you aren't, Fin. You're not alone." My gaze falls to her lips. "I'm here."

"You are." She wets her lips. "You're here."

"I'm here," I repeat. "And I'm not going anywhere."

Slowly, she lifts her chin and presses her mouth to mine, surprising the shit out of me. Salt clings to her lips. It muddies the moment I've dreamed about for years while only making me crave her more. I could've anticipated a thousand scenarios for how tonight would play out, and none of them would've included me in bed with Fin. Not like this. It isn't a soft kiss. It's doused with need. And desperation. And—*fuck*. What the hell is going on? I never thought I'd kiss Fin. Not like this. Not without the excuse of a bet or a dare or a game. But this? My muscles flood with restraint as she keeps her mouth pressed to mine, taking what she wants without promising anything in return, and fuck me if I don't want to let her take it all.

But not yet. Not now. Not when I don't know if her demons are chasing her or if she's thinking of Drew. So, even though it kills me, I slow the kiss, pumping the brakes and cupping her cheek as I force myself to pull away.

Confusion swirls in her red-rimmed eyes as she stares at me, her cheeks glistening from fallen tears. "Griff—"

"Get some sleep," I rasp. "I'm not going anywhere."

"Griff…"

"Get some sleep," I repeat. Wrapping my arm around her waist, I force her closer to me, praying she doesn't misconstrue my actions for rejection. Because that isn't it. Not in the slightest. But she has to understand where I'm coming from and what this would mean, doesn't she? She's sad and heartbroken and overwhelmed, and I can't take advantage of her. Not tonight. Not after the shit day she's had.

It doesn't take long until she gives in, proving I was right to end the kiss because the Finley I know? She would've never stopped there if she really wanted more. Her eyelids flutter, and she snuggles into my side, her warm breath seeping into my T-shirt until slowly, finally, she falls asleep.

CHAPTER SIXTEEN

FINLEY

Incessant buzzing rouses me from sleep. Peeling my eyelids open, I search the dark room, feeling like I'm being pinned to the mattress by a dead body. Nope. It's only Griffin's arm.

Holy shit, it's Griffin's arm. I'm in bed with Griffin.

Flashes from earlier tonight—er, last night?—rise to the surface. I can't believe I kissed Griff. I can't believe he rejected me. I can't believe I slept beside him after he rejected me.

Shit.

The buzzing continues while I try to piece together the here and now instead of drowning in the hazy memory of last night. My phone's on the nightstand. Its screen glows in the pitch black room, blinding me. Slipping out from beneath him, I reach for it, silence the call, and tiptoe into the bathroom to answer it.

"Hello?" I whisper.

"Where the hell are you?" my brother snaps.

I pull the phone away from my ear before bringing it back. "Why hello to you, too, Oscar."

"It's Everett."

"I know it's you." I roll my eyes. "I called you Oscar because you're acting like Oscar the Grouch, which is kind of ironic since you're supposedly on a beach sipping Pina Coladas with your hot girlfriend, so why the hell are you calling me?" I fight a yawn, adding, "And what time is it?"

"Maybe because I'm not on vacation anymore," he replies. "I'm at the house, and you aren't here."

My forehead scrunches, and I wipe at my tired eyes, trying to convince my brain to wake up and compute this conversation. "Why are you at the house? I thought you and the guys were flying straight to Minnesota for the away games after New Year's, then coming back with the team?"

"Mom and Dad told me about the seizure," he mutters. The bastard sounds *almost* apologetic for gossiping behind my back, but it isn't enough to let him off the hook.

Leaning my shoulder against the bathroom wall, I grumble, "Should've known they'd blabber to you."

"You still haven't answered my question. Where are you? And where the hell is Griff? He was supposed to have his meeting this morning."

My heart ratchets at the mention of Griffin. "Meeting?"

"Yeah. With the Tornadoes."

The Tornadoes is the NHL team Griffin signed with during his senior year of high school. He'll play for them after this season. Well, if he plays well on the farm team next season. Man, how time flies. The reminder is bittersweet, and I peek through the barely cracked open bathroom door.

The first rays of morning light filter through the blackout curtains, highlighting Griffin's strong arms and bare chest. The same chest I snuggled up against all night. I'm still not sure how it happened. How I wound up spilling all of my insecurities, kissing him, and managing to fall asleep in his arms after he politely ended the said kiss, even though I'm pretty sure I would've gone all the way with him in a heartbeat. It was a mistake, obviously, but I can't make myself regret it despite his rejection. I needed to be held, and he welcomed me with open arms. No hesitation. No conditions. Just him and me and a night I'll never forget.

I tear my attention from the man's muscular forearm tossed over his eyes and attempt to focus on my conversation. "Why was he supposed to meet with the Tornadoes?"

"Technically, we don't know since he hasn't met with them yet, but there was an injury during last week's game, and since they're well within range of the Stanley Cup, and Griffin plays Caruthers' position, *and* Griffin's been killing it this season, well, I have a hunch."

"Spell it out for me, then," I push. "You know how I feel about all the hockey mumbo jumbo."

"I think the Tornadoes want him to pull out of the rest of LAU's season and move straight to the bench so he can fill in for Caruthers."

"What?" I ask. "I didn't think that was possible."

"It's rare but not impossible," he clarifies.

"Passing up on his degree, let alone missing out on the last quarter of his NCAA career? That's...that's a big deal, isn't it?"

"It's huge, which is why I was surprised neither of you are here," he says, bringing up his original reason for calling.

Oh. Right.

I clear my throat. "Yeah, that's...strange, isn't it."

"Finley," he warns.

My expression pinches. "Oo, someone's bossy today."

"I'm always bossy. Now, where are you?"

"Griffin drove me to see Drew."

"Why?"

I grimace, considering all the things I could say and how much they would piss Everett off if he heard them. Oh, you know, I'm kinda sorta pregnant, and Griffin twisted my arm into telling the father face to face, but it blew up in my face, and now I'm going to be a single mom forever. Yay me. Oh, and PS, I also kissed your best friend last night and slept next to him, so that's new.

"Fin?" Everett prods.

I clear my throat and try to choose my next words carefully. "I, uh, I had a hunch Drew was cheating on me, and I wanted to talk to him face to face, and since my driver's license is now suspended thanks to my seizure Mom and Dad blabbered to you about, the next best thing was to…swing by." I cringe as the words roll off my tongue.

"Swing by?" Everett laughs. "Swing by is a thirty-minute drive. An hour, tops. Drew lives across multiple states, Finley. That isn't a quick drop-in kind of visit. You don't just swing by—"

"Wrap it up, Everett. It's early, and I'm too tired for this conversation."

"Someone's sassy today," he notes, twisting my own words back at me.

"Someone woke up to a grouchy phone call."

"Because someone flew home early from their vacation to check on you," he volleys back at me.

"Fine," I grumble. "Unnecessary, but thank you for being sweet and ending your vacation early even though you most definitely could've called like a normal human being."

"You're welcome," he answers shamelessly. "Besides, it was supposed to rain for the rest of the trip, so we weren't missing too much. Figured flying back with the girls and checking on you was the way to go."

I snort. "Gee, thanks."

"It also doesn't hurt that Raine misses her family," he adds. "Not sure what we're gonna do next season with the Rockets."

"You mean, other than kick butt and make a splash in the NHL?"

"And take her from her family," he mutters.

"Whoa, there. Trouble in paradise, big brother?"

"Nah, we're good. It's just…I dunno."

"Come on," I push, grateful for the topic change. "Pretty sure being a solid sounding board is part of any little sister's resume. Spit it out."

"I dunno," he repeats. "Her ex was good at keeping her from her family. And I know it was always the plan for me to move away and play for the Rockets, but I don't wanna do the same thing. Not when they're finally on good terms again."

Despite Everett not being able to see me, I find myself nodding. He's right. Raine's ex was an abusive asshole who gave her crap anytime she wanted to see her family, so she stopped seeing them. I don't think it happened overnight or anything, but sometimes it's easier to avoid fights than to wade through them. With Raine coming around her family more now, I can see why she might be hesitant to move across the country to be with Everett.

"You're nothing like Drake, though," I remind him. "And besides, there are airplanes, right? I have no doubt you'll bring her back to Lockwood Heights every chance you get."

"Yeah, that's true." He sighs. "But now, she's working with her dad, and…" Another sigh escapes him. "When are you coming home?"

"Subtle subject change," I quip. "And today. We should be home around dinner time."

"Sounds good. I'll make you guys something to eat."

"Don't bother. We can grab food on the way."

"You sure?"

"Yup. No big deal."

"All right. By the way, I know you two have been teetering for a while. How did it go?"

"It?" I squeak. The blood drains from my face as I imagine telling him all the sordid details of what it feels like to kiss his best friend when he interrupts my spiraling thoughts.

"Confronting Drew," he clarifies.

My body sags against the doorjamb. "Oh."

"What did you think I was talking about?" Everett demands.

"Nothing," I lie. "And it went…about as shitty as you would expect." I rub my tired eyes again and replay the last twenty-four hours. The drive. The fight. Drew's callousness. Me slapping him.

"And?" my brother prods.

"We broke up."

It's such a simple statement. Like the sky is blue or caffeine is life. Leaning my back against the counter, I wait for the sting of betrayal to hit me, but it doesn't. All I feel is…the slight tingle of my lips.

"So, he was cheating on you?" Everett prods.

He.

As in, Drew.

Right.

"Technically, he says nothing happened," I offer, "but a girl can read between the lines, you know?"

"Fuck him," my brother curses. "I never liked him anyway."

My lips curve up. "That, you made very clear."

"Yeah, well, I was right, like always."

"So humble," I note.

"It's genetic," he quips, pulling another quiet laugh from me before he adds, "Besides. This'll be good for you."

"What will be good for me?"

"To take a break from guys and focus on yourself. You were with the asshat for so long you never even had the chance to be young and stupid and reckless. Fuck the responsibilities that come with relationships and do your own thing."

"Says the guy who's head over heels for Raine," I toss back at him.

"She's different," he argues. "And I'm older than you. Actually, Raine and I are both older than you."

"Age is only a number, brother."

"I'm just saying there's nothing wrong with enjoying life without needing a guy by your side twenty-four-seven. Do you even know what it's like to be single? You have your entire life to settle down and fall in love. You should enjoy the lack of responsibility. The freedom. The time to be selfish and only think about you. You've never had it."

I'll never have it. Not anymore. The realization is bittersweet. I look down at my stomach, well aware it looks the exact same way as it did two months ago. This isn't about me any more. None of this is. It's about my baby.

I'm going to have a baby.

Deep breath, Fin, I remind myself.

Reading my silence as confirmation that my heart is hurting, Everett adds, "Don't let the asshole get you down. You might've been with him for years, but let's be honest. Most of that time was spent with you two fighting."

"Not *most* of the time," I defend, no matter how pointless it is. He's right. Drew and I fought. A lot. The reminder makes me feel like I'm the failure. The one who was unreasonable. Who screwed up. Who was too stubborn to acknowledge that maybe we weren't a good fit for each other anymore. Maybe I'm not a good fit for anyone anymore.

"Whatever you say, Fin," Everett mutters. "All I'm saying is he was dead weight. You should celebrate."

I roll my eyes. "Celebrate, huh?"

"Yeah. Celebrate," he repeats. "What do you say we have a Game Night tonight? It's New Year's Eve. Might as well help the friends lick their wounds since we had to come home early, and it'll help get your mind off things. It might even be the last one Griffin attends if my hunch is right about the meeting, and he was able to reschedule it."

The reminder of Griffin missing his meeting and my part in it leaves a dull ache inside me. Why would he do that? Why would he potentially piss off the Tornadoes? Is that why he ended the kiss before it had a chance to turn into anything else? Because he knows he's leaving sooner rather than later? Not that the timeline matters. He's moving. Whether it's today or a month from now or even after graduation. He has a life ahead of him. A life he's worked so damn hard for, and he deserves my support.

"I think it's a great idea," I announce. "A Game Night."

"Perfect. I'll tell Reeves to get the ball rolling. Drive safe, yeah?"

"We will. And, Ev?"

"Yeah?"

"Thanks for being awesome."

"Love you, too, Fin."

The call ends, and I set my phone on the counter, grasping the edge of the cool surface. I don't want to go back to bed. The idea of snuggling next to Griffin is a bad idea, especially after the reality check with Ev, but climbing into cold sheets feels like I'm succumbing to my lackluster future. I peek through the cracked door again, giving myself a minute to appreciate Griffin in all his shirtless glory. Moving toward the shower, I turn the stupid thing to its hottest setting, rest my forehead against the cold tile, and wait for the water to heat up.

My pajamas smell like him. Like the guy I slept next to. He's leaving. He has to leave. He has plans. Plans I've known about for years. Plans he's worked so hard for. Plans that have nothing to do with me, and honestly, that's okay. Besides, I'm the one who climbed into his bed. Who threw myself at him. And even though it was a pretty epic kiss last night, maybe that's all it needs to be. All it should be.

A kiss.

I mean, he's the one who pulled away first. He probably already knows pursuing something is a bad idea. It just took me a minute longer to come to the same conclusion. That's all.

I put my hand under the spray, strip down to my birthday suit, and step into the shower, letting the liquid heat flow down my body before grabbing the soap and washing every inch of me.

My brother's right about one thing. I've never been alone, and now that I have a baby inside of me, I never will be. But that's okay. And so is accepting my situation with Griffin.

CHAPTER SEVENTEEN

GRIFFIN

I wake with a groan and cover my eyes with my bicep. "What time is it?"

"Time to wake up, sleepyhead," Finley says. She sounds farther away than I expect. Forcing my eyelids open, I check the bed, but it's empty. She's next to the window, the blackout curtains pulled back, and her long, dark hair damp from what looks like a shower.

"What time did you wake up?" I croak.

Checking the time on her phone, she answers, "About an hour ago," before slipping her cell back into her pocket. "I've showered. I've gotten ready. And I'm officially starting my *I don't give a shit, and I need no man* era."

I sit up a little straighter, pressing my back to the head-board. "What?"

"I want to thank you for last night," she adds. "I really needed…I don't know. A moment to know I'm not alone or something?" She shrugs. "Honestly, I don't even know," she repeats, "but thank you. You seriously gave me exactly what I needed to get through all of this. I even fed Frankie without having a meltdown, and if that isn't the definition of a strong, independent woman, I don't know what is." With a grin, she adds, "I'm going to grab some coffee at the Starbucks down the street. Do you want anything?"

My brows bunch as I study her. "Uh…I'm…good?"

"You sure?" She laughs. "You look tired."

I'm confused as fuck is what I am.

"Uh," I scrub my hand over my face. "Are we good?"

"Yeah, why wouldn't we be?"

"Because we kissed last night, and you're…"

"I'm what?" she asks.

My eyes narrow as I take her in. The perfectly done makeup. The perfectly chosen outfit. The perfectly constructed defenses she's gathered around herself since I fell asleep with her in my arms. There are pros and cons to knowing someone the way I know Finley. Learning what makes a person tick and what constitutes strange behavior, like the doppelganger in front of me. She might look like Finley and smell like Finley, but she isn't Fin. Or, at least, not the Fin I consoled last night. No, this is *fake-it-til-you-make-it-Fin*, and it pisses me off.

"I'll get you a mocha," she decides. "Why don't you shower while I'm gone, then we'll head out?"

She steps closer to the hotel's door, but as she scoots around the edge of the bed, I reach out and grab her wrist, keeping her in place.

"Fin," I say.

She looks down at where I'm touching her. "Yes?"

"What's going on?"

"Nothing."

"What's. Going. On?" I repeat.

"Are you going to cut me off again, or are you going to let me talk?" she demands, stubborn as ever.

I let her go and lift my knee, resting my forearm against it as I stare up at her as if to say, "The floor's all yours."

With a huff, she flips her hair over her shoulder. "Like I said, nothing is going on."

I wait a solid ten seconds, but the girl's mute. "That's it?"

"Not sure what else you want me to say," she hedges.

"You broke up with your long-term boyfriend last night."

"I'm well aware, thank you."

"And you kissed your brother's best friend."

"*And* it was good," she quips. "Like, *really* good. You have one talented mouth, and I'm not trying to blow smoke up your ass, either. Bravo, Griffin." She gives me a slow clap. "Anything else?"

"Not gonna ask why I ended the kiss?"

"Nope."

I hold her stare, waiting for her to cave, even though I know she won't. "You know, for someone who's hella chatty, you're good at dodging questions while saying nothing at all."

"I'm not dodging anything," she argues. "Everything you said is true, but there's no use crying about any of it or overanalyzing any of it, so why bother discussing any of it?" Her shoulder lifts. "Hot or iced?"

"What's going on, Fin?" I push. "We kissed last night, you slept in my arms, and now—"

"Now, it's time to get going," she interrupts.

I hesitate, trying to get my mind to…wake up or something because shit isn't making any sense, and neither is Finley's stiff posture. I ask, "So, we're gonna pretend like nothing happened?"

"Nothing did happen," she defends. "Look, last night was…exactly what I needed. Thank you," she adds with a genuine smile. "But I just got out of a long-term relationship, you're my brother's best friend who's going to be living across the country within the next six months, and I'm going to be a single mom by the end of the summer, so…that's that, don't you think?"

"That's *that*?" I repeat. Seriously, did I enter the *Twilight Zone*? She was sad. She asked me to hold her. We both crossed a line, and yeah, I slowed things down, but now, she's gonna act like it was nothing? Even if she's hesitant to commit to anything or is hurt that I pumped the brakes, which I understand, the blasé attitude messes with my head.

"Yeah. That's that," she returns. Her stormy gaze shoots around the room as she flaps her hands through the air. "I don't expect anything from you. I don't even want anything from you."

"You don't." It isn't a question, but fuck if I'd like some actual answers right now.

She. Kissed. Me.

Clenching the sheets around my waist, I try not to lose my shit as I hold her gaze.

"Nope. I don't want anything from you." She forces her attention to stay pinned on me, her eye twitching. "Except for you to hop in the shower so we can get on the road as quickly as possible. I think the real question is, why are you still lying in bed, lazy bones?"

The girl's so transparent she might as well be glass. And yeah, she's being genuine right now, but something spooked her. Something put her on edge. I just can't figure out what. I know she probably kissed me because she was sad and wanted to be held, which is why I pulled away. I know she would never expect me to jump into a relationship with her, let alone ask me to. But this? This flippant replay, lack of expectation, and aversion to anything real feel…off.

Sometimes, this woman makes me feel like a yo-yo.

Like she can pull me in and push me away but always keep me on a string, ready for her beck and call, and there's nothing I can do about it. It's infuriating.

Did it really mean nothing?

"Fine." I pull the covers off and walk my ass to the shower. And even though I can feel her stare on me as I leave, I know she won't do anything about it.

It's Finley fucking Taylor.

Why did I expect anything different?

CHAPTER EIGHTEEN

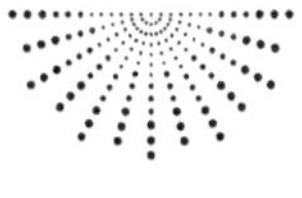

FINLEY

Considering how long I've known Griffin Thorne, he's pretty good at keeping his emotions under wraps. After I disappeared from the hotel room to grab coffee, he's been acting...fine? I think? Maybe a little aloof or something, but I kind of expected him to be pissed at me. Not that he should be. He's the one who put a stop to whatever shenanigans we might've gotten up to, if he'd let me take the lead, so...

Maybe this is just...par for the course when you have a moment of weakness and kiss someone you care about, even though you most definitely shouldn't. Kiss them, not care about them. Obviously, I should care about Griff. He's one of the most amazing people I've ever met. But kissing him, let alone hooking up with him, is a bad idea.

Besides, it's for the best. Last night was...it was... I was hurting. But I'm not about to go down this road with him. Not when he has such an amazing, bright future ahead of him. The fact he missed out on his meeting with the Tornadoes all because I wanted to face Drew head-on? It only solidifies the truth. He deserves more than screwing up his future for his best friend's little sister. Especially when said little sister has a bun in the oven and a neurological disease, which will never be a picnic and will never be a good fit for a guy who travels for a living. I've already settled for someone who wasn't a good fit for me. Doing it twice is a recipe for disaster, isn't it? Still, pretending like last night wasn't a big deal wasn't exactly a walk in the park. I knew Griff and I had chemistry, but our kiss? The feel of his mouth on mine, the tiny groan in the back of his throat? The way his hand practically swallowed the side of my face and his callouses tickled my skin? Yeah... that was a different level of chemistry. So much so my lips are still tingling, and I'm not sure anything will ever beat it.

The drive is boring and quiet, and he doesn't grumble at me when I pick the soundtrack to Disney's *Zombies* movies.

It's my only clue as to whether or not he's lost in his own thoughts like I've been since we left the hotel.

When we pull up to the house hours later, the streets are lined with cars, and Griffin's frown deepens. "What the hell?"

"They flew home early," I explain, cringing. "I probably should've told you, but—"

"You were too busy grabbing coffee?" he offers with a lifted brow.

I nod.

"No worries," he answers, not surprisingly. "What are they doing home?"

"Everett heard about my seizure, so the guys decided flying home with the girls, then traveling with the team for the away games instead of meeting everyone in Minnesota was a bright idea." I shrug. "Figured they'd celebrate."

"What's there to celebrate?"

"Your meeting with the Tornadoes? Oh, wait." I snap my fingers. "You missed it, didn't you?"

His gaze narrows. "How'd you know about my meeting?"

"Seems I'm not the only one with secrets."

"Fin—"

"Everett told me about it." I hide my hurt and pick at my nails instead. "The question is, why didn't you?"

"Didn't know I needed to," he argues. "Besides, it's not a big deal."

Fighting the urge to smack him upside the head, I cross my arms and demand, "You sure? Because Everett made it sound like it kind of was."

His nostrils flare. "Is that why you've been acting weird?"

"I haven't—"

"You have."

"Says the pot to the kettle," I toss back at him.

Before he has a chance to argue any further, Dylan appears from the house's entrance. She skips down the short set of stairs but nearly trips on her own two feet, grabbing the railing for balance while I fight the urge to laugh. Seriously, the girl is clumsier than a baby giraffe. Shoving her glasses another inch up her nose, she lets the iron go and strides closer.

As I lower the passenger window, she calls, "Where's my Frankie? Is he alive? Did he survive? You weren't supposed to take him—"

"Your devil child's fine," I tell her. "I even fed him and everything."

With a relieved sigh, she peeks into the backseat, finds Frankie's terrarium tucked between my backpack and Griffin's duffle bag, and opens the back door so she can reach her precious demon. Good riddance. Scooting into the backseat, she unwedges the terrarium from our bags, and cradles the glass container to her chest as if Frankie is her own flesh and blood. "How's my little guy? Huh, baby?" She dips her head and practically presses her face against the glass to get a better look at the monster. "Did Aunt Finley treat you oh so good, or do I need to sneak you into her bed tonight?"

My lips thin, and I make eye contact with my supposed best friend through the rearview mirror as I roll the passenger window up. "Trust me. That won't be necessary."

"Yeah. Been there, done that," Griffin adds from the driver's seat as he pushes his door open.

Dylan's forehead wrinkles. "What?"

"Frankie jumped out of his cage a couple days ago and wound up torturing me on my bed," I explain.

Eyes bugging out of her head, Dylan almost chokes on her own amusement as she asks, "Are you serious?"

"Careful," Griffin interjects. He climbs out of the car, then bends at the waist so he can hold his sister's stare. "The wound's still fresh."

"Yikes." Swallowing her fresh cackle, Dylan smooths out her expression and clears her throat. "Well, when you finally decide to have kids, I'd be happy to babysit as a thank you."

My lungs squeeze, but I paste on a smile, refusing to acknowledge how close her comment hits home. "Sounds great. I'll definitely hold you to it."

"Perfect! Oh, and, uh," she grimaces, "sorry about the breakup. How are you holding up?"

Keeping my smile in place, I tuck my hair behind my ear, then reach for the door handle. "Never better."

"Why am I not surprised?" She follows my lead and climbs out of the car. The cold breeze hits our faces, turning Dylan's cheeks pink as she adds, "Seriously, Fin.

Pretty sure an asteroid could be headed in our direction, and you'd still find a way to not only handle it but handle it like a freaking pro."

If only she knew.

"I think you're overestimating my abilities," I argue.

"Hardly. And look at the bright side." Dylan's eyes light up. "Now you and Griff can be friends again without feeling guilty, which is actually perfect considering tonight's game."

Closing the driver's side door, Griffin rounds the front of the SUV and asks, "What's tonight's game?"

"You'll see," Dylan replies, still juggling Frankie's terrarium. "Come inside. It's freezing out here, and I don't want Frankie to catch a cold."

"Yeah, wouldn't that be a shame," I quip.

Ignoring Dylan's half-assed glare, we follow her into the house. It's less busy than usual. Still littered with gyrating bodies, don't get me wrong, but there's maybe half of the usual chaos ensuing, and I can't decide if I'm happy about it or not. Part of me could've used the distraction. The other part? Well, I'm too lost in my own head to compute anything but the bare minimum at the moment.

A freshman from one of my classes is at the door. Handcuffs are sprawled out on the table beside him. It's the only hint I can see as to what game we'll be playing tonight.

When I see them, my mouth lifts. "Kinky."

Dylan tosses me a grin over her shoulder. "Raine picked tonight's game, since the last one ended with her crying. Everett suggested we play one of your favorites."

My gaze narrows. "This is payback for when I suggested we play open wide for a nice surprise, isn't it?"

She laughs. "Yup."

"Cuff up, Fin!" my brother calls from the top of the

stairs, well aware of how much I hate being partnered with someone during Game Nights. "You and Griff are on a team."

"I don't get to at least pick my own teammate?" I demand.

"You're too late." He takes the stairs two at a time, meeting us in the entryway. "Everyone else is already paired up."

Standing on my tiptoes, I start searching the family room for a familiar face, muttering, "I'm pretty sure I could find someone to—"

"Griff can take your shots," Everett adds.

Griffin groans beside me, and my face pulls even more as my heels hit the ground. "If he has to take both our shots, he'll be bombed by the second round, and I'll lose."

"I think you mean *we'll* lose," Griffin interjects.

"Suck it up, buttercup," Ophelia calls from the top of the stairs. "It's time for a New Year's Eve Game Night."

"Can I at least take off my jacket?" I ask.

Ophelia shrugs. "You can, but the last obstacle is outside, so…"

"So I get to sweat my ass off *and* get bombed," Griffin grumbles. He shrugs his coat back on while the freshman offers me a set of cuffs.

I take them from him and turn to Griff. We've been partners many times. We've played almost every game in the books together. We've joked and teased and flirted more times than I can count, but after last night? I don't know…it feels different, and I can't help but notice the kaleidoscope of butterflies in my stomach as I force myself to hold his gaze while attempting to act like I don't know what it feels like to kiss him without the guise of a bet or a game.

"What game do you think they picked?" I ask as I twirl

the cuffs around my forefinger in an attempt to look like I'm not replaying last night's events.

Stepping closer, he drops his voice low. "I heard someone ask where they should put the Santa hats and tape, so..."

"That sounds promising."

He nods. "Wanna cuff your right hand and my left so I can have the dominant hand in case we do something like darts or a snowball fight?"

"Yeah, but then I can't throw," I remind him.

He smirks. "I mean..."

With a gasp, I smack his chest. "Rude."

"True," he tosses back at me as Raine appears from the kitchen. A gold medallion hangs from her neck. It's the same one the boys have had since their freshman year at LAU. I can only imagine the games it's overseen and how many people have worn it proudly while picking their own game...with the guys' approval, of course. Everett offers his hand, and Raine takes it, stepping onto the coffee table in the center of the family room.

"Ladies and gentlemen," she announces. "Tonight, we'll be playing a super fun game with several rounds leading up to midnight. But first, everyone, find your partner."

Giving Griffin the side-eye, I sidle up next to him and fold my arms.

"Don't look so excited, Finley." The words are hushed and raspy. They leave goosebumps along my skin, and I press my thighs together, ignoring my body's response. Don't get me wrong. I'm not dead. The guy's turned me on more times than I can count over the years—I literally masturbated to the idea of him earlier this week—but usually, I have a better handle on it.

Seriously, am I blushing?

I fight the urge to touch my cheeks and squeeze my hands into fists instead.

Come on, Fin. You're better than this, I remind myself.

"The first round is pretty straightforward," Raine announces. "All you have to do is wrap a present...blindfolded. Well, one person is blindfolded," she clarifies with a grin. "You get to choose if you want to be the eyes or the hands. The person with the blindfold has to wrap, and the person without the blindfold has to tell the other person what to do."

Everett chuckles and faces the crowd. "Each team will be given a freshman to help judge and keep your team in line. Freshmen, if you're caught cheating for your team, you'll be banned from Game Night for the rest of the year. Let's keep it honest, people."

Raine bumps her shoulder with his, adding, "Shots will be passed out at the beginning of every round, as well as anytime a team finishes wrapping their present. The quicker you pass the round, the less shots you have to take. As a reminder, if you're the one who is not blindfolded, you cannot touch anything, including the shot glasses. Your partner has to feed you the shot and take their own. Oh, and if you spill any of the liquid, you have to take a second shot until your present is officially wrapped. Once a freshman announces your completion,"—I snort, and Griffin elbows me, shaking his head—"you can remove the blindfold and move to the second game."

"On the kitchen table are antlers and Santa hats," Everett explains. "Each of you will grab one. Then, you'll each take a shot, and the person with the Santa hat will jump on the back of their reindeer, who has to run outside and find some mistletoe. It can be hanging from the trees, the house, or...anywhere, really."

"There are a limited number of mistletoe bunches

outside," Raine continues, "and each team must find their own and claim it by standing underneath it. If you fall during your search, you have to take another shot and start over in the kitchen. Oh, and make sure you're standing under the mistletoe by the time the red clock next to the hot tub outside counts down to midnight. Once the timer goes off, you kiss your partner on a body part you both agree on—"

Reeves' laugh cuts Raine off, and Dylan elbows him in the ribs.

"Keep it clean, people." Everett's gaze thins as he stares out at the crowd, making Reeves laugh even harder. Biting the inside of my cheek, I try to keep from joining him, but seriously? It's like Everett's forgotten who his core audience is.

"Aaaand ring in the new year," Raine finishes. "Any questions?"

"I'm gonna get shitfaced, aren't I?" Griffin mutters low enough for only me to hear.

I smirk up at him. "Probably."

"Freshmen!" Everett yells. "Find a team to keep in line. As always, what happens at Game Night stays at Game Night." Stepping closer, he snaps a cuff around Raine's hand, then clicks it around his left wrist, leaving his dominant hand free. "And please don't stab anyone with the scissors. We don't have insurance for this shit." Everyone laughs. "Once the handcuffs are in place, find a spot on the floor. Freshmen, distribute the tape, gift, wrapping paper, and blindfolds for your team. Let's go!"

Griffin's touch is gentle as he follows Everett's orders, brushing his fingers against my bare skin. The cold metal is a stark comparison to his warm fingertips, and a zing shoots up my arm, surprising the shit out of me.

Where the hell did that come from?

Snapping the cuff around my right wrist, he asks, "You wanna be the eyes or the hands?"

"Hands," I decide as our judge for the evening approaches us.

He's scrawny, blond, and still sports braces. I almost feel bad for him until Griffin tugs him in for a bro hug like he's one of the guys.

"Hey, Boyle, what's up?" Griff asks.

"Nothing much, man." He hands Griffin the crimson silk blindfold. "Good luck."

"Thanks, we're gonna need it," Griffin replies.

"I'm sorry. Do you two know each other?" I ask.

"Uh, you don't know Boyle?" Griffin cocks his head. "Boyle helps out at all the parties." He grabs Boyle's bicep and shakes him around like they're best friends. "He's also on the hockey team—"

"I help with the team's equipment," Boyle explains.

"Aw, come on," Griff argues, hooking his arm around the guy's neck. "Boyle's the best. He's also gonna help us win tonight. Right, Boyle?"

"Sure thing." Boyle chuckles. "Good luck, you two."

"Thanks," I say.

After Griffin lets Boyle go, he covers my eyes with the silk blindfold, making my mind spin in circles. One, because Griffin's the captain of the hockey team. He has every reason to be cocky and arrogant and, honestly, kind of a dick. Instead, he's kind. To everyone. Even the people so many would deem beneath him. It's kind of…hot. What else is hot is how he's being so careful right now. Gently, he brushes my hair down along the back of my head, careful to keep the strands out of the blindfold's knot as he loops the fabric together.

"Cuffs *and* blindfolds? Is it my lucky night, or what?" I tease in hopes of breaking the tension I'm currently drowning in. And it's strange because I have no idea if I'm the only one feeling it.

"Yeah, I thought you'd like that," Griffin quips. Prickles race up my arm, making my hair stand on end as his fingertips gently skate against the inside of my wrist, and he hands me the scissors. "Here."

"Here," Boyle adds.

I stand a little straighter, turning toward where I assume Boyle is still standing. "Are you talking to me?"

"He's talking to me," Griffin answers. "He has the present for you to wrap. And thanks, man," he adds, addressing Boyle.

Oops.

Seriously, this no-eyesight thing is rough.

"Three! Two! One! Go!" someone shouts from the opposite side of the room, causing a jolt of anxiety to shoot down my spine.

"Shit, we gotta go."

Moving together, Griffin guides me to kneel on the ground. I blindly search for the roll of wrapping paper, attempt to measure the gift, and cut the correct amount of paper.

"More," Griffin prods.

I roll out another couple of inches.

"A little more," he orders.

I move the scissors another inch or two and wait.

"Perfect," he says.

I cut the paper, dragging the scissors across it until I hit the other side. Then, I drop the scissors on the ground and try to put the oblong box in the center of the sheet, which is weirdly difficult when you can't see anything.

"Yeah, right there," Griffin says. "You're doing great, Fin."

Not gonna lie. I freaking preen at his words, feeling like

I'm pretty much invincible as I fold the paper over the center.

"Tape's by your left hip," he adds.

I fumble for the tape but come up empty.

"Left," he encourages.

"Left. *Right.*" My fingers hit something small and plastic. Confirming it's the tape, I pin the dispenser between my knees and rip off a piece.

"Shot!" someone yells.

"Shit," I drop the tape. "What now?"

"There's a shot glass right in front of you," Griffin says. "Careful."

I feel like an idiot but reach out my hand, trying not to make a mess or bump something I shouldn't.

"A little further away," Griffin guides.

My fingers touch the edge of a glass, and I grab it.

"Bring it to my mouth."

I turn toward his voice. "Where?"

"A little closer."

The back of my finger touches soft flesh, and I raise my opposite hand, feeling Griffin's face while lining up the edge of the shot glass with his lips.

Seriously, why does this feel so intimate?

I shove the thought aside while slowly tipping the glass back, and he swallows the alcohol, leaving the glass empty.

"Fuck," Griff curses, and a sweet but spicy scent hits my nostrils. "Who the hell picked Fireball?"

"I mean, it's cinnamon, right?" I offer. "So, I'm gonna go with Ophelia."

"One more," Boyle orders.

Right.

I move a little faster this time. When my fingers find another glass in front of me, I keep my opposite hand placed on Griffin's jaw and bring the untouched shot glass to his mouth. He lifts his chin and swallows it all. When he breathes out the burn, I feel it against my cheeks. Hell, I can practically taste the cinnamon, and my lips part. Why is this kind of…hot?

"Shot!" Everett yells. At least it sounds like Everett.

Another curse follows, and Griffin's cuffed wrist lifts into the air as I search for another freshly poured alcohol.

"Boyle, where are ya?" I ask.

"A little to the right," Griffin answers for him.

I find the shot glass and search for Griffin again, letting the familiar brush of his five o'clock shadow against the outside of my hand guide me to his mouth. Not gonna lie. It really is weirdly…intimate, and I'm not sure how I feel about it. Actually, I kind of do know how I feel about it, and that's the problem, isn't it?

"One more," Boyle repeats.

"Seriously?" I demand.

Griffin wasn't wrong. He's definitely gonna get shit-faced tonight. Poor guy.

Without waiting for Boyle's answer, I mirror the movement again but tip the glass too quickly, and a light splash hits my hand.

"Shit," Griffin curses. A warm mouth sucks the spilled liquid from around my fingertips, and I swear I can feel it down to my core. The swirl of his tongue. The wet heat of his mouth. There's no way he'd lick me in public. Not if he hadn't already taken a handful of shots. And maybe it's because I'm blindfolded and can't see his face to overanalyze his reaction, but it's the most erotic touch I've ever experienced. Oh, the magic of a mouth. And this mouth? I have a feeling this mouth could do dangerous things if the opportunity presented itself.

"We good?" Griffin asks.

"Uh, yeah?" I choke out, lowering my hand from his mouth. "We're, uh—"

"Yeah, I'll allow it," Boyle says.

Griffin wasn't talking to me.

He was talking to Boyle.

Cool, cool, cool.

"One more piece of tape, Fin," Griffin adds. He must've turned to me because the same familiar scent of spicy alcohol fills my nostrils. It's stronger now. Hell, it's practically fire.

"You got this," he encourages.

I got this. Because we're playing a game.

Right.

Setting the glass down, I wipe my hand against my jeans and rip off a piece of tape from the dispenser still pinned between my thighs, then stick it on the present, smash both ends of the paper, tack on more tape, and wait with bated breath.

"Am I done?" I pause. "It's done, right? It's totally done."

"What do you say, Boyle?" Griffin prods.

The sound of rustling greets me, and I assume Boyle's judging my handiwork, but honestly, I have no idea.

"Boyle?" I prod.

"Looks good to me," he decides.

"Shot!" Griffin yells, announcing to the group that we've finished the first portion of Game Night. Ripping off the blindfold for me, he tugs me to my feet, and I almost trip over myself as he drags me toward the kitchen.

I grab the Santa hat and antlers, placing the antlers on Griffin's head, then slapping the Santa hat onto mine while he downs two more shots from the kitchen island. As soon as the glass hits the granite countertop, I jump on his back and wrap my body around his. It's a little awkward, thanks to our cuffed wrists, but he grabs the backs of my thighs, steadying me. His fingers press little indents into my skin as he hikes me a little higher onto his back, and I swear his touch shoots straight to my core. I blame the open mouthed kiss against my hand. The memory alone keeps my body trembling and my heart racing as I press my chest to his back.

This is only a game.

The door from the kitchen to the backyard is propped open, which I'm sure my parents would love if they knew since they pay the bills, and Griffin jumps over the threshold. Snow falls from the sky. No, floats is probably a more fitting term. It'd almost be peaceful if the yard wasn't scattered with half-drunk, cuffed college students with antlers and Santa hats stumbling through the snow in search of mistletoe. The timer beside the open hot tub blinds us, thanks to the sharp contrast of bright red light and the dark night sky. Or maybe it's because I was blindfolded for the last five minutes. Honestly, I have no idea, but I'm not sure it matters, anyway. There are fifteen seconds. Fourteen. Thirteen. Twelve.

Most of the mistletoe has been claimed. Beneath the tree. By the house. I search for an open bunch, my own competitiveness rearing its ugly head.

"By the hot tub!" I point to one of the last available bunches in the yard. It dangles from a metal pole over the open water.

"You're gonna make me get wet, aren't you?" Griffin grumbles.

"Go!" I kick his sides like he's my own personal horse, and a sting hits my ass. "Hey!"

"Not afraid to spank your ass, Fin," he warns, but he kicks his butt into gear anyway and runs at top speed toward the last bunch of mistletoe available like our lives depend on it.

Maverick and Ophelia cheer us on from beneath a bundle of mistletoe hanging off the gutter while Dylan laughs her ass off a few feet in front of us. She's trying to stay on Reeves' back, her glasses askew, when he tumbles to the icy ground.

"Shot!" I yell as we race past them.

When Griffin reaches the edge of the hot tub, he looks over his shoulder at me, and I nod. "Now or never."

Hot water soaks through our clothes as we stumble into the hot tub and position ourselves under the mistletoe, the timer counting down on the big red clock, contrasting with the dark sky.

Steam swirls around us, and I stare at the bold red numbers.

Five, four, three—

"Happy New Year, Fin," Griffin murmurs.

I lift my head and meet his gaze. His eyes are glassy from the alcohol, his hair is mussed, and a lazy, crooked smile teases the edge of his mouth but doesn't rise to the surface. Not fully. I'm pretty sure he's never been sexier. "Happy New Year, Griff."

He leans closer, and I swear he's going to kiss me, but I turn my head at the last second, letting his lips brush against my cheek instead. My chest caves in disappointment while everyone squeals around me, cheering in the new year.

Everyone but Griffin.

I gave him the cheek. Why did I give him the cheek? Oh, wait. I know why. Because he's Everett's best friend. He has a future. He means something. I did the right thing. I know I did the right thing.

Didn't I?

The air around us crackles as he slowly pulls away.

"You're a good actor, Fin," he rasps. "So good, I almost forgot how well you push people away."

Grabbing the edge of his coat, I force him to look at me. "You're the one who rejected me last night, remember?"

"I'm also the one who held you as you cried and kept us both in check so you wouldn't do something you'd regret. Guess I made the right choice, huh?" Scanning the yard, he yells, "Boyle!" and lifts our cuffed hands into the air. "Where's the key?"

The guy rushes forward. Standing on the edge of the hot tub, he unlocks the handcuffs, careful not to get wet, unlike Griff and me who are soaked from chest to toe. As soon as Griffin's free, he trudges away, his soaked clothes clinging to his body, and even though I'm standing in the middle of piping hot water, both figuratively and literally, I've never felt more cold.

CHAPTER NINETEEN

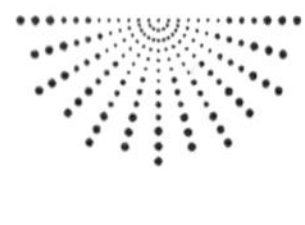

FINLEY

He isn't talking to me. We're back to square one. Only this time, I'm the person to blame. Not Drew. Only me and the baby in my uterus. I stand in front of the mirror and press my hand to my lower stomach. It doesn't look any different. Doesn't feel any different. If I hadn't heard the baby's heart beat, I wouldn't believe it myself. A small part of me still doesn't believe it. I can't be pregnant. I can't be. It's like the size of a blueberry. So small and inconsequential, yet earth-shattering, too, and I know my world will never be the same.

"Knock, knock!" someone calls.

My attention flicks to the locked door. I lower my T-shirt and open it.

"Hi," Ophelia greets me. She's sporting her dad's baseball hat, her messy, strawberry-blonde hair falling around her shoulders.

"Hey."

"So, Dylan and I were thinking…" Her voice trails off.

"Yes?"

"Well, since the girls' side of the duplex is officially

done, and you're moving out next weekend, what if we have a girls' night tonight? Maybe a sleepover in the family room? The boys are leaving for a couple of away games, so the timing is perfect. Maybe you can convince Grandma Taylor to give you the famous chocolate chip cookie recipe, too?" Her eyebrows bounce up and down, making me laugh.

"Sure. I'll see what I can do."

"Yes!"

When she pulls me into a hug, I return it, letting my body sag against hers.

"You good?" she asks.

I nod. "Yeah, just tired. Once I know Frankie isn't across the hall, I'll sleep better."

"You sure living with Everett and Raine won't be worse?"

"To be fair, I'll have a couple weeks of freedom before they move in, but even without the freedom, I think I'd still prefer my brother and his girlfriend living across the hall over Dylan's slimy, green soldier."

She laughs. "Aw, come on. You two didn't bond while we were away?"

"Nope."

"Not even a little bit?" she prods.

I shake my head and shiver. "Not in the slightest."

With a grin, she tilts her head. "How 'bout you and Griff? Things at the party seemed…good, I think? And then…not so good."

My lips bunch on one side. "Is this your attempt at sleuthing?"

"Hey, not all of us are as talented as you, Miss Detective."

"Well, at least you admit it." I pat her shoulder. "And, yeah. Griffin and I are fine."

"You sure? Because he was wearing his pissed-off face this morning, and I have a feeling it wasn't from the extra shots last night." She steps a little closer and glances over her shoulder, confirming we're alone. "Not to sound like a creepy stalker or anything, but I may have noticed how you gave him the cheek last night."

"Pretty sure the Game Night rules applied," I remind her. "Yes, a kiss was part of the rules to win game night, but I got to pick where, and I chose the cheek. So what?"

"Not arguing about the rules, only the reasoning behind them." She hesitates, and a divot forms between her perfectly shaped brows. "I thought you and Drew were through."

"We are through."

"So why not kiss Griff?" She nibbles on the edge of her bottom lip, hesitating. Again. "You and him used to kiss all the time until you started dating Drew."

"We didn't kiss—"

"During game nights, you did," Lia argues. "Truth or Dare, Spin the Bottle, Seven Minutes in Heaven." She lists them off, one by one, and I press my lips into a thin line.

"I also kissed Mav and Archer and Everett's other friends during the games, too," I remind her.

"Yeah, which is why it's weird that you *didn't* kiss Griff last night," she pushes. "You're proving my point for me."

Well, shit.

The girl might be onto something. I've never struggled with meaningless kisses. It's all fun and games. All insignificant. Until it isn't.

"Maybe I'm maturing," I offer.

"Or maybe kissing Griffin isn't a game to you…or *him*." She rocks back on her heels and tucks her thumbs into the front pockets of her jeans. "Just a thought."

"Aaaand, I think you've done enough sleuthing for one day." I fold my arms. "Besides, you're terrible at it."

"Or maybe I'm too good at it," she counters. "I did learn from the best."

"Oh, did you?"

"Mm-hmm." She bounces her eyebrows up and down. "What happened on your little road trip, Fin?"

Not gonna lie. The old me would've told her everything. And maybe I should. But then, I'd have to admit I'm pregnant. Am I so wrong for wanting to keep the lid on that particular can of worms for now?

"So, about our girls' night…" I announce. "Are Raine and Dylan joining?"

Ophelia's lips bunch to one side, mirroring my expression from moments ago, and I have zero doubt she's debating whether or not to let me change the subject.

Try me.

"Fine," she humphs. "I'll drop it. For now." Her gaze narrows. "And heck yes! Of course, Raine and Dylan are coming. We missed you on our trip."

"I missed coming on your big vacation. Trust me," I admit. "But I'm excited for you to tell me all about it tonight."

"We'll give you all the gory details, I promise. I'll even let you pick the movie if you convince Grandma Taylor to let you bake her famous cookies tonight."

"You know, she's your grandma, too," I point out, though it's not like she needs the reminder. Her dad is my dad's little brother.

Duh.

"Yeah, but she likes you more," Ophelia argues.

With a laugh, I counter, "Only because I play the epilepsy card anytime I ask for the recipe."

Our grandma's a crazy person who refuses to let

anyone have her top-secret recipe. I'd say it's old age making her a little looney, but my mom swears she's always been this way. Thankfully, I've made the infamous cookies a time or twenty, so I'm pretty sure I have the recipe memorized, even though I've been sworn to secrecy. In fact, my grandma's so protective of the recipe that she's made me pinkie promise to never write it down for fear of it being stolen. Even though I know the thing by heart, I still call her whenever I'm craving them. Call me a sucker for my childhood, but the cookies will always remind me of summer sleepovers and Mama Taylor's house. Ophelia has the same memories, but since she isn't as interested in baking, she usually leaves the process to me, bless her soul.

"Come on, please?" Lia presses her hands together in a prayer gesture. "I have practice today, so with the hour-long phone call we both know it would take to convince Grandma to give me the recipe in the first place, there's no way I'd have time to make them anyway."

"Fine," I cave. "I'll see what I can do."

"Perfect. Oh, and do you mind if I invite Tatum and Squeaks?" she adds. "They're kind of…in a weird place, and I think the social time might be good for them."

Yeah, I think a weird place is an understatement.

Tatum is Ophelia's little sister. She's a couple years younger than us but has been taking Maverick's twin's death really hard. To be fair, we all have. But I think everyone knows Tatum was in love with Archer, even if he was always too hung up on Ophelia to notice her little sister's affection for him. Not that it mattered. The results are the same. Ever since the accident, Tatum's been spiraling. Hard. With Archer's passing and Tatum holding a grudge the size of Texas against Ophelia and how she treated him, I'm not sure she'll ever stop spiraling. Her parents have tried everything. Therapy. Space. Time.

Nothing has worked, and I'm not sure anything will, especially not hanging out with her older sister when she's so pissed at her.

As for Squeaks? Well, her real name is Rory. She's Maverick's and Archer's little sister and is the caboose baby for our entire friend group. Recently, the girl has basically refused to show her face around anyone. I think it has something to do with Griffin's and Dylan's older brother, Jaxon. Why? Because Rory's been Jax's shadow since she could walk, and lately, the girl's been nothing but a ghost.

So the real question is, what made her disappear? Not gonna lie. I'm curious. So curious I have no problem agreeing to Ophelia's suggestion. I could use the distraction from Griffin, anyway.

"You know they're always welcome," I tell her. "No big deal."

"Perfect." Ophelia sighs in relief. "Now to see if I can twist their arms into coming."

I bite back my scoff. "Good luck."

Go figure. On my one night off, the girls want Rowdy's. It wasn't Dylan's idea, either. She's also a waitress at the steakhouse and didn't plan on coming to work on her night off. To be fair, Tatum and Rory are both underage and don't have fake IDs like the rest of us. So it's not like we could go to SeaBird. Still. I'll take what I can get. Even if the ambiance is all too familiar, it's nice to have a night off. A night away from Griffin. A night where I can bury my head in the sand for a little while longer until I figure out what the hell I'm going to do on the baby front or how the hell I'm going to tell my best friends I screwed up. Twice. Er, three times if we count the whole rejecting Griffin on New Year's bit, but who's counting?

Besides, it's still a toss up on that front. It was a mistake. *Wasn't it?*

Honestly, at this point, I have no idea.

As I sit in the passenger seat, munching on one of the chocolate chip cookies Ophelia insisted I make, Dylan turns down the song on the stereo and lifts her chin toward the front door of Maverick's parents' house. Ophelia and Raine are on the porch, and Raine lifts her hand, knocking on the solid piece of wood.

"Sometimes I forget Raine knows the Buchanans," Dylan says.

She isn't the only one.

"Yeah, it's sort of weird how her parents are kind of close with Mav's," I murmur.

"Right?" Dylan shakes her head and snatches a cookie from the glass container resting on the center console. "Talk about a small world."

Sometimes too small, I think to myself, but only nod as my Aunt Mia opens the door and pulls Ophelia and Raine into hugs.

Minutes later, Maverick's little sister appears. Ponytail swinging, the middle schooler jogs toward us with an awkward wave and climbs into the backseat.

"Hey, Squeaks!" I greet her.

"Never gonna live the nickname down, am I?" she grumbles.

I grin back at her. "Probably not. But hey, I say own it."

"Own me being a whiner?" She rolls her eyes and pulls her phone out. "Gee, thanks."

Giving me a side glance, Dylan mumbles under her breath, "Teenagers."

She's not wrong.

The back door opens, cutting off my response as Ophelia and Raine join us in the car.

"You good if we pick up Tatum, too?" Ophelia asks. She leans forward and grabs a cookie from the container. "I know we'll have to squeeze, but my mom can't drop her off."

"No worries," Dylan says. "We have time."

"Honestly, I'm surprised she's still coming," Lia admits. "The girl's been a recluse since…" Her attention darts to Rory, and she sniffs quietly before setting the uneaten cookie on her thigh as if she's lost her appetite. It makes my chest ache. I don't miss the sheen in Lia's caramel-colored eyes or the way she pastes on a fake-ass smile as she shoves her emotions deep inside her. "So? Who wants to listen to some music?"

Aaaand, that's my cue.

I reach for the knob and turn up the volume.

Thirty minutes later, the cookies are gone, and Tatum's squished to one side of the cab, her shoulder pressed against the back passenger window as we make our way toward Rowdy's. To say the car is eerily tense would be an understatement, and it takes everything inside me not to poke the bear or stir up shit simply for the sake of acknowledging it.

Hey, Tatum, how's the broken heart?

Hey, Squeaks, why have you been MIA? It's kind of lame, but no worries. Happens to us all.

Yeah, I can think of a dozen ways to spark the gasoline-soaked tension. Instead, I keep my lips zipped as Dylan's knee bounces up and down like the Energizer Bunny. At least I'm not Ophelia. Despite the literal buffer in the form of Squeaks and Raine, Tatum looks like she could stab Lia a billion times, and it still wouldn't be enough.

Yikes.

As Dylan brakes at the stoplight, a motorcycle pulls up beside us, and Ophelia sighs. If I had to guess, she's probably thinking about Mav and their daily rides on his bike. I don't blame her. There's definitely something to be said about a man on a motorcycle. I fight the urge to fan myself and announce it to the car, well aware it'll only piss Tatum off more.

Peeking over my shoulder toward Tatum's passenger window, I notice the guy's wearing a leather jacket and a black helmet with the visor pulled down, shielding his face from me. I don't need to see it to know he isn't looking at me, though.

Nope. The guy's attention is glued to Tatum. He lifts his chin as if to say hey, then motions to his face and draws a frowny face before pointing at her window again.

Is he trying to talk to her?

The cab of the car stays quiet, none of us wanting to spook an already grouchy Tatum. When he raises his hand and makes a fist, lifting it three times then doing a sideways peace sign, I realize he's offering to play Rock, Paper, Scissors. I shift in my seat and steal a quick look at Tatum, curious if she's being stubborn or giving this stranger the time of day.

No luck.

Interesting.

The light's still red as I turn my attention back to the side mirror and the mysterious biker's reflection. He makes another fist, and Tatum smiles in my periphery. Okay, smile might be a bit of a stretch, but still. Raising her fist into view, she gives in with a one, two, three. She flattens her hand into paper, and the guy shows rock, throwing his head back and shaking it in defeat. He lost. Paper covers rock. His helmet swivels toward Tatum again, leaving me on pins and needles, and I'm not even the one he's paying attention to. Like seriously. Damn. Slowly, he draws an imaginary smile in the air and gives her a thumbs-up as if making her promise to smile every once in a while. Then, his hand finds the throttle on his bike, and he disappears down the road, his engine whirring and fading in a flash.

"Well, that was…interesting," I decide. "Do you know him, Tate?"

The soft lift of her lips flattens, and she shakes her head, leaning against the window.

"You don't, but I think I might," Raine mutters as her fingers fly across her phone screen.

"Who is he?" Ophelia prods.

Raine hesitates. "Pretty sure that's Pax."

"Pax?" Dylan asks. "As in…?"

"My brother's guitarist," Raine finishes, though her eyes stay glued to her phone, her expression pinched. "It looked like his bike anyway. Hmm."

"Pax has a bike?" I ask.

"The whole band has bikes," Raine answers.

Ophelia shifts in her seat, the corners of her eyes creasing in concern. "Is Pax…trouble?"

"Pax is…Pax," Raine finishes.

"Us Taylor girls." Ophelia shakes her head and gives her sister a reassuring smile. "Seems we're suckers for bikers."

Leaning forward, Tatum glares at her big sister. "Trust me. Our tastes are *nothing* alike."

I grimace and settle back in the front seat. *Yikes.* Don't get me wrong. I get it. Tatum was most definitely in love with Maverick's twin, Archer, before he passed. And even though Archer and Maverick were identical twins, they were pretty much opposites in every way, other than their love for hockey and a certain strawberry-blonde goalie who's currently sitting in the back seat trying not to burn

173

up on the spot from Tatum's blazing glare. Yeah, Ophelia's part in the whole…*situation* is a little complicated, and that's putting things lightly. It's also why Tatum's been so distant since Archer's death. Living in your sister's shadow is one thing. Being in love with a ghost who was in love with said sister is an entirely different—and much more excruciating—story.

Dylan pulls into Rowdy's parking lot and cuts the engine, leaving the rest of us drowning in a silence so thick I swear I could cut it with a knife.

Well, I was right about one thing. I was looking for a distraction from my own shitshow of a life, and apparently, I found it in spades.

CHAPTER TWENTY

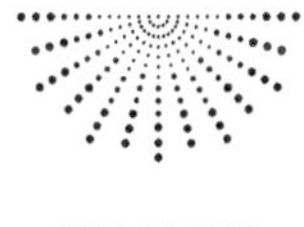

FINLEY

As one of my coworkers sets glasses of water in front of everyone, Dylan drags her drink closer to her chest and asks, "So, Rory. It's been a while. I haven't seen you at my brother's lately. How's life?"

Ophelia blanches and shakes her head, confirming my theory about our dear, sweet little Squeaks making a move on Jaxon Thorne.

Dylan cocks her head, her forehead wrinkling in confusion. "What?" she asks.

"Anyway," Ophelia drags out. "Who's gonna ride the bull later?"

There's a mechanical bull named Bruce who's basically famous at this point, yet isn't half as interesting as Ophelia's weird response or Rory's pale complexion.

"Squeaks, you good?" I prod.

"Yup," she mutters, avoiding everyone's gaze like her life depends on it.

Interesting.

Especially because Rory's basically been Jaxon's sidekick and biggest cheerleader since before she could even walk. Yeah, there's quite the age gap, but he's the only one she's been able to stand being around since Archer's death, and the fact that she hasn't been around Jaxon much lately is…really strange.

"Did something…happen?" I question.

"Nothing's happened," Lia rushes out. "I'm sure Jax has just been busy, you know?"

"I thought Squeaks was the one who's been ditching Jax," Dylan interjects.

Ophelia's head falls forward in defeat, and Squeaks juts out her bottom lip, her eyes welling with tears.

It'd be surprising if Squeaks wasn't…Squeaks. The girl's been a crier since birth. Seriously, I almost feel sorry for her. Not because I think she's weak but because I *know* she thinks she's weak due to her inability to tamp down her emotions like the rest of us. Honestly, I kind of envy it. The way she's so genuine, wearing her heart on her sleeve come hell or high water. So much so I'm pretty sure the girl could be a mermaid for how often the waterworks hit her.

She sniffs and wipes angrily at her eyes. "It's nothing."

"Hey." Lia gives me a warning look and reaches over, touching Rory's hand. "I know Fin can be kind of pushy, but she didn't know she was touching on such a sore subject."

I open my mouth to argue that I most definitely did know I was touching on a sore subject, but Ophelia kicks me beneath the table, and my mouth snaps closed.

"It's okay." Rory twists the napkin in front of her, letting the tears tumble freely down her cheeks. "I just…I feel so stupid, you know?"

"What happened?" Tatum prods, surprising everyone else at the table. The girl's barely said two words since biting off Ophelia's head in the car. Then again, she's probably grateful the spotlight isn't on her for once, but what do I know?

"I, uh," Rory rolls her glassy eyes. "I tried to kiss Jax."

Dylan's jaw drops, and Raine elbows her.

"It's not a big deal," Lia adds. "And Jax didn't return it, obviously—"

Rory squeaks a cry and covers her face with her hands. "Obviously?"

"I didn't mean it like that," Lia says, trying to comfort her.

"Now, who's the one putting their foot in their mouth," I mutter under my breath.

Tatum scoffs. "It isn't Lia's fault she doesn't have a heart. She's never experienced unrequited love, so—"

"I *did* love Archer," Ophelia snaps. Dylan jumps in surprise and scoots closer to me as Lia turns her glare on Tatum. "Okay?" Her expression twists with pain and anger and remorse. She slaps her hands against the table, leaning closer to Tatum. "I loved the shit out of him, and if you would just let me explain everything instead of shutting me out and painting me as the villain when I already feel like shit as it is—"

"Hey, are you ready to order?" Mindy, the waitress, asks before realizing exactly the kind of shitshow she just stepped in. Clicking the back of her pen, she clears her throat and hooks her thumb over her shoulder. "I can always come back…?"

"I don't think that's necessary," Squeaks chokes out. Her bottom lip wobbles. "I'm not very hungry."

"Neither am I," Tatum decides without breaking her staring contest with her older sister.

I suck my lips between my teeth in an attempt to keep

from calling everyone out for having their heads up their asses, well aware it isn't the time or the place to let my acidic tongue run wild, especially when Tatum has plenty to go around.

Nostrils flaring, she tears her gaze from Ophelia and turns to Rory. "Squeaks, do you want to sit at a different table with me while I hire an Uber to take us literally anywhere but here?"

The same familiar sheen of regret fills Ophelia's eyes. It swallows her frustration from seconds ago as she stares at her little sister helplessly. "Tatum," she pleads.

Standing, Tatum sets her napkin on the table as Rory joins her on her feet, and they stroll away, slipping into one of the booths furthest away from ours. And it's kind of funny. Seeing them together. How opposite yet similar they really are to each other. Tatum's once long, blonde hair is now black and hangs just beneath her jaw. Her nails are black and chipped as if she's been chewing them. And the books I'm used to her carrying around like a security blanket since she was a kid are long gone, along with her ability to cry. Okay, the last part is only a hunch, but she's more stabby than woe-is-me, while little Rory Buchanan looks two seconds away from literally crying me a river as she sports her pink scrunchie, white polo, and tennis skirt, despite the cold weather.

"Well, damn," I mutter. "So much for time healing wounds and mending bridges and shit."

"It's been five months, Fin," Ophelia reminds me as if I've forgotten. Joke's on her. Archer wasn't only close to Ophelia and Tatum. He was close to all of us. And yeah, I know I lean a little more on the morbid, dark humor side of things when it comes to coping, but I'm not heartless. And I do miss him. More than most people know.

"I'm pretty sure it could be five years, and Tatum still wouldn't let me mend bridges and shit," Ophelia continues. "It doesn't matter how much I apologize, if I try to put on a brave face, or...anything. I'll always be the bad guy in her story, and that?" She sniffs and wipes beneath her nose. "That's a burden I'm pretty sure I'll have to carry for the rest of my life. But, it would be easier if Tatum would at least let me...talk to her."

"You made a mistake, Lia," I reply. "You're allowed to make mistakes. And whenever Tatum's ready to let you in again, you'll be here. I think it's all that matters."

"Fin's right," Dylan adds. "And for now, Tatum can lean on Rory. Pretty sure they could both use a friend."

We all watch Tatum and Rory from across the restaurant, surprised and enthralled by the two of them side-by-side. It's like they're magnets, and it's literally a toss-up as to whether or not they'll be brought together or pushed apart depending on the day. And thanks to their broken hearts, they're clinging to each other.

"At least they aren't pushing each other away," I add, studying them.

Biting the inside of her cheek, Ophelia tucks her hair behind her ear and sits back down. "Look at you, focusing on the positive."

"Someone has to," I joke.

Raine and Dylan give me pity laughs and open their menus.

"Don't get me wrong. I get it, you know?" Ophelia sniffs and plays with a straw wrapper, staring at it like it holds the answers to all her problems. "I get that our history is messy, but...I'm just so...exhausted." The paper wrapper skids across the top of the table as she flicks it away from her. "Knowing my little sister will never forgive me, let alone move on and be happy, even if it feels impossible. And trust me. I know how impossible it feels."

"I know you do," I offer carefully.

Pressing her fingers to her lips, Ophelia nods. "After Archer's death, Mav and I started going to therapy, and it's been hard, you know? Hard dealing with survivor's guilt and all the things we wish could be different while knowing that it's out of our hands. But then I see Tatum, and she just…isn't trying." Her hand falls to the table. "And I know I shouldn't say that, but she bottles everything up, shoves it down, and refuses to make any room for real emotions. I feel like it's all my fault, but there isn't any way to fix it. To fix any of this."

She's right. There isn't. Only time will heal the wounds from Archer's passing, but only if we let it. Tatum? It's like she's picking at the wound, refusing to let the scabs mend her broken heart. Instead, she'll be left with scars. Irreparable damage. And I'm not the only one who knows it.

"Okay, we should change the subject," Lia begs. "Please? Anyone? Give me something else to think about."

"So, uh, did Rory really try to kiss Jax?" Dylan asks. "There's like a ten-year age gap, not to mention a very illegal aspect to the whole thing. What else did she expect?"

I laugh and cover my face. "I mean, Jax *is* hot. I can see it."

"Hey, you're talking about my brother," Dylan argues before a Cheshire grin takes up half her face. "Although, speaking of my brothers…"

Clasping my hands in front of me, I clear my throat. "So, are we really going to let Rory and Tatum leave with an Uber?"

"Subtle subject change," Raine notes.

With a gasp, I clutch at my chest. "Excuse me, but those two girls are under our care, thank you very much."

Dylan snorts. "Yeah, I'm with Raine on this one. Subtle subject change, Fin."

Crossing my arms, I lean back in the booth. "Doesn't mean I'm wrong, though."

"You're all right," Ophelia interjects. "Fin, you're being dumb for avoiding a very simple and juicy question. One we'll most definitely be pressing you on later, and you're also being logical by pointing out our current predicament with the two teenagers across the room who hate me."

"To be fair, I'm pretty sure only Tatum hates you," I quip.

"Hey, be nice." Dylan reaches for the straw wrapper and tosses it at me, but it falls flat, spiraling toward the table like a dying bird, and I hold back the urge to make fun of her for it.

Instead, I turn back to Ophelia. "And, if we're really trying to assess that girl's emotions, I'm gonna go out on a limb and say your little sister hates everyone, so don't take it too hard."

"She's right," Raine adds. "Tatum's mad at the world. Not just you."

"Thanks," Lia mutters, though she doesn't look like she believes us. "But even if it's true, it's not like Tatum is going to let me in the car with her again." She pauses. "Actually, I have an idea. Dylan, will you take the girls home, and I'll have Mav swing by and pick me up?"

"You sure?" Dylan asks.

Nodding, Ophelia pulls out her phone, and, I assume, sends a quick text to her boyfriend. "Yeah. Yeah, I think it's probably the best idea for everyone. Maybe Rory will even come with us?"

"Let them bond," I say, tilting my head toward their

booth. "Tatum might be a little older, but they could use each other right now."

I'm right. I know I am.

Ophelia looks up from her phone and frowns. "So, what? It's only me and Mav?"

"And me," I quip. "I could use some space from drama for now, too."

"Why?" Raine prods. "So you can avoid Dylan's questions about you and Griff?"

"There is no me and Griff," I remind her.

"Sure there isn't." Raine shares a look with Dylan, making me want to smack them both.

"Stop making those faces," I grumble around my straw.

"Why? Because you know we're right?" Raine challenges.

Dylan adds, "He's been pissy since you rejected him last night."

"I didn't—"

"You did," Ophelia chirps. "We all saw."

"You saw nothing," I argue.

"I saw Griffin hungover as shit this morning," Raine offers.

"Because he had to take all *my* shots *and* his," I point out. "Maybe if you picked a different game, none of this would've happened."

"Yeah, sure. Blame the game," Ophelia says.

"Griffin doesn't drink. Not really," Dylan notes. "Yet, there was a bottle of Jack in his room."

"Why were you in Griffin's room?"

"I'm his sister," she defends. "And you're missing the point."

"The point is, you all need to get out of here." I push Dylan's shoulder, urging her to stand up. "Go. Take the girls home."

When she's on her feet, she faces me again, her gaze narrowing from behind her glasses. "Don't hurt my brother, okay?"

"You act as if I'm capable."

"Oh, I think we all know you're plenty capable," Ophelia argues.

"She means that in the nicest way possible," Raine adds.

"Sure, she does." I snort. "You do know you're saying this to the girl who was cheated on, right?"

"Yeah, and look who bounced right back," Dylan says, refusing to budge.

Part of me wants to smack the girl. The other part? I guess I get it. I'm a good liar. So good, it seems I've fooled my own best friend. Honestly, I should give myself a pat on the back or some shit, even if her perception of me is a bit warped. Then again, maybe it's a good thing. Appearing impenetrable. Better to not have a heart than to risk having it broken, right? And yeah, I might not be feeling the ache of Drew's absence, but the possibility of losing Griff? It's enough to make me twitchy, which is the last thing I need.

Rocking back on my heels, I wiggle my fingers at my friends. "And on that note, toodle-oo, ladies."

"Look, I'm not trying to be a bitch, I'm just saying—"

"I know what you're saying."

"No, you don't," she rushes out. "My brother might seem like he's laid back and good at going with the flow, but he's more than a rebound kind of guy when it comes to you, Fin."

My lips press into a thin line as the girls each give me their own looks of disapproval.

"She knows," Ophelia finally answers for me.

And that's the problem. I do know. And I already crossed that line.

My toes curl in my boots at the memory of our kiss before my face is lit on fire by the recollection of last night. When I gave him the freaking cheek. Seriously? Who does that? Me, that's who.

"Come on, Dyl. You've made your point." Raine bumps Dylan's shoulder with hers and hooks her purse over her forearm. "Let's go."

CHAPTER TWENTY-ONE

GRIFFIN

Where are the damn pain meds?

I shouldn't have drunk last night. Or the previous night. Or any other night since New Year's. But I'm on edge. The Tornadoes want to reschedule our meeting. I know what they're going to ask, and my head's too fucked to come up with an answer. Finley went out with the girls while I was away, and from what I gathered from my conversation with Dylan, she did not tell them about the baby. We got home last night, and even then, I couldn't help but drown out my questions in alcohol as soon as I stepped through the door. I don't drink. Not much, anyway. Yet here I am, acting as if the alcohol is fucking water, and I'm nothing more than a goldfish.

A stupid. *Stupid.* Goldfish.

"You might want to be more subtle when you're butthurt," Finley announces behind me.

I slap the cabinet closed and face her, folding my arms with a glare.

"Like that," she quips. "How were the games?"

Rounding the center island, she searches the cupboards for a glass in nothing but a pair of boxers and a baggy T-shirt. It'd be innocent on anyone else, but Fin? Somehow, she manages to make the ragged clothes look like fuckin' lingerie. When she stands on her tiptoes, her calves flex, and I can't help but notice her bubblegum pink toenails.

"They were fine." I tear my attention from the view, letting my stare linger on her round ass briefly, and clear my throat. "Heard you had a girls' night while I was gone."

"So?"

"So, you haven't told them yet."

She glances at me, then peeks over her shoulder toward the main hallway to confirm we're still alone. Satisfied, she finds a glass, answering, "I have no idea what you're talking about."

"Denial," I note. "Why am I not surprised?"

"What do you mean?"

"I mean, you're awfully good at avoiding shit, Fin." I step closer to her until her ass hits the counter. Call me a dick, but after the rollercoaster she's had me on since the hotel, my patience is less than none.

She gulps but keeps her head held high. "Not sure what you're referring to, but—"

"You mean, other than the baby?" A humorless laugh escapes me. "I'm referring to you climbing into my bed at the hotel and then rejecting my kiss on New Year's."

Her eyes widen in surprise. Probably because I don't usually talk to her like this, but after the radio silence and her walking around the house like everything's normal, then being around her brother for the past few days, shit's messing with my head. I'm tired of playing her game. Of letting her make the rules.

"Where's my brother?" she demands.

"Tell me why you gave me the cheek."

She bites the edge of her mouth, looking cagey as shit. "Griff, I didn't—"

"You did."

Her tongue darts out between her pretty pink lips. "You really want to play this game?"

"I'm not the one playing," I remind her. "You are."

"Fine. I didn't want to send you mixed signals."

"I think it's a little late for that," I growl. "You kissed me first."

"Yeah, and then you rejected me."

"I didn't reject you," I all but snarl. My fingers dig into the countertop behind her, and I take a deep breath. This girl is infuriating. "I…figured we should take things slow," I grit out. "So you wouldn't regret anything."

"What's there to regret?" she offers. "Nothing happened."

"You're right. It didn't."

"Exactly," she quips. But her eyes? Her eyes say it all.

They fall to my chest like she can't even look at me. Like she's guilty. Like she's embarrassed.

Ashamed.

And damn, if it doesn't get to me.

"You ever hear Reeves say he doesn't like the miscommunication trope?" I demand.

A divot forms between her brows. "What?"

"The miscommunication trope."

"I know what it is," she defends. "Although, I'm surprised you do. You're not usually one to read."

"I think I can understand basic English, Fin."

"Fine," she huffs. "What's your point?"

"My point is, I think Reeves might be onto something because this?" I wag my finger between us. "This miscommunication bullshit is driving me insane."

"Who says there's a miscommunication?"

"Stop being a smartass for once, Fin." I reach up and brush her hair behind her ear, my gaze falling to her lips as regret and confusion swirl through my veins. "Why didn't you let me kiss you?"

A flicker of…something, flashes in her gray eyes before her tongue darts out and wets her bottom lip. "Because you're my brother's best friend."

"I've been your brother's best friend since you were born," I remind her. "And we've kissed plenty of times during games, not to mention you being *very* interested in kissing me when we were at the hotel." I dip closer, caught between rage and lust as I stare down at her. So fucking perfect. So fucking infuriating. "Try again."

"I'm done having this conversation." She moves to the left, but I grab her bicep, keeping her in place.

"Like I said," I growl. "Not a fan of the miscommunication trope."

"Pretty sure this would be classified as lack of communication, not miscommunication," she argues.

My hand itches to smack her ass, but I fight the urge, fisting it instead. "Guess I'm not a fan of either of them, then. Regardless, after everything these past two weeks, I think I deserve some clarification, don't you?"

Sucking her lips between her teeth, she stays quiet but doesn't try to dodge me again, so I loosen my grasp on her arm, dragging my fingers to her wrist, then letting her go. "Why didn't you let me kiss you, Fin?"

The same familiar flicker of emotion and indecision hits her gaze before she whispers, "I don't…I don't want you to ruin your life." It's so quiet I'm surprised I even hear her. Hell, maybe I didn't, and I only read her lips. Maybe I only read her mind.

"Who says you're ruining my life?" I murmur.

"Well, let's see." She stands a little taller and lifts her

chin, locking up the glimpse she'd given me of her vulnerability and leaving me aching for more. "Off the top of my head, what if this doesn't work out, Griff? Hmm? I'm not stupid, okay? I know there's been a pull between us for years, and neither of us has ever acted on it. Not really. And then I was sad, and you were there, and I kissed you, and yes, it was amazing, but you're still my brother's best friend."

"So?" I push.

She cocks her head. "You really wanna talk about this?"

"Yeah, I really do," I snap. I feel like I'm on a fucking carousel and we're going round and round in circles like we always do. And I'm tired. So fucking tired of this game. But not enough to get off the ride. To let go of her. Not yet. "Talk to me, Finley."

"Fine," she seethes.

She pushes away from the counter, but I stand my ground, refusing to give her an inch, let alone the space she thinks she wants.

When our chests touch, she steps back again, leaning against the counter as she glares up at me.

"Not so used to me standing my ground, are you, Fin." It isn't a question.

"I think we can both agree that we've never crossed the line because whether or not we actually had the conversation, we both knew if things went south, your friendship with Everett would never be the same, and that is the last thing I want. That's why you were smart to end the kiss at the hotel, and that's why I gave you the cheek on New Year's."

"Because you don't want to risk my friendship with Ev."

"Exactly."

I lift my shoulder. "Maybe I think you're worth the risk, Fin."

Her lips part, and her chest expands on a sharp inhale, causing her breasts to brush against me. She's surprised. By my candor. My easy admittance. But only for a second. Heaven forbid she let someone in long enough to show them her actual thoughts and feelings for more than a milli-fucking-second.

And just like that, it's gone.

Shaking it off, she argues, "You say that now, but what if it doesn't work out? And my brother is only the tip of the iceberg. What if the Tornadoes ask to reschedule your meeting, you move away, and I only see you a few times a year? I just got out of a long-distance relationship. I'm not exactly interested in taking that route again. Oh, and let's not forget about the baby in my uterus, right? This isn't only about me and you anymore. There are no guarantees in this, Griff. None. This is a recipe for disaster, and I care about you. I want you to have an amazing, successful life without me dragging you down in the background."

Maybe it's my throbbing headache, but I swear I'm hallucinating. This girl wears her confidence like a second skin, and has never been afraid to go after what she wants. Not once. Hearing her put aside those wants for me and my future is not only off-brand, it's fucking delusional. Especially twice in one conversation. Add in her confession about caring for me, and I'm pretty sure I have a concussion I didn't know about.

"Did you say you're afraid of dragging me down?" I ask.

"That's exactly what I said."

My mouth twitches. "You wouldn't drag me down."

"Yes, I would! I'm not stupid, okay, Griffin? I'm aware my epilepsy makes things more complicated than the average relationship. Add in a baby, and I'm basically a walking thousand-pound bag of luggage no one deserves to lug around."

My attention falls to her lips again. I want to ask if she's serious. If she honestly believes all the bullshit she's spewing. Like she's a burden to be around when she's always been the most confident and fucking gorgeous girl in the room. Does she really not see it? The way I want her? The way I've always wanted her?

Gripping the counter on either side of her hips, I offer, "Maybe I want to lug you around."

She snorts. "No one wants to—"

I kiss her, swallowing her tiny gasp of surprise as my mouth moves over hers. Perfect. She's fucking perfect, and if I have to shut her up by kissing her so she stops spiraling over bullshit lies like I wouldn't be the luckiest bastard in the world to claim her, then I have no problem doing exactly that. My hands find her waist, and I tug her into me, letting her curves meld against my body. It's dangerous doing this. Here. Now. Sure, it's early, but anyone could walk in. Anyone could see us. But I can't make myself stop. Can't make myself regret anything else when it comes to Fin and me. Haven't we already wasted enough time?

I kiss her harder, dragging my tongue along her bottom lip until she opens up for me. A tiny whimper slips out of her as she touches her tongue to mine, and she grabs onto my sides, fisting the fabric of my T-shirt like her life depends on it. Depends on me. As she tilts her head up even more, I grunt in response and shift my leg between her thighs. Fuck, she tastes incredible. Just like all the other times I've tasted her, but even better because there are no witnesses. No games. No bullshit excuses. Just Fin and me and years of pent-up attraction. I dive in deeper. Sucking her tongue into my mouth, my fingertips dig into her waist as I hold on for dear life. All I want to do is pick her up, put her round ass on the counter, shove her underwear aside, and bury myself inside her like I've imagined for years.

Not here.

Damn. I'm surprised my self-preservation kicks in at all, let alone is loud enough to cut through the haze of lust pulsing through my veins and shooting south now that I'm kissing her. Now that she's kissing me.

Being caught kissing her is one thing. Fucking her is probably frowned upon. At least in public. Or in general, now that I think about it. But I'm too turned on to care.

Letting go of my shirt, her hands press against my chest, and she slowly pushes me away, her long lashes fluttering over her delicate skin as she peeks up at me, making my heart thump faster with every inch of distance.

Don't you dare push me away again.

CHAPTER TWENTY-TWO

GRIFFIN

"What was that for?" Finley asks.

The quiet question cuts through my racing thoughts as I take in her flushed cheeks. "Someone had to shut you up," I rasp. "When are you gonna realize I care about you?"

"Griff—"

"As more than a friend," I interrupt. "More than my best friend's little sister. More than the annoying girl who loves driving me insane. I care about you, Fin."

She wets her lips. "Caring isn't the issue, Griff…"

"You're right. Because even if you won't admit it, I think you care about me, too. I know I can't guarantee love. I can't guarantee forever. But I can guarantee that my feelings are real—have been real for a long fucking time— and they aren't going anywhere." I push her hair away from her face, letting my thumb skate across her cheek instead of pulling away like I've done so many times before.

"Damn." Leaning into my touch, she peeks up at me. "You weren't kidding about refusing to play into the whole miscommunication thing."

"Smartass." My mouth lifts. "I know the timing is shitty, but I want a chance. A real chance. With you and the baby and…"

Just say it.

"I *want* you, Fin. Now, stop overthinking shit, and let me have you." My mouth slams against hers again, not giving her a chance to respond. With my hands on her waist, I walk her backward toward the hall and into my room. She goes without protest. Once we're over the threshold, I close the door and press her against it.

Fuck, these curves. I've dreamed about them. Fantasized. Played out a thousand scenarios of what I could do and would do if the opportunity finally presented itself. Now, here she is. Right in front of me. Moving closer, I grip the backs of her upper thighs and lift her up, grinding myself against her heat as my tongue duels with hers.

I should've known she'd kiss like this when there isn't an audience. Greedily. The girl's never been afraid to take what she wants. But neither am I. Not anymore. Not when it comes to her. Sucking Fin's tongue into my mouth, I shift against her, letting her feel every single inch of me. A soft moan slips past her lips, and I set her down. I can't help it. I'm tired of taking things slow. Of overthinking shit. I want Fin. And I want her *now.* Fumbling with her hot pink boxers, I shove them down her legs and fall to my knees.

"Griffin, what are you—"

Her words end on a breathless hitch as I spread her folds and lick her center. I always imagined what this would be like but never thought it would happen. Are we really doing this?

"Griff," She gasps. "Griff, keep doing that."

Fuck, yeah. We're really doing this.

Hooking her leg over my shoulder, I grab her ass and

force her other leg into place. Her back presses against the door, and I use it for leverage, eating her pussy like it's my last meal. I breathe her in, sucking her clit and slipping my finger inside of her. So tight. So greedy. She bucks against me, her channel squeezing me and her juices drenching my tongue and dripping off my chin. I like her like this. Needy. Exposed. Real. Weak. But only for me.

"Griff," she pleads.

My scalp burns as she threads her fingers through my hair and tugs. Twisting it in her fists and pulling me closer to her center, forcing me to eat her the way she wants. I smile against her, craving her neediness more than my own.

"You like my mouth, Fin?" I continue fingering her, adding my middle finger and scissoring back and forth inside of her. She's like silk. Fucking silk. So soft and wet I want to wrap her around me.

Her head rolls forward as she meets my gaze. "I like your mouth more when you're using it to please me."

I crook my fingers, causing her to moan. "You seem pretty pleased to me."

"Lick me again," she orders.

Bending forward, I drag the tip of my tongue along her clit and squeeze her ass with my opposite hand.

"Yes," she breathes out. "Yes, yes, yes. Fuck, Griff, I could let you do this to me all day."

Hot air hits her clit as I chuckle against her before latching on and flicking my tongue over the little nub over and over again.

Yeah, I could do this all day, too. And night. Fuck, I could spend the rest of my life worshipping her like this. Shutting her up with my mouth. My cock. The image of her on her knees in front of me, taking every inch as I bury myself between her thighs is almost enough to make me come in my pants, and I groan, lapping at her folds.

Her spine bows, and she falls apart against my lips. Nah. Explodes is more like it. It makes me feel like I'm king of the fucking universe.

Yeah, baby. I did this.

I made you fall apart.

I made you come.

Me.

A string of expletives falls out of her as she grinds her pussy against me, her thighs pressed along either side of my head like if I even think about pulling away, it'll be the last thing I do.

Joke's on her. I'm not going anywhere. Ever. Not if I can help it.

When her legs finally start to relax, I remove my fingers from her core, give her one more kiss against her center, and set her feet back on the ground. I can't believe I just licked Finley's pussy.

Finley fuckin' Taylor.

I smile and wipe at the corner of my mouth with my thumb. Best damn taste I've ever experienced. Without giving me a chance to stand to my full height, she falls to her knees and pushes against my chest until my back is pressed to the floor.

"What are you doing?" I ask.

"I mean, if we're really doing this, we might as well cross everything off the list, right?" Those gray eyes pin me in place as she fumbles with my jeans and tugs them down my thighs. My cock springs to life an inch from her mouth, and she grins, holding my attention hostage as she swallows me down, one inch at a time like I'd imagined.

I wait for her to retreat. To pull away. Instead, she deep throats me like a fucking porn star, and my head falls back.

Holy. Fucking. Shit.

Staring at the ceiling, I slide my fingers through her long hair, then cup the side of her face. I want to thrust. I want to force myself inside of her. Instead, I let her take the lead when we both know it's exactly what she needs. A moment of control. Power. And considering how much has been ripped away from her lately, I'm happy to give it. I've imagined this a thousand times. What it would be like. How she would look. How deep she would take me. My imagination is shit.

Tiny mewls vibrate up her throat as she sucks on the head, dragging her tongue along the slit and swirling it around the head of my cock again as I try to steady my breathing.

"Never thought I'd have your mouth," I groan. "Never thought I'd have any piece of you."

I move my hands from her face and press my palms into the ground, fighting for restraint. For self-control as the cords along my neck tighten.

Diving back onto my cock like her mouth was made for it, she hums around me, her hands finding my balls. She's so damn gentle as she rolls them around, tugging softly and driving me insane. It's like she was made to please me. To make me come. To make me fall apart.

Fuck, I think I might be right.

Closing my eyes, I savor the feeling, not knowing if or when I'll ever get it again. But if this is my only chance, my only opportunity, I'm not gonna squander it.

"Finley, come here," I order.

With a quiet pop, my cock slips from her mouth, and she tilts her head. "So help me, if you tell me we should stop, I'm gonna—" She squeals as I hook my arms beneath her and pull her up.

"You want to know what it's like, remember?" I growl

against the long column of her throat. "What it's like to be with someone other than that immature prick who couldn't see what he was letting go." Kissing her neck, I tug us to our feet, then guide her toward the bed as she hooks her arms around my waist. When the backs of her thighs hit the edge of the mattress, she tumbles onto it, bringing me with her. "Let me give you a glimpse."

The girl's like silk as I grind against her. Fuck, I feel like I'm losing my damn mind, and I'm not even inside her yet.

"Okay, this feels really good," she whimpers. "I'm gonna need you to get inside me like right now."

Smiling against her mouth, I reply, "You read my mind." I press the head of my cock against her center but pause as the last of my sanity makes one final plea. "Fuck, a condom."

"Already pregnant, remember?" she jokes.

"Fin," I warn.

"If we're being stupid, we might as well go for gold, right?" My cock twitches between us, and she grins. "Come on, big boy."

"I'm clean," I promise her.

"Me, too. Promise."

With a single thrust, I push inside of her and drop my forehead to hers. Fuck. She's tight. And wet. So fucking wet. My eyes roll back in my head as I force my body to not rip her in two, but it's hard. Really fucking hard.

"Damn, Griff," she pants. "I know I called you big boy, but, uh, *ouch*."

A dry laugh escapes me. "Sorry, Fin."

"No you aren't." She laughs.

I lift onto my forearms and stare down at her. "You're right. I'm not."

And it's true. The idea of marking her, of making her sore enough to think of me any time she moves tomorrow, is almost as addictive as being inside her. Feeling every inch of her. Her shallow breathing. The slight angle of her heel pressed against my ass.

Dragging her trimmed nails along my spine, she whispers, "You can move now."

Pleasure shoots through my balls as I slowly pull out of her, the friction better than anything I've ever experienced until I thrust into her again. And again. And again.

"You feel so good," she whispers. "I didn't think you'd feel this good."

"I knew you would," I admit. Pressing my mouth to hers, I kiss her again, taking control instead of letting her take the lead like before. I time my thrusts with my tongue, mirroring the movements as her core constricts around me. When the headboard bangs against the wall, I groan, sliding my hands beneath her ass and picking us both up. I hate how I have to hide it. This moment. This connection. This experience. If I'd given in at the hotel, this wouldn't be an issue, but here? It's only a reminder of how precarious the situation really is.

"What are you doing?" she asks.

"If your brother comes home and hears us, he'll kill me." With one hand, I keep Fin pressed to me, our bodies still connected, and grab the comforter on the bed with my opposite one. Once it's spread on the ground, I lay us down, keeping our bodies connected.

Sweat breaks out along my hairline as I stare down at her parted lips. "You have no idea how long I've been waiting for this," I breathe out.

Her nails scrape against my back, proving she's close, and I dip down to kiss her harder, branding her mouth with my own and swallowing her gasp as she squeezes my cock like a vice.

"Why do you feel so good?" she whispers. "Why is it so different with you?"

My sternum aches at her words. At what they mean, even if she doesn't know it. Isn't willing to recognize it.

Sitting us up, I lean my back against the edge of the bed, push the hair away from her face, and cup her jaw. I could joke about the size of my dick. I could tell her everyone's different. I could tell her a lot of things. But the truth is…I don't know why. Not really. She's always called to me. Always. I don't know why I've craved her more than anyone else—more than anyone I've ever been with. I don't know why I like the way she crawls under my skin. The way she drives me insane. The way my chest squeezes when she smiles at me.

I don't know a lot of things, but I do know she'll always be different. This thing between us will always be different.

"Been searching all my life for that answer," I admit. "If you figure it out, will you let me know?"

Her eyes dance with amusement, and she kisses me.

Rolling her hips, she rides me like a seasoned pro, and my eyes fall back in my head, too lost in the feel of her to analyze the pull between us. Especially now. When I'm so fucking close. As she burrows into the crook of my neck, I grab her waist and guide her movements, my balls tightening with every aching thrust until I can't take it anymore. My cock jerks inside of her, and she bites the side of my throat, sucking on the flesh as her core milks me for every damn drop. Her muscles tighten before she melts on top of me like a hot stick of butter.

"Fuck," she pants.

I laugh. "Fuck."

I might not have ever had a girlfriend, but I've never been one to turn down a casual hookup, and now that I'm here with Fin. Each and every experience in my past is laughable. This girl? This girl means more than she'll ever know.

"Did we, uh"—she sucks her bottom lip into her mouth—"did we really just do this?"

I flex my softening dick inside of her. "Pretty sure."

"And, uh, what are the odds you'll let me sweep this under the rug and pretend I didn't just sleep with my brother's best friend?"

"I'm gonna go with a zero percent chance." I squeeze her thighs. "But I'm okay if you want to wait to announce it to the world."

"Oh, so now there's an announcement needing to be made?"

"Add it to the list, right?" I offer dryly.

She sobers. "Good point."

"You could always let me be by your side, and we could air everything out at once."

"Or we could take things slow, and you can be patient with me while I…figure everything out."

"Everything…" A stone falls in my gut, and my amusement dissipates. Don't get me wrong. I didn't think we were gonna ride off into the sunset or some shit, but the reminder of how she isn't as invested in this as I am burns. I fight the urge to move her off me and pull her closer, caught between two conflicting feelings and what they would mean if I followed through with either of them. Rejection is the last thing she needs right now, but it's the last thing I need, too.

"Griff, I really do like you, and I really liked what we just did, but it's not only me anymore."

She won't look at me. Maybe she can't. Too busy drowning in all the unknowns of her future while adding me to one or two of the possibilities and analyzing whether or not my addition is a good idea. And I hate that

I get it. I understand her reservations. Fuck, I had no intention of sleeping with her when she walked into the kitchen this morning, but I don't regret it, and I sure as shit would never take it back. I meant what I said. I care about her. I want her. And if it means I have to go at her pace or risk another rejection on the off-chance she gives us a real shot, then I'll do it, even if it's a bitch.

Grabbing the side of her face, I urge her to look at me. "Finley, you're not alone in this."

Her lips smash together as she forces herself to hold my gaze. I know she doesn't believe me. I can see it in her eyes. Feel it in her silence. And in a way, she's right. I *don't* know. Not fully. I can't. I'm not Finley. I haven't been in her shoes, and I sure as shit can't ever become pregnant. But if she thinks I don't grasp the severity of her situation, or how weighted it really is, she doesn't know me as well as I thought she did.

"Finley, you're not alone in this," I repeat. "I'm not going anywhere."

"What if we…" She bites her bottom lip. "What if we wait to tell people?"

"Wait," I repeat.

"For a little while." She slips her hands beneath my shirt, drawing circles along my chest. The gentle scratch of her nails against my bare skin feels like fucking heaven. Goosebumps scatter along my spine and out to my limbs. "A month. Two, tops," she offers.

"Are you talking about us, or are you talking about the baby?"

She hesitates. "Both? I think? My family's already going to freak out when they find out I'm pregnant. Add in a very new…something…between me and my brother's best friend, and… You have to see where I'm coming from. Besides, I read online that most people don't announce their"—she gulps—"pregnancy until they're out of the first trimester anyway, so really, I'm not even too far behind the average girl. And in the meantime, we can…feel things out. See if this is…what we think it might be before signing our families up for heart attacks."

I want to tell her no, I don't want to wait. Hiding shit isn't going to make it go away. But I know this girl, and agreeing to feel out whatever this is between us instead of fighting it is already a big concession on her part.

"Fine." I grab her wrist, preventing her from moving. "We'll give it to the end of the month."

"Deal."

CHAPTER TWENTY-THREE

GRIFFIN

My legs shake as I lower into one more squat.

"Come on, man, you got this," Everett encourages me.

We've been waking up early and hitting the gym for as long as I can remember, but I've never felt more tension than today. Sweat beads along my forehead, but I lower into my squat for the set, squeezing the metal bar across my shoulders.

Muscles burning, I push up through my heels and stand. The weights clang as I slide the bar into place and step back, shaking out my tired legs.

Mav's working beside Reeves at the leg press, and I take note of the weight he's using. He might not be on the team anymore, thanks to his medical condition, but he's stronger than he used to be. Not where he could've been if fate hadn't fucked with his body, but still. Stronger.

"How do you think he's doin'?" Everett murmurs beside me, keeping his voice quiet so only I can hear him.

I lift a shoulder. "He'll never be one hundred percent, but he's better."

"Yeah." Everett gives a slow nod. "Pretty sure none of us will ever be one hundred percent after Archer."

He's right. We won't. Losing a best friend is never easy. Losing a best friend the way we lost Archer? It fucked with all our heads in a way I don't think any of us really grasp. But it doesn't matter how much time I spend analyzing what went down. I don't think I'll ever be able to accept it. Any of it.

I don't have a chance to respond as my phone begins vibrating in my basketball shorts, and I pull it out.

"Who is it?" Ev asks.

I shrug again and slide my thumb across the screen. "Hello?"

"Hello, Griffin Thorne?" an unfamiliar voice questions.

"Yeah, that's me. How can I help you?"

"Hello, Mr. Thorne. This is Teresa with the Kansas City Tornadoes."

Everett's expression lights up, and he gives me two thumbs up. I turn to face the opposite wall, ignoring him.

"Hello, Teresa," I say.

"Hi," she repeats. "How's your family?"

My forehead bunches until I remember the lie I told her when I canceled my last meeting with the Tornadoes' General Manager.

"They're, uh, they're good," I lie.

"Well, that's good to hear. I'll be sure to pass along the update to the team and everyone here at the organization."

"Uh, thanks?" I shake my head. "Thanks."

"Of course." I can hear the woman's polite smile through the speaker. "I'm calling to reschedule your meeting with Mr. Deemwater," she adds.

I tug at the collar of my T-shirt, then wipe my forehead with the back of my hand. Deemwater is the team's General Manager, the guy I bailed on so I could drive

Finley to see Drew. The reminder leaves me on edge, but I shove the feeling aside, answering, "Uh, yeah. Sure. When's a good time for Mr. Deemwater?"

"Well, he'll be in Lockwood Heights next Saturday. Would you be interested in meeting with him before LAU's game? He could meet after, as well," she continues. "He plans to attend either way."

"The game?" I choke.

"Yes?" I can hear her confusion.

Scrubbing my hand over my face, I clarify, "He's coming to LAU's game?"

"Is there a…problem?"

My head shifts left and right on reflex. Stopping myself, I lift the hem of my shirt and dab at my forehead. "Uh… you tell me, I guess?"

Seriously, is it hot in here?

"He simply wants to watch his rising star in action," she explains. "You've been playing very well this season."

"Thanks," I mutter, but the tightness in my chest doesn't loosen. "Can I ask what the meeting is about?" I cringe. "Sorry, I guess I'm just a little curious why he wants to talk to me before the season is even over. Are there any problems with my contract or anything?"

"Oh, no. Nothing like that," she rushes out. "Quite the opposite, actually. You're a prime asset to the Tornadoes organization, Mr. Thorne. No off-the-ice drama, especially in the"—she clears her throat—"female department. Your stats are incredible, and I'm sure you heard about Caruthers' injury before the holidays."

"Yeah, I did." I squeeze the back of my neck. "Tough break."

"Yes, well, Mr. Deemwater and the rest of the board have been considering their options for next season. I'm sure they'll give you all the specifics at lunch. Does two o'clock work for you?"

I nod. "Uh, sure."

"Perfect! He'll meet you at Rowdy's. Are you familiar with the establishment?"

My head bobs again. "Yeah, that works."

"Perfect!" she repeats. "Nice chatting with you, Mr. Thorne. Go, Hawks!"

"Go, Hawks," I reply, ending the call. As if my arm weighs a thousand pounds, it drops to my side, and I turn around, finding my friends staring at me.

"What'd they say?" Everett asks.

"They rescheduled my meeting with Mr. Deemwater since I couldn't make the last one."

"Yeah, 'cause you were driving Fin across the country," Reeves interjects. "How'd that go, anyway?"

With a shrug, I move to the squat bar and get into position again. "It was fine."

"You beat Drew's ass?" Everett challenges.

I lower into a squat, my muscles screaming as I push back into a standing position. "Wanted to, but Fin beat me to it."

I squat again, and Everett grins. "Should've known. Glad you had her back, though. Any idea what Mr. Deemwater wants to talk about?"

We've had this conversation. Made our own assumptions. But after I bailed on the last meeting, I didn't expect another one. Not when Caruthers' backup was on the ice the weekend after I got home with Fin.

Puffing out my cheeks, I bend my knees, keeping my feet wide, then squeeze my ass up again. "They aren't gonna pull me from LAU."

"Thank fuck," Mav interjects.

Everett glances at him.

"What?" Mav replies. "You already lost two of your best teammates at the beginning of the season. LAU would be screwed without their captain for the end of it."

Reeves tilts his head toward Mav. "He's not wrong."

Pausing mid-set, I huff out, "I think—" *Breathe.* "I think they wanna have me skip the farm team and move straight to the Tornadoes next season."

Reeves' eyes widen. "No shit?"

Copping out, I set the bar back into place, my chest heaving. "It's only a hunch," I pant, "but Mr. Deemwater's coming to Saturday's game to watch, so"—I take another deep breath—"yeah. I think they want me on the Tornadoes' roster this fall."

"Well, damn." Slapping me on the shoulder, Maverick grins. "That's awesome, man. You've earned it."

"I dunno. We'll see," I mutter, wiping the sweat along my hairline.

"What do you mean, we'll see?" Everett interjects. "This is what you've always wanted, isn't it?"

Something sharp hits between my ribs, but I don't rub the pain away. "Yeah, for sure, but looking so far into the future is…a lot."

"What do you mean?" Everett laughs. "We've been dreaming about this since we were kids."

"I know," I reply. "And I'm excited. I just have to think about finals and graduation before thinking about next season, you know?"

"Yeah, 'cause moving straight to the NHL is such a hard pill to swallow," Reeves chimes in.

"I know," I repeat, feeling like a parrot or some shit. And I do. I know this is a huge opportunity. I know I'm being seen for my talent on the ice, not my father's, and they want to reward me for it. I know any of my friends and teammates would give anything to be in my position.

To have an opportunity like this. A chance to slingshot the trajectory of my career instead of spending years on the farm teams proving my worth. But even taking all of that into account, I can't help but think of Finley, too. Here. Alone. I shove the thought aside and glance at my friends. "It'll be great."

With a nod, Mav claps his hand on my shoulder. "Fuck yeah, it will. Now, move aside. It's Ev's turn."

CHAPTER TWENTY-FOUR

FINLEY

It's weird. Pretending like the biggest thing on my mind is whether or not my red and black face paint looks on point when my world feels like it's turned upside down. As Lia, Dylan, Raine, and I get ready for the game, complete with LAU jerseys and said red and black face paint—which looks phenomenal, by the way—my stomach grumbles.

"You good?" Dylan asks.

I touch my gut through the jersey tied below my breasts. "Yeah. I'm hungry, I think."

"We just ate," she says with a laugh.

She's right. We did. I had a bagel with cream cheese, sausage, two eggs, and fruit on the side. I should be stuffed.

My stomach grumbles a little louder, and Raine rolls her eyes. "Finish your mascara while I grab you something from the fridge. What sounds good?"

I hesitate, my lips bunching on one side as I consider my options. "Can I do a tomato sandwich?"

"A what?" She screeches to a halt and stares at me over her shoulder.

"Tomato, mayo, salt, pepper, and bread." I smile sweetly. "Actually, yeah. That sounds delicious."

"Okay, weirdo."

She starts down the hall, and I add, "Oo, and pickle! Don't forget the pickle!"

"Dill or sweet?" she calls.

Popping my head outside the bathroom door, I quirk my brow. "Obviously, there's only one right answer."

"Dill!" Dylan clarifies for me with a grin.

"Thank you!" I chime in, leaning closer to the bathroom mirror to apply the rest of my mascara.

As I swipe the wand against my lashes, Dylan notes, "So, you look especially cute today."

"Um, I always look cute."

"I said *especially*."

Slipping the wand back into the tube, I twist it into place and give my best friend a once-over. "So do you. I like the face paint."

"You did the face paint," she points out.

"No wonder I like it." I wink. "But for real, you look hot. Reeves is gonna die when he sees you."

Her mouth lifts in a shy smile, but she sobers slightly.

"Okay, what did I say?" I ask. "Because you went from looking as happy as a clam to looking like I kicked your puppy."

"I don't have a puppy, and what kind of saying is that, anyway?" Her nose scrunches. "Ollie says it, too."

I lift a shoulder. "No idea where the saying came from, but I knew I liked Reeves. Great minds think alike and all that."

"Mm-hmm."

"So?" I prod. "What's wrong?"

Her lips bunch on one side, and she scoots her glasses a little further up her nose. "Can I ask you something?"

"Yeah, of course."

"Was it ever like...*this* for you and Drew?" she asks.

"You mean like rainbows and butterflies and over-the-top cuteness?"

She nods.

Digging my teeth into my bottom lip, I play back a few of my most potent memories with Drew at the beginning of our relationship, then pop a shoulder. "Honestly? Things with me and Drew were never like"—I wave my hand toward her—"*this*. We were like two puzzle pieces who kept trying to mash ourselves together in hopes of fitting. Sometimes, I could almost believe it worked, but then...I don't know. It's like I could feel the crumpled edges I was trying to convince myself were as sharp and intricate as in the beginning. Does that make sense?"

She nods again. "Yeah, I think it does."

"So, see? You and Mr. Reeves are the real deal, and I'm not the only one who can see it, so don't stress."

"Thanks." Her lips lift. "How are you holding up on the whole Drew front, anyway?"

My body sags against the edge of the bathroom counter. "You've already asked me this, you know."

"Yet, I never feel like you give me the real answer," she volleys back at me.

"We're good."

"We?"

My face scrunches. "Talk about a Freudian slip, am I right?" I try to laugh it off as I push my hair behind my shoulder and give myself one more quick assessment in the mirror. "I meant me and Drew. We're better off apart, and honestly? Considering all the time I wasted with him, I kind of thought I'd be sadder, but I'm not. I'm..." I press my lips into a thin line, mentally finishing my sentence. *Too distracted by the baby in my uterus and sneaking around with your older brother to give my ex much thought.* "I'm good."

"Just know I'm here for you," Dylan says. "And so are Lia and Raine. I know you think you have to put on a brave face and be Miss Independent and all, but we're here."

"Thanks." I pull her into a hug, squeezing tight.

"Even Frankie," she adds.

With a laugh, I shove her away from me. "Sure, he is. Come on. I bet my sandwich is ready."

BY THE TIME I SHOVE THE LAST BITE OF MY TOMATO sandwich into my mouth, Dylan's pulling into the rink. Reeves caught a ride with Everett when Ev dropped Raine off at the duplex, letting Dylan use his car to bring us here since none of us girls have our own vehicles at the moment. I should probably figure out what I'm going to do about that soon, though. I make a mental note as I scan the area.

We're early, but even so, the parking lot is still brimming with fans. They're here to watch the guys warm up on the ice like the rest of us, and boy, is it a sight. The men in their gear, stretching and chatting and lazily skating across the ice like it's what they were made to do. Don't get me wrong. I'm a sucker for a good game, but watching the players without their game faces has its own appeal.

Hooking my purse on my shoulder, we head inside the arena. It's already buzzing with anticipation as I stand in line to order popcorn and make my way to our seats. When I enter the stands, I catch the girls at the glass chatting with the guys, so I watch my feet, careful not to fall on my ass as I make my way toward them.

"Want some?" I tilt the cardboard box toward Raine. She pops a kernel into her mouth.

"Extra butter?" she asks.

I nod. "Obviously."

She laughs and wiggles her fingers toward my brother. Skating closer, Everett gives her a fist bump against the glass, and she returns it with her own.

"You look pretty," he calls.

With a grin, she motions to her face. On it is a cute little hawk beside her right eye. Its wings are spread, and in the center of its chest is Everett's jersey number. Cheesy? Yes. Adorable? Also, yes.

"Your sister's quite the artist," Raine muses.

"You can blame Ophelia's mom," I tell her. "My Aunt Blakely is the queen of face paint." My chest puffs up with pride. "Taught me everything I know."

Everett's eyes stay glued to Raine. "You know I'm gonna mess it up later, right?"

My nose wrinkles. "Gross."

"I meant with my hands," he replies, finally gifting me with a crumb of his attention. "Get your head outta the gutter, Finley."

"Yeah, okay." I snort as Dreggs skates toward us.

"Hey, Fin!" he calls.

Balancing my popcorn in my opposite hand, I wave. "Hey, Dreggs."

"A little bird told me you're single."

My gaze flicks to Griffin near the blue line before I can stop myself, then I turn back to his teammate. "Sure am."

"When's the last time someone took you on a date?"

"A date?" I ask.

"Careful, Dreggs," Everett growls. "She's my baby sister."

"I'll be a complete gentleman, I swear," he offers.

"Yeah, and I'm the Pope," I tease.

He clutches his chest like I've sucker punched him, and my lips quirk.

He's a flirt. He's always been a flirt. I know it. Dylan knows it. Everett knows it.

Everyone knows it.

Still, it is amusing. Or at least, it would be if I was actually single and less like a ticking time bomb.

"Come on. One date," Dreggs pleads, pressing his hands into a prayer gesture and everything. "You and me."

"Gather up, team!" Coach Sanderson yells from the bench.

I wiggle my fingers in another half-assed wave. "And on that note, toodle-oo, boys. Good luck!"

"See you around, Finley!" Dreggs calls. "That's a promise!"

I grab another piece of popcorn, toss it into my mouth, and grin. "Bye, Dreggs." Turning on my heel, I head up the stairs toward my seat, with the girls following.

When we reach our seats, I yell, "Go Hawks!" and sit down, balancing my sneakers on the empty chair in front of me.

"Did Dreggs seriously ask you out?" Raine asks.

I shrug, digging through the cardboard box for an especially buttery piece of deliciousness. "Apparently."

"He's cute," Dylan chimes in.

"He's very cute," I agree. "He's also very much Everett's teammate, and I'm very much recently out of a relationship." *And kind of currently in a secret one,* I silently add to myself.

"So?" Raine interjects. "I believe you're the one who told me the best way to get over someone is to get under someone else."

"And then you fell for my brother." I grin up at her.

"You're welcome, by the way. See? I'm the queen of face paint *and* romantic advice."

"Yet you're shit at taking it," she volleys back as she collapses into the chair next to me. "Go figure."

"Har, har. Let's watch the game," I announce.

"Mm-hmm."

Dylan leans forward. "Hey, PS—did you hear about the house?"

I frown. "What about it?"

"The inspection guy finally gave us the green light to move back in."

"Us?" I challenge, batting my lashes at her.

She scoffs. "Okay, when I say us, I mean you, Raine, and Ev."

"Yeah, since you've been shacking up with your little boyfriend and all." I wink. "Reeves must be quite the performer in the bedroom."

Untucking her pale blonde hair, Dylan tries to hide her blush, but the girl's practically glowing with embarrassment. "No comment. Now, watch the game."

"Mm-hmm," I hum, mimicking Raine from seconds ago. "So, Raine. Does Ev know about the occupancy status update?"

"Yeah, but we probably won't move in until all the furniture arrives, which should be in a couple of weeks."

"Well, I'm moving in ASAP," I announce. "Don't get me wrong. I love living next to two fuck buddies." I pause, giving Dylan a pointed look. "But my earplugs can only take so much wear and tear, so the more space, the better."

"Gee, you're so funny," Dylan quips.

"I'm hilarious," I agree.

"Yeah, Dreggs thinks so, too," she tosses back at me.

With a hmph, I fold my arms and turn to the game.

CHAPTER TWENTY-FIVE

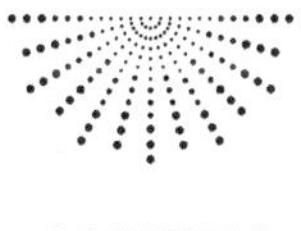

GRIFFIN

"Yo, Thorne," Cameron calls.

I tear my attention from Finley at the glass. A generic LAU jersey is tied beneath her breasts, leaving her stomach on display beneath a black leather jacket and dark jeans. Her lips are painted red, and a smudge of matching crimson, black, and glitter covers her right cheekbone, though she's too far away for me to make out what it says. LAU maybe? It could be Hawks. I pass the puck to Cameron and glance at Fin again.

My jaw locks.

What the fuck is Dreggs doing talking to her?

She rolls her gray eyes and tosses some popcorn into her mouth before those red-painted lips form a response.

Dreggs clutches at his chest like a wounded animal, shifting his hockey stick from one glove to the other and lifting his chin.

"Gather up, team!" Coach calls from the bench.

I don't move from the blue line, though. With a playful wave, Finley and the girls head to their seats, and Everett skates away from the glass with Dreggs in tow.

"Hey, you comin'?" Ev asks as he reaches me.

I throttle my stick and nod, moving beside him and Dreggs.

He's always been kind of an ass and has had a thing for Finley and every other girl in the friend group since the beginning of the school year. The reminder doesn't exactly make me feel better.

I barely hear a word Coach says as he gives us a pep talk. There are too many things on my mind. Finley. Dreggs. Deemwater.

I met with the Tornadoes' General Manager for lunch earlier today. I was right, too. They want me to take Caruthers' position. And even though my agent pushed me to take it, I declined.

Fuck, I can't believe I declined.

My attention shoots to Deemwater in the crowd. Part of me wondered if he'd even bother coming to the game after our lunch, but he's here. Front and center. Guess it means I haven't entirely fucked up my future. Not yet, anyway.

What the hell am I doing?

"Thorne, anything you want to say?" Coach asks.

Shit. How long has he been talking to me?

Clearing my throat, I force myself to focus on someone other than the girl in the stands and my precarious hockey career.

"Uh...don't fuck up," I tell them.

The team laughs, and I force a smile, squeezing my stick in my hands.

"Excellent captain's speech," Sanderson mutters dryly. "Now, come on. Let's show our fans what we've got."

Then, we take the ice.

I scan the crowd, finding Deemwater staring at me from behind the glass, when my eyes fall on Finley. She's sucking down an Icee, and I don't need to see inside the cup to know it's cherry-flavored. I tear my attention from her, forcing myself to focus on the game and how important this game is now that the man who literally holds my future in the palm of his hand is in the stands.

We're playing the Hammers. They're a decent team, but nothing to write home about. Lining up on the left-hand side, I watch Everett skate to the center, preparing to go head-to-head with the HMU Hammers' center.

The ref stops short in front of them, balancing his whistle against the edge of his bottom lip, and drops the puck. Everett misses it, and the Hammers' center slaps the puck toward his waiting left wing. Bardot snatches the puck, not allowing it to make it to the intended player, and chips the puck off the boards. Racing toward it, I spin around the defenseman in my path and dribble it down the side, smacking the puck across the center of the ice toward Reeves. As soon as it hits the edge of his stick, Reeves passes it to Everett like a well-oiled machine. Hurrying into position, I wait for Everett to notice me as one of the defensemen blocks his path. Everett taps the puck through his legs, and I catch it on the opposite side, slapping the puck into the left pocket. Sirens wail around us, the red light glowing as the score updates to one to zero.

Pumping my fist into the air, I glance at the stands, searching for the coach but finding Finley on her feet instead. Her hands are cupped around her mouth while she and the rest of the girls cheer us on. When my gaze connects with hers, the girl's smile grows, and my heart pounds faster as I return it with one of my own.

We got this.

The rest of the first period goes by in a blur. After Everett slips the puck into the pocket within ten seconds of the buzzer, leaving the score two to zero, we file into the locker room for our first break. With my helmet tucked under my arm, I steal one of the water bottles, drinking half its contents.

"Come on, man," Dreggs says. "It's one date."

"Not gonna happen," Everett growls.

My ears perk, and I turn toward my best friend.

Dreggs is straddling the bench, gripping the sides with his bare hands, his gloves haphazardly tossed in front of his crotch as he stares up at Everett.

"One date. It's not a big deal."

Everett rolls his shoulders and catches me eavesdropping. "Will you tell this asshat to leave my little sister alone?"

"Leave his little sister alone," I say around the edge of the water bottle and finish what's left of it.

Dreggs scoffs. "What? Afraid it'll mess with my playing or some shit? 'Cause I'm pretty sure that's the only reason my captain would be allowed to have any say in who I do or don't date."

Jealousy hits my sternum, and my fingers squeeze into the water bottle as I force my expression to remain indifferent. Part of me wants to kick his ass for insubordination. For thinking he has a chance with Finley in the first place. For recognizing that he has every right to ask her out because he has no idea she's already taken. Already mine.

Wiping my hand with the back of my mouth, I dig deep for indifference and point out, "Everett has a stick up his ass when it comes to his baby sister. You know this."

"It's one date," Dreggs argues.

"Yeah," Everett grunts, spreading his legs wide. "One date too many."

Dreggs scoffs. "She dated her boyfriend for how long?"

"Too long," I offer.

"She deserves to have some freedom," Everett explains. "Especially after being tied down to a dick like Drew."

"Then let me take her out…show her a good time…give her a glimpse of what it's like to date a real man." Lifting his arms, Dreggs flexes his biceps as if to give us a physical representation of what a real man looks like, and my forehead furrows in disgust.

"She isn't interested," Everett tells him.

"She looked interested," Dreggs argues.

My best friend scoffs. "No, she didn't."

"Did you hear her say no when I asked?" he counters.

My stomach bottoms out, and I set the empty water bottle with the rest so they can be washed and refilled for the next period.

She didn't say no?

What the fuck, Fin?

Trying not to lose my shit, I take a deep breath.

"Enough begging, Dreggs," Everett warns. "Your captain said no."

"Is that right?" Dreggs counters. His focus shifts to me. "You're really pulling the captain card, man?"

"Looks like it," I mutter.

With a grin, Everett stands and slaps his hand against my shoulder pads. "Glad to see someone has my back."

"Glad I can be of service," I grumble.

But even then, I can't erase Dreggs's words from haunting me.

Did you hear her say no when I asked?

Fuck. She really didn't turn him down?

I scrub my hand over my face.

We agreed to keep our relationship quiet, not to act like it doesn't exist in the first place. Is she really interested in seeing other people?

"One minute," Coach calls from his office. Lifting his

pointer finger into the air, he makes a tiny circle, adding, "Wrap it up."

We head back to the ice and win the game, three to one. I wind up in the penalty box. Twice. Once for roughing a player and another time for high sticking. It was a dick move, but I couldn't help myself. I'm too amped up. Too frustrated. Too caught up in my own head and what Dreggs meant versus what Finley wants and where the hell I fit into it.

But the worst part? Is knowing the Tornadoes' GM saw me play like shit for the last two periods of the game after I had already declined his offer to move me up to their team for the remainder of the season. But I can't make myself care. Not when I'm so wrapped up in my best friend's little sister.

CHAPTER TWENTY-SIX

FINLEY

They won. It was a good game, and my throat is officially sore from cheering so loud. Everyone's already in the hall. Everyone but Griff.

"Are we having a Game Night or what?" Reeves asks us. "My phone's been blowing up with people asking since the first period ended. Pickles?" he prods, using his favorite nickname for my best friend.

Dylan shrugs and loops her arms around his neck, pulling him in for a quick peck. "I'm good with whatever."

"I'm okay with a Game Night," Raine adds. "What do you think, Ev?"

My brother nods. "Works for me." Glancing at the closed locker room, he frowns.

"Is Griff still in there?" I ask.

His head bobs again. "I don't know what's taking him so long."

"Probably pissed he lost his head in the second and third periods," Reeves interjects. "Did you hear the Tornadoes' GM was here?"

Everett's brows hitch. "You noticed, too, huh?"

223

"Yeah," Reeves answers. "It would fuck with my head, too."

"Fuck," my brother mutters. "Let's give him some space. Fin, you wanna ride with me and Raine back to the house?"

"A friend from one of my classes texted and asked if I wanted to catch up after the game," I lie as my attention moves from the closed locker room door to Everett. "I'll see if she can give me a ride to the house."

"You sure?" he asks. "I don't mind waiting."

"I'm good, promise." Rising onto my tiptoes, I kiss his cheek. "But thank you for being a super duper overprotective brother who always looks out for me."

"Yeah, yeah," he grumbles. "Be safe."

"I will. Oh, and"—I snap my fingers—"on the off-chance she can't drop me off, I'll just text Griff since it seems like he'll be here for a while." I tilt my head toward the locker room. "No biggie."

Everett hesitates but winds up nodding as I pass hugs around to the rest of the group like they're confetti. Once I'm finished, my friends head toward the exit. I start in the opposite direction before peeking over my shoulder and slipping into the men's locker room when the coast is clear.

The door is heavy and creaks in protest as I push it open, praying I don't get caught. The musty, stale scent of sweat and leather mixes with the humid air, and my stomach curdles. Either I've forgotten how smelly a locker room can be, or these pregnancy hormones are messing with my sense of smell. Regardless, I press my hand to my stomach and inch further into the space. One of the showers is on. The familiar whoosh of rushing water echoes off the cinder block walls as I tiptoe past the coach's office. It's empty. Everyone's gone home for the day. Most of the lights are off, leaving an eerie glow as the steam spills out of the showers.

With a squeak from the pipes, the water cuts off, and I call out, "Griff?"

Silence.

"Fin?"

I can hear the confusion in his voice, and my lips tug up. "Yeah, it's me."

Peeking into the showers, I find a very bare backside topped by a very muscular back. Seriously. How can one man be so damn good-looking? It's like not only did God smile upon this boy, but so did all of his angels.

Turning around, Griffin faces me in all his naked glory.

My teeth dig into my bottom lip as I shamelessly check him out. "Well, damn. Is it my birthday, or did I win the lottery and no one told me?"

He drops his gaze and reaches for a towel on the hook beside him, drying off his body, then rubbing the damp, white towel against his light brown hair without even bothering to cover his half-raised cock.

"Pretty sure you aren't supposed to be in here," he mutters.

"Pretty sure you shouldn't be complaining."

He knots the towel around his waist and cocks his head. "Oh, I shouldn't?"

"Not when this place is empty, and my goal is to bring a smile to your grouchy face." I step closer, lift my hand, and cup his jaw. Urging him to look at me, I add, "I heard about the Tornadoes' GM attending today's game. I'm sorry if you didn't play the way you wanted to."

"I don't care about the game," he mutters.

"You don't?"

He shakes his head. "Or the GM."

"Well, color me surprised." I lower my hand and pat his

chest. "Consider this a celebratory blow job for today's win, then. Although if you're feeling generous, I'd love to kneel on the towel—" I reach for the knot above the outline of his erection, but he grabs my wrist and stops me.

"I don't want your mouth, Finley."

My brows pinch. "What?"

"I said I don't want your mouth."

I peek up at him, not bothering to hide my confusion. "I'm sorry, but I'm pretty sure I need my hearing checked because no guy in the history of guys has ever turned down a mouth. Just sayin'."

"This isn't a joke, Finley."

The pain in his eyes makes me pause. The hurt. The distance.

What the hell?

My mind whirs, and I try to piece together what he isn't saying.

My tongue darts out between my lips. "Did I…" I lean back. "Did I do something wrong?"

"Why didn't you tell Dreggs no?" he demands.

Dreggs? This is about Dreggs?

A breath of laughter escapes me. I start to pull my wrist away from him, but Griff doesn't let me go.

"Something funny?" he growls.

"Are you serious right now?" I challenge. "You're mad because I didn't flat-out refuse Dreggs when he asked me out? That's why you're acting like this?"

"I want to know why."

"Because you and I agreed to keep this thing a secret, remember?"

"Add it to the list, right?" he offers dryly.

"Okay, pause. Are we discussing the whole…" My mouth snaps shut, and I point to my stomach. "Or are we discussing this?" I wiggle my finger between us. "Because those are two very different things, and only one of them technically involves you, so I suggest you choose your next words wisely."

I sound like a bitch. I know I do, but he's being unfair, and I'm not going to simply roll over and take it.

His jaw tics, but he lets out a slow breath, his expression softening. "Me and you, Fin. I wanna discuss me and you."

"Okay." I sigh. "Well, for starters, that was a wise choice." His mouth twitches. "And secondly, you're not allowed to be mad at me. I might not've said no, but I didn't say yes, either, okay? I have no desire to date—or to be with—anyone but you, which is why I came in here. To be with *you*," I emphasize. "Not Dreggs. Not any other guy. Only you."

His grasp on my wrist tightens, and he tugs me into him, surprising me with a bruising kiss I can feel from the top of my head to the tips of my toes. I moan at the contact, letting my hands roam every dip and flex of his muscles beneath my touch. "I like you like this," I whisper against his mouth, finding the knot in the towel. It drops to our feet. "All needy and jealous." Lifting my chin, I let him kiss me again. It's softer this time but just as desperate. I like him like this, too. Seeing him care. Seeing him give a shit when he's so laid back most of the time it's impossible to tell whether or not he's affected by…anything, really. His cock bobs between us, and I grasp it softly, running my fingers over the head like it's a delicate flower, well aware of exactly how much I'm teasing him.

A groan of frustration hits my mouth, and he leans away with a warning look. "You playing with me, Fin?"

"Is that what I'm doing?" I ask innocently.

"Gonna fuck that smart mouth of yours again one of these days."

"I mean, I did offer," I quip.

"And if we were anywhere else, I'd take you up on it." His hands find the loop of my jeans, and he tugs me toward him, grinding his cock against my bare upper stomach, thanks to the knotted jersey beneath my breasts. "Do you have any idea how much this has been killing me?" He slips his hands around my waist and along my spine, causing goosebumps to spread over my skin like wildfire.

Leaning closer, he sucks on the patch of skin just beneath my ear, and I tilt my head as he unbuttons my jeans and slides them down to my knees. I never felt this with Drew. This...intensity. This...completely unhinged desire to throw caution to the wind, no matter how stupid it is. Because let's be real. Hooking up in the men's locker room isn't the brightest thing either of us has ever done, yet here we are, desperate to feel each other. To touch each other. To come apart with each other. Because of each other.

Spinning me around, he orders, "Hands on the wall."

I peek over my shoulder and place my open palms on the tile as he fists his hard cock, spreading the pre-cum along his shaft.

My core clenches at the view, and I bite my bottom lip, wiggling my ass in front of him. "Any day now, Griff."

His chuckle is dry and low as he steps closer, lining himself up with my entrance. "You're a pain in the ass, you know that, right, Fin?"

With a nod, I arch my back, trying to push him inside of me, but he pulls back, rubbing the head along my slit but not entering me the way I want. The way I need.

"Speaking of pain in the ass," I muse. "Are you gonna fuck me or not, Griff?"

He smirks. "You've been teasing me all day. Figured I'd return the favor."

I laugh and slip my hand between my thighs, playing with myself before dragging the moisture to the head of his cock still tucked against my center. "Do you have any idea how wet I am for you?"

Griffin's head falls forward, and he groans, reaching around me. A sting hits the back of my hand as he slaps me away and envelops my wrist. With his opposite hand, he grabs my hips, ramming himself inside of me, pushing my face into the tile wall and hitching my hand behind my back. The icy surface seeps through my jersey and makes my nipples harden with anticipation. This. I never knew it could be like this. That *he* could be like this.

My jaw drops at the intrusion, the delicious stretch making my knees weak as I try to catch my breath.

"This pussy is mine. This body is mine. This soul is mine." He pulls out, then thrusts into me again, hitting me so deep I could scream.

"Fuck," I gasp.

"Yeah," he rasps against the shell of my ear. "Fuck."

Moving my hair to one side, he sucks on my throat, rutting into me hard and fast and wild. His fingers slide around my waist, find my clit, and I combust around him. The nails of my free hand scrape against the tile surface as stars erupt behind my closed eyes. Never, and I mean never, have I been fucked like this. So raw and animalistic. It's the hottest thing I've ever experienced, and when his cock jerks inside of me, I want every fucking ounce. I crave it. Need it. Need him.

His heart rams against my chest as we both catch our breath, his forehead resting at the base of my neck, when all of a sudden, I hear a cold, detached voice from the shower's entrance.

"What the fuck?"

CHAPTER TWENTY-SEVEN

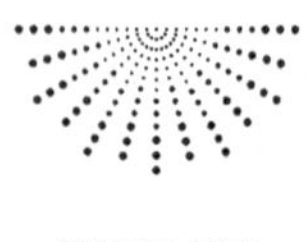

FINLEY

Griffin's softening cock slips out of me as he blocks my half-naked body from my older freaking brother.

Shit.

My stomach bottoms out, and I squat down, grabbing my jeans and sliding them back into place as my face burns like it was dipped in acid. I don't get embarrassed. Not really. But this? My brother catching me with my pants literally down as his best friend fucks me in the men's locker room was not the way I wanted to end my day.

Well, the fucking part I'm cool with, but the brother catching me part? Not so much.

His footsteps are slow but oh-so deliberate as Everett moves toward us.

Step. Step. Step.

They echo off the tile walls, and I fight to steady my breathing. I've pissed my brother off more times than I can count in my short life, but this? Yeah. This takes the cake.

"What. The. Fuck?" he demands.

Peeking around Griffin's very naked body, I start, "Everett, calm down."

"Is this the *friend* you were coming to see?" he spits. His sneakers threaten to touch Griffin's bare toes as they stand chest to chest. Face to face.

Lifting his hands in surrender, Griffin starts, "Look, Ev—"

His head snaps to the side from Everett's sucker punch, and my hands press against his bare back as he stumbles into me. Holy shit. Did my brother really just hit Griff?

Yup. Yup, he did.

Once he's steady, I move around Griff and shove my brother in the chest. "Back the hell up, Everett!"

"Don't start with me, Fin."

Craning my neck, I glare up at him. "No, don't start with *me*." I jab at my sternum. "I know this is a little bit of a shock to you, but you are not allowed to walk in here and act like Griffin was defiling me or whatever. I'm a grown adult."

"How long have you been fucking my best friend, Finley?" he growls.

The words are like a lash. So cold and heartless, my body reacts on its own, and I flinch back. The disgust in his voice? The hurt? I guess it hits different, doesn't it? And I don't...I don't know what to say.

"Back up, Everett," Griffin warns. The heat of his chest seeps into my back as he moves behind me, wrapping his arms around my shoulders.

My brother's attention snaps from me to his best friend. "Using my sister as a shield, asshole?" He scoffs. "Fucking coward."

Griffin's chest expands on a slow breath, but he doesn't pull away. Doesn't move me aside. Just stares at his best friend as if contemplating how to handle this situation now that the cat's out of the bag. Well, one of the cats, anyway. There's still the doozy of the bun in my oven, but hey. One surprise at a time, right?

It would probably help the entire situation if Griffin's bare cock wasn't nudged against my jeans-covered ass, though. I glance at the towel splayed on the ground behind Everett but decide it isn't worth the effort. Not at the moment.

Silence surrounds us. Heavy. Thick. Toxic.

Seriously, I've never been speechless like this. I've never not known what to say. But right now? Standing between my brother and his very naked best friend? I don't know what to say or how the hell I can fix this. If I can even fix this. This was the look I'd been hoping to avoid. The one tainted in disappointment. Disgust. Betrayal.

Shame unfurls inside of me, and I cross my arms. "Ev," I start. "I know you're disappointed, but—"

"Disappointed?" Another laugh escapes him. "I'm more than disappointed."

"Let me handle this, Fin," Griff murmurs. "Ev, I know you're pissed, all right? And you have every right to be, but don't put this on her, and don't act like you're oblivious to my feelings for Fin."

Nostrils flaring, Everett's attention snaps from me to Griffin. "What the hell are you talking about?"

With a low chuckle, Griffin dips his head over my shoulder, skates his lips across my cheek, and steps around me with a confidence I honestly envy, especially while sporting his birthday suit.

"I've had a thing for Finley since she was a freshman in high school," Griffin tells him. "Remember?"

My brother's expression falls, but he doesn't back away. Doesn't give his best friend any room as Griffin bends down and grabs the towel from the floor. It's probably dirty, and I have no doubt that under different circumstances, there isn't a chance in hell he'd wrap that thing around his waist again, but considering his current predicament, it's the least of his worries. The least of mine, too.

"And what did you tell me, Ev?" he pushes, knotting the fabric to cover his impressive cock.

Not the time, Finley.

I tear my attention from Griffin's bulge in time to witness my brother's teeth grinding, and for the first time ever, I have enough empathy to not want to sweep this under the rug or make light of his overbearing theatrics. Ev has every right to be shaken, and if I'm being honest, so do I. This entire situation is…a little much. But even so, I can't make myself regret it.

Also, did Griffin just admit he had feelings for me since high school? Be still my pattering heart. Seriously, I would swoon if I wasn't terrified of Everett throwing another punch at his best friend because of me.

"You told me if I touched her, I could kiss our friendship goodbye," Griffin continues.

"You said you were joking," Everett defends.

"Yeah, well, I wasn't."

My sternum aches from the pressure his words bring, and I press my fist against it. He's telling the truth. Everett threatened him? Seriously? I mean, I guess I shouldn't be surprised, but still. Knowing they actually talked about me is kind of…flattering in a really twisted, messed-up way, but also a little heartbreaking because…well, because I know how much their friendship means to each other, and here I am, coming between them.

With a wave of his hand, Everett snaps, "And here you are, fucking her in plain sight."

You read my mind, brother.

"Not exactly how I would've wanted our coming out party, but it is what it is." Griffin offers his hand to Everett. "And yes. I'm aware that if I hurt her, you'll kick my ass."

My brother only stares at it. "So, you two are official?"

"We haven't gotten that far," I interject.

Griffin's hand falls, and he glances over at me. "Your sister's stubborn, and since she just got out of a relationship, she wants to take things slow." It's a lie. Partially. I mean, yes, I'm stubborn, and yes, I just got out of a relationship, and I want to take things slow, but the truth is, being pregnant and trying to navigate through all of this is messy and confusing and overwhelming, and I've never liked Griffin more for taking all of it into consideration without holding any of it against me.

"Let me get this straight," Everett demands. "You're saying that taking shit slow is fucking her in the men's locker room?" Another scoff escapes him. "You shouldn't have touched her until you were both ready to commit."

"Funny because if you played by those rules, Raine would've taken your virginity," I snap. "Now, get off your high horse, Everett. I'm allowed to sleep with whoever I want."

My brother's nostrils continue flaring, and he opens his mouth to say something when Griffin cuts him off. "I'm in this for the long haul, man. I promise. And despite the shit your sister's spewing, I wouldn't have touched her if I didn't think she felt the same. I wouldn't do that to you."

Without a word, Everett turns on his heel and storms out of the locker room. The door slams against the cinderblock, and I flinch at the sound, moving toward a frozen Griffin at the center of the room.

"I'm sorry," I whisper. "And thank you. Again. Seriously." I touch his shoulder and move in front of him.

"Shouldn't have touched you here," he mutters.

A smile teases the edge of my lips as I peek up at him. "Pretty sure I found it hot as hell until my brother walked in."

Like a dam, his stoic expression breaks, and his shoulders vibrate with amusement as he scrubs his hand over his face. "I can't believe Ev walked in."

"I mean, I could've been sucking you off, right?" I offer. "So, you know, look at the bright side."

He shakes his head. "That's what you call a bright side?"

"I mean…"

"Your brother seeing me balls deep inside of you is better than you swallowing my cock?" he challenges.

With a grin, I shrug. "Well, when you put it that way, I guess it's kind of debatable, isn't it?" I press my hand over his bare chest. "To be fair, it's not like Everett's one to talk. He had a sex video circulating not too long ago, remember?"

"Yeah, but,"—he lifts his hands in air quotes—"*to be fair, it wasn't his fault.*"

The man makes a good point, but I don't back down.

"Well, neither was this," I argue. "The door was closed, so…in a way, this is kind of on him, if you think about it."

He cocks his head. "Are you always this stubborn?"

"I think we both know the answer to that," I volley back at him. Tilting up my face, I wait for him to lean closer and kiss me, curious if he'll take the bait after everything that just happened. When he does, I swear I feel it all the way down to my toes.

Pressing my body against him, I tug at the towel around his waist but keep it wrapped around his hips, teasing, "Don't tempt me, Griffin, or I just might seduce you again."

"Is that what you're doing?"

With a nod, I smile against his lips. "That's exactly what

I'm doing." My heels hit the ground a second later, and I add, "So, are we good?"

"Good?"

"You know...are you still mad at me?" I prod.

"Are you gonna go out with anyone other than me?"

I shake my head. "You're the only one I want, Griffin Thor— *Ouch!*"

With a loud smack against my ass, I yelp.

"Then, we're good," he replies, squeezing the tender flesh with his massive hands. "And now that your brother knows, does this mean our little secret has been blown out of the water?"

I shouldn't find the spark of hope in his eyes so damn endearing, but I can't help myself. Nibbling on the edge of my lip, I murmur, "I'm thinking...it might be, but we probably want to give my brother a day or two to warm up to the idea before we announce it to the world."

"Yeah, you might be onto something," he agrees. "Maybe we keep a wide berth from each other until tomorrow when I can talk to Ev?"

I nod. "Sounds good to me. But, uh, I did tell our friends you'd drive me to the party."

"So, now you try for honesty?" he quips.

"Pardon me, sir, but the trick with lying is to weave them with as many truths as possible." I give him a cheeky grin. "Now, get dressed. I'm almost finished chatting with my"—I lift my hand and do air quotes—"*friend* and could really use a ride home."

He rolls his eyes but steps toward a row of lockers so he can get dressed. "You know, it's a good thing you're not an evil mastermind or anything."

"Don't worry!" I reply, shamelessly checking out his broad shoulders and tan skin on full display. "I only use my powers for good." I hesitate. "Well, most of the time."

His laughter bounces off the cinderblock walls. It turns my insides into goo as I soak it up. Because that sound? I did that. Even after tonight's game and my brother walking in. I still managed to make Griffin smile. And it makes me feel lighter than air.

CHAPTER TWENTY-EIGHT

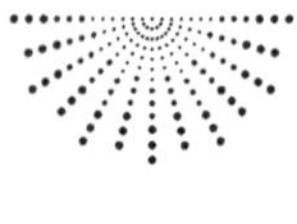

FINLEY

There are pros to not touching alcohol. Remembering the night before. Saving money. Always being the designated driver. No one questioning why you're not drinking tonight and if it's because you're most definitely pregnant.

See? Pros.

Taking a deep breath, Griffin and I walk up the steps to the house when someone almost knocks into me as they stumble to the edge of the porch. Falling to their knees on the freshly shoveled cement, their body lurches forward near the bushes, and they spew vomit all over the snow-covered plants, staining the white with an orange-ish red.

My stomach churns as I watch helplessly.

Aaaand, there's another pro.

No vomiting in public. Scratch that. No vomiting. Period. Yup. Sounds like a solid win to me.

Speaking of which, I kind of think I might puke. The putrid smell clings to my senses, and I press my fingers to my mouth in an attempt to keep from joining the inebri-ated partygoer on the ground when Griffin grabs my side.

Tugging me closer to him, we give the stranger, who clearly doesn't feel well, some extra space as he leads me inside the house.

"Boyle!" Griff calls. "Go check on the person out front. If they need an Uber, let me know."

"Will do." The freshman rushes outside, and Griffin drops his hand from my waist. A frown threatens to take over my expression, but I keep it in check. Because we're pretending again.

Right.

Not sure why it feels weird to not feel Griffin's hand touching me when I've gone my entire life without it, but hey. It's totally normal.

Now, if I could only get my stomach to calm down after the near-vomit sesh, I'd be golden.

"You good?" Griffin murmurs. His voice is low and raspy as he stares down at me.

Peeking up at him, I force a smile. "Yeah, why wouldn't I be?"

"You look like you're gonna be sick." His forehead stitches with concern. "Do you want me to—"

"I'm fine." I grab his hand to keep him from touching my face and lower it to our sides, releasing a slow breath. "Promise."

His brows pinch even more. "You sure? You look pale."

"I'll be fine, I just"—I take another slow breath and let go of his hand—"need a minute."

He tugs me to the side of the entryway, keeping us from blocking the front door as he peers down at me. "Fin…"

"Seriously," I murmur. "All things considered, I'm pretty lucky. That was my first bout with—" My eyes pop, and I clamp my lips shut.

He nods, clearly filling in the blank without needing me to spell it out for him.

Morning sickness.

That was my first bout with morning sickness.

And holy shit, I almost said morning sickness in the middle of a freaking college party. Want to talk about fast-spreading rumors? Yeah, pretty sure that thing would catch like wildfire.

I've heard it's a bitch—morning sickness, not being the star in a rumor mill, although I doubt either is pleasant. If I'm being completely honest, it's been strange to not experience the rite of passage. So, this? This is only a small hiccup. In fact, it's already dissipating now that I'm not outside, and the putrid stench of vomit has been replaced with sweaty bodies, alcohol, Febreeze, and Griffin's cologne. My lips form a small "o" as I let out another slow breath and smile up at Griff.

"Your color's coming back," he notes.

"Maybe you're just good at making a girl blush."

His eyes fall over my body, then meet my gaze again. "I can think of a thing or two that could make you blush."

With a smirk, I lift my chin. "Oh, really? Care to tell me?"

"I could show you," he offers, moving closer, but I press my hand to his chest.

"You could if we weren't supposed to be lying low, remember?"

He frowns. "Fuck."

I laugh.

"I almost forgot," he mutters.

"You almost made *me* forget," I offer. "And we both know I'm stubborn and not afraid to stick to a plan."

"And go down with it, even if it's a shitty one," he quips.

With another laugh, I shove his shoulder. "Hey!"

"Just calling it as I see it."

"Pretty sure we both agreed to keep a wide berth for tonight."

He leans closer, towering over me. "Pretty sure I'd claim you in front of everyone right here, right now, if you let me."

He would. I know he would. The idea alone makes my heart all but thump right out of my chest, and I suck my lips between my teeth, considering it, but tear my attention from his face and stare at the LAU logo on his shirt instead.

"Yo, Thorne!" someone calls from the kitchen.

Griffin looks down at me, appearing torn. I don't blame him. He was inside me thirty minutes ago. Now, we're supposed to pretend like we're only friends? Yup. This is weird.

"Offer's still on the table," he murmurs.

"Go on, Thorne." I shove him again, keeping my tone light. "You can come find me later."

"Is that an invitation or…?"

"Go," I say, exasperated.

"I mean, I'd prefer if I *came*, but whatever you say, Fin." He lifts his chin toward whoever was calling him from the kitchen and moves past me, letting his fingers brush against mine as he leaves. Tingles race up my arm, and I bite the inside of my cheek to keep from chasing after him and insisting he pin me to the nearest wall.

The firm muscles beneath his T-shirt bunch and flex with every step he takes away from me. I shake off the view, clear my throat, and scan the area for a distraction when I spot some of my friends. Dylan's tucked near the fireplace. Reeves' arm is around her shoulder as he nurses a beer while Mav and Ophelia stand across from them, creating a half-circle. Together, they laugh with each other like it's just another Game Night. And maybe it is... for now.

The question is, where's my brother? And has he already told everyone about what happened in the locker room? Not that I would care. Now that the cat's out of the bag, it's...out of the bag. Isn't it? So why am I pretending I'm not into Griff? And even if they don't know, they will. Eventually. So...why put off the inevitable?

Forcing my feet to move, I head to my friends near the fireplace. Once they're within earshot, I call out, "Don't worry. You can start the party now. I'm here."

Ophelia turns around, laughs, and pulls me into a hug. "Hey!"

"Hey! So, what'd I miss?" I ask.

"Nothing much," Ophelia answers. "Only that Dylan finally got a call from her lawyer."

She lets me go, and my jaw drops as I turn to Dylan. "Are you serious?"

Nodding, Dylan scoots her glasses along the bridge of her nose, her relief palpable. "Yup."

"And?" I prod. "The drug possession charge?"

"I'm officially off the hook. I mean, I was already officially off the hook, but now I'm officially *officially* off the hook."

"What about Reeves' dad?" I continue, mentioning the asshole who not only planted cocaine in the back of Reeves' car in hopes of screwing him over, only for Dylan to take the fall instead, but also used his position as a police officer to torture his son for years until Dylan came to his defense. Yeah, there's a thing or two I'd love to do to Reeves' father, and most of them involve a rusty spoon and the man's balls.

"That's the best part," Reeves interrupts with a shameless grin. He hooks his arm around Dylan's shoulders and tugs her into his side. "They kicked my dad off the force."

My jaw drops. "Are you serious?"

"Yup," Dylan answers. "We never have to worry about him or any of the messes he made ever again."

"No freaking way!" I squeal. Tackling them in the middle of the family room, I give Dylan and Reeves a huge hug. Lia joins me, forming a Dylan and Reeves-centered sandwich as we celebrate their gigantic win. Seriously. This is amazing, and I couldn't be happier for both of them.

Squirming, Dylan says, "Okay, okay, let me go! I can't breathe!" through bouts of laughter. After we follow her order, she fixes her skewed glasses again, smooths out the LAU jersey swallowing her whole, and turns back to me. "So, how was your chat or whatever?"

"Chat?" My brows bunch. "Oh! Yeah, it was good," I lie. "Have you guys seen Raine or Ev by chance?"

"Yup," Lia answers. "Everett looked like a constipated moose as soon as he walked in, and Raine followed him to the back of the house. Then they both left like bats out of hell."

"Cool, cool, cool." I rock back on my heels and pull my phone out to text Raine.

"PS, we were just talking about you," she adds.

My thumbs stop moving across my screen, and I peek up at my half circle of friends. Each of them is staring at me, and boy, would I give my left boob to know what they're thinking. Okay, that's a lie. Griffin likes my left boob. He likes my right boob, too, but it's beside the point.

Tucking my phone back into my pocket, I ask, "Oh?"

"Yeah," Reeves answers. "Dreggs wants me to give him your number. Dylan says it's against the girl code, but

Ophelia says it would be good for you." He crosses his arms. "What do you think I should do?"

I tilt my head toward Lia. "It would be good for me, huh?"

"Dude, we were literally talking about this at the game, so you already— Oh. Uh. Hey!"

A throat clears behind me, and I peek over my shoulder. "Speak of the devil."

"Hey, Fin." Dreggs offers me a Red Solo cup. "Thirsty?"

Taking the cup from his grasp, I peek inside, taking in the amber liquid, then look up at him. "Is this beer?"

Dreggs nods. "Yeah. Figured you could use a drink."

"Unfortunately, I don't drink," I remind him. "But Reeves does."

"Oo, thanks." He grabs the cup from me and swallows it back.

I turn to Dreggs again. "Epilepsy ruins all the fun, am I right?"

Squeezing the back of his neck, Dreggs mumbles, "Shit. I forgot about the whole, uh, epilepsy thing."

"Just wait 'til you see me drop to the ground and start convulsing," I quip with a wink. "Then it'll be etched into your brain for eternity."

His eyes bug out, making Ophelia laugh as she pulls me into her. "And here I thought Dylan was the awkward one." She squeezes me tight. "Ignore her, Dreggs. She's joking."

I'm not, but I get why my best friend's trying to soften my crazy. What she doesn't understand is that I need Dreggs to see it. I need him to become uninterested and soon because if he keeps talking to me after everything that went down in the locker room, Griffin is going to see, and if Griffin sees, whatever ruse we're still clinging to will explode into a bazillion pieces.

"Definitely not joking," I announce. "Hell, ask Griff. He

saw it firsthand over winter break. It was a real hoot, let me tell ya."

"Shit." Dreggs tugs at the collar of his T-shirt, appearing almost as uncomfortable as a man who was just asked to turn and cough.

Wee lamb.

If he thinks talking about epilepsy is messy, he should try dating someone with it.

"How, uh,"—he clears his throat—"how are you doing after…it?"

"You mean my seizure?" I pat his chest. "I'm fine. But I should probably go find me a non-alcoholic drink. Nice chatting, though."

As I start to slip past him, he grabs my wrist, preventing my escape. Not aggressively, mind you, but, uh, confidently? Yeah. I'll go with confidently. Like I'd be a fool to turn him down. And maybe I am a fool because this guy? He doesn't do it for me. At all.

"Playing hard to get, Fin?" Dreggs challenges.

I smirk back at him. He is cute. And if I wasn't already most definitely interested in someone else, I could see myself testing the waters just for shits and giggles…and maybe to educate him on chronic diseases. But he's too late. And he isn't Griffin.

My attention drifts to the kitchen, where Griffin disappeared. He stares at me, his jaw tight and his biceps bulging as he folds his arms. All of the humor from our little flirting session a few minutes ago is completely void from his expression. He doesn't look pissed. He looks…uninterested yet still…observant.

I'm not surprised. Maybe I should be, but I'm not. Now that we've been hooking up, I can see past the laid back facade. The one he uses to protect himself. Like, if he can convince others he doesn't care, then maybe he won't, either. He does the same thing with hockey. Pretend a loss isn't a big deal, and maybe he won't beat himself up about it.

He still does, but...I don't know. He tries, at least. Not to care. But for some reason, the idea of him not caring in this moment isn't comforting. In fact, it's kind of terrifying. The idea of Griffin looking at someone else like this instead of me. He's been so patient with me. More patient than I deserve. And I know we both agreed to lie low. To give Everett time to wrap his head around us dating, but...I don't know if I care anymore.

"Fin?" Dreggs prods.

"Surprisingly, I'm not playing at all," I murmur, looking back at him. "Nice chatting with you, Dreggs. Now, if you'll excuse me..." I twist out his grasp and slip through the crowd, holding Griffin's unreadable gaze.

He's still watching me. The realization spurs me on. It's like he's a homing beacon. Like the world is nothing but a blurry canvas around us, and all that matters, all I can focus on, is getting to him as quickly as possible. He looks so...unflustered. So laid back and in his element surrounded by people. Strangers mostly. Or maybe they've been friends for years. You'd never know the difference. He's kind to everyone. Patient with everyone.

Patient with *me*. So damn patient with me.

When I finally reach him, I don't stop. I close the last bit of distance, rise onto my tiptoes, and kiss him in the middle of the party. Without caring who can see or what assumptions they might make. I kiss him with everything inside of me. Every fantasy. Every selfish thought. Every ounce of pent-up desire and whispered what ifs that've filtered through my mind for years. *Years.* Claiming him in front of everyone and letting everyone in the vicinity know I've been claimed, too. Even if I didn't expect it. Even if I didn't want it. Not in the beginning. But Griff? Well, I think we've danced around this long enough to know what wasting time feels like. And right now? I've never wanted anything more than to say, fuck it. I like Griffin Thorne, and he likes me.

He's stunned for a millisecond before his hands find my waist, and he kisses me. Hooting echoes from the family room, and I have zero doubt in my brain it belongs to Reeves, Ophelia, and Maverick. Dylan's probably grinning, too, but the girl's too quiet to hoot. I smile against Griffin's mouth as I imagine it, and he pulls away, his forehead bunching. "What's so funny?"

"You really want to know?" I ask.

He nods.

"I imagined Dylan hooting like the rest of our crazy friends."

"They were hooting?" He looks over my head toward our friends, and his mouth splits into a shy grin. "Oh, so that's why you kissed me."

"I kissed you because I'm tired of letting people believe I could possibly want anyone who isn't you when I've already wasted years with the wrong person. Is that a problem?"

He tugs me closer and steals another kiss, making my toes curl in the process. When he finally pulls away, he answers, "No problem."

I smile back at him. "Didn't think so."

"So," Reeves interjects.

Glancing over my shoulder, I find the rest of the gang trailing behind him. "This is new."

"Or is it?" Dylan questions.

"Does your brother know?" Maverick interjects.

Griffin frowns, then answers for me. "He might've found out earlier tonight."

"And you're still standing?" Mav scratches the scruff along his jaw. "I guess Raine really did help with Ev's short fuse."

"It might not be as short, but it's still there," I offer, threading my fingers through Griffin's and wrapping him around my body like a blanket. "You should've seen his face when—"

Griffin clears his throat next to my ear, so I zip my lips and throw away the proverbial key, pulling laughter from Dylan and Ophelia.

"You gonna smooth everything out with him?" Reeves asks Griffin. "'Cause, uh, I've been on Everett's shit list. Zero out of ten stars. Do not recommend."

Chuckling, Griffin's focus falls to me. "I'll take care of it. Promise."

I peek over my shoulder at him. "I know you will."

"Now, let's celebrate!" Dylan offers. "Because Finley and I are going to be sisters!"

Laughter echoes around us, and I shove my best friend on the shoulder. "Careful with the assumptions, Dyl. You might scare me away."

An arm squeezes around my waist as Griffin shifts me from his front and into his side. "Nah. I'm not letting you go anywhere. Sorry, Fin, but now that you've ripped off the Band-Aid, it looks like you're stuck with me."

Welp. When he puts it that way…

Lifting my chin, I wait for him to meet me halfway, and just like the mind-reading genius he is, he does.

CHAPTER TWENTY-NINE

GRIFFIN

Scratching my jaw, I head into the gym. It's early and so cold my balls want to retreat into my body as I slip on my coat's hood. The roads are icy, and it's still dark outside. So dark, if I didn't know this was the only place I was sure to find Everett so I could talk to him, I might've even stayed at home in Finley's bed. We stayed in the same room last night. We're out in the open. Me and Fin. The air is clear. Mostly. No sneaking around. No lies. No alibis. The memory of her tight little body wrapped around me this morning makes me nearly groan, but I force it back and tug the heavy glass door open.

There he is. Just. Like. Clockwork.

It's arms and chest day. Everett grunts as he does a bicep curl. The veins pop out beneath his skin, proving he's already earned his pump.

He's been here for a while.

As I approach, the rhythm of his curls staggers, but he doesn't look at me. Not directly or in the mirrors lining the gym's walls. Nah, he's pretending I don't exist.

Real mature, man.

Tucking my hands in my coat pockets, I ask, "Hey, can we talk?"

Metal clanks together as he sets the free weights down and adds another forty pounds to each side of the bench press without acknowledging me.

Yeah, the guy's pissed.

He should be. I not only went back on a promise I made when we were kids, but I did it without giving him a heads-up, and, knowing how this guy operates, it's the worst way I could've handled everything.

Stepping closer, I squeeze the back of my neck. "Ev, I know I fucked up."

He scoffs. "You think?"

"Not about kissing your sister, but—"

He scoffs again. "Is that all you were doing, Griff? Kissing her?"

My head falls forward, and shame fills my gut. At this point, it's familiar, but it doesn't make the feeling any less potent or crippling. Doesn't mean he needs to be an ass about it, though.

"I know I should've told you I was going to make a move before I went through with it," I admit, "but it just… happened, all right? And then, she wanted to keep it a secret, and…I'm sorry."

"Let me get this straight," he challenges, giving me his full attention. "You're not sorry for failing to ask me permission, but you're sorry for not keeping me in the loop when you crossed a line? That's the angle you're gonna take?"

I shrug, unsure what else to say. "Guess so."

"Good to know." He turns back to the weights and lies on the bench press, preparing to work his chest. I make a mental note of the amount of weight he's using, then get into position to spot him without waiting for a request.

The guy might be pissed, but he isn't Superman.

"Look, your sister's a grown adult, and whether or not you want to admit it, you have nothing to do with her dating life, and you sure as shit shouldn't have any say in it."

"And here I thought you were apologizing," he mutters under his breath as he grips the bar.

"I'm apologizing as your friend, not your sister's boyfriend," I clarify. "You know I'd never hurt her."

He glares up at me, his knuckles turning white as he squeezes the bar in his hands. "And what happens when you leave? You sure that won't hurt her?"

"I'm not going anywhere."

"What about the Tornadoes? Your contract? What then?" He lowers the bar toward his sternum, his nostrils flaring. "She's already done long distance once." Everett shoves the bar back up. "You really think she deserves to be dragged through that hellhole twice?"

"It isn't up to you," I remind him. "It's Finley's decision, and it's not like I coerced her or some shit. She cares about me, too."

"Of course she does." His face reddens as he does another rep, staring at the ceiling. "She's had a thing for you since she was a kid."

"Then what's the problem? You hated Drew, but even with him, you didn't put up this much of a fight, which, if we're being honest, is a low blow, Ev," I mutter. "Why do you not want me with Fin?"

His jaw locks. "I never gave a"—another rep—"shit about Drew because I knew it wouldn't last. I knew he wasn't the one for her."

"And I am?" I challenge.

He lowers the bar again, then shoves it up, making sure to keep his elbows from locking. Gotta give the guy credit.

He must be tapping into his inner Hulk or some shit because he's bench-pressing more weight than I've ever seen.

Still refusing to look at me, he grunts, "You have. The power. To break her."

"I won't."

Setting the bar back onto the hooks, he pulls himself to a seated position and stares up at me. "But you could."

"But I won't."

He pushes to his feet and meets me chest to chest. Eye to eye. We've always been pretty matched for height and weight, but after the last thirty minutes Everett's spent imagining all the ways he could kill me while channeling all the pent-up energy into weight lifting, the guy's muscles are fucking swollen. It makes him look at least fifteen pounds of pure, lean muscle heavier. And right now, he also looks like he wants to rip off my head.

"But you *could* hurt her," he repeats vehemently.

I stay quiet, letting his words hit their mark. He's right. I could hurt her. I won't, but I could. And that's the problem. I get it. I get his need to protect her. To keep her safe. To look out for Fin and everyone else around him. It's who he is. He can't just…turn it off. Even with friends and family. Especially with friends and family. And here I am, putting him at odds because we're best friends, but his sister is his *sister*. And I could hurt her.

"You know me better than that, Ev," I murmur. "I wouldn't have pursued Fin if I thought there was even a chance she'd be hurt in the process."

"And what if she breaks you?" he demands. "You're my best friend, and Finley's…Finley."

I cock my head. "Afraid she'll get bored?"

"Afraid she'll be impulsive and do something she shouldn't."

"Like sleep with your best friend?" I offer.

"More like dump your ass."

I chuckle. "Give me a little more credit."

"Fin's young. She has her whole life ahead of her."

"Yeah, and by some miracle, she wants me in it for the time being. You really blame me for shooting my shot?" His attention shifts from one of my eyes to the other, bouncing around my face until his head dips in a sharp nod, his molars still grinding. "Why now?" he questions. "I know she was with Drew before, but you're leaving…"

"I couldn't fight it anymore."

Another nod. Not like he accepts my reasoning, only my sincerity, but I'll take it anyway.

"And what happens if you can't fight *for* her?" he pushes.

"I'll always fight for her," I promise. "Always. No matter what. No matter the cost."

"You sure?"

"If anything, this conversation with you should prove it firsthand," I argue. "You're my best friend, and I knew this would hurt you, but I still went after her. I saw the opening, and I took it. And you can be pissed at me all you want, but you know me. You know I'd do anything for her. *Anything.*"

His attention darts over my features again as he searches for whether or not I'm telling the truth. When I realize how much he looks like Fin when he does it, my mouth twitches, and I promise, "Not gonna hurt her, Ev. You have my word."

"Fine." He backs away and sits on the bench. "You gonna spot me again or what?"

CHAPTER THIRTY

GRIFFIN

The girls' side of the duplex smells like fresh paint. I make a mental note to open some windows and air out the place as I stride into the kitchen with another of Finley's boxes. I thought the smell would have faded some by now since the construction company finally finished the renovation while Finley and I were on our road trip. It felt like every time we turned around, they threw us yet another curveball. But as soon as the city announced this side of the duplex was livable, Finley pulled the trigger on moving back over here early, despite the lack of furniture. In spite of the strong smell tainting the air, she's anxious to gain some space from the two fuck bunnies across the hall.

Her words, not mine.

I'm not complaining, though. Now that everyone knows about us, we could use the space without Everett breathing down our necks. Don't get me wrong. Ever since our talk at the gym, he's been…supportive. Or at least, Ev's version of supportive.

But being respectful when I'm finally able to touch

Finley the way I've always wanted to is harder than I expected, and my blue balls can attest to it. Hell, this is the first time we've been together since the party without feeling like we have to walk on eggshells, and the moment's never been sweeter.

"Is it weird that I kind of love how empty the place is?" Finley asks. With her arms open wide, she spins around the empty family room. Thanks to the smoke from the fire and water damage from the sprinklers, the furniture had to be replaced, though the new stuff won't be delivered for another two weeks.

"Never pegged you for a minimalist," I say as I set yet another box on the kitchen counter. We spent the last couple of hours packing her stuff into boxes, and carrying them over here. Her mattress is in her room, but the majority of small boxes containing things like clothes and toiletries are scattered along her bedroom floor and have now spread into the kitchen.

Yeah. Minimalist isn't a term I'd use to describe the girl in front of me, for sure.

With a smirk, Finley sways toward me, wrapping her arms around my neck. "Gotta put these muscles to work, Griff."

"Are you using me for my body?"

"I mean...can you blame me?" She drags her hands down my biceps and squeezes before snaking them along my trap muscles, noting, "Although you are a dirty boy."

With a laugh, I wrap my arms around her waist and sway us back and forth. Her feet are bare, and her baggy, hot pink sweats hang low on her hips. I splay my fingers against her lower back and memorize the feel of her silky skin in my hands. "Are you complaining?"

"Hardly." Rising onto her tiptoes, she kisses me softly. "I like it when you make me dirty." Her heels hit the ground, and she rests her head on my chest as I chuckle quietly. This girl. To say she's a handful is an understatement, but I've learned to crave the chaos. The smartass remarks. The teasing. Fuck, I crave everything about her.

"I also like it when you dance with me like this," she adds with a wistful sigh.

"Is that what we're doing?"

"I mean, I could always use some music, but…"

Keeping her pressed against me with one hand, I fish in the front pocket of my joggers, pull out my phone, and open Spotify. As an IndieCent Vows song filters through the speaker, I set my cell down on the kitchen counter and pull Finley closer into me.

Her laugh is light and airy as she lifts her head, smiling up at me. "Smooth."

"I can be smooth."

"I'm aware. You're very smooth. Why else do you think I let you into my pants?"

"So, it wasn't my charming personality?"

She snorts. "Nah. It was definitely the body that got you into my pants, but it's the personality that won you a season pass, so you're welcome."

I throw my head back and laugh. "Are you saying I'll have to renew in a year?"

"You'll be gone in a year," she points out.

With a frown, I lean back, making sure I can study her expression. "You really think I'm going anywhere?"

"Uh, I know you'll be going somewhere." She fake-coughs. "Tornadoes." *Cough, cough.*

Her nonchalance would kill me if I didn't know her better. The way she ticks. The way she hides her vulnerability behind a thick coat of sarcasm. Yeah. I know Finley Taylor. And this girl? She's kind of attached to me, too.

At least the feeling's mutual.

I tuck her long dark hair behind her ear. "We'll figure it out."

She stays quiet, sucking her bottom lip between her teeth, then gives a slow nod. "Careful, Griffin. If you keep dancing with me like this, I just might believe you."

I lean in for another kiss, and she raises her chin, meeting me halfway. It's been like this for a while now. Tiptoeing around my contract with the Tornadoes, and the expiration date accompanying it. After our lunch meeting, my agent reached out to Deemwater. He wanted to confirm I hadn't pissed the GM off by rejecting his offer before I played like shit against the Bulldogs. By some miracle, the Tornadoes are still anxious for me to represent their organization. It should make me feel better. Instead, I'm preoccupied with what-if's.

Finley's whole life is here. And mine? Mine's waiting for me a thousand miles away. Closing my eyes, I drag my tongue along the seam of her lips, memorizing the shape. The softness. The taste.

A quiet sigh escapes her.

"Question," she murmurs against my mouth, then pulls away, peeking up at me.

"Yeah?"

"Do you, uh..." She hesitates, and her eyes become nothing but slits.

"Am I in trouble?"

With a slow shake of her head, she explains, "I'm debating something."

"And what are you debating?"

"Something...personal."

I stop us from swaying. "What is it?"

"I haven't decided if I'm going to change my mind or not."

Smothering my amusement, I argue, "You can't do that."

"Do what?"

"You can't dangle the bait like that."

"What bait?"

"Don't play dumb."

"Who says I'm—"

My fingers dig into her sides. The girl almost crumbles like a deck of cards, but I keep her in place, tickling the shit out of her as her legs buckle beneath her.

"No tickling!" she yells through bouts of laughter, squirming against me, her elbows fusing to her sides. "You're gonna make me pee!"

I stop my assault and cock my head. "Are you gonna tell me?"

The same mock glare takes up her expression as she finds her feet. "Fine." Brushing herself off, she grabs my wrists, places them at her lower waist, then wraps her arms around my neck again, urging me to continue our dance.

Once we're swaying again, I warn, "Three. Two—"

"Do you..." She pauses again and peeks up at me through her dark lashes.

Hell, it's like she's fucking begging me to kiss her, but I stay strong and push, "Yes?"

"Do you...want to go with me to my neurologist appointment next week?"

I pull back, surprised. "You want me to come?"

"I mean, no pressure, obviously, but yeah. Yeah, I think I do. He's gonna talk about the baby, and we're gonna come up with a game plan, and since you're the only one who knows about everything, I figured..."

"I'd love to." My fingers dig into her spine while I fight the urge to kiss the shit out of her all over again. This is big. She might not know it. Might not want to acknowledge it. But the invitation? Fuck, I wouldn't miss it for anything. Not even the Stanley Cup.

Her forehead wrinkles. "Really?"

I laugh. "Yeah. Of course, I would."

"You're sure?"

"I told you you're not alone, remember?"

"And you're not saying this just because I asked and you want to get into my pants?" she challenges.

I smack her ass, and she yelps, squirming against me all over again, but I hold strong, continuing to lead our dance.

Her eyes narrow, but she gives in almost instantly. As her body relaxes against me, she points out, "You're right. You could've gotten into my pants without agreeing to go to my doctor's appointment."

"I'd go to your doctor's appointment even if what's in your pants wasn't on the table," I counter. "You know that."

"I do," she agrees. "And that's why I'm inviting you."

I capture her mouth with another kiss, lost in the feel of her against me and the way her lips move with mine. This girl. This fucking girl.

When she pulls away and licks her bottom lip, I rasp, "Wouldn't miss it for the world, Fin."

Another warm smile spreads across her face. "Good. Now, are these your only dance moves? Or—"

I spin her around, then pull her closer, dipping her over my arm. When her long, black hair nearly touches the floor, she laughs. "Whoa there, mister."

"Sorry, but it sounded like a challenge."

Twirling her around, her tinkling amusement mingles with the music until the moonlight filters in through the windows, and it's like everything else with her.

Fucking perfect.

CHAPTER THIRTY-ONE

FINLEY

y knee bounces as I sit on one of the red cushioned chairs. We're late. Three minutes, to be exact. Maybe the doctor is going to reschedule? It isn't unheard of. Although I would feel bad wasting Griffin's time and all, but he's a big boy, and it's not like he was doing anything anyway, so it'll be fine. Completely. Totally. Fine.

"You nervous?" Griffin asks.

Jumping at the sound, I twist my hands in my lap and glance at the receptionist's desk. "I can't decide."

He smirks. "You can't decide whether or not you're nervous?"

"I mean, I've already heard the heartbeat," I point out as the memory of my emergency room visit not so long ago rises to the surface. Man, it feels like a lifetime ago. I shake it off, adding, "So, it's not like they're going to tell me anything too crazy, right?" My teeth dig into the inside of my cheek. "Although, I did go down the rabbit hole a couple of days ago about everything that can go wrong during a baby's development, and it didn't exactly give me any warm fuzzies, so…"

Griffin reaches for my hand in my lap and squeezes softly. "So that's why you're anxious."

I shift toward him in my seat. "Am I so obvious?"

"The bouncing knee gave it away." His grin softens. "You and the baby are going to be great, Fin. All the neurologist is going to do is make sure you and your brain and your baby are all in perfect condition. It'll be fine."

When his lips brush against my forehead, I hum, "Mm-hmm," though I'm not entirely convinced. Not yet. And now that I've officially had some time to warm up to the idea of being a mom, the idea of losing the opportunity kind of *really* sucks.

"Finley?" a nurse calls. "Finley Taylor?" She must be new because I don't recognize her. I know everyone at my neurologist's office, thanks to my consistent visits since I was a baby. Dr. Reed and Dr. McDougal kind of split their duties as my primary neurologist thanks to moving in middle school, then winding up back here a few years later. Pretty sure both of them know me as well as my grandparents do, and that's saying something. But the nurse? The nurse is new, and it feeds my anxiety. Short, curly silver-blonde hair. Baby blue scrubs. Probably my mom's age. I'm sure she's nice, but what if—

Stop. Obsessing. Over. Nothing.

My legs wobble as I stand. Griffin joins me on my feet, keeping our fingers threaded together as we walk toward the nurse. She smiles, her eyes flitting over our hands, and she guides us to one of the rooms at the end of a long hall-way. Doors line each side, and she stops at a scale, motioning for me to step onto it.

Once the numbers are recorded, she leads us to the last

room, takes my vitals, and asks about any changes in medication and if I've had any other ER visits. Picking at my nails, I answer each and every question as the nurse makes notes in my file.

Satisfied, the nurse adds, "Dr. Reed will be right in."

"Thanks."

As she closes the door behind us, Griffin takes a seat on one of the vacant chairs and rubs his hands along his thighs, his eyes scanning the exam room with unrestrained interest.

I climb onto the large leather chair in the center of the room, cross my legs, and lean back on my hands. "Like what you see?"

"Just curious."

"About what?" I prod.

"Don't get me wrong. I know you're an open book when it comes to epilepsy, but seeing the other side of it is…"

"Intriguing?" I offer.

His gaze falls to me, and he smiles. "Just like the woman herself."

I laugh. "You know everything about me. Not sure the term *intriguing* fits. Not anymore."

"Pretty sure I could spend the rest of my life with you, and I'd still find a secret or two."

"Are you saying I have…layers?" I quip.

He smirks. "Are you about to quote *Shrek*?"

"Like an onion?" I continue, ignoring his completely accurate assumption. "Am I an onion, Griffin?"

"You're more like cake." He stands, moves closer, and grips the sides of my chair, shifting closer. "Everybody loves cake."

"Nah, I'm an onion," I argue as my eyes fall to his mouth. "A big, stinky—"

A knock cuts me off, and Griffin jerks away from me like he was caught with his pants down.

Ha! Been there, done that.

"Hello," Dr. Reed greets us. He hesitates, scanning Griffin's tense posture and my red cheeks. "Did I interrupt something?"

"Only me and my boyfriend about to make out since you were taking so long," I quip.

"Ah, so you're the infamous Drew?" Dr. Reed offers his hand. "It's nice to finally meet you. I've heard—"

"This is Griffin," I interrupt. "Griffin Thorne."

Dr. Reed's big eyes bulge behind his thick, black frames. "Oh. Of course. I apologize."

"Don't," Griffin deflects. He takes Dr. Reed's hand and shakes it. "Finley's a hot commodity. Had to snatch her up while I could."

Relief shines back in Dr. Reed's expression as he lets Griffin go. "Of course. I assume it's why you tied her down with a baby, too?"

Griffin opens his mouth to correct Dr. Reed, but I cut him off. "I mean, he's a hockey player. It's his job to slip one past the goalie, am I right?"

Griffin's eyes cut to me, and he tilts his head.

Giving him a smile, I turn back to Dr. Reed. "And speaking of babies, I believe you owe me a congratulations, Dr. Reed."

His laugh is warm and inviting as he shakes his head back and forth. "Congratulations, Finley. Do your parents know?"

"Not yet," I answer. "I'm waiting until I'm out of the woods."

He frowns. "Then you'll be waiting a long time."

My lips part in confusion because that's the last thing I expected him to say. I'll be waiting a long time until I'm out of the woods? What? Why? How? I thought…I thought the first trimester's a doozy, but after that, everything would be…smooth sailing. Am I wrong? And if I am, what else—

"What do you mean?" Griffin interjects.

"Well," Dr. Reed unlocks the iPad in his arms and begins scrolling through what I assume is my chart. "I've looked over the file the ER doctor sent, and even though things looked good at that point, because of your epilepsy, your pregnancy is considered high-risk."

My brows crease. "I'm sorry, high…risk? What does that mean?"

"It means because of your medication, you have a slightly increased risk of miscarriage, but—"

"Can I stop taking the medication, then?" I ask.

He shakes his head and folds his arms, pressing the iPad to his chest. "I don't recommend it, no."

"For my safety or the baby's?" I challenge.

"Both," he answers simply. "But don't stress, Finley. I've dealt with plenty of patients who have gone on to have full-term, healthy babies, including your mother. Rarely is there an issue. Honestly, I'm not very worried about you or the baby, but you know me. I'm upfront, and I don't beat around the bush. You're young. This is your first pregnancy. And you have epilepsy. The combination makes for a high-risk pregnancy, but the label doesn't doom you to failure. Have you found your obstetrician yet?"

I shake my head. "It's been on my to-do list, but I figured I could wait until twelve weeks or…whatever."

"Not a problem, but I do suggest you find one sooner rather than later. Would you like me to recommend someone?"

I nod, feeling like a deer caught in headlights. "Obviously."

With a warm smile, he replies, "I can do that for you."

"What precautions can we take?" Griffin asks. "Is there anything we can do to mitigate any potential challenges to make sure they're both safe and…healthy?"

"Excellent question." Dr. Reed rocks back on his heels. "Take it easy. Don't overexert yourself. Listen to your body. Continue taking your medication. Don't forget your prenatals. And I want to make sure you're checking in with me or your obstetrician on a regular basis. No missing appointments," he warns, eyeing me over the thick rims of his glasses.

I look at Griff and hook my thumb toward Dr. Reed, overwhelmed and close to hyperventilating as I paste on a fake smile. "Would you look at this guy? It's like he doesn't even trust me."

"I know you," Dr. Reed interrupts. "I know you far too well."

"Mm-hmm," I hum, praying he can't see the way my body shakes or the sheen I can feel hitting my eyes.

High-risk.

My pregnancy is high-risk.

Take it easy. No exertion. So, what? Am I just supposed to sit still and do nothing? Can I even go to classes? What about work? Do I quit? I mean, I can if I need to. I…oof. This just became a lot more…real, and I feel a lot more… alone.

A warm hand encompasses mine, and I look down, finding Griffin's fingers tangling with my own in my lap. My attention trails up his strong forearm and lands on his kind, reassuring gaze. "We got this," he murmurs.

I gulp, unable to convince my vocal cords to work no matter how much I want them to. He looks so confident. So…solid. Like a rock. A handsome, optimistic, and dangerously positive rock.

Okay, not literally. He's still Griff. The boy next door. *My* boy next door.

"We got this," he repeats. "Promise."

"Now, enough of the gray cloud conversation," Dr. Reed suggests. "Let's talk about the fun stuff."

CHAPTER THIRTY-TWO

GRIFFIN

Fun stuff is subjective. The doctor has Finley's blood drawn. A bunch of stats are thrown her way. And the whole time, she's lost in her own head. I can see it. Feel it. The glazed eyes. The "I'm sorry, can you repeat that?" over and over. The way she can't stop chewing on the inside of her lip or making sarcastic remarks.

She isn't the only one, though. As soon as she didn't correct Dr. Reed when he called me the dad, I was lost. Lost in what ifs. Lost in a different world. One where I was the father. Where I was going to be a dad. One where I didn't have to wonder if I was crossing lines or obliterating boundaries when I have no idea where they are in the first place. Part of me wants to ask her. What she wants. The other part is too afraid of her answer.

Finley's stubborn.

So damn stubborn.

And I know if push comes to shove, she'll carry the world on her back if only to prove she can. Even when she shouldn't. Even when it can hurt her or the baby.

High-risk.

Like a neon sign, the two words flash through my mind as I drive us back to her place.

She might not be okay. The baby might not be okay. And I don't care how fucking strong Finley is. There's no way a word of caution like that can't affect her or mess with her psyche.

Glancing at her in the passenger seat, I find Finley chewing on the edge of her lip, her eyes as glazed as they were during her appointment while she stares out the windshield. It's snowing. Hell, it's a blizzard. As if the dark clouds and thick blanket of white falling from the sky are an accurate depiction of the situation and the mood we're both drowning in.

Without bothering to look at me, she asks, "Do you know what sucks?"

"What?"

"Your first game," she murmurs. "My brother's first game."

"What about them?"

"Unless they're against the Lions, I'm going to have to miss them." A divot forms between her brows. "There's no way I'm going to be able to travel with a newborn. And the playoffs this year? I might as well kiss attending them goodbye right now, if the whole high-risk label sticks."

My chest caves, and I squeeze the steering wheel, caught between confusion and flattery that hockey is where her head's at as her comment washes over me.

"We'll figure it out," I promise.

"Yeah." She nods absently and sighs. "Do you think I'll have to move in with my parents once they find a place?" Her frown deepens before a pathetic laugh slips out of her. "Talk about backsliding, am I right?"

Reaching toward her, I squeeze her knee. "We'll figure it out."

"There's that *we* again." She gives me the side eye.

"Is that a problem?"

With another sigh, she places her elbow on the passenger window and rests her head against her hand. "I haven't decided yet."

I want to ask what she means, but I stop myself. Now isn't the time. She needs my reassurance, not the other way around. "We'll figure it out, Fin."

Her lips press together. "Yeah. Of course *we* will."

She doesn't believe me, and honestly, a small part of me doesn't believe it, either. Not entirely. Things are precarious at best, and with so many unknowns, it's hard to predict the future, let alone affect it or control it the way I'm itching to.

"You ready to tell your parents?" I prod.

"And upturn their life more than I already have by being their daughter?" A pathetic laugh escapes her. "And that's if it's even necessary, right?" She wipes beneath her eyes, her armor finally cracking. "The baby might not even make it in the first place, so—"

"Don't talk like that, Fin."

"How can I not, Griff?" Her lower lip wobbles. "The doctor said so himself. I'm high-risk."

Snow crunches beneath the tires as I find a secluded spot, pull over, and grab her face, forcing her to look at me. "High-risk doesn't mean shit."

A ghost of a smile teases her lips. "It actually kind of does. Literally. It means...shit. This is a shit pregnancy, and—"

"Stop spiraling," I order. "This isn't you."

She shakes her head. "Maybe it is, Griff. Maybe this is

who I really am when I can't pretend to be strong anymore."

"Stop."

"I can't." Her voice cracks. "I can't stop thinking about it. I can't stop blaming my stupid brain—"

Slamming my mouth to hers, I kiss her. To shut her up. To force her to stop belittling herself and voicing aloud her ugly thoughts when they couldn't be further from the truth. Her muscles freeze for a moment, then her teeth clash with mine, and she bites my bottom lip, kissing me back. Fighting me. Forcing all her pent-up frustration and anxiety into the kiss until I can fucking taste it.

Ripping my mouth from hers, I growl, "Don't you dare blame yourself."

"Then, distract me," she demands. "Because I am so caught up in my own head and all the what-ifs that could absolutely destroy me, I'm not sure what else to do. Griffin, I'm begging—"

I swallow her plea and reach around her, unlatching her seatbelt as the windshield wipers slash left and right. She needs a distraction. A distraction and a fucking release. The girl's wound so tight after the appointment, she just snapped, and not in a good way. But I can fix this.

I can fix this.

Lifting her oversized sweater, my fingers fumble with the top button on her jeans. Once they're undone, she shimmies them down her thighs while I massage the outside of her bare thighs with my left hand. I lick at her lips, forcing our mouths together and prying hers open.

Tearing away from me, she pants, "Fuck, Griff, just—" She dives in for another kiss and spreads her legs wide as I drag my knuckle along the damp underwear covering her. The girl's soaked.

Cupping her center with my left hand, I drag the heel of my hand against her clit, then grab her cheek with my right, angling her head and thrusting my tongue into her mouth. She sucks on it, mewing quietly as I push the scrap of cloth aside and drag the tip of my finger along her entrance.

She wants it. Fuck, I know she does by the way her hips buck, but I don't slip into her. Not yet.

"Griff," she warns.

I dip my finger to my first knuckle, then retreat, adding pressure to her clit.

"I need this," she begs. "I need you. Please."

My cock aches from her words, and I shift closer to her, swallowing her pleas as I slowly dip my forefinger inside of her again, this time to the second knuckle. The girl whimpers, grabbing my wrist tucked between her thighs as she rides my hand. Hips rocking, she urges me deeper, and I add a second finger, crooking them inside of her and rubbing my thumb along her clit. If I didn't think she needed this right now, I'd toss her into the back and eat her out like she's my last meal.

My mouth waters from the thought alone while Fin continues sucking on my tongue as if it's my cock. I've never seen her like this. This desperate. Not only for me but also for a release. For a moment of respite. A moment of quiet.

Pressing my forehead to hers, I watch her lips swallow my fingers. "Do you have any idea how beautiful you are?" I rasp. "How fucking perfect?" I tear my focus from her bare pussy to her face. "You're perfect, Fin."

"Just keep...keep doing that," she begs, leaning in for another kiss.

I suck on her bottom lip as I crook my finger inside of her, searching for the little bundle of nerves inside her channel I know drives her wild. When I find it, her hips buck even more, and her jaw drops open on a moan.

"Fuck, Griff. Fuck, you have no idea how good this feels."

"You can do no wrong," I murmur, convinced I might actually come in my fucking jeans as I swirl my fingers inside of her, adding more pressure to her clit. "This body can do no wrong, Finley Taylor. And I know you can't control everything. Neither of us can. But look what your body can do. Look how pretty it is when it swallows my fingers."

Her core clenches around me, her fingernails digging tiny crescent shapes into my wrist as she throws her head back. She's gonna come. Her cheeks are flushed. Her lips are parted. Fuck, what I wouldn't give to shove my cock between those pretty lips and watch her suck me dry. What I wouldn't give to push inside of her right now, see her take every inch. My breathing turns ragged, matching hers as she writhes in the passenger seat, her thighs quivering.

"There is not a single thing wrong with this body, Finley. It's perfect. And so are you. Trust it. Trust yourself. Trust me. We're gonna get through this."

I keep the same pace, pushing in and out, drawing tiny circles, spreading her juices from her center to her clit before pressing back into her and crooking my finger.

Her body tenses, her core squeezing my two fingers as she falls apart, moaning my name, and fuck if it isn't the sweetest sound I've ever heard.

"Thank you," she whispers.

Slowly, I pull out of her and suck on my fingers, closing my eyes as I savor the taste of her.

"I'd do anything for you," I murmur.

And fuck if I don't mean it.

CHAPTER THIRTY-THREE

GRIFFIN

Tugging at the tie around my throat, I stare at the tall black door in front of me. I've debated this since Finley's doctor's appointment, and if I'm being honest, long before then. But I never thought I'd go through with it. Never thought I'd have the guts or the justification. And maybe I still don't have them, but now that it's here. Now that I've called and set up the meeting, I feel like I'm standing on the edge of a knife, and one wrong move could ruin everything. Everything I've worked for. Everything I've wanted for as long as I can remember.

Maybe I already have ruined it.

My knees bounce as I rest my elbows on them, staring at the marble tile beneath my Oxfords.

I still remember when I got the call. It was years ago, but right now, it feels like it was yesterday. The Tornadoes wanted to sign me. Ev already knew he was going to play for the Rockets. He'd looked over contracts a few weeks prior. Same with Mav and the Lions. But me? My agent was ironing out the details, determined to get me the best contract possible because he thought I was worth it and was convinced the Tornadoes thought so, too. Little did they know, I would've signed anything as long as it guaranteed I could be on the ice and follow in my dad's footsteps without looking like I was riding his coattails.

Don't fuck this up.

I've thought long and hard about this. With all the shit going on with our families, the idea of leaving. Of moving away. It feels wrong. Even before I slept with Finley, it felt wrong, and I couldn't figure out why. I kept telling myself it was because of everything that happened with Archer and Mav. Then, everything went down with Dylan and Reeves' dad, and Raine's ex beat the shit out of Ev, and now I'm with Fin, and she's pregnant, and I can't...I can't leave. I also don't have a choice. Not if I don't want to lose everything I've worked for. But there's no way I can walk away and move across the country. Not anymore. Can I? She needs me. She doesn't want to admit it, but she does. So, here I am, doing the only thing I can think of, no matter how stupid it is.

Don't fuck this up.

"You can go in now," the receptionist offers. Erica's been a family friend since I was born and has worked for my Uncle Henry at Buchanan Enterprises for decades. But even the familiar smile does shit at calming my nerves.

The media can be a bitch in this line of work. If I had a dollar for every time someone said shit about my talent on the ice, blaming my familial connections for my success instead of the blood, sweat, and fucking tears I've shed for this sport and my future, I'd be as rich as my Uncle Henry. Now, here I am, calling in a favor and giving each and every accusation merit.

They're gonna have a field day with this.

I shove the thought aside, hook my finger in the silk noose around my throat, then stand.

As I step into Uncle Henry's office, he looks up from his desk and smirks. "This feels official."

"Thanks for meeting with me."

"Anytime." Fingers steepled in front of him, Maverick's dad, the owner of the NHL Lions, watches me approach the armchair across from his desk and motions to it.

My spine is straight as I sit on the edge of the cushion and hold his stare.

"So?" he prods.

Just. Say. It.

"I need your help," I announce.

"Figured as much. What can I do for you?"

"I need you to trade me to the Lions."

His brows kick up. "Pardon?"

Shifting in the leather seat across from Henry, I repeat, "I said I need you to trade me to the Lions. There's an opening on the team, thanks to Mav's"—I clear my throat —"early retirement, and I know there's been talk of you wanting to rebuild the Lions from the ground up. Ask the Tornadoes to trade me for Erickson."

"Erickson's a good player," Uncle Henry argues, mentioning the Lions' right wing.

"He's an old player," I argue. "I'm young. Healthy. I'll be on the team for years, and I will win you a Stanley Cup. I promise."

His eyes thin. "Did Everett put you up to this?"

Blindsided by my best friend's name, I pull back. "What?"

"He came in last week asking for the same thing, though he went with trading Collins instead. Same idea, though. Rebuilding the team. Making some unconventional moves. Shaking things up a bit."

Fuck. Everett wants to be traded to the Lions, too.

I didn't know this. And by the look on Henry's face, he

knows I was also left in the dark as soon as the words were uttered.

"He wants to stay close to family," Uncle Henry explains. "Wants Raine to stay close to her family and her career at the tattoo shop."

Hating myself more and more with every passing moment, I nod. We're after the same spot. Everett and I are after the same spot. The room spins, and I dig my fingers into the armrests. Shit just got a hell of a lot more complicated, but I can't back down. Not now. Not with Fin. Not with the baby.

"I don't suppose this has something to do with Caruthers' injury before Christmas, does it?" Uncle Henry prods.

"The Tornadoes want me to play out the rest of their season."

"And in the process, kiss your degree goodbye, as well as the rest of your season with the Hawks," he realizes.

My chin dips in a grudging nod.

"When did you talk with them?" he prods.

"I met with them for lunch before the Bulldogs' game. They wanted to meet before then, but I was…unavailable."

"Unavailable?"

"I was on a road trip with Fin," I clarify.

"Finley, huh?" A smirk tugs at the corner of his mouth. "Should've known that hellraiser would be involved if it meant skipping something important. That girl's giving Mack and Kate a run for their money."

He has no idea.

"Yeah." I clear my throat. "Guess you could say that. But about the contract…"

"It's quite the opportunity." He pauses, considering the Tornadoes' proposition. "Risky, though. You do have leverage on your side." He shifts from Uncle Henry to the infamous business shark, Henry Buchanan, in the blink of an eye. "Have you negotiated a bonus at least?"

"There's no need. I turned them down."

His eyes widen. "And why would you do that?"

"Because I'm needed here."

"Which is why you want me to extend you an offer to play for the Lions," he concludes.

"Yes." I clear my throat. Again. "And I know Everett makes a good case with his personal situation, and I know family's important. Family's everything," I clarify. "But Finley's circumstances are a little more precarious than Raine's family and her internship at her dad's tattoo shop."

Concern flashes across his features, and his head tilts. "What's wrong with Finley?"

Fuck. I didn't want to play this card. Didn't mean to. It just slipped but...*fuck*. I don't want to betray Finley's trust. But I don't have the month Finley requested until we tell the family about the baby. Things are moving too fast. And if I want my career without sacrificing my relationship with Fin, then I need to make my move. Now.

"What's wrong with Finley, Griffin?" my uncle demands.

"She's uh…" I tug at the knot at my throat and rest my forearms against my knees. "You need to give me your word that this stays between us."

His eyes narrow. "I'm not sure I can until you tell me what this is about."

"Uncle Henry," I push.

His sigh is forced, and so are his next words. "Is it life-threatening?"

I hesitate. "Not at the moment, no."

"Not exactly painting me a pretty picture, Griff."

"I need your word," I repeat, well aware I'm pushing my

luck but too stubborn to give a shit. Not now. Not when Finley's trust in me is on the line.

Scratching his jaw, he finally murmurs, "Fine."

"She's, uh, she's pregnant."

If I wasn't raised with Uncle Henry, I would think he's unaffected by my declaration. But I *was* raised with the guy, and I know him well. Well enough to see the tension in his jaw. The slight shift of his muscles. The minor twitch of his right eye. Yeah, this is the last thing he would've guessed, I'd say. Jokes on both of us, though.

"And who's the father, Griffin?" he demands. "I heard you two are dating."

"I need you to trade me to the Lions," I repeat, dodging his question. "She needs to be close to her neurologist and her obstetrician and her family. She'll need support with the new baby while I'm at away games. I won't be able to leave either of them without knowing she has her family around while I'm gone."

The same twitch hits at the corner of his right eye. "And what makes you assume I can do this for you?"

"Because you're Henry Buchanan," I remind him.

He scratches his jaw, his gaze never leaving mine. "Your stats are good, Griff. Hell, they're on par with your father's when he was at LAU, but I have to take into account my current roster. My current players. I need defensemen, not right wings or centers," he adds. He's right. Mav plays defense. Ev and I are forwards. It's not an even swap.

"Like I said, we both know Mav's contract fell through," I murmur. "And I know shit is complicated, but I wouldn't be here if I didn't need this favor."

His sigh lingers in the air, leaving me even more anxious as he continues holding my stare. I can see the wheels turning. The calculations we both know he's weighing. The pros and cons and everything in between.

"Uncle Henry, please."

"I'll only be able to take on one of you, and that's if I can convince the coach to trade one of our offense for a current defender to make room for a rookie." He grits his teeth. "Erickson and Collins might be older, but they still have fight in them. Convincing the GM to let them go and make room for a rookie, even a rookie with incredible stats," he gives me a pointed look, "isn't an easy feat."

"I know."

"I can't make any guarantees."

"Your willingness to try is more than enough," I reply.

Leaning back in his desk chair, he asks, "Does anyone else know?"

I shake my head.

"Well, then." He stands and offers his hand. When I take it, he adds, "Congratulations, Griff. Being a parent is…" He swallows thickly, and I know he's thinking of Archer and Maverick and Rory. About burying his son, canceling the other's NHL contract, and raising his youngest, who's going through the thick of it with no end in sight.

Suddenly, I feel like shit. For letting him make assumptions about my paternal involvement. For swaying the situation in my favor instead of Everett's. For using a sore spot against him. All of it. But I bite my fucking tongue. Because if I don't. If I tell him I'm not the biological father, there's a chance I won't be able to stay in Lockwood Heights, and the idea of Finley being alone as she raises a baby on her own is more than I can handle.

"You're a good dad, Uncle Henry." I wipe my sweaty palms against my slacks. "One of the best."

His dark eyes turn to glass, his Adam's apple bobs in his throat, and he nods. "When are you going to tell the family?"

I lift a shoulder. "I'm letting Finley take the lead on that front."

He nods again. "Well, if you need anything in the meantime, let me know. I'll see what I can do on my end."

"Thanks, Uncle Henry."

"We're here for you, Griff." As I smooth out the front of my dress shirt and stand, he adds, "And Griff?"

"Yeah?"

"I'll have my GM and the coach, if I can swing it, come to tomorrow's game and see what they think. If you impress them, it'll help your chances." He gives me another pointed look. "Don't screw it up."

"I won't."

CHAPTER THIRTY-FOUR

FINLEY

It's early. And cold. I tuck my toes between Griffin's calves as he lays on his back. The guy doesn't even flinch from the temperature, but his chest rumbles under my cheek. "You're freezing."

Yesterday afternoon, he sent me a text asking if I wanted to binge murder documentaries and eat junk food. Obviously, I obliged, then jumped his bones and fell asleep on his chest. Now, here we are. Sharing a bed and soaking up each other's warmth as the morning light slips through the blinds.

Lifting my head, I look up at him. "Good thing I have my own personal heater to share a bed with me." I grin. "How'd you sleep?"

"Okay." He hesitates and rubs at his tired eyes. "You?"

"Just okay?" I nudge the divot between his ribs. "Figured last night's orgasm would've knocked you out."

A low chuckle reverberates through his chest. "It should've." Trailing his hand along my bare spine, he dips lower and squeezes my butt. "You're good at knocking me on my ass."

"So, what's up?" I ask. "Are you nervous about today's game?"

He nods. "Something like that."

He's lying. Or, at the very least, dodging my question. He should know I can read him better than this. The bags under his eyes? The cadence of his breathing? He's nervous.

Why are you nervous, Griffin?

Resting my chin on his chest, I push, "Okay, for real, what's going on? Is the Tornadoes' General Manager going to be at the game again? Is that why you're acting weird?"

His silence rings loud in the quiet room, and I sit up even more, letting the blankets pool around my naked body. As his eyes fall to my boobs, I arch my brow. "Better look your fill, boyfriend, 'cause after Everett and Raine move in, you can kiss this view goodbye."

Lifting his head from the pillow, he kisses the tip of my nipple, and my breath hitches. Seriously, this man owns my body, and I doubt he even realizes it. As he lays back on the bed, he hooks his hands behind his head and replies, "Then it looks like neither of us are moving for a few more hours."

With a laugh, I smack his chest playfully. "You're ridiculous. And you're also avoiding my question." I bend forward and kiss him, not even caring about our morning breath. Not when I have someone like Griffin Thorne in my bed. "Talk to me."

"It isn't the Tornadoes' GM who will be there."

My forehead crinkles. "Then who?"

"The Lions' GM."

"Why would you care if the Lions' GM is going to be at the game?" He stays quiet, and I jab his pec. "Tell me."

"I did something."

"Something," I repeat.

"Yeah." He scrubs his hand over his face. "Something."

"And what did you do?" I prod, caught between my own curiosity and how cute the guy looks when he's squirming.

"I, uh, I asked Uncle Henry if the Lions would be interested in a new right wing."

With a frown, I point out, "But you're signed with the Tornadoes."

"The Tornadoes are across the country." Reaching up, he brushes my hair away from the side of my face, pulling it over one shoulder while leaving the opposite side of my neck fully exposed as he stares up at me. He looks... nervous.

Why are you nervous, Griff?

"The Lions are here," he explains. "With you. And your doctor. And your friends. And your family. And LAU."

My lips part as I register his words. "A-are you trying to see if you can stay in Lockwood Heights?"

"I know I should've talked to you—"

"Griffin, tell me you're staying," I push.

"I'm doing everything I can to—"

I press my mouth to his, cupping both sides of his face. His scruff tickles my palms while his own hands trail down my spine. His grasp tightens, and he picks me up, forcing me to straddle him. Not that I care. Honestly, my mind is spinning. I can't believe he talked to Uncle Henry. He's so big on not riding the coattails of his infamous hockey god of a father, yet he called in a favor? It's confusing and flattering and...a little unbelievable.

Pulling away from him, I rub my thumb against his bottom lip, trying to keep my emotions—and hope—in check as I hold his soft gaze, memorizing the flecks of navy in his eyes. "You're really staying?"

"I told you I wasn't going anywhere, Fin," he rasps. "There's only one...problem."

"Other than your contract with the Tornadoes?" I offer dryly.

He forces a smile, then sobers. "Everett also asked to be traded."

"What?" I pull back. "Why?"

"I'm not the only one leaving people I care about in Lockwood Heights, Fin."

Shit.

He's right. Everyone Everett and Griffin care about is in this small town. Moving across the country to chase your dreams isn't easy, and it sure as hell doesn't come without sacrifices. I guess I always figured they were okay with it, though. The sacrifices. That the pros outweighed the cons, and we'd be nothing but a speck on their radar as they chased their dreams. Their futures. The ones they've been building for as long as I can remember. Knowing it isn't entirely the case is…sobering, I guess.

Chewing on the edge of my thumb, I finally ask, "And what are the odds of Uncle Henry trading for both of you?"

Griffin hesitates. "I'm gonna go with…not great."

I grimace, hating how I'd already reached the same conclusion. "Well, that's…inconvenient."

"You could say that."

"Maybe I can bribe Uncle Henry with Grandma Taylor's cookies," I offer. "Think it would work?"

Running his hand up and down my bare back, he chuckles softly. "Worth a shot. Might wanna wait until I've told Ev I'm his competition, though."

My eyes bulge. "He doesn't know?"

"Not yet."

"Does he know you know?"

He shakes his head.

"Well, are you gonna tell him?" I prod, caught between

being impressed with the man's audacity and a little scared for his life because Ev? He's not someone you want to piss off, and he sure as shit has no problem holding a grudge. Add in my relationship with Griffin, and we're already treading some pretty tumultuous waters. Now, this? This is…bad.

Griffin's jaw clenches, and I have zero doubt he's thinking the same thing.

"Maybe after the game," he mutters. "Or…after the Lions make a decision. Or…" He scrubs his hand over his face. "I dunno."

Climbing off him, I rest my back against the headboard. "Pretty sure Everett hasn't even come to terms with us dating yet. Add in the competitive side of things and the possibility of him losing or disappointing Raine, and he is not going to be happy."

"He'll get over it."

I look down at Griffin, his mussed hair, the worry creases around his eyes. He's worried. He might act like he isn't, but he can't fool me. And he knows Everett all too well.

"Get over it?" I challenge. "We're talking about my brother, right?"

With a groan, Griffin tosses his forearm over his eyes. "Fuck, don't remind me."

Grabbing his wrist, I force his arm back to his side and laugh, hoping to lighten the little dark cloud of chaos surrounding us. "It'll be fine."

"You sound so sure," he mutters.

"One of us has to be, right?" I shift forward and kiss him again in hopes of softening the stubborn divot from moments ago. When I pull away, I realize it hasn't done shit. Yup, the thing is so deep it's basically a gulch. Running my thumb along the mark, I murmur, "For now, it'll be our

little secret. Focus on the game. Do your best. And we'll…
play the rest by ear."

He nods slowly, grabbing my wrist, bringing my fingers
to his lips, and kissing them softly. "Yeah. Yeah, it'll be fine.
Add it to the list, right? But first, we have to help your
brother and Raine move in."

My nose scrunches. "Damn. I kind of forgot about that."
With a groan, I collapse onto his chest and snuggle into his
warmth. "Or, we could hide away until Reeves has done all
the heavy lifting."

With a laugh, he squeezes me softly. "All right, one
more hour, then we gotta get up."

"So bossy," I note, letting out a sigh and breathing in his
familiar scent.

CHAPTER THIRTY-FIVE

FINLEY

"So...who thought it would be a good idea to move a bunch of shit the day we have a game?" Reeves grunts. He's carrying a bunch of new furniture from the U-Haul and into the opposite side of the duplex—my side—with the rest of the guys.

It's kind of weird to think that a few months ago, this space belonged to me, Ophelia, and Dylan. Now, Ophelia shares Maverick's room, and Dylan is staying with Reeves, leaving me as the only official resident. Or at least, I was until Everett and Raine offered to move in while they wait for a house to go on the market on the same street. It's what they tell me, anyway. I don't think they'll be going anywhere, though. Not when Everett will be moving across state lines to play for the Rockets at the end of the school year. They're really going to buy a second house, just so they have a landing spot when they visit Lockwood Heights?

Then again, Raine's family is here. Her job at Etch 'N' Ink is here. Maybe they won't be moving too far after all, especially if he earns the open spot on the Lions' roster. I wonder if Raine knows what Everett's doing behind the scenes to keep them in Lockwood Heights.

Not gonna lie. I don't exactly want to live with my brother and his girlfriend. Actually, I *really* don't want to live with my brother and his girlfriend, but it's just the way the cards fell, and now that I'm pregnant and need to figure out a new game plan, I'm grateful for the free roof over my head until I'm forced to admit the truth. I am so screwed.

Deep breath, Fin.

"At least there isn't too much to move," I point out. "Griff and I already handled the majority of things, so really, you only need to move Everett's and Raine's things."

"Says the girl who insisted she needed a new dresser when you moved into our place," Maverick quips.

"Uh, I'm sorry, but my house basically burned down, so…"

Mav moves closer, shifting a small box to his other side. "Your kitchen burned down, so…"

"*And* my dresser had smoke damage, so…" I point my finger at him and twirl it around, adding a mock death glare for good measure as he throws his head back and laughs.

Sidling up beside me, Griffin reaches for the cardboard box in my arms. "Here. Let me—"

"I've got it," I say.

His eyes narrow. "Fin…"

Batting my lashes at him, I say, "I'm a big girl, Griffin. I think I can handle carrying a few boxes."

He moves closer. "I think you should take it easy."

"Why should she take it easy?" Lia asks from the kitchen.

"The seizure," Griffin explains, and honestly, I'm impressed. He had that one locked and loaded. Must've learned from the best. Even so, it doesn't mean I'm going to let him get away with bossing me around, even if he's sexy as hell when he does it.

"I'm fine." I lift Raine's clothes-filled box a few inches higher into the air as if to prove my point, then step onto the shared front porch of the duplex while ignoring Griffin's heated stare along my back.

Yeah, yeah. You've made your point clear.

Lifting boxes is probably a no-no when pregnant, but seriously. It's clothes. I'm not stupid, and I'm not going to put the bun in my oven in danger, even if I am sporting the high-risk label for the foreseeable future. Pretty sure Mr. Thorne needs to take a chill pill, especially when said bun is still most definitely on the down-low.

"Reeves, after you're done with the mattress, wanna help me carry the dresser from Fin's old room?" Everett calls. "I'll be upstairs."

Carrying a piece of furniture out of the U-Haul, Reeves grunts, "Sure thing. Be there in a sec."

Thankfully, Raine and Everett are taking the top floor of the duplex. I already invested in some noise-canceling headphones, so we should be good to go…until Griffin decides to sleep over and Everett has another aneurysm. I guess I'll just sleep at his place instead of mine. Until the baby is born.

Dread and anticipation fill every crevice inside me as I set a box on Everett's and Raine's bare mattress. Once the baby's born, do I ask for a second room? Do I kick them out and take the upper floor? Do I try to fit a crib in here? I scan the decent-sized space, imagining where I would fit a crib. Beside the window is okay, I guess. But what if the light bothers her? Or him? Maybe next to the closet would be better, but—

"Where the hell is she?"

"Ev, calm down," someone says. *Mav, I think?* "What is…" His voice trails off, and my heart ratchets up.

What's going on?

"Oh, shit," someone else mumbles.

Curious, I peek into the hallway, finding a red-faced Everett storming toward me up the stairs, his hand fisted at his side. Now, don't get me wrong. I'm used to pissing people off, Everett included. But after the last time we spoke, I'd hoped to stay on his good side for at least a week or two before poking the bear, especially after Griffin's truth bomb this morning. So, why is Ev looking like he's seconds from blowing a gasket? Then, I see it. The pregnancy test. In his fist.

The one from the room. The one I never thought to look for after seizing. He must've found it when he was moving the furniture.

Shit.

Do pregnancy tests last this long?

Blood drains from my face, and the world spins around me as all of my repercussions for keeping this from everyone hit at full force. I lean against the doorjamb, searching for balance as he lifts the stupid stick into the air.

"What the hell is this, Fin?"

I keep my expression blank. "How am I supposed to know what—"

"Bullshit."

"Ev?" Dylan calls from the base of the stairs. The rest of my friends file in from the front door, leaving the family room and kitchen way more crowded than I'd like at the moment. Then again, if crime documentaries have taught me anything, it's that witnesses are a good thing if you're about to be murdered, and since I have no desire to kill my brother, and he looks two seconds away from strangling me, well, maybe they can stay after all.

Like a rabid dog, Everett turns on the stairs to face Dylan and lifts the test into the air. "Is this yours?"

"Is what—" Her eyes pop behind her glasses. "Holy shit."

Reeves' jaw drops. "Dylan, are you pregnant?"

Finding her boyfriend, Dylan presses her hands to his chest and shakes her head. "It's not mine, I swear."

"Ah, man." He slips his hands around her waist and gives her an Eskimo kiss. "I'm almost disappointed."

Dylan rolls her eyes, and wiggles from Reeves' grasp before searching the room for any other potential culprits. When her gaze falls on Ophelia, she asks, "Lia?"

"Nope, I had my period last week," Ophelia announces.

"Yeah, I can vouch for her," Maverick adds.

"Ew," Dylan mutters.

With a wink, Reeves says, "Kinky."

"Pretty sure that's my line," I quip from the top of the stairs before regret fills every single crevice of my body.

Whoops.

So much for flying under the radar.

Silence ensues as everyone turns their stares to me. My heart races in my chest, ratcheting faster and faster with every curious look. Every unspoken assumption. I can't decide if it would be easier if I was still with Drew or if this is the best way to handle things. Just me, myself, and I. Because even if Griffin and I are a thing—a really amazing thing—the little nugget in my stomach is very much mine and mine alone.

Speaking of which, where the hell is he?

"Seriously, someone say something," Dylan pleads as she searches everyone's expressions. "Because, uh, a positive pregnancy test is kind of a big deal, and…"

"Well isn't this a delightful game of whodunnit?" I

announce. Rubbing my hands together, I paste on a fake smile. *Just say it.* "Yup. The cat's out of the bag. I'll take the congratulations now and will be registered online, thank you very much."

Everett's frown hardens as he reaches the top step. Hell, it's freaking concrete. He lowers his hand. Not effortlessly, mind you. Nope. This guy is so close to the brink of a mental breakdown I can almost taste the shift in the air as he forces his arm to lower like he's the Tin Man from *The Wizard of Oz.*

"You're pregnant," he states.

It isn't a question. It doesn't need to be. I already confirmed it.

"I believe the next words out of your mouth should be, *'Congratulations, baby sister, I'm so excited for you.'*"

"What the fuck, Fin?" he demands.

I grimace. "Apparently, I need to have my hearing checked because that sounded nothing like—"

He slams his hand against the wall, and I flinch.

"I thought you said you broke up with Drew," he growls.

"I did break up with Drew."

"So, is he *not* the father?"

I blink. Twice. "What?"

"I assume he isn't the father, or else why the hell would you break up with him?" His eyes darken. "Were you cheating on him with Griff? Is it his? Because the timeline sure as shit is murkier than it should be."

"What?" I screech. "No—"

"Or were you telling the truth when you first got home from your little road trip, and Drew really was cheating on you?" His nostrils flare. "You were, weren't you? He was cheating."

"Ev," I start.

"I'm gonna kill him," he decides. "I'm gonna fucking—"

"Ev," Raine interrupts. Slipping beside him, she touches his cheek and forces him to look at her. "You need to breathe, and you need to stop overreacting."

"Pretty sure I'm not overreacting, Storm," he rasps, but the muscles in his shoulders soften, and he leans into her touch, forcing his gaze back to me. And the disappointment. The resignation. It stings.

"Fuck, Fin."

"Yeah, that's pretty much how it happened," I joke.

The guy's mouth doesn't even twitch. "How could you be so…"

His voice trails off, but I could fill it in with a thousand different words, and none of them would take away the sting.

"Fertile?" I offer dryly. "Well, apparently, it runs in the family since mom got pregnant before she was married, too, and you turned out okay, so…"

Unamused, Everett folds his arms. "Does this mean you're planning to marry Drew like Mom did with Dad? Because at least with me, I had both my parents."

"I thought you hated Drew," I point out with a smirk in hopes of dissipating the bundle of nerves making me feel like a livewire under his scrutiny. I want to tell him that I know it was stupid. I know *I* was stupid. I know this whole situation is messed up. I know I made a mistake, and I'm terrified of what comes next. Of how I'm supposed to handle this.

"It isn't funny, Fin. It isn't a joke." My brother scrubs his hand over his face. "How could you be so irresponsible?"

And there it is. The word I was waiting for. The word I knew would cut me and solidify my biggest assumption. He thinks I'm irresponsible. And in a way, I am. I forgot to pack my birth control when I visited Drew, and the rest is history. But it doesn't soften the blow or the knowledge that I'll never be enough. I'll never be looked at as someone who knows how to handle their shit. Nope. I'm just the girl who screwed up by getting pregnant before I'm even allowed to legally touch alcohol.

Fantastic.

"Everett," Raine snaps. "This could happen to anyone—"

"Yeah, and the rest of us would handle it like adults instead of sweeping shit under the rug or pretending it isn't real or cheating on our significant other or—"

"Don't you dare accuse me of cheating!" I yell, but my asshole brother barrels over me.

"Or letting the fucking sperm donor off the hook! Does Griffin even know? How could you do that to him? I was worried he'd fuck you over, but you're the one—"

"It's mine," Griffin interrupts.

The lie hits like a punch to the gut, and I crumble forward, searching the sea of friends for my boyfriend's face. There he is. At the front door. Sandwiched between Maverick and Ophelia. His expression is…grim. And I hate that it's there because of me. My mistake. My screw up.

"Griff," I plead.

"Fin, it's okay," he says.

"What?" Everett's neck swivels left and right as Griffin approaches us, the stairs creaking beneath his weight.

"You already know we've been seeing each other—" Griffin starts, but Everett cuts him off.

"Yeah, but for how long, Griff? You knocked my sister up?"

"Personally, I'd think he'd be happy about it," Ophelia chimes in, mumbling to Dylan like they're watching a soap opera or something. "At least she isn't tied to Drew for the rest of her life, am I right?"

"Sh…," Dylan murmurs. "They're getting to the good part."

"There is no good part," Everett snaps. "I thought you two were…new." His lip curls. "How long has this been going on?"

"Why? Because the math isn't mathing?" I toss back at him then give Griffin a pointed look.

"A while," Griff answers for me. "We were keeping things quiet until we knew it was the real deal, and then she wound up pregnant, and—"

"So, wait. *You* were cheating on Drew?" Dylan interrupts. "With my brother?"

"Why do you think Drew wanted Fin to cut me out?" Griffin challenges.

Seriously, is the room spinning? It feels like it's spinning.

Although, bravo because this is an excellent lie. Too good, really. And if I didn't have a conscience, I just might go along with it, but I do have a conscience, and it's rearing its ugly head. I can't do this to Griff. I can't hijack his entire future all because I wound up pregnant even if things are going pretty freaking perfectly on the relationship front. It isn't fair to him, and it isn't fair to my baby.

Is it?

How the hell am I supposed to get out of this?

By opening your freaking mouth, Finley, I remind myself.

Shaking my head, I push away from the wall and call out, "Okay, enough bullshit, all right?" I move closer, wedging myself between Griffin and Everett at the top of the stairs. "First of all, you're a dick. I'm not sweeping shit under the rug. I'm trying to come up with a game plan since I'm well aware having a baby is kind of a big deal, but thank you so much for the vote of confidence. You're a real jackass. You know that, right?" I jab my brother's sternum with my forefinger. "Second of all, Griffin is—"

"We need to talk," Griffin interjects. "Right. Now."

Unease swims in my gut, and my head snaps to my brother's best friend. "Griff—"

"Please."

It's the *please* that does me in. The way he's looking at me like he might fall to his knees if it would give him what he wants, which, apparently, is a minute alone with me.

Without taking my eyes off the man in front of me, I murmur, "Everett, can you give us a minute, please?"

The floor squeaks beneath his weight as Everett steps away from us and down the stairs. Once we're the only two on the second floor, Griffin follows me into Everett's and Raine's room. The quiet click of the latch reverberates throughout the room as I force my lungs to work, praying the oxygen will bring some clarity with it, but nope. This situation is just as messed up as before.

Turning to Griffin, I whisper, "What the hell are you thinking?"

"Give me two minutes," he begs.

"Two minutes." A delirious laugh bubbles out of me, and I collapse onto the bed. "Sure. Why not? You have two minutes until we go out there and clear things up. Start talking, Griff."

CHAPTER THIRTY-SIX

GRIFFIN

Two minutes. She's giving me two fucking minutes. What I deserve is a round of applause for this.

I lock the bedroom door and press my back to it. The girl's cagey. Flighty. Anxious. Her eyes bounce around the walls, and she wrings her hands in front of her as she sucks her lips between her teeth.

"What the hell was that, Griff?" she finally demands.

"That was me saving your ass."

She scoffs. "No, it was you sticking your nose where it doesn't belong."

Ignoring the sharpness in her words, I murmur, "You don't need to feel stupid."

Her jaw drops. "I don't—"

"You do. It's why you're acting like a brat."

Hurt hits her eyes, but she only lifts her chin in defiance. "Maybe acting like a brat comes naturally to me."

"No, you're using it as a defense mechanism," I argue. "And even though I usually find it cute as hell, I'm gonna need you to breathe."

Glaring at me, she snaps, "Don't tell me what to do!"

"Your brother's out of line, Fin."

"Duh." She folds her arms, avoiding my gaze and looking...small. Uncomfortable. Hurt.

"And he had no right to call you irresponsible," I add, "especially when we both know he's hooked up with a shit-ton more people than you ever have."

"Yet it's always the girl's fault for winding up pregnant, right?" She scoffs again and stares out the bedroom window. "Talk about a double standard."

"You're right. And I'll talk to him about it—"

"I don't need you to stand up to my older brother for me. I'm more than capable of putting him in his place."

With a smirk, I step closer. "No one's doubting you."

"Yet here you are, telling people you're the father?" She laughs and covers her face with her hands. "Seriously, Griff? Don't get me wrong. I appreciate your...chivalry or whatever, but no one's going to believe—"

"Why not?"

She drops her hands to her lap and looks up at me. "Well, like I already pointed out, the math doesn't exactly add up. I mean, we could probably get away with it for now until the baby comes two months early, you know? Wow, that's a pretty big preemie, guys," she mocks.

"Already covered that," I argue. "We lie and say we slept together before you officially broke things off with Drew."

"So, I cheated."

"You and Drew took a break, which is when you fell for my charm. Then, Drew came groveling back, and because you have a heart of gold, you decided to give him another chance. But, when he found out about our little... rendezvous, he asked you to keep your distance from me." Stepping closer, I nudge her chin up with my knuckle and give her a lopsided smirk. "It works out that your ex was a controlling dick who didn't want us to be friends anymore."

"And I'm not a cheater."

"Exactly."

Her lips purse. "Okay, let's say they do believe it. It still makes zero sense for you to make up something like this. I know you care about me, and I care about you more than you'll ever know, but…"

"But what, Fin?" I push.

Grabbing my wrist, she lowers my hand from her chin and wets her lips. "What if it doesn't work out?"

"It's gonna—"

"You don't know that," she argues. "Yes, things feel pretty freaking perfect right now, but why in the world would you sign up to be my…beard or whatever? And to what end? Ope." She snaps her fingers and drops her voice a couple octaves. "Looks like you and I aren't as great of a fit as we'd thought, and I fell in love with someone else *and* found my future wife. Peace out, fake baby mama." The girl gives me two thumbs up. "Yeah, that sounds like a brilliant idea with zero chances of blowing up in our faces."

"Who says this won't work?" I demand. "And who says I'm gonna fall in love with someone else? Look, you told me you're scared to do this alone—"

"I am scared of doing this alone, but that doesn't mean I'm not capable of it."

"You're plenty capable, Fin." I grab her face, forcing her to look at me again. "You are. But just because you can do something by yourself doesn't mean you should have to. I care about you."

"For how long?"

"Well, if we take our history into account, I'm gonna go with a long fuckin' time, especially when I'm already in the process of figuring out how to stay here. With you. Like you asked me to just this morning," I remind her.

"I know I did," she whispers. Reaching up, she touches the back of my hand as I cradle her face. She doesn't remove it this time. Instead, she leans into my touch, sandwiching my hand between her palm and cheek as she peers up at me with the most vulnerable gaze I've ever witnessed. "And I do want you to stay, Griff. I want it more than you know, and you know I'm all for secrets, but this one could affect the rest of your life. I don't know if I can... I don't know if I can do that to you. This is new and terrifying and..."

It hurts more than I expect. Her lack of faith in me. In us. I'd give up anything for Fin, and the fact that she can't see it? That she refuses to see it? It isn't fair. Not to me, or to her.

"How long have we known each other, Fin?" I demand.

She shakes her head. "That isn't the point."

"Answer the question," I push. "How long have we known each other, Fin?"

Her lips part, the mint of her breath hitting my face. "Forever."

"And have I ever, in your entire life, let you down or broken a promise?"

My heart wars in my chest, and irritation heats my limbs as a smokescreen falls over her eyes.

"That's the thing, Griff," she whispers, pulling away from me again. "I know you wouldn't let me down, and I know you're pretty much incapable of breaking promises. It isn't in your blood, and it's one of the things I love most about you, but this is your entire future." She lifts her shoulder in defeat. "If we let people believe this baby is yours, and it doesn't work out, I won't be able to live with myself. You're unselfish, Griff. But me?" She pats my chest. "I'm looking out for number one here."

My mouth lifts as I stare at her. Taking in every curve of her face. The slight dip of her brows. The pout of her bottom lip.

"I'd be lucky to be your baby's father, Fin."

"And this baby would be lucky to have you as their father, but I'm not going to let you take the blame for knocking me up," she counters.

So. Damn. Stubborn.

"Yeah, well, maybe I need you to, to save my ass," I argue. "Ever think of that?"

With a frown, she leans back on her hands. "Since when does your ass need saving?"

I squeeze the back of my neck, hating the precariousness of the situation and how I feel like I'm about to walk the plank despite my best intentions.

"Griffin, tell me," she pushes.

"You know the whole…Uncle Henry thing?"

"Yes?"

"I, uh, I may have told him about the baby."

She blanches. "Griff—"

"I know."

"Why would you do that?"

"Because after the doctor's appointment, I couldn't imagine being away from you, so I told him the truth."

"That I'm pregnant," she finishes for me.

I give her a sharp nod. "Yeah."

"Anything else?"

I squeeze the bridge of my nose, hating myself more and more with every passing second. "I let him assume I'm the father."

She gasps, her eyes popping even more as she registers my confession and everything it means. "You didn't."

"I did."

"Griff—"

"I know, okay?" Dropping my hand to my lap, I look down at her. "I know I fucked up, but the idea of leaving you…it's not an option for me, Fin. Not after everything we've been through. Not when the future is…what it is."

"So, you lied."

I hesitate. "I omitted."

"Griffin," she pushes.

"Okay. Yeah. I lied. And if we tell Everett or anyone else I'm not the biological father, there's no way Uncle Henry will trade for me, and then I'll lose you, and I can't lose you, Fin."

Eyes softening, she peers up at me. "I can't lose you either, Griff."

Like a balm, her words ease my fear, and I reach for her hand, lacing our fingers together. "Then, will you do this for me?" I ask. "Let me step up? Let me be the guy you deserve?"

Her mouth bunches on one side, but she stays quiet, studying me. Not giving in, but not telling me to fuck off, either. I don't blame her for being caught off guard. This is a big risk. A big potential fuck up. And it doesn't only involve me and her anymore. It involves our friends. Our family. Her baby.

Our baby.

The thought makes my heart pound against my sternum, but not in the way I expect. Hell, it isn't dread pushing me. It's excitement.

We could do this.

We could make this work.

Me. Her. The baby.

And I want to. I want to make this work. I want a life with Finley. Forever, if she'll have me.

"You're not gonna say anything?" I ask.

"I'm debating," she muses.

With a low laugh, I shake my head. "So stubborn."

"I'd blame the pregnancy hormones, but I think we both know me better than that."

I laugh again and kiss her softly. "So is that a yes?"

"You're sure you won't regret this?" she pushes.

"Not possible." I kiss her forehead. "We're gonna get through this."

Closing her eyes, she leans into my touch again as if letting me carry some of the weight she's been shouldering on her own for way too long, but damn if I'm not ready to take it.

"And you're gonna tell your parents," I add.

Her forehead scrunches beneath my lips. "So bossy."

Smiling against her, I squeeze her tighter. "Never claimed I wasn't, Fin."

"Yeah, but you're supposed to be the nice guy, remember?"

"I'm not nice?" I challenge.

With a mock glare, she pulls away and looks up at me. "You're bossy."

"I can be bossy *and* nice," I offer. "But only after we smooth things over with everyone."

"Fiiiine," she groans but raises her chin for another kiss.

Bending down, I give it to her.

CHAPTER THIRTY-SEVEN

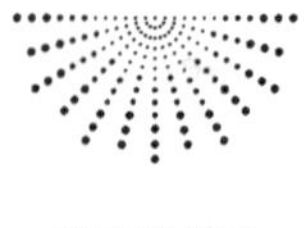

FINLEY

Joke's on us. The house is empty by the time Griffin and I reappear. No notes. No texts. Only a positive pregnancy test on the kitchen counter and a stone of guilt in the pit of my stomach.

"Any suggestions on what we should do?" I ask, turning to Griffin.

He checks the time on his phone and sighs. "Not sure, but—"

His phone buzzes in his hand.

Leaning closer, I see his mom's face flashing on the screen, and my eyes dart to his. "You gonna answer it?"

With a nod, he reaches for my hand, squeezes softly, and heads into the family room, lifting his cell to his ear. "Hey, Mom."

I tiptoe back to my room, close the door behind me, and pull up Everett's contact info. Pressing call, I wait for him to pick up, but it goes straight to voicemail, confirming my suspicion. He's pissed. I get it, but still.

I dial his number again and lift my phone to my ear.

Ring. Ring.

"This is Ev. Leave me a message—"

Hitting end, I open my messaging app and click on my conversation with Everett.

ME

I know you're mad, and you have every right to be, but if you could not be an ass and let me explain myself, that would be great.

I hit send, then stare at the delivered notification at the bottom, waiting for it to shift to read. When it doesn't, my teeth dig into the inside of my cheek.

Three little bubbles pop up, and I hold my breath, waiting for his response.

EV

Can't talk now. Gotta get my head on straight for the game. We'll talk later, though. I'm sorry I was an ass, and I love you.

ME

Love you, too.

Tapping my cell against my chin, I squeeze my eyes shut. One down. One billion to go.

Before I can talk myself out of it, I pull up my friends' group chat and type out a message.

ME

So...I probably owe you girls an explanation...

Before everything exploded, we agreed to meet outside the arena for the game, but still. The radio silence? It feels off. I need to fix this. I need to clear the air. I need to...do something. I feel disconnected now more than ever, and I know it's my own fault. I should've told them. I should've smoothed things over. I should've...I should've done so many things.

My phone buzzes in my hand, and my heart leaps as I find a text from Ophelia.

OPHELIA

Oo...already?! I was kind of thinking we were giving you space until the game, but we're ready whenever you are for the explanation if you want to give it.

DYLAN

Yup. We're definitely ready whenever you are. No pressure, though.

ME

Not sure I'll ever technically be ready since this is kind of a doozy, but I was wrong for keeping this from you guys. I screwed up.

With a deep breath, I hit send, anxious to clear the air so I can finally breathe.

DYLAN

Don't get me wrong. I think we all would've liked to have been in the loop, but I can't imagine being in your position, Fin. I think it's normal to spiral a bit after getting news like that, you know? You had every right to keep this close to the chest until you were ready to tell people.

My phone buzzes with a second text.

RAINE

I agree with Dylan. And I'm sorry your brother was an ass. I promise I smacked him upside the head after dragging him out of the house. You're still coming to the game, right?

ME

Planning on it. And thanks for smacking Everett, even though I kind of deserved the freak-out.

OPHELIA

No one deserves a freak-out like that. I think the real question is…when are you going to let Everett back into the house since you guys all live together? Lol

ME

Har, har. You're SO funny, Lia.

DYLAN

Pretty sure she gets it from you, Fin.

I roll my eyes.

ME

I repeat: Har. Har. And I didn't kick him out. You guys all disappeared. What the hell?!

OPHELIA

We figured you could use the space for a minute, and you know you love us. PS- How are you feeling?

I hesitate, considering her question, and type my response.

ME

Freaked out, but also kind of excited.

RAINE

As you should be. And can I tell you how excited I am to be an aunt again? It's the best title ever, and I know Everett and I aren't even close to getting married or anything, but am I allowed to claim the title anyway?

DYLAN

Oo, me, too! Maybe I can buy your baby a frog once you get home from the hospital!

ME

So help me, I will murder you.

DYLAN

Then who will babysit?

OPHELIA

I volunteer as tribute!

My mouth lifts as I type my response.

ME

Of course you do.

But seriously, thank you. For not ripping my head off for keeping you guys in the dark.

OPHELIA

We forgive you, Fin. You're kind of stuck with us.

RAINE

ALL of us ;)

ME

Thanks, ladies.

RAINE

Honestly, I should be thanking you. Now I
don't feel like I need to impress your
parents anymore, because as long as I
don't wind up pregnant, I'm golden, lol.

OPHELIA

I should thank you, too. We're all going to
be aunties!!! Do you have any idea how
excited I am?

DYLAN

You're excited? I'm already shopping for
frog onesies online ;)

Pinching the bridge of my nose, I let out a quiet laugh when a soft knock hits my door.

"Hey," Griff murmurs.

I set my phone on my nightstand and sit up. "Hey."

"Something funny?"

"Just...the girls," I admit. "They're crazy but awesome. And supportive," I add, "which is kind of a miracle. What did your mom say?"

"She called about the game and asked how you're doing." Walking toward me, he wiggles his cell phone back and forth. "And I ,uh, I told her."

My eyes pop. "You told her how I'm doing or you told her...about the baby?"

The mattress dips as he sits down beside me. "They're kind of synonymous, aren't they?"

"I mean..."

"I'm sorry," he murmurs. "I guess I was tired of keeping secrets."

"So you created more?" I counter.

The warmth of his palm spreads across my belly as he palms my stomach. "I know it's a technicality, but now that we agreed to do this, I can't imagine not being this baby's dad in every sense of the word other than blood, and even that feels…so fucking small in the big picture." He leans in, kissing my temple. "Did you try calling Ev?"

"Went to voicemail," I mutter. "He texted me, though."

"What'd he say?"

"That he loves me, he's sorry for being an ass, and we'll talk after the game."

Griffin nods, digesting my words. "Good."

"I think so," I agree."

"You gonna tell your parents yet?"

My face scrunches. "Or, hear me out. We go to tonight's game, then come home, eat junk food, and watch movies in bed. Eh? Eh?" I give him a wide smile and bat my lashes. The man folds in an instant.

Tossing his arm around me, he tugs me into his side. "I'm gonna let you take the lead on when to tell your parents, but now that mine know, it's only a matter of time until your phone rings, though I did tell them you want to tell them yourself if you can help it."

"So, basically, you gave me an unofficial deadline." I give him a mock glare. "Gee. Thanks."

"Can't hide from this forever, Fin."

"I know."

"For now, I'm gonna head out and see if I can smooth shit over with Ev before the game. You still driving with the girls?"

With a nod, I give him a squeeze. "Yup."

"And you're good?" he prods.

"Never better."

"That's my girl."

CHAPTER THIRTY-EIGHT

GRIFFIN

I've given a lot of pre-game speeches. More than I can count if I'm being honest. Sometimes, they hit. Sometimes, they don't, but with everything riding on the game and no one knowing about any of it, I'm wound so fucking tight I might actually puke.

Everett isn't talking to me. I figured as much, but when I entered the locker room, and the asshole stonewalled me, it only solidified the shitty situation. He's pissed, and he has every right to be. I know Ev, though. Forcing him to talk when he isn't ready could easily blow up in my face, but so could keeping him in the dark. With the baby. With the potential trade. He glances my way, then turns to Dreggs and nods, acting as if he's paying attention to whatever our teammate is saying.

I make a note to corner him before the game, then climb onto one of the benches, making myself a foot taller than everyone else in the room. Right now, I need to get my head in the game, and I need to make sure my teammates are as invested as I am in playing our best tonight.

"Listen up!" I yell. The metal clanging and low hum of chatter in the locker room quiet.

Now or never, I remind myself.

"There are moments in life," I boom. "Average moments. Moments taken for granted. And tonight might look like one more game for the books, but we're twelve games away from playoffs. Twelve. Games." I pause and rotate slowly, confirming I have everyone's attention. "Twelve games to make a difference. Twelve games to up our stats. Twelve games to break records and to wear LAU's name on our jerseys before the season ends. We might be a shoo-in for the championship, but let's play like it's our last."

The team hits their helmets against the lockers, and the sound reverberates through the room. It's so loud, I have no doubt they can hear us in the arena, but I welcome it. The energy. The solidarity. The brotherhood we've forged in this very room over years of blood, sweat, and tears. From wins to losses, both on and off the ice, these are my brothers.

Glancing at my best friend, guilt claws at my insides. He's my brother, too, and I've done what I swore I never would. I've lied to him. And I might not be able to rectify everything, but I can start somewhere. I jump off the wooden bench and open my locker, grabbing my skates and lacing up. He's still talking with Dreggs. I'll smooth shit out in a minute. I hate to. Before the game. Before he has another reason to hate me. Before I move our friendship another step in the wrong direction.

"Hey, man," Reeves says. Slapping his locker closed, he slips on his gloves and palms his stick. "Nice speech."

"Gotta say something to keep the spirits up," I lie, though I'm not exactly wrong, either. I do need to keep their spirits up. We've been stagnant lately. Going through the motions. And yeah, we're winning, but where's the heart?

"Your dad here?" he prods.

I shake my head. "Why?"

"You seem…" Hesitating, he scans me up and down. "More nervous than usual. You're only like this during playoffs and when your dad's watching."

He's right. I'm always more on edge when my dad or brother are in the stands.

Nothing like being the youngest boy in a long line of overachievers. And yeah, the list includes Jax, too. He might've passed up on his career as a professional player to coach the Ladyhawk's team, but it wasn't because he couldn't hack it. It was because he wanted a challenge, and building an organization from the ground up is no easy feat. Regardless, I should be grateful. I'm used to the pressure. The need to show up and perform and kick ass when it counts. And today? Today, it counts.

"You hear the Lions' GM is in the stands?" Reeves asks.

Finished tying my skates, I look up at him and grab my gloves from my open locker. "Do you know why he's here?"

"Nah, but I was hoping you would."

"Why would I know?"

With a shrug, he leans against the closed locker beside me. "Just curious."

Oliver. Fucking. Reeves. The man is way more astute than any of us give him credit for. The question is, does he already know the answer, or is he searching for the puzzle pieces so he can connect the dots? And when he does—cause it sure as shit isn't *if*—what then?

"He not talking to you?" Reeves adds, glancing at Ev.

I shake my head but don't answer.

"Figured." He slaps my shoulder. "Congratulations, by

the way. I know shit hit the fan earlier, but we're happy for you. Me. Mav. Ev."

I scoff. "Liar."

"Okay, maybe not the Everett part." He grins. "Not yet, anyway. He'll come around, though."

"Guess we'll have to wait and see."

"Nah, he will. Lia was right. Fin being tied to Drew for the rest of her life would've been a bitch. You?" He shrugs. "You'll take care of them."

A lump lodges in my throat, but I swallow it back, appreciating his confidence in me more than he knows. I will take care of them. I'll do whatever it takes. I have to.

"Thanks, man," I mutter. "I, uh, I appreciate it."

"Listen up!" Coach booms when he appears from his office. The team quiets, some gathering their helmets and sticks, others already prepared to take to the ice as we turn toward Coach Sanderson. The legend. Other than the shaved head and a few more wrinkles, he looks the same as when he coached my dad and Uncle Theo. Yeah. Talk about trying to live up to a person's expectations.

I shake the thought off and try to focus.

Arms folded, Coach continues, "I know you already heard your captain's speech, but Thorne's right. Play every game like it's your last, and we'll keep making a name for LAU. Let's go!"

As we head down the tunnel toward the ice, I trail behind the team, playing out every potential outcome of today's game and if I'll be able to get through it without fucking up things with Everett or Finley or Uncle Henry. My attention slides to Ev. I wonder if he knows the Lions' GM is here. Probably. If Reeves knows, there's no way Everett doesn't, right? But even then, does he know the guy is here for *both* of us? Does he know we're pitted against each other? That I pitted us against each other, even if it's the last thing I would've wanted?

Shit, I don't even know what to do anymore. What's right. What isn't. If I'm being selfish or deceptive or loyal.

He would want me to look after Finley. Especially with a baby on the way. I know he would. If I could only explain myself. The situation. Make him understand.

"Ev, wait up!" I call.

Looking over his shoulder, he eyes me warily and sighs. "Not now, man."

"Listen—"

"I need my head in the game, Griff. Especially this one. Just...leave it alone, all right?"

"I need to talk to you—"

"Yeah, and I need to play well tonight," he interrupts. "Don't worry, though. I won't be a dick on the ice. Let's just play. We'll talk about you and my sister later."

Leaving me behind, he quickens his pace down the tunnel, and I stand dumbfounded.

This isn't only about me and Fin. It's about the game, too. It's about the Lions' GM Everett thinks is here for him when that isn't necessarily the case. Maybe he is. Maybe he isn't. But either way, I'm fucked, and so is Ev. He just doesn't know it yet.

The familiar roar of the crowd rumbles through the arena, and the announcer's voice booms over the speakers. When he calls my jersey number, I glide onto the ice and tighten my grip on my stick, feeling the familiar grooves under my gloved fingers. Searching the stands, my attention lands on the Lions' GM for the briefest of seconds until a poster with red glitter and the words, "My boyfriend is hotter than yours," steals my attention a few rows below. Finley raises the poster a little higher into the air, her smile growing as soon as our gazes connect.

"You. Got. This," she mouths, and I swear I can hear her fucking words.

I got this.

The bright lights pound down on me. I head to the bench with the rest of the team until Coach gives me the green light to hit the ice. As I skate into position, the crowd's roar surrounds me, a cacophony of excitement and anticipation.

I got this, I remind myself.

My heart pounds in my chest, adrenaline surging through my veins as Everett lines up for the face-off.

The puck drops, and I'm off, my skates cutting sharp lines into the glassy ice. I weave through the opposing team's defense, stickhandling with precision when my eyes lock onto the net. Almost there. I approach the goal and stop short, waiting for the inevitable pass I know is coming.

Come on, Ev. Come on.

Ice sprays, and I twist around in time to catch Everett winding up and chipping the puck off the boards. I catch it, and with a quick flick of my wrist, the puck sails past the goalie's glove, hitting the back of the net with a satisfying thud.

"Yes!" I yell.

The crowd erupts, and I raise my stick in triumph.

One down. Who the hell knows how many to go.

I've got this.

Chest heaving, I skate around the edge of the rink, refusing to look at the crowded stands and who I know is watching.

When I almost reach Everett, he slows, letting me catch up to him.

"That was quick," he says.

His hand hits my padded shoulder, and I grin back at him. "Play like it's our last game, right?"

Reeves skates between us, whooping. "Fuck, yeah! And look at you, leading by example and shit." He presses the handle of his stick to his chest. "O Captain! My Captain!"

"Stop celebrating!" Coach yells from the bench. "The game's only getting started. Get back in position!"

He's right. The game's barely started, but fuck, we're gonna play like it's our last.

The next two periods are a blur, but Everett scores once, and the Bulldogs score twice after a fuckup by Cameron and a lucky shot by the Bulldogs' center right before the buzzer, leaving us tied by the third period.

My muscles ache. Sweat pours down my face. And my mind races. As we skate back into position, I ignore the prickles along my spine and the mounting pressure. Before I can stop myself, my attention drifts to the stands for what feels like the thousandth time.

There he is. Shawn Burrows. His eyes are glued to the ice as Everett stands at the blue line. His posture is crouched and ready, waiting for the ref's whistle to blow. He's had a hell of a game. Seriously. I'm fucking impressed, even if it does contradict my own self-preservation. If Ev makes the team, he's earned it, but I sure as shit am not going down without a fight.

Seconds later, the puck slips from the ref's fingers, and this time, the Bulldogs steal possession and dart toward our goalie. The Bulldogs' center attempts a wraparound, but our goalie makes a glove save, and one of my teammates rebounds it, opting for a dump and chase, sending the puck flying past the blue line. I catch the pass, but a hard check from a defender sends me sprawling onto the ice. The puck slips just out of reach when Reeves rushes after it and saves my ass. I scramble back to my feet, my skates cutting through the ice as Reeves chips the puck off the boards toward Everett when it's intercepted.

"Fuck!" I yell.

As the seconds tick down on the clock, my breath comes in ragged gasps, and with a final burst of speed, I lunge forward, my stick meeting the puck with a satisfying crack. Sweat drips down my hairline, wetting the back of my neck as I push my body to the limit and race back to the goal, the crowd screaming at the tops of their lungs while the shot clock counts down. The defense closes in, but I deke left, then right, slipping past them.

"You got this, you got this, you got this," I chant under my breath. With a powerful slap shot, I send the puck flying. It rockets past the goalie, and the red light flashes.

Three to two. We did it.

My teammates swarm me, their congratulations ringing in my ears.

We did it.

We. Fucking. Did. It.

So, why do I feel like shit?

CHAPTER THIRTY-NINE

GRIFFIN

"Game Night?" Reeves suggests, shifting his attention from me to Ev as he slides his T-shirt on in the locker room. "You in?"

Everett smiles, then looks down at the ground. "Yeah, yeah, I think we're in. Let me talk to Raine and make sure she's good with it."

"Yes." Reeves pumps his fist into the air, cups his hands around his mouth, and yells, "Game Night at our place! See you there!"

Our teammates cheer, more than ready to replay the game with our friends and celebrate tonight's win. Coach gives us a congratulatory speech, and we jump in the showers and get dressed. There's always a high in the locker room after a good game. And a buzzer beater like tonight? It has us even higher than usual.

Or at least, most of us. I'm too lost in my own head to enjoy it. Pulling my phone from my locker, I check the screen for any messages from Uncle Henry or Finley or even the Lions' GM, but there isn't anything.

"Good game tonight," Ev says.

Tucking my phone into my pocket, I clear my throat. "Yeah, man. You, too. Look, uh…"

"Let me ride the high, yeah?" he interrupts. "I know shit is messy with…everything, but I could use my best friend right now."

I hesitate. "What is it?"

"Do you know what tonight means?"

"What?" I ask.

"It means…" His smile stretches, and he tips his head back, yelling, "Fuck, yeah!" Turning back to me, he explains, "I wanted to tell you, but, uh, after shit went down at the house, I didn't know what to say."

"Ev—"

"Let me finish." With a laugh, he scratches his jaw, shaking his head like he's in disbelief. "Did you hear the Lions' GM was in the stands?"

I nod, unable to look him in the eye.

"Yeah, well, I asked Uncle Henry if, uh, if they'd be interested in trading with the Rockets for me, and after tonight's win?" I catch his grin in my periphery. "Let's just say I think it looks good."

Fuck.

Unease floods my veins as I stare at my gloves hanging in my locker. "I heard."

"And?" He shoves my shoulder, forcing my attention back to him. "Come on. I know we have our shit, but I thought you'd be happy for me."

"Look." I sigh. "You're not the only one who, uh, who thought it might be a good idea to stay in Lockwood Heights."

He frowns. "What are you saying?"

Fuck!

My hands tighten into fists at my sides as I fight to find

the right words, knowing there aren't any. "I, uh, I wanted to tell you before the game, but you wouldn't listen."

Moving closer, he demands, "What did you do?"

"After I found out about the baby, I knew I had to do… something, so I…"

"What did you do, Griff?" he growls.

Sensing the shift in the air, the teammates start filing out of the locker room, grabbing their shit and getting the hell out of dodge. Part of me wishes I could do the same. The other part? Well, I'm pretty sure this conversation is long overdue.

Facing Ev, I force out, "I asked Uncle Henry if he'd be willing to trade for me, but I didn't know you reached out to him, too, all right? I didn't know until I'd already asked."

"And you didn't back off?" he challenges.

"Your sister is pregnant."

"Raine's entire family is here."

My head falls forward. "I know."

"Her nieces, her nephews, her parents, let alone her job."

"I know," I repeat, lifting my head and holding his gaze. "And if the circumstances were different, I would've kept my head down, but—"

Teeth grinding, he slams the locker closed and leans against it, staring blankly in front of him. "Did he make a decision?"

"Uncle Henry?"

Everett gives me a jerky nod, but refuses to look at me.

"Not yet. Or at least, not that I know of," I clarify. "You kicked ass on the ice tonight, though. And if you make the team, you know I'll be happy for you, but…" I scrub my face from forehead to chin. "But that doesn't mean I couldn't sit by and *not* try for the spot, too."

"Of course, you couldn't." He scoffs. "When did you ask him?"

"As soon as I found out Finley's pregnancy was high-risk."

Turning to me, his expression falls, his frustration melting into concern. "What do you mean, high-risk?"

The memory of the doctor's appointment floods to the surface and leaves me queasy, reminding me how helpless I really am. "The doctor wants to keep a close eye on her and the baby."

"Are they okay?" he demands.

"So far, so good," I answer vaguely. "But it's still early, and I couldn't *not* do something, man. I'm sorry, though. I feel like shit."

He closes his eyes, his defeat matching my own. It swirls around us. Ruining the high from tonight's win and leaving me hollow as I stare at my best friend.

"I'll pull my name," he decides.

"Ev—"

"Don't," he grumbles. "Tell Fin I love her. I gotta make a call."

"Ev," I repeat, but he doesn't listen. He only walks away.

CHAPTER FORTY

FINLEY

The walls shake as Griffin guides me out the front door. We played beer pong, which I usually thrive at, thanks to subbing the beer with Diet Coke. But after losing my reigning champion title to a couple of bombed puck bunnies, I decided to call it a night.

Yeah, I'm a sore loser. So sue me.

There are benefits to living next door to your boyfriend, and when I'm peopled out, a short walk like this is definitely one of them.

Okay, peopled out is probably the wrong term. More like bone tired with a side of my-brain-feels-like-it-was-dipped-in-pudding-and-thinking-straight-is-impossible, but hey. Semantics. After celebrating tonight's win, being bombarded with a billion questions and congratulations from my friends, and not-so-subtly noticing my brother's absence at the party, I'm officially exhausted.

"You talked to Raine, right?" Griffin asks for what feels like the millionth time.

I nod. "Yeah. How was Ev at the game? What'd he say?"

"He's...handling it," Griffin mutters. "Really wish he'd answer my calls, though."

I'm not the only one who's been distracted by Everett's absence. Griffin's been glued to his phone all night. Texting. Calling. Trying to reach Everett despite my conversation with Raine.

"You're not exactly making me feel better," I point out. "When I spoke with Raine, she said he's okay, and they were staying home to celebrate on their own." My nose scrunches. "Which, when I put it that way... Maybe I should sleep at your place."

I wait for Griffin's familiar laughter or, at the very least, an invitation to spend the night, but when I'm only greeted with silence, I glance at him. His nose is still in his phone, and he looks...stressed.

I grab his wrist, forcing him to lower his phone-wielding hand. "Hey."

"Sorry."

"Don't apologize." Rising onto my tiptoes, I brush my lips against his. "You played well tonight."

"Thanks."

"And you wanted to play well," I continue.

"I know I did."

"So, what's wrong, Griff?"

With a quiet sigh, he pulls me closer, letting me steal his body heat as the cold breeze seeps through our coats. "Ev said he's gonna pull his name."

My brows raise. "What?"

"I wanted to come clean about the Lions thing, but when I told him, he said he was gonna pull his name, and—"

"He can't do that."

"I know he can't."

"That isn't fair to him."

"I know it isn't," he murmurs. "I've been trying to get a hold of him all night, but…"

"But he's ignoring you because he knows you're going to try and talk him out of it," I finish.

"Yeah."

"Shit."

He frowns. "Yeah. Shit."

"Well, then he probably isn't doing much celebrating with Raine." The cold metal handle causes a shiver to race up my spine as I start to push the front door open. "Let me see if I can talk to him." I hesitate and turn back to Griffin. "Are you okay if I do this alone?"

"You sure you don't need me?"

"I mean, I'll always need you, but yeah. I think it's best if I have a sisterly chat with him, one on one."

"Whatever you think, Fin." He bends closer and kisses me softly. "I'll keep my phone on me. If you need anything, let me know."

"I will," I promise.

THE HOUSE IS QUIET. TIPTOEING DOWN THE HALL, I GO TO the bathroom and give myself a mental pep talk when a soft squeak from my bedroom catches my attention. Moving closer, I peek through the cracked door, finding Everett sitting on my bed.

The hinges creak as I push the door open the rest of the way and lean my shoulder against the doorjamb. "Hey."

"Hey," Everett grumbles.

"What are you doing in my room?"

"Wanted to…talk."

"Talk," I repeat. "Okay, so…talk."

"Not sure what to say." His head continues hanging

between his shoulders as he stares at his hands. Hell, he's a statue. A very grumpy looking statue.

"Are you still mad at me?" I ask.

"Disappointed."

Rolling my eyes, I push myself away from the doorway and walk into my room. "Not sure that's any better, but thanks."

"In myself, not you," he clarifies.

"Are you serious?" My frown deepens. "Why are you disappointed in yourself?"

"Because I pride myself on being a good big brother, and I fucked up in every. Single. Way." He shakes his head. "I couldn't have handled today in a worse way, Fin. I yelled. I stormed off. I made you feel like shit."

"You didn't—"

"I did," he argues. "I know you don't like to talk about your feelings, Fin, but I know I hit below the belt today."

He's right. He did. But seeing him like this? It doesn't make me feel any better. Honestly, it makes me feel even worse. He's always been hard on himself. The man who thinks he can carry the weight of everyone's world on his shoulders, come hell or high water. And it appears right now is no different.

"You were angry I lied to you," I offer. "You had every right to feel that way."

"You're not irresponsible, Fin."

The reminder is like a knife twisting between my ribs, but I fight the urge to rub at my sternum and face my brother. "I mean…" My shoulder lifts in a half-assed shrug. "I did get pregnant way too young."

He chuckles dryly, finally gifting me with a glimpse of his eyes that match our father's. "Yeah, but you're you. Of course, you did shit backward. But you're *you*," he emphasizes. "I should know better than to assume you can't handle whatever's thrown at you. You've been doing it your whole life, Fin. Your epilepsy. Dealing with me as a brother." He smirks. "You're going to be a great mom."

A burn hits the back of my eyes, and I collapse onto the bed beside him, surprised by the waterworks and how much his words mean to me. I've always been closest to Everett. I mean, yeah. My half-sisters are awesome. But the age gap made Miley and Hazel feel more like aunts than actual siblings. But Ev? He's my ride or die. Always has been. And hearing something as simple as his confidence in my ability to be a good mom means more than he'll ever know. Especially right now. When it couldn't feel further from the truth.

Me? A mom? Let alone a good mom? The title feels so…unattainable. Like I've received a job offer not only way out of my league, but I didn't even apply for it in the first place.

"I like the vote of confidence, but I don't know about—"

"I do." With a reassuring smile, he wraps his arms around my shoulders and pulls me close. "You're going to be a great mom, Fin. Those are the first words that should've come out of my mouth, but they didn't, and that's on me. I'm sorry."

"You're more than forgiven," I murmur.

"Good." He lets me go. "And I'm gonna be a kickass uncle."

"You already are," I point out, reminding him of Miley's and Hazel's kids.

"Yeah, I know. But this kid?" He pauses. "This little kid is gonna be spoiled rotten." Leaning closer, he drops his voice lower. "And my favorite. I promise."

With a quiet laugh, I look down at my stomach. It's still the same. Part of me wishes it would look different. Like I swallowed a watermelon or something. That I could skip the pudgy stage and go straight to the *that girl's definitely pregnant* stage. Maybe it would make this feel more real. Less unknown. Instead, I'm caught in the between. The what ifs. The maybes.

Sobering, I admit, "It's scary."

"I know it is." He pauses. "I'm here for you."

"Thank you." I lift my gaze and smile. "Seriously."

"And, Fin?" he adds. "I'm happy for you and Griff. I know I've been a dick on that front, too, and I know you're not one to need my approval on shit, but you have it."

My smile widens, and I bump my shoulder against his. "Thanks, Ev."

"Did he, uh, did he mention potentially being traded to the Lions?" he prods.

I nod. "Maybe."

"And how do you feel about it?"

"I feel..." My brows bunch as I honestly consider his question. The idea of Griffin staying. The idea of us raising this baby together. Close to family and friends and doctors and school. "Honestly, if it works, I think it would be great."

"You two are solid?"

"Solid as we can be, considering the circumstances."

"Good." He gives me a hesitant smile. "He's a shoo-in."

Pressing my lips together, I study him carefully. The creases at the corner of eyes. The slight twitch of his jaw. "What about you?" I question. "Griff mentioned that you also reached out to Uncle Henry."

"He did, did he?"

"Mm-hmm."

"I'll be all right."

"That isn't an answer," I argue.

"You really think I'd put my career on the line for anything?"

He starts to stand, but I grab his wrist and hold him in place. "For the people you love? Yes. Yes, I do."

"My career is just fine, Fin."

Bullshit.

I'd laugh if he wasn't such a terrible liar. There are pros and cons to voicing what I've heard through the grapevine instead of keeping it close to the chest, but I don't bother weighing them. Why? Because there aren't enough pros in the world to potentially stand in the way of everything my brother's worked so hard for. Not when I've had front-row seats to every practice. Every early morning weight session. Every game. Not to mention being up close and personal when it comes to his relationship with Raine. Before they met, Ev was even more bullheaded, convinced that if he wasn't the one to carry his loved one's burdens, then he had no use in the world. Yet here he is, reverting back to his chivalrous—and very problematic—habit of being the martyr.

I won't let him.

Not even for me.

And so, before I can talk myself out of it, I blurt out, "Griff said you're gonna pull your name."

His jaw locks, but he doesn't look at me, proving me right. "Of course he did."

"You can't."

"Fin, I'll be fine."

"Let me clarify. I won't *let you* do that."

"You're not the boss—"

"Uh, first of all, I'm one hundred and ten percent the boss, but it's cute you don't think I am. Now, if you don't promise me—"

"It's too late."

My expression falls as my body tenses, and the familiar beat of my heart echoes in my ears. Too late? It can't be too late. He can't throw his future away all because of me. All because I'm pregnant, and Griffin lied, saying he's the father so he can stay close to me. To us.

"Ev—"

"I'm good, Fin," he interrupts. "Raine's good. I already talked to her, and—"

"No. No, you're not good, and Raine's not good, and I'm not good—"

"Fin—"

"Don't *Fin* me," I snip, losing my earlier sass and replacing it with full-blown bitch mode because this is ridiculous. He can't fall on a proverbial sword and sacrifice his future for me. It isn't fair to him or Raine or...anyone. With a huff, I argue, "Yes, I am having a baby, and yes, it would be more convenient if Griffin was here, and yes, I would love to keep my same doctors, but I'm a big girl, and I'm more than capable of handling this pregnancy no matter where Griffin plays next season, so don't you dare bend over backward under the guise of helping me when I'm the one who got into this mess in the first place, do you hear me?"

He smiles. It stretches slowly across his face and is almost genuine enough to cover the smallest hint of disappointment and resignation shining back at me. Almost.

"Love you, little sister."

"Did you already pull your name?" I demand.

"Fin."

"Did you already pull your name?" I repeat, elbowing him in the ribs. "Answer the question."

"Not yet, but—"

"No buts," I snap. "And no talking. Not until I'm finished."

His eye twitches, but he keeps his mouth shut.

"Good," I say. "Now, you know me, and you know I can

be a hell of a lot more stubborn than you if I need to, so listen up and listen closely. I am a big girl. And you are a big boy. You are going to let me handle my future like a grown-up, and I'm going let you handle your future like a grown-up. Independently of each other. Do you know what that means?" I don't wait for him to answer. I simply barrel forward. "It means you are not going to call Uncle Henry and pull your name. You're going to accept the fact that you and Griffin played incredibly well tonight, and you are going to accept the fact that either one of you would be an excellent fit for the Lions. You're also going to accept that, no matter the outcome, all parties will be excited for one another. And lastly, you are going to accept the fact that I do not need to be babied to be supported. You telling me you love me and offering to spoil my baby is all the support I want. Do you understand?"

His brows kick up as I finish my monologue. "Am I allowed to talk now?"

"Depends. Are you going to give me a hug and say you agree to my terms, or are you going to try and overstep your bounds like you usually do despite Raine's insistence that you really are getting better about the whole overprotective thing?"

Eyes narrowing, he scratches his jaw. "Does Griff really find this cute?"

With a cheeky grin, I toss my hair over my shoulder. "First of all, I'm adorable—"

"And a pain in the ass."

My grin grows. "Obviously. Now, stop trying to change the subject. Promise you won't pull your name."

"Fin." Rubbing at the corner of his eye, he sighs.

"Promise me," I push.

"I want you to be happy."

"Glad the feeling's mutual," I quip. "And I will be happy as long as you don't pull your name."

Another low sigh escapes him. "Fine."

"Fine...?"

"Fine, I won't pull my name," he grumbles.

"Promise?"

With a groan, he drops his head back and stares at the ceiling. "Yes. I promise."

My mouth splits into a grin. "Thank you."

"I'd say you owe me, but..."

"But I already saved you from making a huge mistake?" I offer. "Yeah. I know. I'm awesome. Now, give me a hug."

Wrapping his arms around me, he pulls me close, his muscles softening. "Love you, little sister."

"Love you, too, big brother."

CHAPTER FORTY-ONE

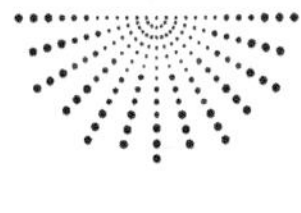

FINLEY

Vmmm. Vmmm.

My phone vibrates against my nightstand, and I shift toward it against my better judgment. I just got off my shift at Rowdy's, only to wind up craving a solid veg night instead of meeting up with everyone at SeaBird. Call me a baby, but the chaos from…everything is still fresh, and I don't have it in me to be social for once. My mom's name flashes across the screen on the nightstand. Squeezing my eyes shut, I bring it to my ear, answering the call.

"Yes?"

"Hello to you, too," my mom replies.

I sniff and shift my phone to my other ear. "Hi, Mom."

"Hey, baby."

Baby.

I almost choke on my scoff but stay quiet. It's a trick I learned from the woman herself. Sometimes, not blurting out whatever's on your mind is the quickest way to read the other person's. And I have a hunch I already know the reason for her call.

"So," she murmurs. "How are...*things*?"

"Sneaky," I note.

"Things are sneaky?"

"No, your innocent question is sneaky," I muse.

"Who says I'm trying to be sneaky?"

"Did Everett call you?" I push.

A short pause follows, and it doesn't take a genius to figure out I'm right.

"Maybe," she finally answers.

"And?"

"And this is my interrogation, missy," she quips. "How are things? How are you?"

"Not gonna ask about the baby?"

Her breath hitches. "You are my baby."

My bottom lip wobbles, so I suck it between my teeth and bite down. Hard.

"Sweetie, I'm so sorry—"

"Mom—"

"Let me finish," she says. "I'm so sorry you've had to carry this on your own."

I squeeze my eyes shut, and a tear slips down my cheek.

"I love you so much, Finley. Your dad loves you, too. We love you, and...and damn. This is quite the doozy."

With a pathetic laugh, I wipe the moisture from my cheeks. "Something like that."

"How are you feeling? Does the doctor know? How far along are you? Man, I could ask you a thousand questions." She takes a deep breath. "Okay, let me try this one more time."

I laugh again. "Okay, I'll start."

"I'm ready," she announces.

"Hello?" I offer.

"Hey, Fin. I miss you," my mom says.

"I miss you, too. I'm glad you called."

"Yeah?"

"Uh-huh." A lump lodges in my throat, but I swallow past it. "I, uh, I actually have some news."

"Oh?"

"Yeah, uh," I wipe beneath my nose with the sleeve of my shirt. "I'm, uh, I'm pregnant."

"You're pregnant? Oh, baby, I'm so excited for you!" she gushes. "Let me put you on speaker so you can tell your dad the amazing news, too."

My watery eyes look at the ceiling as another feeble laugh slips out of me.

"Fin?" my dad's voice crackles through the speaker. "Fin, you there?"

"Uh, yeah," I choke out. "Yeah, I'm here."

"Your mom says you have something you want to tell me?"

Digging my teeth into the inside of my cheek, I whisper, "You're gonna be a grandpa…again."

"Fuck, baby." His voice cracks, and just like that, my heart shreds into a million pieces. Because it isn't filled with disappointment. It's filled with awe. And pride. And love. So much fucking love I can feel it. "I'm so happy for you, Fin."

I close my eyes, soaking up his words and exactly how much I needed to hear them. This is why my parents are the best. The way they're so accepting and welcoming and nonjudgmental. I wipe beneath my nose with my forefinger, grateful I have them to look up to. To ask for parental advice and support. Griffin's right. I should've told them a long time ago.

"When's your due date?" my mom chimes in.

"I'm, uh, I'm about eight weeks."

"And how have you been feeling?" my dad prods.

"Normal," I answer honestly. "So normal, it's almost freaky."

"Not freaky. Amazing," my mom replies. "Honestly, I'm jealous. I was puking my guts out during the majority of my pregnancy with you."

"Yeah, if anything, I'm more hungry," I admit, sorting through the last few weeks for any other symptoms, no matter how abnormal they are from what I'd anticipated. "And I want Grandma Taylor's chocolate chip cookies."

Their laughter echoes through the speakers, and I catch myself smiling. I missed them. My mom and dad. And the fact that we're talking about my pregnancy like it's the most normal thing in the world is so damn refreshing I could cry. Hell, I *am* crying.

"Why is that funny?" I ask.

"Because it's the only thing your mom really craved with you and Everett when she was pregnant," my dad answers. "Must be in your blood."

"Must be," I murmur.

"Have you made your first appointment yet?" he prods.

"Not with the OB/GYN," I admit. "I should, but I'm procrastinating."

"Yeah, you should probably get on that," my dad teases. "Gotta make sure my grandbaby is growing big and strong."

"I will," I promise.

"That's my girl."

"How's the epilepsy side of things?" my mom continues. "Is that what triggered your episode around Christmas?"

Shifting onto my stomach, I bend my knees, cross my ankles in the air, and rest my chin on my folded arms. It's crazy. How much has happened. It's a whirlwind. Catching them up on everything feels...cathartic, but also...like it isn't enough. A recap of what happened when they should've been by my side throughout all of it. If only I hadn't pushed them away.

"Fin?" my mom prods. "You still here?"

"Yeah, I'm here, and, uh, it's actually when I found out. I saw the test results, kind of had a mental breakdown, and it's the last thing I remember."

"That must have been really scary," my mom murmurs.

"It was." Tears cling to my lashes, and I squeeze my eyes shut, blocking out the memory and all the changes since then. "Griffin was there, though, and…and he's been really sweet."

"Aw, baby," my mom gushes. "He's a good egg."

"He is," I agree.

"Have you talked to your doctor yet? Confirmed your epilepsy medication won't affect the baby or anything?"

I nod even though she can't see me. "Yeah, I think so. It's still early, so we're just…playing things by ear, I guess."

"Well, that's good," my dad interjects. "How's, uh, how's Griff handling things?"

I cover my eyes with my hands and bite back my amusement. "Are you asking if he's a little nervous to be tied to me for the rest of his life?"

"I'm just asking," he hedges.

"Yes, Griffin's handling everything…way better than any other guy in the world," I answer.

"Figured as much," my dad replies. "If he wasn't, Everett would put him in the ground."

"Which is a very healthy response, by the way," I quip.

"He loves you," my dad argues.

With a sigh, I admit, "I know he does. And it's a good thing I love him back because he's definitely thrown a wrench in my love life. Did you know he told Griffin to stay away from me when we were younger?"

"That surprises you?" My mom laughs. "The boy's been

overbearing and overprotective since before you could walk, Sweet Pea. You really think he was going to be okay with his best friend dating you? No offense, but we both know if push came to shove, your brother would pick you over anyone, and I mean anyone." She hesitates. "Okay, before Raine, he'd pick you over anyone else."

"Ouch," I say with a laugh.

"Don't worry. It's the beauty of true love. He'll never have to, but you get my point."

"I guess," I say, my voice tainted with disbelief. "Although, you didn't have to make it sting so much. My own flesh and blood choosing their girlfriend over someone as awesome as me? Rude."

"Whatever," my mom returns, not even the tiniest bit phased by my sarcasm. Bless her soul. "The good news is, Everett knows Griffin would never hurt you."

"And we know it, too. Although you could've told us," my dad chimes in.

"So, you're okay with it?" I prod. "Me dating your friends' son?"

"Honey, we've been rooting for you two for a very long time," my dad clarifies.

"Thanks," I murmur. "I, uh, I should get going, though."

"No worries," my dad replies. "We just called to catch up and say we love you."

"Love you, too," I answer.

"And congratulations!" my mom adds. "We're so excited it's not even funny."

With a smile, I sigh. "You have no idea how good it is to hear you say so. I'll talk to you later."

"Bye, babe!"

"See you."

As I hang up the call, a text appears.

GRIFFIN:

Not to sound creepy and shit, but I can
hear you through the wall.

Seriously?
"Tell me you're joking," I call.
My phone buzzes.

GRIFFIN

Not joking.

Another text follows right after.

GRIFFIN

We should've had the contractors check
the insulation because this is borderline
creepy.

"Borderline?" I ask aloud.

GRIFFIN

The good news is you'll never have to
masturbate alone again. Just say the word,
and I'll be there in the blink of an eye.

I laugh, take off my shirt, leaving me exposed in a hot pink, lacy bra, lift my phone, and snap a picture. After hitting send, I hold my breath, listening.

A muffled, "Fuck," echoes through the wall, followed by a door being slammed as I cover my amusement behind my hand. Seriously. It's like taking candy from a baby. Keeping my eyes glued to my bedroom door, I count to thirty, and sure enough, there he is. Griffin Thorne in all his masculine glory.

He doesn't wait for an invitation. Hell, the picture was probably invitation enough. He simply jumps onto the bed and climbs on top of me, hooking his fingers around my wrists and bringing them above my head until I'm sprawled beneath him.

"Glad they took the news well," he murmurs.

"Me, too."

"Glad they didn't suggest neutering me, either."

I grin up at him. "I mean, the news is still fresh, so…"

With a low laugh, he grinds into me. "And how would you come if I was neutered?"

"To be fair, I'm pretty sure you keep the dick and lose the balls when neutered, so…"

He rubs himself against me again, and I spread my legs wider, biting back my groan of appreciation. Seriously, though. How does this man make me so freaking weak, and we're both still fully clothed?

"So, as long as I have my cock, you won't complain?" he quips.

"Don't get me wrong. I do like your balls." I slip out of his hold on my wrists, slide my hand between us, and cup him softly through his joggers. "I also like your mouth and your fingers." My grip tightens, and his dick twitches in my hold, exactly like I guessed it would.

Eyes rolling back in his head, Griffin thrusts into my hand as he cages me in, resting his weight on his elbows. "Anything else you like, Fin?"

"I mean, you're kind of easy on the eyes, too." I lift my chin and nip at his lips. "I also like your determination. And your thoughtfulness. I like the way you hold me and how you're always thinking of others." My hand glides along his erection again before I let him go and wrap my arms around his neck. "But most of all, I like your heart, Griffin Thorne."

"Just like, huh?" Eyes crinkling, he dips closer, kisses my nose, moves onto his haunches, and reaches for my bottoms. I don't know how he does this. How he manages to turn me on and make me wet with barely a minute of foreplay. Maybe it's because I know what's in store. Maybe because I've had a bit of a shit day, and I know he can take care of me. Maybe because I spent so long telling myself no when it comes to all things Griffin, it's refreshing to not have to hide anymore. To be open and vulnerable and…ready. So ready to feel him inside me again.

Slowly, Griff pulls my pants down, and I lift my hips, helping him shimmy them off me until I'm left bare beneath him. As his eyes find my core, his mouth parts, and his gaze meets mine. "My heart likes you, too."

"Just like, huh?" I ask, tossing his own words back at him.

"You want the truth?" Shoving his joggers down, he reveals his rigid cock, and my mouth waters. With a slow nod of my head, I watch him fist his thick erection—once, twice, three times. Then, he lines up the head with my entrance. Usually, I'd tease the guy for not making sure I'm a ready and willing participant, but he knows me too well, and right now, I'm freaking dripping.

He must feel it, too, because his knuckle brushes against my slit for the briefest of seconds. The corner of his mouth quirks as he pushes inside of me, one inch after another, watching as his cock disappears into my heat. My heels dig into the mattress, and I lift my hips to meet him, anxious to feel the familiar burn and stretch. I love this part. The closeness. The rhythm. The way my breathing turns ragged, and his pistoning movements push me over the edge.

"Pretty sure you own this heart, Fin," he rasps.

"Pretty sure you can stop with the sappy stuff," I tease. "You're already getting laid, Griff." I wiggle beneath him, proving my point. "Now, are you gonna fuck me or what?"

His chuckle is low and raspy as he shakes his head back and forth. "Not gonna fuck you, Fin."

I close my eyes, savoring the way my body stretches around him while silently willing his body to start moving. "Then, what would you call this?"

"This is making love."

"Did you…" I gasp as he fully seats himself inside of me. "Did you just get super corny on me?"

"Telling you I'm making love to you is corny?"

"I mean…" His cock drags out of my channel, and he thrusts into me again. It isn't hard and fast. It's torturously slow, causing my lungs to bottom out with need and frustration and want. So much fucking want it's not even funny. Fisting the sheets, I peek up at him and point out, "Well, would you look at that. This is doing it for me. Apparently, corny and horny are a good mix."

He snorts. "Did you just rhyme?"

"I don't know, maybe? Corny. Horny. Thorney. Ha!" I smack his butt, urging him to keep his pace. "Come on, Thorney. Make me come, Thorney. You're such a peach, Thorney." I grin up at him. "Yup, I'm definitely a poet in the bedroom. Now, come on. Pick up the pace, boyfriend."

"I like it when you call me boyfriend."

"And I like it when you fuck me."

He stops moving. "Not fucking you, remember?"

"Feels like fucking," I muse. "Or at least, it would if you kept thrusting these hips, boyfriend." I grab his ass and squeeze, but the bastard doesn't budge.

"Say you love me back," he orders.

"I'm sorry, did I miss that part?" I bat my lashes up at him. "Because I'm pretty sure you didn't drop the L-word."

"I alluded to it."

"Alluded, huh? Sounds like a technicality to me."

"Not gonna say it?" he prods.

My eyes narrow. "Say what?"

His mouth twitches along with his cock, and I nearly choke on my moan.

"I see what you're trying to do here," I grit out.

"And what am I trying to do?"

"Trying to get me to admit it first. Very sneaky, Thorney."

With a scoff, he eases into me again, driving me insane. "Please tell me that nickname doesn't stick."

"Leaving me horny while being corny, Mister Thorney." I laugh. "I mean, the poem practically writes itself."

Leaning closer, he drags his teeth against my throat, then laps at the small scrape. "Pretty sure I should find poetry while my cock's buried inside you a turn-off."

"Yet here you are,"—I skate my fingernails beneath his gray T-shirt up and along his spine—"stalling because you don't want to be a two-pump chump, am I right?"

Lifting his head, he quirks his brow. "Are you rhyming again?"

I grin. "Maybe."

He grips my thigh and tugs it higher around his waist. With a hard push of his hips, he thrusts deeper into me until I'm pretty sure I can feel his cock in my eyeballs.

"Ooookay, sir." My jaw drops at the intrusion, and he rocks his hips, pressing his pubic bone against my clit. "Yup. That'll do."

His mouth finds my neck again, and he sucks softly. "I love you, too."

My eyes fall back in my head as I try to focus on our conversation instead of the fact that I'm pretty sure he's never been deeper. "I didn't say it."

"Yeah, but we both know you're thinking it." He lifts his head and kisses me, thrusting his tongue into my mouth while I suck at it greedily. When he pulls away, I groan in frustration, and he adds, "Who else would appreciate this smart mouth?"

My face scrunches. Because first of all, he most definitely appreciates my smart mouth. When it's on his cock, or when I use it to get myself into trouble. Like right now. Because boy, am I in trouble when it comes to my feelings for this man. And it's funny, because he has no idea. How many times I would say something snarky or sarcastic or just plain old ludicrous, and Drew would only return it with a look that made me feel...stupid. And I never let it get to me. I'd simply shrug it off, assuming it's a normal reaction. But with Griff? It's different. It's always been different, and I always wrote those differences off, telling myself it's because he's known me longer. Of course, he understands my sense of humor, but now? Now, I see it for what it really is. Yes, he's known me my entire life, but he doesn't just get my sense of humor. He gets me. All of me. My quirks. My perception of things. My sense of humor. My beliefs. And he doesn't simply understand it. He accepts it. He values it. He values me.

Lips bunching on one side, I stare up at him, slipping my hands out from beneath his shirt and skating my fingers across his five o'clock shadow as he slowly pumps into me.

"Say it again," I whisper.

"I love you, too, Fin."

Too.

Smartass.

"Hey, Griff?" I murmur.

"Yeah?"

I tighten my grip on his jaw and tug him into me. "I love you."

"I know you do."

Kissing him, I pull him into me even more. Until we're

chest to chest. Skin to skin. Heart to heart. And it's never felt more real or genuine. This moment. This connection. I've never had it with anyone else, and I refuse to ever take it for granted again.

He's right. This isn't fucking. This is making love, and until this moment, I never knew the difference. The bed squeaks as we move together on the mattress, and within minutes, I can feel the familiar buzz beneath my skin. The tremors of my core. The unsteady breaths echoing off the walls. We're close. Both of us. Our pace quickens as he brands my mouth in a punishing kiss, digging his fingers into my waist as he pushes me higher and higher.

My back arches as I fall apart beneath him, letting him use my body any fucking way he wants until the familiar twitch of his cock and tightness of his muscles proves he's coming, too. Seconds later, he collapses on top of me, careful not to squish me entirely as he catches his breath against the nape of my neck.

"So fucking much."

"Hmm?" I ask with a laugh.

"I love you so fucking much," he clarifies.

My smile stretches, and I close my eyes. "So fucking much, Griff."

CHAPTER FORTY-TWO

GRIFFIN

I haven't heard from Uncle Henry yet. Neither has Everett. It's been a little while since the Lions' GM watched us play, but all we've had is radio silence. We've tried to play it off. Like neither of us is thinking about shit when it couldn't be further from the truth. We won the last two away games. Both of us played like our lives depended on it. And in a way, maybe they do. Our futures. Our goals. Our girls. They all hang in the balance.

We've been gone the past two days, traveling for hockey, and the distance has only solidified my resolve to stay in Lockwood Heights. We've talked. Texted. But nothing compares to holding my girl in my arms, and damn, I've missed her.

After yesterday's win, Reeves suggested we go to SeaBird and celebrate with everyone. I texted Fin to get her opinion, and she said she was fine with it as long as she could go in sweats since real clothes make her feel like the Pillsbury Doughboy.

Her words, not mine.

Leaning against the doorjamb, I watch her apply lip gloss in the mirror. We got home a couple hours ago, each of us separating and promising to meet at SeaBird at eight, though now that I'm here, the idea of leaving when I could spend the night in with Finley grows less and less appealing with each passing second.

As she leans close to her reflection, her ass pops back, and I swear the girl's doing it on purpose. Driving me nuts. Making me want to grab her waist and grind against her just because I can. Just because she's mine. Just because she's stolen one of my sweaters, and it hangs off her shoulder, giving me a glimpse of her creamy skin. If our friends weren't waiting for us, I'd do it. I'd take her. Right here. Right now.

"Like what you see?" she quips, well aware I'm practically salivating at the view in front of me. However, the hot pink sweats I'd expected when she announced that denim is officially dead to her have been replaced with a pair of gray joggers. They look eerily familiar.

As I scan her up and down, I ask, "Are those mine?"

She peeks over her shoulder, grins, and slides the cap on her lip gloss. "Maybe."

"Did I say you could steal my clothes?"

"It's adorable how you think I need to ask permission." Her hips sway as she moves toward me, locking her arms around my neck. "PS, can I tell you how bummed I am that I didn't get to see you kick ass against the Rangers last night? I heard you were amazing."

Part of me wants to ask if she honestly thinks I didn't notice the not-so-thinly-veiled subject change or how she has no issue stealing my shit. The other part? Well, I find her arrogance hot as fuck, and I think we both know it.

Giving in, I kiss the tip of her nose and loop my arms

around her waist. "It was a good game. And you can watch me kick ass against the Rangers the next time they're at LAU."

"Always. You know I refuse to miss any home games, so you're kind of stuck with me." She pats my chest. "Sorry, big boy. Besides, who else is going to cheer you on and keep the puck bunnies from encroaching on my territory?"

"You don't need to worry about puck bunnies."

"I know I don't. Although, I do like bragging that you're mine."

My grin grows. "Is that why you ordered an LAU jersey with my name?"

"Mm-hmm."

"I think I like my name on you."

"I thought you might."

"It matches Dylan's," I add, mentioning the jersey Reeves asked Fin to make when the puck bunnies were giving Reeves a little too much attention for her liking. Now, the girl is almost never seen without it at the games. Pretty sure it's the highlight for Reeves each and every time we hit the ice. Now that I've seen Finley wearing one with my name, I get it.

When I caught Fin in it the first time, I had to resist the urge to storm up to her seat and kiss the shit out of her in front of everyone. Somehow, I managed to keep the urge in check, though I did ask Dreggs if he liked my girl's new jersey. Thankfully, the asshole only laughed it off, telling me I was a lucky guy. And fuck, if it isn't the truth.

Finley's eyes dance with mirth as she toys with the hair on the back of my neck, causing goosebumps to break out along my spine. "I got the same guy to make this one for me. Now, Dylan and I are twins. Well, except hers says Oliver, and mine says Thorne, but you get it."

"Yeah, I get it." I laugh, leaning closer and planting another kiss against the tip of her nose. "What do you say we stay in tonight instead of meeting everyone at SeaBird?"

"You sure you don't want to celebrate?" she questions.

"I can think of other ways we can celebrate," I offer.

The corner of her mouth lifts. "Oh, really?"

My hands find her waist, and I sway us back and forth. "Maybe."

"Again with the no music," she teases.

"Just wait 'til I have you moaning." I nip at her plump lips, the taste of strawberry teasing me, when a loud knock echoes from the front door. With a frown, I guide us into the hallway and glance toward the front of the house.

My stomach bottoms out.

Through the window framing the front door, I see the one and fucking only Drew standing on the doorstep, holding a bouquet of red fucking roses.

What the hell is he doing here?

Finley peeks around me, her eyes bulging. "What the hell is he doing here?"

"Excellent question." I stride toward the front. "I'll find out."

"Wait." Reaching for my arm, Finley pulls me to a stop. Her fingers drag across my lower back as she steps past me, heading for the door.

"Fin," I warn.

"Give me two minutes."

She reaches for the door handle, and I watch helplessly from behind her. There are moments. Moments that feel like a lifetime. Moments where you can feel yourself at a crossroads. Hell, you can see it. The inevitable fork, giving you two paths forward. And this? This one feels like it might lead to a cliff, and it's up to Finley to choose whether we go down it or not.

I've felt helpless before. More times than I can count. But right now? Right now, I've never felt more helpless in my life, and there's nothing in the world I can do to stop it.

CHAPTER FORTY-THREE

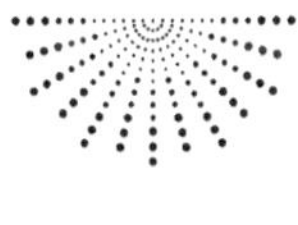

FINLEY

My jaw feels unhinged. Like it might literally tumble to the ground, and my ability to speak will be gone forever. But seriously. What. The. Hell?

I haven't heard from this man since he told me to have an abortion. Now, here he is on my front fucking porch?

Hands shaking, I reach for the handle and twist it, opening the door. Yup. I definitely wasn't hallucinating. Drew, in all his preppy freaking glory, is on my doorstep with a dozen red roses. Like he wants to apologize. Like he has any right to apologize. Like he has any potential chance to be with me again.

Honestly, if I wasn't so shocked, I'd find the entire thing laughable. Instead, I can't convince my vocal cords to work properly. I feel like a fish out of water. Like my tongue is ten times its usual size, and my eyes might pop out of my head if I stare too long at the mess in front of me.

"W-what are you doing here?" I whisper.

"I came to…" Drew squeezes the back of his neck. "Talk."

"Talk." A crazed laugh bubbles out of me. Yeah, I'm not surprised anymore. I'm freaking pissed. Like seriously. Is this real life right now? "I'm sorry, I must've misheard you. Did you say you want to *talk?*"

"Finley, I—"

"You don't get to talk," I decide. Propping my hand on my hip, I glare at the last person I'd ever want on my front porch. "Yeah. I like that. You don't get to talk. Sorry."

Drew pulls back. "Excuse me?"

"I said you don't get to talk. Not after I drove across the country and found you cuddled up next to Mollie—"

"I never touched—"

"It doesn't matter!" I screech. "That's the crazy part about all of this. It doesn't. It literally doesn't matter. I don't care what you do. I don't love you. You don't love me. We're over."

"Finley, you're pregnant—"

"Am I?" I spit. "You told me to get rid of it, remember?" I march over the threshold, moving closer to him. "Who says I didn't?"

He pales. "Did you?"

"It. Doesn't. Matter." I jab my finger into his chest. "Get off my porch. *Now.*"

"Finley," he pleads.

"You know what's funny?" I ask. "This?" I wave my hand at him. "This used to do it for me. The way you said my name. The designer clothes. The way you were so driven and so obsessed with your future that you somehow convinced me it would be mine, too, and I felt lucky." I laugh. "I felt lucky to be part of it. Until you decided that not only was our baby not a good enough reason to shift said future, but you also decided you didn't want a future with me, period."

"*I* decided?" he scoffs. "Since when did you let me decide anything, Finley? You're bossy and controlling and—"

"I don't need to have this conversation with you." I turn on my heel and head inside my house, rage licking though my veins as I come to terms with the fact that this asshole had the audacity to knock on my door after everything we've been through. Gripping the edge of the door, I start to slam it when Drew slaps his hand against the solid piece of wood, stopping me.

"See, that's where you're wrong," he murmurs. "Because whether or not we're together anymore, the kid is mine."

"You don't want him," I remind him.

"It doesn't matter what I want. He's my responsibility. I can't just…"

"Walk away?" I finish for him. "No, I think you can. Actually, I think you're pretty good at it, so really, it shouldn't be too much of a problem for you. Just turn around. Get back in your rental car. And leave me alone. See? Simple. Now, if you'll excuse me—"

"What happens when he asks about me? When he wants to know who I am or if I hate broccoli as much as he does? Huh? What then?"

My chest aches, and my eyes well with tears as his words wash over me, painting a picture so fucking heart-breaking I could crumble right here. Right now. Because I can't lie to myself. I've thought about it. What he or she will look like. If people will notice the differences. If they'll question Griffin's involvement in the baby-making process. If my baby will question whether or not Griffin's their father. The last thought makes me sick to my stomach. Makes me want to double over and retch all over the icy concrete. I'd give anything to make it real. To gift my baby Griffin's genes, keeping them as far away from Drew as possible. But that's the problem. It's too late. All of this is.

"Finley, I'm here because I want another chance with you," Drew continues. "I'm here because I handled everything so fuckin' badly the first time. I'm here because I want the family we dreamed about. You. Me. And the baby. And I know the timeline doesn't fit what we'd planned, and I know I should've responded differently, but I'm here now. I'm here, and I'm not going anywhere."

He pulls a little black box out and falls to one knee, making my eyes bug out of my head as he opens it. Inside is a round, glittering diamond on a thin silver band.

It's beautiful. It is. And it makes my heart break even more.

The floor creaks behind me, and I turn around, finding Griffin's broken gaze pinning me in place. Tearing his attention from me, he stares at the ground like he wants to bolt. Like he wants to respect me and my conversation with Drew. Like he knows he was just caught eavesdropping.

Instead of leaving like I expect, he steps through the thin gap between me and the door, his muscles rigid as he approaches Drew on the porch.

"Get off your fuckin' knee," he growls.

"Griffin, wait," I murmur.

"This guy doesn't deserve you, Fin."

Drew scoffs. "Stay in your own fuckin' lane, asshole."

"Drew," I seethe. "If you want to hear my answer, I highly suggest you shut your freaking mouth."

Teeth grinding, he digs his fingers into the black box in his hand but stays quiet.

Satisfied, I turn back to Griffin. "Give me thirty seconds, okay? Trust me."

His frigid gaze shifts to me, and he cocks his head, waiting. I wonder if he's caught between respecting me and my decisions and throwing me over his shoulder, claiming me for his own.

It's kind of adorable, I'm not going to lie. If my ex wasn't three feet away from me, I'd throw my arms around Griffin's neck and kiss him until next Tuesday, promising I'm his and only his. But, alas.

Moving closer to Drew, I crouch down beside him and close the little black velvet box in his hand. "You and I are over, Drew. We were over long before I found out I was pregnant, so you can let go of whatever guilt convinced you to buy a ring, get on a plane, and come to my house after the way we left things. I'm not holding a grudge, and I sure as hell don't need you to propose out of guilt, especially since I now know what an actual loving relationship feels like, so can you please just...leave?"

"And the baby?" he demands.

"She'll send you a postcard," Griffin answers from behind me.

Tossing him a smirk over my shoulder, I give Drew my full attention. "We'll get there when we get there. *If* you're even still interested in being part of their life once I actually give birth. But for now? There's no use dragging shit out and playing the happy family when, if we're being honest, it's the last thing either of us wants. So, tell me the truth. Why are you really here?"

It's a gamble. A painful and potentially humbling gamble. Making an assumption like this. Acknowledging that he doesn't want me or the baby. Not really. Even if he is here. Even if he is down on one knee, begging me to take him back. He doesn't want this. There's no way he wants this. I can't erase the memory of the look I saw in his eyes when I told him about the baby. The contempt. The anger.

There's no way all of those emotions would disappear. So, what is it? Why is he here?

"Answer me," I push. "Why are you here, Drew?"

He closes his eyes, proving I'm more spot-on than either of us really wants me to be. "You want the truth?"

"I think I deserve it, don't you?"

His Adam's apple bobs. "I-if my parents find out I abandoned a kid, they'll cut me off."

"Cut you off?"

"You know how religious they are. If they found out I got you pregnant and didn't marry you, they'd kill me. My schooling? My allowance? It would all be gone, Fin, and you know how much pressure they put on me, let alone if anyone finds out about…everything. I can't live with myself. I can't live with them. They'd never forgive me. Never give me another chance. I'd be fucked, Fin. You know I would be."

With a slow nod, I suck my lips between my teeth.

I should've known greed would be the culprit. Greed and shame. Like those are honorable reasons for buying a ring and stepping up as a father. I can't decide if I'm hurt or relieved. Both, I guess. Neither one changes the situation, though. Or the outcome.

Squeezing his bicep, I murmur, "I have good news, Drew."

"What is it?" he pleads.

"You can walk away without feeling guilty. I don't want to ruin your future any more than you want me to. I'm not going to come after you. I'm not going to tell your parents. Besides, everyone thinks the baby is Griffin's, anyway."

He frowns, his attention sliding to someone behind me. "Not everyone."

Curious, I follow his gaze and look behind me. Griffin is on the doorstep with his hands tucked in his pockets.

And behind him, at the base of the stairs, is my brother, his face twisted with rage.

"Why the fuck is Drew here?" Everett demands.

My muscles seize, and the blood drains from Griffin's face as he turns around to face my brother.

Shit.

CHAPTER FORTY-FOUR

GRIFFIN

There are moments like this, too. When you know you've fucked up. When you know you've been caught red-handed, and the reasoning behind your decisions doesn't matter anymore. Only the fallout.

"Everett," I start.

My best friend moves closer. His steps are slow and calculated, too deliberate to be natural. "Why. The fuck. Is Drew here?" Leaving barely an inch of space between us, he glares at me, though I doubt he wants an answer. He already knows. Hell, Finley just laid it out for him to hear.

I'm not the father. Even though everyone thinks I am. Or at least, they *did.*

"Drew," Finley's voice echoes behind us. "I need you to leave. Now."

"Nah, stay," Everett orders. His attention flicks over my shoulder toward the porch. "Good to see you again, fuck face."

Hands raised in surrender, Drew stumbles out, "L-look, I don't want any trouble, all right?"

"Seems like it's a little late for that," Everett points out. He moves past me. "Did you knock my sister up?"

Ignoring her brother, Finley seethes, "Drew. Get off my porch. Now."

"Nah, stay a sec," Ev interrupts. "I think you and I need to have a quick...chat."

Turning on my heel, I face the shitshow as my adrenaline pulses through my veins like I've pounded a dozen energy drinks.

"If you want to have a chat with anyone, I'm pretty sure it's me," Finley argues. "And if you'll let me explain..."

"Let me get this straight." Scratching his temple with his forefinger, Everett cocks his head. "Griff isn't the father. You are."

"Exactly." The asshole fucking beams like he won the lottery or some shit. And maybe he did. Because while he was burying his head in the sand, I was busy painting a target on my back, and I'm not sure there's anything I can do to erase it. Not after everything I've done. Everything I've lied about. Everyone I've lied to.

"Ev," I start.

Without facing me, Everett lifts his index finger, urging me to give him a second as he continues his interrogation. "You cheat on her, too?"

The blood drains from Drew's face. "Wait, I didn't—"

"You tell her to get rid of the baby?" Everett prods.

"Ev," Finley pleads.

"Answer the question," Everett pushes.

"I, uh..."

"That's all I need to hear." Glancing at me, Everett asks, "You gonna do the honors, or do I need to?" Surprise flashes through me, and Everett must see it because he drops his voice lower, his eyes shining with defeat. "We'll deal with our shit later."

I give him a nod, then face Drew. My need to avenge Fin for all the shit he said to her the last time they spoke drowns out the familiar guilt of betrayal as it pulses through me. He really is a sniveling little bitch. He's here because he's scared of his parents? What an asshole. Fisting my hand at my side, I growl, "If I see you on this porch again without an explicit invitation, I'll beat the shit out of you. We clear?"

"Y-you're not the boss of—"

A bone-crunching sound echoes on the porch as I deck Drew in the nose and watch the blood pour onto his pressed button-up shirt. "Get off Finley's property. Now."

As he stumbles away, I unclench my fist and stretch my fingers wide. The familiar ache of my bruised knuckles spreads across the back of my hand. It's a good hurt. A deliberate hurt. And if I'm feeling it, so is Drew. Good. If only it would distract me from my best friend's pissed-off presence.

Tires squeal seconds later, and I force my body around, facing Everett and the love of my life.

Finley's pale. Her bottom lip trembling. Because this is the moment. The one we've dreaded. The one we both hoped would never arrive, yet here it is. Glaring down at us. The truth is exposed for everyone to see. And to judge. And to fucking twist until there's nothing left.

"Ev," Finley begs.

Ignoring her, Everett demands, "Now we'll deal with our shit. Why'd you lie?"

It's the crux of everything, isn't it? Why did I lie? Even now, I wish I had a better answer. One he would understand. One he would empathize with. But he's my best friend, and I fucked up. It's as plain and simple as that.

"All I want. All I have ever wanted," I clarify, "is for Finley to be happy and safe and healthy, same as you."

"Then why'd you lie?" he repeats.

It's a good question. One I've asked myself a hundred times. The problem is, I'm not sure there's anything I can say to justify it. I lied. To everyone. My best friend. My family. Uncle Henry. I screwed up.

As I stand motionless, Finley reaches for me, lacing our fingers together while putting on a strong front. A strong front both of us desperately need if we want to get through this.

"Start. Talking," Everett grits out.

With a sigh, I tear my focus from our interlocked hands and hold my best friend's glare. "I thought the only way I could see Fin happy and safe and healthy is to be close to her family and her doctor."

"Still doesn't answer the question," he points out. "Because technically, my sister can be happy and safe and healthy and be close to her family and her doctor"—he moves closer, his chest heaving—"with or without you. So, why did you lie?"

"Back the hell up, Everett," Finley snaps. Placing herself between us, she jabs at his chest. "You have no idea what you're talking about, do you hear me?"

"Fin." I tug on our laced fingers, pulling her back from going head-to-head with Everett. When she looks over her shoulder at me, her eyes blazing with fury, I murmur, "I gave you a minute to clean shit up with Drew. Mind if you give me a minute with Ev?"

Lips pressed together, she keeps her eyes locked on mine, then turns to her older brother. "You hit him, I kick you in the balls. We clear?"

His hands stay fisted at his sides.

"I mean it," she pushes. "I'm not afraid to check your knuckles after all this is said and done, so don't test me."

Squeezing Finley's fingers, I say, "Go, Fin. I'll meet you in your room."

"You have five minutes." She brings my fingers to her lips, kisses the knuckles, then lets me go and disappears down the hall, leaving me alone with my best friend turned enemy if I didn't know any better.

With another sigh, I walk toward the couches in the family room, wipe my hands on my jeans, and collapse onto one of the cushions. "Take a seat, Ev."

"Why should I?"

"Because whether or not we're able to salvage our friendship, I'm gonna be your brother-in-law one day, so we might as well sort our shit out."

Grudgingly, he strides toward the opposite sofa and sits down but doesn't say a single fucking word.

"I'm in love with your sister," I announce. "I know it's no excuse, but I am. And honestly, in a fucked-up kind of way, all of this should make you happy."

He scoffs. "Bullshit."

"I'm serious," I push. "If you take anything away from this fucked-up situation, it's the knowledge that I'd sacrifice anything for her. Including my career. My reputation. And you." I look up from my bruised knuckles. "My best friend. My *brother*. That's how much I love Finley. How willingly I'd do anything to keep her safe and to make her happy. It's all you ever wanted for her, right? To find someone who would do anything—be anything—for her, and I promise you, I will."

"I'm not arguing with you on that front. I'm pissed because you lied to me."

"Did I?" I question.

Another scoff escapes him. "Seriously, man? That's the bullshit stance you're gonna take?"

"If we're going by hard facts, you're right. Biologically,

I'm not the father. But in every way that matters, I will be this baby's dad. Every. Fucking. Way."

"I don't doubt it, but—"

"Look at my mom, man," I growl. "Look at the way she raised Jax. Yeah, Jax's birth mom is still in the picture, but my mom has claimed him since day one. He might not be hers by blood, but she is every bit his mom as she is mine, and we both know she would burn the world to the ground if anyone tried to keep him from her. She'd also fucking neuter you or anyone else," I clarify with a pointed look, "if she ever heard someone try to tell her she isn't Jaxon's mom or the blood running through his veins holds any kind of weight to the love she has for him. You know it, and I know it, so get off your high horse."

His molars grind, but he stays quiet, knowing I'm right. We were raised together. Everett. Me. My older brother, Jax. He saw the way my mom treated us. Treated all of her kids. Like we were equals. And fuck, if it isn't the truth.

"Finley's baby is mine," I continue. "It doesn't matter whose name is put on the birth certificate. Doesn't matter whether or not Drew is in the picture. I love every piece of Finley, including the pieces she's passing on to her unborn child. So you can be pissed at me all you want, but nothing, and I mean nothing, is going to change my stance on this." I hesitate and lean back on the cushions, spreading my legs wide as I stare at my best friend.

"You're missing the point," he mutters. "I get how much you care about her, Griff. And I can even get behind you wanting to raise the kid like your own. But you lied. To me." He punctuates his words with a sharp shake of his head. "And you can say whatever you want about your reasoning, but if you'd told me the truth, if you'd told everyone the truth, you would've still had our support. *That's* why I'm pissed. Why I can't even look at you.

Because if we were as close as I thought we were, you would've told me. And you sure as shit would've told Uncle Henry. Now? Now, I feel like I don't even fucking know you, and after the way you lied to me, I feel like you don't know me, either."

"You're right," I mutter. "I fucked up. I didn't trust you enough to tell you everything, and I should've."

"Yeah, apparently, it's a theme lately," he offers dryly.

"Apparently." A low laugh escapes me. "I'll work on it."

"Good." He hesitates. "And I'll work on not losing my shit when things don't go according to plan." Scratching along his jaw, he adds, "Doesn't help I just got off the phone with Uncle Henry when I overheard shit going down on the front porch." He drops his hand to his lap.

"What'd he say?"

"That he's working on shit, but he's not a miracle worker."

"I'll tell him the truth," I rush out.

"You will," he agrees. "But only because Uncle Henry deserves to know."

"Maybe he'll—"

Everett shakes his head. "The position's gonna go to the right guy, Griff. The Lions need you. My sister needs you. The baby needs you." Standing, he walks toward me and offers his hand. When I take it, he pulls me to my feet. "Raine and I are excited for our future, wherever it takes us. Promise." His mouth lifts. "I even got her a gift for our new place once we move."

"What's that?"

"Drake, uh, he destroyed one of her drawings when they were still together. I pieced it together and had it framed." His mouth lifts. "We're gonna be fine, man."

"You sure?"

With a soft thud, his hand lands on my shoulder.

"You're not the only one who would sacrifice anything for their girl. We'll be good. Promise."

I nod. "Thanks, Ev. For everything."

"You're my brother, man." Tugging me into a hug, he slaps his hand against my upper back before letting me go. "Now, go check on my sister and show her I didn't beat the shit out of you, all right? I don't feel like having my balls kicked in tonight."

With a laugh, I shake my head. "See you later."

"See ya, man."

GRIFFIN

"Congrats, man." Jax hands me a cup of coffee and motions to one of the nearby oak tables. The Bean Scene is a coffee shop near campus. It's been here forever. Rough brick exterior. Heavy glass doors. Metal chairs with polished oak counters and tables spaced far enough apart to offer a little privacy. Their coffee is always good, and the girls are obsessed with their pumpkin spice lattes in the fall, but I'm sticking with a plain black coffee today.

After my big brother found out about the baby a little while ago, he reached out, offering to buy me coffee, but thanks to both of our busy schedules, this is the first time I've been able to take him up on it.

"Thanks." I start to take a sip of my drink but nearly burn my tongue off, pulling a dry chuckle from Jax as he watches me. Sometimes I forget he's only my half-brother. He looks so much like our father, it's hard to place any of his mom's traits at all. Dark, wavy hair. Green eyes. He's built like him, too. Broad shoulders. Tall. Hell, I feel like

I'm looking at a younger version of my dad, and I'm about to get a lecture.

"Seems we have a lot to catch up on," he adds with a grin. "Apparently, you take after...*Mom?*"

Should've known he wouldn't want to beat around the bush.

"You heard about that, huh?" I grumble, unable to look him in the eye. I should. He's my big brother. The rock in the family despite all our best efforts to follow his path. But maybe that's the problem. The reminder that his shoes are impossible to fill. Both on and off the ice. Jax is a legend. Hell, he's a god. Never makes mistakes. Never fucks up.

As we take a seat across from each other at the empty table, Jax adds, "Really wish my brother would've told me about it."

"I know I should've told you. I'm sorry."

"It's all good." He leans back in his chair and spreads his legs beneath the table. "How are you handling it? Taking on the role?"

"It's easier than I would've thought," I admit. "Sometimes, I even forget that I'm not..."

I can't finish it. The sentence. Because it doesn't feel accurate. I'm not the father? Bullshit. It feels like a cop-out when I'm so wholly invested in being in Finley's baby's life. However, clarifying their blood relation to me is a waste of breath but a necessary one, and if that isn't a contradiction, I don't know what is.

"Fin's lucky to have you," Jaxon replies. "And so is the baby."

"Thanks." I hesitate. "Can I ask you something?"

"Yeah, whatever you need."

Wiping my palms on my jeans, I shift forward and rest

my elbows on the table's cool surface. I've wanted to ask this question a hundred times, but I've always stopped myself, afraid the answer might break me or throw another curveball at my plans, and I'm not sure if I can handle another one. Not anytime soon. "Was it…weird?" I ask. "Your relationship with Mom?"

"Weird?"

"You know, having two moms while the rest of your siblings only had one."

Jaxon's mom, Eleanor, is a great woman, but she was always very deliberate with relationships. Part of me thinks she was afraid that if she extended too much of an olive branch to me and Dylan, she'd be stepping on my mom's toes or something, but it's only a theory. It's not like we ever went to her house with Jax when we were little or anything. She'd bring us Christmas presents, and slurpees on our birthdays. But other than that? Nothing but a polite hello whenever she'd pick up or drop off Jax, depending on what week it was. Then, when Jax hit middle school, Eleanor remarried. Her husband received a promotion, requiring them to move to London, and Jax chose to stay with our dad instead of going with his birth mom. He said it was because he wanted to continue playing hockey and follow in our dad's footsteps, but I like to think it's because of me and Dylan. I'm not sure what I would've done if my big brother had left us behind.

"Yes and no," Jax returns. "Sometimes, I felt like I was split in two. Like, I had two different lives, and in a way, I guess I did. Two bedrooms. Two families. Two curfews. Two sets of rules." He pauses, his eyes growing hazy as if he's assessing his childhood in search of answers. Blinking, he focuses on me again and takes a swig of his coffee. "But they did the best they could, you know? Mom, Dad, *my* mom. They did their best and…life wasn't perfect, but it was enough. More than enough. It'll be different with you, though," he adds.

"How so?"

He shrugs. "From what I hear, the dad wants nothing to do with Fin or the baby. Is that true?"

"For now, yeah."

"That's good, I think," he decides. "If he changes his mind, you can come up with a new game plan, but for now, I think you're handling everything exactly how you should."

"You think?" I grasp my cup and let the heat seep into my palms. "Sometimes, the idea of screwing up and shit… it's a lot of pressure."

"Take it from someone who had the most amazing bonus parent on the planet. Showing up is enough. And you, man? You've never had a problem showing up."

He's right. About my mom. She's always there. Always a phone call or a short drive away. Then again, so is my dad. They're the best people I know. And if I've learned anything from them, it's that their example has made me the man I am today. And maybe, just maybe, I'll be enough to fill the dad role and claim the title, even when I haven't earned it yet.

"Thanks." My lungs expand on a deep breath, grounding me. "I needed this conversation."

"Figured you might." He smirks. "Not gonna lie, though. I always figured I'd be the first to be a dad."

"Yeah, my money was on you, too," I joke. "Funny how life has way of…fucking us up while working itself out in the process."

"You could say that." The steam swirls in the air as he takes another sip of his drink. "And sometimes, it only fucks us up."

The bell on the entrance jingles, announcing an

incoming customer, and the blood drains from his face as his attention catches on someone behind me.

Curious, I turn around and find a guy in a navy blue suit and white dress shirt ordering a coffee at the register. It's Uncle Henry. "Shit."

Tearing his attention from our uncle, Jax turns to me and cocks his head. "*Shit?* You, too?"

"*Too?*" I ask. "Since when are you avoiding Uncle Henry? Forget to pay rent or something?" Jaxon moved into our Uncle Henry's penthouse by campus last summer, but they've always been close. The idea of Jax avoiding him makes less than zero sense. Then again, so does me lying to all of my friends and family, so it's not like I have any room to talk.

"Not exactly." Tugging at the collar of his T-shirt, Jax sinks a little lower in his chair. "He's been hounding me about Squeaks ever since…"

"Since she tried to kiss you, and you rejected her 'cause she's a *kid*?" I finish for him.

His head falls forward in defeat. "Something like that. What about you? Why are you avoiding him?"

"Not sure if he's heard through the grapevine about the baby's birth father yet," I mutter.

Jaxon arches his brow. "So?"

"So, I may have bent the truth when I asked to be traded to the Lions so I could stay close to Fin."

His eyes bulge. "No shit?"

"Yeah," I mutter.

"*Fuck.*" He throws his head back and laughs. "You're in even deeper shit than I am." His attention shifts back to Henry and his smile falls. "He's coming over."

I gulp and sit a little straighter, shame burning through my insides. I've been dreading this since before I lied in his office, knowing it would catch up with me, but too selfish and short-sighted to rectify it. Especially now.

"Hello, boys," Uncle Henry greets us.

Craning my neck, I look over at him and fake a smile. "Oh. Hey, Uncle Henry."

"Hello," he repeats.

I search his face for something. A hint. A clue. A fucking lifeline. But just like always, his expression is on lockdown. I shouldn't expect anything less, but damn if he couldn't have thrown me a bone for once. It's not like I'm some stranger he's doing a business deal with. I'm family. But so is he. And I lied to him.

"You good?" he challenges. "You look like you've seen a ghost."

"Uh, yeah," I clear my throat. "Yeah, I'm good. I've been meaning to call—"

"Mind if I take a seat?" The chair scrapes against the polished concrete floor as he drags it away from the table without waiting for an answer.

"Yeah, you know you're always welcome," Jaxon interjects. "What are you doing on campus?"

"I had a meeting," Uncle Henry answers before he turns to me, pinning me with the same stone-cold expression. His mouth twitches. "You're lucky you're family, Griffin. Watching you squirm is entertaining, but I'll put you out of your misery. Your dad caught me up on everything. Would've appreciated it if you'd done it yourself, but I understand why you..." He hesitates, lifting his coffee to his mouth and swallowing. "Bent the truth."

With a quiet laugh, Jaxon looks down at his beverage. *Asshole.*

"I know I should've been up front about the situation when I asked for the trade, and I'm sorry. Genuinely. I fucked—screwed up."

Stealing another sip of his drink, he stares at me from

above the rim. "You did, but I understand why. You should have a little more faith in your family, though."

"You're right. I should. You've always been nothing but supportive, and..."

"And we've been through this before." His attention cuts to Jax. "If Ashlyn can do it, you can, too. Of that, I have no doubt."

Jax shifts in his seat, appearing uncomfortable. I don't need to ask why. Even with the welcoming arms, part of me still wonders if he views himself as the black sheep. The outsider.

Shifting my attention back to Uncle Henry, I murmur, "Thank you."

"You're welcome. Now, let's move on to business. I made some calls," Uncle Henry continues, "and considering the circumstances, the organization thinks you'd be a great fit for the Lions, so we negotiated with the Tornadoes to bring you on. What do you say?"

"I, uh...what did you say?"

"I said we want you to play for the Lions. What do you say?"

Shock. Elation. Confusion. They all battle for the spotlight as I choke out, "Yeah. Yeah, I'd love to. Are you...are you sure?"

"If I wasn't, I wouldn't have made the calls," Uncle Henry returns.

Relief and trepidation wash over me as I register his words and how weighted they really are. The combination is so potent I'm afraid I would've fallen on my ass if I hadn't already been sitting.

"Seems you're staying in Lockwood Heights, Griff. Congratulations."

Seems you're staying in Lockwood Heights.

I'm staying in Lockwood Heights.

I don't have to move.

I don't have to leave Fin.

I don't have to leave the baby.

I get to stay.

I get to stay.

I get to stay.

But that means…

Shifting in my chair, a wave of nausea knots my stomach, and I ask, "What about Ev? Did he…"

Uncle Henry holds my stare as a muscle in his jaw twitches. "Not a miracle worker, but I'm looking at some options."

It's not a no.

It's *not* a no.

I hold onto the glimmer of hope.

"Thank you."

"You're welcome." He taps his knuckles on the coffee table, then turns to Jax. "And speaking of children, have you heard from Rory recently?"

Jax shakes his head. "No, why?"

Uncle Henry sighs. "Tatum put it in her head that they should go to boarding school together next year."

"She's leaving?" Jaxon demands.

"Mia and I are discussing our options. We've tried talking some sense into Rory, but…a fresh start is the only thing we haven't tried yet."

I've heard the rumors. After Rory's brother's death, she's been in therapy and has a tutor to help her keep up with her classmates so she doesn't fall behind. I thought it was going okay, but then she tried to kiss Jaxon, and that's when things went to shit.

"Seems she's pulling away from everyone," Uncle Henry

murmurs. "Including you, Jax. And that was the last thing I would've expected, even after…everything." His attention snaps to my big brother. "If you hear from her, or if she mentions boarding school, will you let me know?"

"Of course," Jax answers.

"Thank you."

CHAPTER FORTY-SIX

FINLEY

It's been a weird week. A good week but a weird one. We came clean to everyone about the baby's paternity. No one even batted an eye. Pretty sure Everett warned them beforehand, but I'm not going to complain. Nope. Instead, I'm going to bask in the lack of drama for once because man, it feels like it's been a lifetime since I haven't felt on edge. If only it lasted longer.

Right now, I'm crabby, I don't feel good, and I want to go home. Or maybe I'm grouchy because the guys are down two to one. The tension is palpable, even from the stands, and I know I have a two-hour drive home after it ends. The Lady Hawks have a game at home, so I'm here with my parents. Griffin's parents are here to cheer him on, too, but they couldn't get seats with us, and I gave up searching for them in the crowd, too distracted by my achy body. If only we weren't losing, then I'd at least have something to be happy about. Now, I just feel…blah.

As Everett heads to the blue line, meeting the waiting ref and the opposing team's center, my dad squeezes my knee beside me.

"Hey, you good?" he asks.

"Crampy, but fine."

He frowns. "You sure?"

"Yeah. I Googled it. It's normal."

"No dizziness?" my mom prods from his opposite side.

I fold at the waist, sneaking a peek at her from around my dad. "No dizziness. Just a little crampy and hungry."

"Want me to grab you a pretzel?" my dad offers.

I shrug. "Maybe after the second period."

With a soft nod, my parents turn back to the game, and I do the same, just in time to watch the puck drop from the ref's fingers. Everett immediately rears his stick back, ready to steal it from the opposing center. Sticks clashing and bodies crashing into the boards, Everett passes the puck to a waiting Reeves.

Suddenly, near the center of the ice, Paulson, a burly defenseman known for his physical play and assholery all game, delivers a hard check to Griffin. With a gasp, I jump to my feet along with the rest of the crowd. Griffin stumbles but quickly regains his footing, turning to face Paulson with a glare I swear could cut through steel.

Shit.

The tension between the two has been building throughout the game since Griffin scored our only point through Paulson's skates during the first period. Now, it looks like it's finally reached a boiling point, and Paulson's pissed.

Without hesitation, Griffin drops his gloves, and Paulson does the same, his gloves hitting the ice with a thud. I used to love this part. And maybe a part of me still does, but the other part? Well, no one likes seeing their boyfriend get hit, even when I know he can hold his own. The game is forgotten. Now, all that matters is my man near the glass, his hands fisted. His expression twisted with fury. The ref's whistle blows, ringing throughout the arena, though I've attended enough games to know it won't do shit.

Nope. These two have been pissing each other off all night. Pressing my hand above my pubic bone, I shift from one foot to the other, ignoring the cramps that've been plaguing me all day, and hold my breath, preparing for an all-out brawl.

Eyes locked with his opponent, Griffin throws the first punch. His right hook glances off Paulson's helmet, and Paulson counters with a jab to Griffin's chest, followed by an uppercut that catches Griff on the chin. The crowd erupts, a mix of cheers and gasps filling the arena, as I cover my mouth.

Ouch. Er, double ouch.

Yup. There's another cramp. I press my hand above my pubic bone as the fight intensifies, both players trading blows with ferocity while I watch from the stands. Then again, it's not like I could join in and rip the two apart, but part of me wants to, just to keep Griffin from getting hurt.

"It's only a game," I whisper under my breath, rising onto my tiptoes in hopes of getting a better view.

Griffin grabs Paulson's jersey, pulling him off balance and landing a solid punch to the side of his head as I hook my arm around my dad's bicep, using him to keep me steady while we watch the chaos unfold. Paulson responds with a flurry of punches to Griffin's midsection, each hit landing with a dull thud, and I wince. Blood trickles from a cut above Griffin's eye, but he doesn't back down as my brother races toward the chaos with the rest of his team.

Yup. We're seconds from an all-out brawl, and I swear I can feel every hit all the way up here in the stands.

My mouth forms a small 'o' as I breathe out another sharp pain above my pubic bone.

Yeah, that one hurt.

The referees, now close enough, step in to separate the two. It takes a few moments, and the help of other players, but they finally manage to pull Griff off Paulson, their faces flushed with exertion and adrenaline.

As the refs escort them to the penalty boxes, the crowd roars with excitement. Griff sits down on the bench, his hands still fisted. He gives Paulson one last glare—the glass separating them not enough to dampen their animosity—then he looks up at the stands, searching for me.

Once he meets my gaze, I mouth, "You okay?" and give him a thumbs up, my brows stitched with concern. When another cramp hits me, I press my hand to my stomach again, fighting the urge to fold in half and vomit all at the same time.

Oof. That was a rough one.

Cramps are normal, I remind myself. They're super normal. But this? This feels...this feels wrong.

Griffin's smirk falls as he stands, looks up at me through the glass, and presses his hands to the see-through barrier separating us.

"Are you okay?" he mouths, holding my gaze across the ice.

My teeth dig into my bottom lip as I force a nod and sit down.

"Fin," my dad murmurs.

Pressing my hands to my thighs, I take a few slow, deep breaths. "I'm fine."

The game resumes, the tension still through the roof, but I don't see any of it. I'm too busy overanalyzing the inconsistent sharp pangs of discomfort cutting through my uterus. This doesn't feel like normal cramps. But if it isn't normal, what does it mean?

"Fin," my dad repeats.

"Baby, you okay?" my mom adds.

"I, uh, I think I need to go to the bathroom."

"I'll come with you."

Clutching my midsection, I hobble to the bathroom, my mom trailing behind. As I close the stall door, my eyes well with tears, and I unbutton my jeans. It's strange. They always talk about mother's instincts, but I've never prayed to be wrong. Not until this moment.

My hands tremble as I slide the thick denim down my legs and sit. Squeezing my eyes shut, I let my head fall forward and let out another slow, cleansing breath.

"Baby?" my mom murmurs outside the stall. I can hear the question in her voice. The hesitancy. The fear.

Forcing my eyes open, I look down at my underwear.

Blood.

There's blood.

It isn't a lot, but it's there.

"Baby?" my mom repeats.

"I'm, uh, just a sec." Resting my elbows on my knees, I pee, telling myself the liquid is only urine as I dig my nails into my hands. Once I'm finished, I grab the toilet paper, ignoring the way my body shakes, and reach between my legs, wiping myself. When I look down, a sob breaks free, and my chest caves.

"Baby," my mom repeats. But the question's gone. The question is fucking gone. How does she know? How does she fucking know?

"It's going to be okay." My mom hesitates, and the sound of rustling fabric hits my ears. "Hey, Mack," she murmurs. She must've called my dad. The realization leaves me even more anxious, but apparently, I'm a glutton for punishment because I only strain my ears more, trying to focus on her conversation with my dad instead of the image of blood on toilet paper ingrained in my memory.

"I need you to get the car. We're going to the hospital." *Pause.* "I'm not sure, but, uh, please hurry. We'll meet you out front."

CHAPTER FORTY-SEVEN

GRIFFIN

Whooshing hits my ears as Finley stands from her seat. The red game clock shines behind her, highlighting the score and my girl's hunched body. Her hand presses into her belly as she scoots past her dad. Uncle Mack says something to Aunt Kate. She nods at him and follows Finley up the concrete stairs. Their movements are slow. Forced. Pained.

My attention darts to Uncle Mack again, waiting to see if he follows. He's a paramedic. He wouldn't leave them alone if he was worried. Would he? He stares at the tunnel the girls disappear through, wiping his palms along his jeans and shifting back into the plastic seat while turning to the ice. It should make me feel better. Maybe she ate some bad food or something. But it doesn't do shit at easing the tightness in my muscles or the pressure in my chest.

The minutes tick by at a snail's pace until the penalty box timer goes off, and the ref opens the door, letting me free. My skates cut through the ice as I head to my position, gripping my stick while trying to get my head back in the game.

When I miss a pass, Coach Sanderson yells, "Thorne! Get your head outta your ass!"

I shake my head and scramble for the puck, but it crosses into the enemy's territory, and I look up at the stands again.

Mack's gone.

Where the fuck is Mack?

Ice sprays against my calves as Ev stops short in front of me. "Hey, you good?"

"Something's wrong." The realization hits like a truck, and makes my heart pound faster and faster with every passing second. Racing to the bench, I barely cast my coach a glance. "Family emergency. I gotta go."

"Thorne," Coach starts, but I don't stop as I rush down the tunnel toward the locker room.

A text with a hospital address is waiting on my phone. Adrenaline buzzing through my veins, I grab my street clothes and start changing when the locker room door slams open, revealing a pissed-off Everett. "What's going on? Where'd my family go?"

"Hospital," I answer as I rip off my jersey and pads.

Ev kicks his ass into gear and opens his locker as the word rolls off my tongue. "Seizure?" he asks.

I shake my head while replaying the image of her hobbling up the steps. "I don't think so."

"Baby?"

Unease twists in my gut as I reach for my T-shirt and shove it over my head. "Just hurry."

"You gonna call your parents?"

I send them a quick text, then jerk my skates off.

I'm coming, Fin.

~

AFTER MEETING MY PARENTS IN THE PARKING LOT, I PUNCH the hospital's address into my GPS, and my dad speeds toward it. My dad drops me off with Everett at the entrance, promising to meet us inside once they find a parking spot. Uncle Mack's waiting for us since Everett had the foresight to give him a heads-up we were on our way.

When he sees us, he motions to his left. "Third door on the right. She just changed."

"Take Griff," Everett offers. "I'll wait for Uncle Colt and Aunt Ashlyn by the entrance."

With a swift nod, Uncle Mack guides me down the hall toward Finley's room. The smell of cleaning supplies hangs in the air, making my nose scrunch.

I haven't been back to a hospital since Finley's seizure. Before that? Archer's passing and Mav's surgery.

I shake off the foreboding feeling and ask, "She okay?"

He squeezes the back of his neck but doesn't answer me immediately, making my pulse race even faster.

"Uncle Mack—"

"She is, yeah."

"And the baby?"

"Not sure yet. We're waiting on the doctor."

It's not a no. I cling to his words.

Not a no.

Relief spreads through me, and I look up at the ceiling, saying a silent prayer of gratitude.

"Not outta the woods yet, Griff," Mack warns. "There's a lot of blood."

A chill races down my spine, and my heels dig into the ground outside the third door on the right.

There's a lot of blood.

She's in there. Anxious. Scared. In pain. Probably going out of her mind with unanswered questions.

There's a lot of blood.

The words haunt me as I stare at the closed door separating me from my everything. Since when is there blood? Did it start during the game? Has it been going on for a while, and she didn't tell me? How can I fix this? I need to fix this. I need to make sure she's okay. That the baby's okay.

"I need to fix this," I voice aloud, though I'm not sure who I'm telling.

Stepping closer, I reach for the door, but Uncle Mack grabs my bicep and stops me. "Sometimes, we can't fix things, Griffin."

My gaze slices to his. He looks…scared. And my Uncle Mack is never scared. He's like a moat. A quiet protector. He surrounds the people he loves, giving them room to grow and to be safe and to fucking thrive. But he's never scared. Not even when Maverick dropped to the ground at a family party last summer. So, what the hell is this?

"Don't say that," I grit out. "Don't tell me I can't fix this."

"I just want to make sure your expectations are where they should be," he warns.

Like a punch to the gut, the air sputters from my lungs. I want to scream. I want to hit something. I want to run into Fin's room and carry her out of here. Far away. Where nothing can touch her. Not even fate. The same familiar burn spreads from behind my eyes to the back of my throat, and I fist my hands at my sides. "What do I do, Mack?" I rasp, looking at Finley's father like he holds all the answers because I sure as hell don't. Not right now. Not in this moment. I feel helpless, and I hate feeling helpless. Like my hands are tied behind my back. Like it doesn't matter what I do, I'm still spiraling. And so is Fin. I need to get to her. I need to…do something. Anything.

"You be the man my baby needs." His voice cracks, and my chest splinters at the sound. Because if Mack is worried? If Mack's worried, then there's something to worry about, and I have no fucking clue if I'm strong enough to handle what's on the other side of this door. My shoulders hunch as if I'm carrying the weight of the world, and maybe I am. Because if Fin's okay, but the baby isn't, I'm not sure how to handle it. If I can handle it. And if Fin's not okay? I won't survive it.

"Go on," Mack mutters. "I'll wait for everyone out here."

My body feels like sandbags are tied to my limbs, but I force myself to move, knocking my split knuckles against the door, then I slowly push it open.

Aunt Kate's sitting in a chair next to the hospital bed. A hospital gown covers Finley, and itchy sheets are spread out along her legs as she talks to her mom over the beeping machines. When Kate's gaze lands on me, Finley follows it, her lips parting on a gasp when she sees me.

"Griff?" Her brows crash together, like she doesn't trust her eyes. "What are you…what are you doing here? What about the game?"

Rushing toward her, I sit on the edge of the bed, careful not to jostle her as I cup her face. "Are you okay, baby?" She looks pale, her gray eyes stormier than normal, her bottom lip trembling before she sucks it into her mouth.

"I, uh,"—a sheen hits her eyes—"I'm gonna go with no. I'm not okay."

Pulling her into me, I hold my broken girl against my chest as her hands twist in my T-shirt.

"Stupid question," I mutter against the top of her head, and she laughs softly.

"Kind of, yeah. But don't worry. I forgive you."

Hot tears seep into the fabric, and I squeeze my eyes shut, hating how lost I feel. How fucking helpless. I hate this. I hate this so fucking much, and I don't know how to fix it.

A soft knock cuts through Finley's quiet sobs, and she lifts her head, turning to the sound. A doctor in a pair of black scrubs stands at the entrance, his expression stoic but unreadable.

"Hello, I'm Dr. Brandish. I hear you're having some cramping and bleeding?" He steps into the room.

Wiping the tears from her face, Finley answers, "Uh, yeah."

"And how long has this been happening?"

"Uh,"—she licks her lips—"the, uh, cramping started a little bit last night but got progressively worse, and the, uh,"—she lets out a slow breath, her body tensing as another cramp hits her—"the bleeding started about..." turning to her mom, Finley gives her a questioning look. "Thirty? Maybe forty-five minutes ago?"

"And how far along are you?" Dr. Brandish prods.

"Um." She presses her fingers into the corners of her eyes, then wipes beneath her nose. "Eleven—"

"Twelve weeks on Tuesday," I finish for her.

Dr. Brandish turns to me. "And you're the father, I assume?"

The question hits as hard as it did the last time we were in a hospital together. When everything was so different, yet I wanted the answer to be the same, regardless. The reminder that whatever perceived control we convince ourselves we possess couldn't be further from the truth is still very present. The realization that our lives, regardless of outcome, are about to be irrevocably changed, and there's nothing I can do about it.

"He is," Finley answers.

The doctor's head bobs up and down. "Well, cramping and a bit of bleeding can be completely normal, but I think it's best if we do an ultrasound to see how everything's going."

Sitting up a little straighter, Finley wipes at her cheeks again. "Uh, okay. Whatever you think would be great."

"Perfect. I'll have a technician come by in a few minutes."

"Thank you," I tell him.

As he disappears, Everett and Macklin step into the room, their shoes squeaking on the linoleum floor.

Hands tucked in his pockets, Everett mutters, "Hey, sis."

"Hey."

"You, uh, you doin' okay?"

A pathetic laugh slips out of her. "I've been better."

"Anything I can do?"

She shakes her head. "Not really, but thanks for coming. You didn't have to miss your game."

"Are you kidding?" He chuckles. "Our asses were getting kicked. At least now I can blame it on our absence and let Reeves take the fall, right?"

The same pathetic laugh pushes past her throat as she dabs at her eyes with the edge of her hospital gown. "Glad I can be of service."

He steps closer and scoops up her free hand, squeezing it softly while plopping down in the last vacant seat. We sit in silence, exchanging worried glances every time Finley bows forward or wrinkles her forehead in discomfort despite the IV plugged into her arm pumping pain meds and fluids. It's more often than I'd like to admit.

Something is definitely wrong.

A few minutes later, a young woman arrives. She's sporting the same stoic expression as the doctor, and it doesn't make me feel any better.

Not gonna lie. I'm scared shitless, and I'd give anything to go back on the ice. To see Finley's big grin up in the stands. To hear Reeves' Game Night ideas. Instead, we're here. Waiting. Helpless. Fucking spiraling at all the potential what-ifs our future may or may not hold anymore. It's torture.

Nah. Even torture is better than this. This…unknown.

"Hi, I'm Beth," she says, introducing herself. "You're far enough along that we don't need to do the ultrasound vaginally, so if you'll lift up your gown, we can get started."

"Aaaand, I'm gonna wait outside," Everett announces. He gives Fin one more squeeze, then heads out the door as Finley's parents look at each other carefully.

Finally, Kate murmurs, "We'll stay or go. Whatever you'd prefer."

"Uh…stay. I guess?" she answers.

"And me?" I prod.

She looks up at me with watery eyes. "Don't you dare think about leaving, or I swear I'll kick you in the balls."

Despite the ache behind my eyes, I smile and kiss her forehead, caught between gratitude and fear. Fear of losing her. Fear of knowing that some things are out of my control even when I'd give anything to fix this. To take away her pain. Her discomfort. Everything.

"All right, then," Beth offers. "I'm ready whenever you are."

"Oh. Right." With a nod, Finley shimmies the gown up but hesitates at the last second and looks up at the ceiling, sucking her lips between her teeth.

"What's wrong, baby?" I murmur.

"Uh…"—she shakes her head—"I can feel the blood…" Her voice cracks, and she bites the inside of her cheek before letting out another slow breath. "I can feel the blood coming out when I move."

"Do you want to use the restroom first?" Beth interjects.

Finley shakes her head back and forth again, her tears falling freely down her cheeks. "I'd rather have an official answer from you first."

The technician's expression falls, and I hate that I see it. The glimpse of pity hidden behind her stoicism. She's seen this before. Probably more times than I can count. Yet here we are, pretending like everything might be fine.

Fin's right. The quicker we do this ultrasound, the quicker we can see past the unknown and grieve or celebrate the way we need to.

A lump forms in my throat as I help Finley lift her gown a little more, noticing the deep crimson stain on the bottom edge of the fabric from where she'd been sitting on it. My hands shake as I move it to the side, covering the blood-soaked splotch with some excess blanket while making sure her stomach stays uncovered in the process so Beth can do what she needs to, and we can get some answers. Grabbing Finley's hand, I thread our fingers together, and bring them to my lips, kissing her soft skin.

Fuck.

Fuck!

I want to hit something. I want to rip the world apart. I want to burn the building to the ground. I want to throw Finley over my shoulder and carry her away. Where she's safe. Where nothing can hurt her. Nothing. But that's the shitty thing about life. It has a way of catching up with you. And I hate how a small piece of me. A piece I don't even want to fucking acknowledge. Already knows the truth.

It's too late.

A burn hits behind my eyes as the technician squeezes some goop onto the wand, then presses it to Finley's bare midsection right above her pubic bone. She drags the screen a little closer to her, keeping it angled away from us while wiggling the wand back and forth in hopes of gaining a clearer picture.

"Is the baby okay?" Finley whispers.

The technician hesitates, refusing to look away from what I assume is a grainy image. Or at least that's what was on the ultrasound last time. Just a grainy, black-and-white picture and the promise of an indescribable future. Fuck, it feels like a lifetime ago. When we were here. Together. Seeing the baby for the first time.

Please be okay.

"The doctor will be in to look at everything and can give you an update," the technician offers.

"Tell me he's okay," Finley pushes. It's a plea.

Without a word, the technician lifts the wand, wipes the goo off with a tissue, and offers one to Finley. It hangs in the air between them as Finley releases a shuddering breath.

"Tell me my baby's okay," she begs.

Reaching for the tissue, I help Finley clean up as the technician leaves the room, and it's all I need to know the truth.

The baby's gone.

Fuck!

CHAPTER FORTY-EIGHT

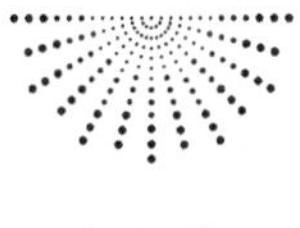

FINLEY

Dr. Brandish promised my epilepsy had nothing to do with it. I want to believe him. I do. But sometimes…sometimes, it sucks. Not knowing. They offered to do a D and C, which is basically a procedure where a doctor goes in and scrapes out your insides while you're under anesthesia. However, thanks to the ultrasound, it didn't look necessary. My body is already doing its job. That's what the doctor said. Like it's normal to *not* carry a baby to term. Like it's normal for a body to abort an innocent human all on its own instead of being a safe haven for an embryo to grow and thrive.

Because that's what a normal body is supposed to do. To protect. To nurture. Not to destroy and discard. The reminder makes my stomach lurch, leaving me nauseated and disgustingly exhausted.

Griffin hasn't left my side.

Neither have my parents.

And I know they love me. I know they want me to be safe and comforted. But there isn't any comfort in this.

I should be happy, right? That's what the little voice

inside my head keeps saying. I should be happy about this. I don't have to be a mom at nineteen anymore. I don't have to put my life on hold.

Instead, I'm heartbroken. Heartbroken and nauseated and crampy and…shit. I need to go to the bathroom again. The pad's already soaked. I swear I've changed it ten times since we made it home and I convinced my parents to give me some space.

They're sleeping in the guest bedroom. Well, sleeping might be a bit of a stretch. I'd bet a thousand dollars they're holed up in there with their ears pressed to the door, waiting and ready in case I need anything.

I should find it sweet. Instead, I find it suffocating.

As I push myself to my feet, Griffin murmurs, "Hey, you okay?"

"Bathroom." Slowly, I waddle toward the bathroom like I'm wearing a fucking diaper. Then again, that's basically what it is, thanks to all the blood. I hate this. I hate this, I hate this, I hate this.

My phone's been blowing up since the game. Everyone was begging for updates, and I was too angry and depressed to give them one, so I asked Griffin to do the honors.

I'm not sure what he said. I've been too terrified to check my phone and see the truth on my screen, but the texts have stopped, and for that, I'm grateful. I should be used to the feeling. Being coddled. Treated like glass. Yet here I am, splintering apart and surrounded by amazing people who are desperate to keep me together, even when it's useless.

I'm not just splintering. I'm fucking shattered.

After I finish using the restroom, I shuffle back into the family room. A murder documentary is on the television, and for the first time since I stumbled onto the genre, it isn't comforting. Actually, it only makes me want to cry more.

Fighting the urge to collapse on the cold, hard ground, I whisper, "Turn it off."

Griffin reaches for the remote, and the screen goes black. When he looks over the back of the couch, his eyes are red-rimmed and bloodshot. The sight cuts me even deeper. Because I'm not the only one hurting. I'm not the only one affected by my stupid, broken body that can't even do what it was made to.

Digging my fingernails into my palms, I bite the inside of my cheek, tasting blood.

"Finley, come here," Griffin urges. "Come sleep."

"You can go home if you want."

"What?" he rasps.

"I said, you can go home. If you want."

"I'm not going anywhere, Fin."

Shaking my head back and forth, I whisper, "You didn't sign up for this."

"Fin—"

"I'm serious," I push, shoving my hair away from my face. "You didn't sign up for this. You should go home and get some sleep. You should—"

"Fin." Standing, he rounds the edge of the couch and reaches for my waist.

I shake my head again, pulling away from him. "I can't…I can't do this. I can't do anything. I can't…"

The words hang in the air, and if he's hurt, he doesn't show it. No, the guy's too perfect for that. He simply looks at me. His hands at his sides. His eyes glassy. His jaw slack.

"I love you, Fin." It's so matter-of-fact. So direct. Like the sky is blue or grass is green. It only breaks me more. My shoulders heave as his words wash over me. "I love you, Fin," he repeats. "Every piece."

Bottom lip trembling, I bite the edge of my lip and whisper, "I love you, too. I just..." I shove my hair away from my face again, tugging at the roots while hoping and praying the sting is enough to distract me from the pain inside of me. The one ripping me to shreds.

"Hey," he coos, grabbing my hand and forcing my fingers to relax so I don't rip my hair out one brutal handful at a time.

He's right. What am I doing?

I slowly shrug out his hold, the tears falling freely as I press my fingers to my lips. "I, uh, I need to get my head on straight."

"I'm here."

I nod. "I know." I hesitate. "Just so you know, I'm not mad at you, okay? I just..."

"I know you're not."

"I know you know, I just..." I lick my chapped lips. "I just need...fuck, I don't even know what I need." My teeth dig into the inside of my cheek, hitting the tender flesh all over again and I tongue the wound, hating myself more and more. "Actually, that's a lie." I squeeze my eyes shut, desperate to ease the deep, sharp, *excruciating* pain inside my chest. "I need my baby, Griff."

He catches me as my legs give out and cradles me against his chest, rubbing his hand along my spine as I sob my eyes out. When he realizes I've gone into full-blown mental breakdown mode, he cradles me to his chest and carries me to my room as I ramble against the column of his throat. "I didn't even want the baby, you know? Not in the beginning. And now?" I claw at his clothes, burying my head against his chest. "Now, I can't believe he's gone. I can't believe I'm not gonna be a mom anymore. I can't believe any of this."

"Sh..." He sits on the edge of my bed and rocks me back

and forth like I'm a child. I'd find it ridiculous if I wasn't falling apart so completely. But dammit, this hurts. It hurts so much. I can't breathe. I can't think. I can't do anything but succumb to the pain and the knowledge that there isn't anything in this world that will take it away.

"I knew my body was broken, you know?" I cry. "I knew I was fucked, but I didn't think…" I sob even harder. "I didn't think it would betray me like this."

"Fuck, Fin." He slips his hands beneath my shirt, splaying his hands along my bare skin as he pulls me even closer. "Your body's perfect, Fin. Every inch of you is perfect."

"It's not, though." My voice cracks. "If it was perfect, I wouldn't have epilepsy. I wouldn't need my medication. I wouldn't have lost the baby." My body shakes in his hold. "I'd still be pregnant, and we'd still be in this together, and—"

"We *are* in this together. Do you hear me, Finley Taylor? I'm not going anywhere." He squeezes me even tighter, practically melding my body against his. "I promise I'm not going anywhere. And I promise we're gonna get through this, okay? You and me."

I let go, my chest wracking with sobs until my throat is raw and my eyelids are heavy.

And then, when it's too much, I slip into oblivion, the steady beat of Griffin's heart lulling me to sleep.

CHAPTER FORTY-NINE

GRIFFIN

I sent a text to everyone when we were at the hospital. Everett helped spread the news, too, offering to stay at the cabin with Raine for the night so Fin could have some space. After Fin fell asleep, I carried her to bed and called my parents. My mom cried. My dad asked if I needed anything. I didn't know what to say. I still don't know what to say.

You be the man my baby needs.

Uncle Mack's words filter through me, acting like a beacon. Like it's the only thing I can hold onto. The only thing I can trust. *Be the man my baby needs.* Fuck, I'm trying. But it's hard. I'm so used to fixing things that not being able to is a special kind of torture. One I wouldn't wish on anyone.

As the morning light slips through the window, a soft knock echoes from the front of the duplex, and I slip my arm from beneath Finley's head. We've been awake for an hour, but she hasn't moved. I think she's afraid to. Afraid she'll see more blood. More evidence of the baby we lost. She scared me last night. Telling me to leave. That I should go home. The words were like a dagger to my sternum, but I know her better than that.

Knock, knock.

My eyes feel like sandpaper as I rub at them and climb out of bed. "You want company today?" I rasp.

Fin shakes her head. "Not today."

With a nod, I step into the hallway and toward the front door. A suit comes into view through the side window, making me freeze until I force my body to move.

The hinges squeak as I open the door. "Uh, hey."

Uncle Henry and Aunt Mia stand on the porch with a bouquet of Gerber daisies.

My chest cracks even more, and I reach for the flowers. "I assume you heard about the baby."

Uncle Henry sighs. "We did."

I give a slow nod, my fingers digging into the edge of the door to keep me from falling on my ass and crying like a little kid.

"Do you mind if I…?" Aunt Mia's voice trails off as she peeks around me toward Finley's room.

"She doesn't want company," I murmur.

"Totally get it. How about I put these flowers in a vase, then we'll be on our way?"

"Uh. Yeah. Sure," I concede.

"Perfect." Aunt Mia slips into the kitchen and begins opening cabinets in search of a vase.

Numb, I turn back to Uncle Henry on the porch. "Thanks for stopping by," I mutter. "I've, uh, I've actually been meaning to call, so…"

"Yeah?" His brows lift in surprise. "About what?"

"About the position," I continue. "Now that, uh, the baby's gone and everything, it looks like you can give Ev the spot, so…"

"Not gonna do that, Griff."

A splinter shoots through my sternum. Or maybe it's always been there. Ever since the hospital. It flares, and I rub at the spot. "Well, you should."

"Not gonna happen," he repeats. "That being said, since you brought up the Lions, I have news, if you'd like to have a conversation?"

I nod, not really giving a shit anymore. Even though hockey was my life before this, now it's only a blip on my radar. Because nothing—and I mean nothing—else matters but the girl holed up in her room, refusing to see anyone.

A heavy strain tugs at my muscles as I glance down the hall. It's second nature. Like a weird tick or some shit. But even though I just climbed out of bed with her, the need to check on her is overwhelming.

"Uh, sure," I offer, forcing myself to keep my feet planted where they are instead of giving in to my compulsion. "Whatever…whatever you want to do."

"I'll keep it quick since you obviously have more pressing concerns on your mind," Henry offers. "Bluntly put, Everett's on the team, too."

My eyes widen. "What?"

"The GM agreed that we haven't seen this kind of synergy on the ice since your dad played with your Uncle Theo. We want both of you playing for the Lions next year."

"I don't…I don't know what to say."

"Say you're not giving up."

I close my eyes. "I'm not giving up."

Grasping my shoulder, he squeezes. "Good man. The more you say it, the more you believe it. We love you, all right?"

I nod, my body heavy, as Aunt Mia returns. Wrapping her arms around my waist, she gives me a hug and kisses my cheek. "He's right. We do love you, and if you need anything, and I mean anything, we're only a phone call away."

If only a phone call could fix this.

Rubbing at my eye's inner corner, I reply, "Thanks, Aunt Mia."

"Anytime."

CHAPTER FIFTY

FINLEY

It's been two weeks. Two long weeks. We met with my obstetrician. He did another ultrasound, confirming I'm healing properly, then reiterated Dr. Brandish's assumption. This had nothing to do with my epilepsy. Not my medication. Not my diagnosis. It was simply…a shitty and really heartbreaking event.

I should feel better. After receiving a confirmation like this. That it was out of my control. That I couldn't have done anything to prevent it. Instead, I bawled my eyes out as Griffin drove us around town, then stopped at a burger place and grabbed me some food. We ate it in the car while listening to *High School Musical*. Pretty sure I've never loved the man more.

I didn't know I could cry this much. Honestly, I'm pretty sure I'm giving Squeaks a run for her money in the waterworks department, but I can't stop.

The smallest things are triggers, too. Like a stupid puppy video or a crosswalk sign next to an elementary school. I hate it. I hate crying. I hate feeling this way. And I hate feeling like no matter what I do, I'll never be happy again.

I know it isn't true. I know this will pass. But then I feel guilty for wanting it to pass. And then I feel scared of potentially getting pregnant again and having to relive this hellish nightmare. I just…I don't know what to do.

Griffin's been amazing. Surprise, surprise. It's been nice, though. Having him as my self-proclaimed shadow. He even missed his last game to be with me. It didn't help with the guilt side of things, but the idea of being without him for a night was more than I could handle.

My professors have been great, giving me a leave of absence. Griffin's are letting him take his classes online, so I don't have to be alone.

It sucks.

Everything sucks.

Everything but me and Griff.

Okay, that's a lie. Our friends and families have been pretty freaking awesome, too. But other than that? I only want to sleep and cry and sleep and cry and snuggle with Griffin and, you guessed it, sleep and cry.

As we pull up to the house, Griffin parks the car and rounds the front, opening my door and offering his hand. Once we're inside, he asks, "Bedroom or couch?"

Covering my yawn, I check the time on my phone, surprised to see it's almost midnight. "Bedroom."

"Okay." He kisses the back of my hand. "I'll be right back."

"What? Where are you going?"

"Give me five."

"Five?" I jut out my bottom lip. "Five seconds? Five minutes? Five hours?"

With a low chuckle, he walks toward the door. "Minutes."

"But it seems like so long," I whine.

Glancing over his shoulder, he gives me his signature lopsided smile, then walks away.

Like a lost puppy, I mosey to my room and collapse on the bed, staring at the ceiling. And that's all it takes. A few seconds of being alone to realize exactly how much I need the guy. He's been sleeping with me every night. Holding me. Making me smile, even if it's for short periods of time. I've almost forgotten what it's like to sleep in my bed alone.

Craning my head, I listen, caught by the quiet thump of…something on the other side of the wall.

My mouth lifts. "Griff?"

The rustling stops, followed by a muffled, "Yeah?"

"Still creepy," I call.

Pause.

"Yeah."

"I miss you."

"Miss you, too, baby."

Baby. Part of me wondered if I'd ever be able to stomach the word again without being bombarded with loss. But when Griff says it? It makes me feel warm and fuzzy and ooey-gooey inside.

Touching my lips, I realize I'm smiling, and it's all because of him. "You coming back or what?"

"I said five minutes," he reminds me through the thin sheetrock.

"Fine, but I'm putting on a timer." I take out my phone and set the clock to three minutes, rounding down for good measure. "Two minutes!" I call once I reach the mark. The seconds tick down, one after another. "One minute!"

The steady *thump thump* of feet greets me seconds later, followed by the squeak of my bedroom door opening, revealing a sexy, half-naked Griffin with a poorly wrapped gift in his hands.

"What's this?"

"It's a present." He offers it to me. When he senses my amusement, he adds, "You'll have to cut me a little slack on the wrap job. Someone was timing me."

Taking in the crumpled paper and skiwampus tape placement, I cock my head and peek up at him, biting back my grin. "Did you wrap it blindfolded?"

"Nah, that's your job, remember?" he quips, referring to our New Year's Eve Game Night.

"Man, that feels like a lifetime ago," I admit.

"Still can't believe you gave me the cheek." He shakes his head in mock disappointment, then sits beside me on the bed.

"Still can't believe you drove me across the country to tell Drew about our little secret."

"Our?" he challenges.

"I think it was always you, even if I didn't want to acknowledge it in the beginning. I mean, even Drew could tell, you know?"

"Yeah." He nudges my hand. "You gonna open it?"

"Depends. What is it?"

With a low laugh, he shakes his head. "Not telling. Open it."

Curious, I slip my finger beneath the crooked tape and unroll the black box from the pink and blue polka dot wrapping paper.

"Griff," I whisper.

"Open it."

I lift the lid and gasp. Inside is a silver necklace with a small circle that has a date stamped on it. My eyes well with tears. It's the day I miscarried. The day I felt like I lost everything. "Griff..."

"You can add the rest of our babies' birthdays as we go."

A tear slips past the corner of my eye, but I don't bother

wiping it away as I replay his sentence. "Rest of our babies?"

"What? You think we'll only have one more?" He chuckles dryly. "Come on, Fin. I think we both know we want at least three."

"Three, huh? That's an awful lot of assumptions you got going there." My mouth lifts, and I look down at the necklace again, realizing there's a second small circle. "What's this?" I flip the medallion around, noting the date. "I'm sorry, is something happening five years from now?"

"Yeah. It's the day I'm gonna marry you."

My heart lurches. "It is?"

"Mm-hmm." He leans closer and kisses my neck.

"What if I'm busy that day? Hmm?"

"I think you can rearrange your schedule."

"And where's the ring?" I challenge, trying not to get too lost in his open-mouthed kisses, especially when we can't have sex for at least another two weeks, but boy, is he making it difficult.

"Ah, you see, it's a secret."

"A secret, huh?"

"Yup." He scrapes his teeth along my throat, and I nearly moan.

"Who says I was okay with you having a secret without me?"

"I mean, I told you the wedding date, and no one else knows that one, so…"

"So that's your loophole?" My brow arches. "You have a secret, and we have a secret?"

"Add it to the list, right?" He kisses along the underside of my jaw and nips at the edge of my lips. "Want to know another secret, Finley Taylor?"

"Hmm?"

"I've never loved anyone else. Not ever. You're the one

for me. And even though the last few weeks have been a bumpy ride, I wouldn't want to be with anyone else. I love you."

"I love you, too."

"That's my girl. Now, let me put this on you."

As I lift my hair from my neck, he takes the simple chain and clasps it around me before pulling me into his arms and kissing me like it's his last. And honestly? I wouldn't have it any other way.

EPILOGUE

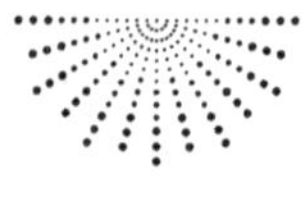

FINLEY

A few months later...

Sometimes, it blows my mind. How fast time can fly, yet drag at the same time. The last three months have been the hardest of my life. I've been in a fog, blindly stumbling through it while juggling classes and friendships and families and work. Now, here we are, in the Bahamas, celebrating the end of spring semester and the boys' graduation. The guys are playing volleyball in the sand while the rest of us soak up the sunshine.

After spreading out a pink and yellow towel between Dylan's and Raine's, I plop down and tug my hair into a messy bun on top of my head.

"Dude, I'm already hot," I point out.

Fiddling with her black bikini top, Raine says, "You and me both. I love it, though."

"Me, too." I lay down and arch my back, stretching out on my towel, when I catch Griffin smirking at me. With a wry grin, I wiggle my fingers at him.

Dylan gags beside me. "He's still my brother, you know."

"And he's still my boyfriend, so, suck it up, buttercup."

"Yeah, yeah, whatever. You're just lucky I left Frankie at home."

A shiver races down my spine as I move onto my stomach and rest my chin in my hands, letting the sun hit my back. "And who's watching your little demon, anyway?"

"Tatum," Dylan answers. She's only half paying attention since her gaze is glued to Reeves' half-naked body as he winds up to serve the volleyball over the net.

Then again, I don't blame her for being distracted. Those boys are creating quite the stir. People are pausing on their walks, watching the friendly game like it's an Olympic sport, and the view isn't too shabby.

Ophelia snorts beside Dylan, stealing my attention. "Then, good luck. Hope you don't mind buying another frog after my little sister starves Frankie."

"Hey!" Dylan tosses some sand at Ophelia.

Laughing, Ophelia squeals, "Hey, watch it!"

"You're the one who joked about my baby's death, thank you very much." She blanches and turns to me. "Shit. I didn't..."

"You're good," I rush out. "I know you didn't mean anything by it."

"I know, but still. It was super insensitive."

Reaching toward her, I grab her knee and move it back and forth. "Seriously, you're fine. I promise. And honestly? It's nice. To just...be here with you guys, you know? The last few months have been a blur, and I'm excited for a fresh start this next year."

"I don't blame you," Raine offers.

"So, how are things?" Ophelia asks.

I shrug. "They're good, I guess. Still weird, but...at least

I don't have anyone telling me it's for the best or my baby's in a better place or any of that other bullshit. Not that it's their fault when they say those things," I add. "But sometimes, I just wish more people would've told me, 'That sucks, and I'm sorry.' You know?"

"After everything went down with Archer, comments like that were so refreshing. Like sometimes life sucks. And there isn't a reason for it. It just…sucks."

"Exactly." I smile at her. "And I had a few months that sucked, is all. But it is what it is and…it is what it is," I repeat.

"And how are you and Griff?" Dylan prods.

"We're good." A smile hits my lips. "Really good, actually."

"I'm glad. Now I can cross you off my worry list," Ophelia replies.

"And who else is on the list?" Raine interjects.

"Let's see…" Tapping her finger against her chin, Ophelia rattles off names like they're confetti. "Rory, Jaxon, Tatum, and…not you anymore." She gives me a smile. "Thank goodness."

"Glad I can be of service," I quip. "But what's wrong with Jax?"

"Technically, nothing, but he's worried about Rory, who's basically blacklisted the poor guy, and therefore, I'm worried about both of them," Ophelia admits. "At least I don't have to put up with him during practice anymore. He was always checking his phone and asking me to ask Mav for updates and stuff. Honestly, it was sweet. Like he was a big brother and just wanted to make sure she was okay. The problem was, Rory explicitly told me and Mav that we're not allowed to even utter her name to Jaxon anymore, which made things"—she grimaces—"a little tricky."

"Rory's still MIA?" I prod.

"Not literally," Dylan answers. "But from what I heard, the girl is either at school or in her room twenty-four-seven, so…"

"Yeah, you aren't the only one who fell off the face of the earth for a little while. Not to mention Tatum," Lia adds.

"Where is Tatum?" Dylan interjects. "I'm pretty sure I haven't seen her since we went to Rowdy's and she bailed."

"Yeah…" Ophelia leans closer before glancing at the guys still immersed in their volleyball game. Confirming we don't have any eavesdroppers, she adds, "After being suspended for drawing a penis in her school's auditorium, she convinced my parents to ship her off to a year-round boarding school."

"What?" I screech. "I mean, don't get me wrong. I know I've been a little preoccupied, but seriously? When did this happen?"

"Two weeks ago," Ophelia answers. "And don't worry, I was going to tell you—"

"Good because I'm a sucker for some juicy gossip, and this is gold." I laugh. "Also, what do you mean she convinced your parents? Isn't boarding school usually a threat the parents make to keep their kids in line?"

"Are you kidding?" Ophelia laughs. "My parents have been begging Tatum to open up to them for almost a year now. The idea of shipping her off is literally the last thing they want."

Putting myself in Aunt Blakely and Uncle Theo's shoes, I sober slightly, drawing Tatum's name in the sand. "Maybe it'll be good for her, though," I offer. "A fresh start. Fresh faces."

"Maybe," Ophelia mutters. "Rory's begging to go, too, but Mav's parents haven't given in yet."

Dylan pulls her knees to her chest, her eyes wide. "No shit?"

"Yup." Ophelia pops the p at the end. "Bet you twenty bucks she'll be there next year, though."

"Why?" I ask.

"Any excuse to be as far away from Jax as possible."

"And I repeat, why? Don't get me wrong. I get it. I get why she's embarrassed and stuff, but like…it was one rejection from a guy who would be in jail if he returned it in the first place, so…"

"Exactly," Raine murmurs.

"Besides," I continue. "Squeaks is gorgeous. If she could just let her silly crush go and move on, she'd realize there are other guys out there who are her age who would treat her like gold."

"Yeah, and they'd be lining up in an instant to have a shot with her," Raine adds.

Brushing off the sand from the edge of her blanket, Dylan chimes in, "True. But to be fair, I get it. Rory might not be as shy as I was when I met Reeves, but she has to be feeling like a lost puppy at this point. She followed my brother everywhere, and now…"

"Now, she feels like she has no one," Raine realizes.

"No one but Tatum," Ophelia finishes. "My parents said Rory's the only person Tatum talks to. Not like it's a daily thing or whatever, but still. That's why I think Rory's going to wind up at the same school. Maybe they can be room-mates or something."

Raine shrugs. "I guess we'll have to wait and see."

"That's gotta kill Aunt Mia and Uncle Henry, though," I point out. "Rory's all they have left, and after Archer's death, they have to be hesitant to let Rory live across the country."

"True," Dylan murmurs. "But I also think they're even more anxious to see their daughter heal, you know?"

I nod. "Yeah. I get it."

"Me, too," Raine adds.

Ophelia drags her fingers along the edge of the towel. "Me, too."

"We should get in the water," Dylan decides. She peeks at her bare shoulders growing pinker and pinker with every passing second. "I'm roasting."

On a laugh, Ophelia repeats, "Me, too. Come on." She stands, wiping the sand off of her, and offers her hand to pull me up.

As I take it, she yanks me to my feet, and I grab Dylan's hand on my opposite side. Catching onto the trend, Dylan loops her arm through Raine's, and we all race toward the water's edge, our feet digging into the sand with every hurried step. Cold water licks at our ankles within seconds, but we don't stop there. Instead, I yank everyone further into the waves until the last thing I hear is Dylan's protests.

"My glasses!" Her words are swallowed by the water as I tug us under. Warm, salty ocean envelops us in an instant. When our heads break the surface, laughter ensues, and it's music to my freaking ears.

"Pickles!" Someone yells. "My pickles!"

What the hell?

I look over at the guys, finding Reeves jogging toward us.

"Dude, we're in the middle of a game," Everett calls from behind him.

"Gotta avenge my girlfriend first!"

"Ah, hell." Griffin drops the volleyball and chases after him, kicking up sand with his footsteps. Gotta give the man credit. He's good at knowing when he's needed, and given the fake death glare Reeves is directing at me, I'm gonna say I could use Griffin's protection.

Dodging Griffin's pursuit, Reeves argues, "This doesn't concern you!"

"My girlfriend. My concern." He lunges for Reeves again, both of them laughing as they play a game of tag like a couple of kids.

"I'm only gonna splash some salt water in her eyes. That's all," Reeves quips.

"Yeah, and I'm only gonna make you eat a little bit of sand," Griff volleys back.

Giving Dylan the side-eye, I ask, "Do you think they'll ever grow up?"

"Says the girl who just dragged me into the water," Dylan counters.

"Touché." I cup my hands around my mouth. "Hey, boys!"

"Yeah?" they return in unison.

"How 'bout we settle this like grown adults."

Reeves must be intrigued by my suggestion because he stops his little game of tag with Griffin and crosses his arms, his biceps bulging. Not gonna lie. He's a good-looking dude, but the poor bastard doesn't hold a candle to the man next to him. Yup. Griffin Thorne has my whole heart, and I'm not sure there's anything I could've done to stop him from stealing it. Not that I would've, mind you. He's pretty freaking perfect, and despite the last few months we've endured, I wouldn't have wanted to survive it with anyone else.

Sporting a lopsided grin making my chest swell every single time it's directed at me, Griffin prods, "Go on."

Oh. Right.

"How 'bout a chicken fight?" I suggest. "Me and Griff

against Reeves and Dylan. First girl to land in the water loses."

"Hey, I wanna play!" Lia interjects. "Mav! Ev! Get down here!"

"You sure you wanna go against me and Ev?" Raine teases beside her.

With a wink, Lia replies, "Yeah, I think I can take you."

The waves lap at our waists as the boys race toward us like a group of water buffalos, the ocean splashing around them with every step. Okay, describing them as water buffalos is probably a little dramatic. Pretty sure they could star in Baywatch, thanks to their rippling muscles and sunkissed skin, though there's no need to inflate their egos even more than they already are. But, I digress. Reeves reaches us first. Wrapping his arms around Dylan's waist, he tackles her into the water like he's a professional linebacker, and I squeal with laughter.

Okay, now that was funny.

When she comes up sputtering a few seconds later, she slaps his shoulder and wipes at her eyes. "Oliver freaking Reeves! I thought you were coming to avenge me, not replicate the reason for avenging!"

Throwing his head back, Reeves's chest rumbles with amusement. "Sorry, Pickles. I saw an opportunity, and I took it."

"Of course you did," Dylan glares at him, her glasses askew, but the wide smile she's sporting doesn't exactly help her case. "Now, get over here so I can climb on your shoulders."

"And here I thought I'd climb on yours." His bottom lip juts out in a mock frown.

"Whatever." Rolling her eyes, Dylan pats his shoulders and tries to shove him down, but he barely budges. "Oh, come on," she begs.

Giving in, he crouches down so she can climb onto him as Griffin moves toward me.

Wrapping his arms around my waist, he pulls me in for a hug, and I lift my chin, kissing him softly before my attention cuts to Reeves. "And that's how you treat a lady."

"Lady." He scoffs. "You do know we're talking about Finley, right?"

I flip him off, and he laughs even harder. "Yeah, yeah. Whatever, Fin. Come on. We're about to take you down. Ain't that right, Pickles?"

"Bring it on," Dylan says.

With a smirk, I turn back to Griff. "You know, I almost feel sorry for them."

"Me, too." He glances at the couple while the rest of our friends prepare for their own chicken war a few feet away. "Sorry, little sister, but we're not gonna go easy on you, so if you want to surrender now, we completely understand."

Dylan's jaw drops. "Who said you need to go easy on me?"

"I once saw you trip over nothing," I point out. "You weren't even walking. You just…fell over like a dead tree."

With a low laugh, Reeves squeezes Dylan's calf and cranes his neck back so he can look up at her as she sits on his shoulders, and I'm not going to lie. The adoration in the man's gaze is adorable as hell.

"It's okay, Pickles. I won't let them win," he promises.

Her face scrunches. "Yeah, well. Neither will I."

"Sure, you won't," Ophelia calls, pointing to me. "Enjoy beating her because after I take care of Raine, you and I are gonna tango, missy."

"So much talking, so little fighting," Raine interjects from on Everett's shoulders. He widens his stance and motions for Ophelia and Maverick to bring it on.

It's ridiculous and silly, and I'm not gonna lie. I love it.

The banter. The sass. The camaraderie. It just might be my favorite thing in the world.

Warm hands hit my waist as Griffin steals my attention. I can see the question in his eyes. The silent check-in. Am I good? It's what he's asking. I nod and lift my chin again, waiting for a kiss. When he meets me halfway, I close my eyes and bask in the gentle brush of his lips against mine, knowing it'll never get old. This. Me. Him. Surrounded by family and friends.

I didn't know if I'd ever feel this way again. Light. Happy. At home. I didn't even think it was possible.

And honestly, maybe I never would've felt this way again. Without Griffin's push. Without my family's support. And it makes me grateful. So damn grateful. That I have these people in my life. People who make me smile. Who make me laugh. Who put up with my bullshit without batting an eye.

And even though there are dark days, and I have no doubt there will be many more in my future, it's moments like this, surrounded by loved ones, when I realize it's still worth it. This life. The bumpy ride. The earth-shattering moments. Because if I have this, then it's enough.

It will always be enough.

And I hope one day, my future children will be able to find the same thing. A support system. A family. A home they can take with them across the world.

But for now? For now, I'm going to bask in the sunshine with my best friends while we play a ridiculous game in the warm ocean and balmy summer breeze.

"All right, Griff." I pat his shoulder, and he squats down so I can climb onto them. "You and me. Let's do this."

"You read my mind."

HIJACKED EPILOGUE

TATUM

A few years later...

"Seriously, I cannot believe you did this," I muse.

"It's your birthday, and you're my best friend," Rory reminds me. "I literally had to do this."

She didn't, but I appreciate her thoughtfulness nonetheless.

I kind of hate my birthday. I kind of hate a lot of things, but I especially hate my birthday. It's another reminder that a year has passed and he's still gone. To be fair, a lot of things remind me of Archer Buchanan's absence. Specific dates. Holidays. Smells. Books. Honestly, my birthday is pretty low on the totem pole, all things considered. Doesn't make it easier, though.

Slipping out of the Uber, I hook my arm through my best friend's, who also happens to be Archer's younger sister, and peer up at the venue. Rough brick exterior with glowing windows peppered across the front. Music echoes through the air. The band must've already started playing. Tilting my head, I listen to the familiar beat while the scent

416

of weed mixes with the beer and sweat clinging to the air. Not a great combination, but I won't complain. There are so many people here. They crowd the front of the building, creating a long line from the main entrance out to the dark road. This is insane. The energy really sells the place, though. Hell, it's electric. I bite the inside of my bottom lip to keep from grinning like a full-blown lunatic.

"See? I knew you'd love this," Rory adds.

"Who are we seeing?" I ask. "Because it kind of sounds like…" I pause, listening to the muffled, almost-familiar chorus filtering from the building.

"Like…your favorite band?" Rory finishes for me.

My jaw drops, and I stop midstep, twisting my best friend to face me fully. "Are you serious?"

"Maybe."

With a squeal, I grab Rory's biceps and jump up and down. "You have no idea how excited I am!"

"I thought you might be," she laughs.

"Are they headlining?" I hesitate. "What am I saying? Of course, they aren't headlining. Doomsday isn't big enough for that. If they were, I'd know about it. Who are they opening for?"

Looking down at the ground, she kicks a pebble with her sneakers. "Well, uh, IndieCent Vows, actually, but…"

My brows pull down, and she peeks up at me.

"Don't worry. I didn't call in any favors, if that's what you're thinking," she rushes out. "We can even slip out before Dodger and the guys take the stage if you're really worried about it. But it's your twenty-first birthday, Tate, and Doomsday is your favorite. I would've made this happen even if they were playing in a ditch across the world."

She's right. She would've. Rory's sweet like that. Thoughtful. Caring. Maybe even a little self-sacrificing to a fault, if I'm being totally honest. She's the opposite of me in every way, and I couldn't be more grateful. Honestly, I can barely stand my own presence most days. Having two of me in a friendship? Yeah, we'd kill each other.

Lips pursed, I push, "You promise you didn't call in any favors?"

"Promise. I even got the tickets on a shady site instead of calling Raine or Dodge to get them for free, so if my credit card info is stolen, it's all your fault."

With a laugh, I loop my arm through Rory's and walk us toward the entrance, grateful our whereabouts are still hidden from my family, thanks to a shady website and Rory's bravery. "Come on. It sounds like they're already playing."

"Yeah, because *someone* couldn't get her butt in gear at the hotel."

"When you said our activity started at seven, I thought you meant it in a it-starts-at-seven-but-the-cool-kids-show-up-at-nine kind of thing."

"No, I meant it in a get-your-butt-in-gear-because-we're-going-to-miss-your-favorite-band-if-we-aren't-on-time-but-I-don't-want-to-ruin-your-birthday-present-so-I'm-trying-to-play-it-cool kind of thing."

My mouth lifts. "You've ruined nothing. And thank you."

"You're welcome."

Let me be clear. I have nothing against IndieCent Vows. Actually, their music is pretty awesome, but the main singer, Dodger Anders, is the older brother of Raine Anders, and Raine Anders is best friends with my older sister, and well, let's just say, the connection is a little too close for comfort when I haven't had an actual conversation with my sister in who knows how long, and I'd like to keep it this way. It isn't personal, it's just… Oh, who am I kidding? Of course, it's personal. It's Ophelia. The one person who's shadow I'll never be able to step out of. Like a piece of hot coal, my phone burns a hole in my purse, acting as a reminder of the unanswered text Ophelia sent wishing me a happy birthday.

I shake off the mental intrusion as we open our purses for security, walk through the metal detector, and head toward the ushers scanning tickets.

After Rory shows the tickets to an old man with a bushy white mustache, he says, "ID please."

"ID?" Rory squeaks.

The bored expression vanishes from the usher's face, and he looks us up and down with newfound interest. "This is a twenty-one and older venue."

Well, shit.

Without a word, Rory stands there like a deer in the headlights, so I move closer.

"I'm sorry, it's what?" I answer for her.

"A twenty-one and older venue," he repeats. His eyes bounce from me to Rory, then back again. "Do you have IDs?"

"Oh. Uh. Yes, but, uh… One second." Red hits Rory's cheeks as she fumbles in her purse for her ID, her hands shaking more and more with every passing second. I don't blame her. The line is building behind us, and it doesn't matter how long she tries to stall, her ID still won't magically show an earlier birthdate than the one I know it sports. Even though it's my twenty-first birthday, Rory won't be eighteen for another two months.

"You know what? I need to pee," I announce. "We'll be right back." Reaching for Rory's fumbling fingers, I drag us away from the line and back toward the curb in front of the building.

"Tatum, I am so sorry," Rory squeaks. Tears fill her eyes,

and she dabs at the corners, careful not to ruin her makeup. "I swear, I had no idea!"

"Rory, breathe." With a light laugh, I roll my eyes. Not because it's fun to watch my best friend cry, but because if she didn't shed a tear or two by the end of the night, I'd be convinced she'd had her body snatched by an alien or something. "Seriously, Rore. Breathe," I tell her.

"Yeah, but it's your birthday, and I was trying to surprise you, and—"

"Trust me. I'm very surprised."

"Don't be a smartass." Her bottom lip wobbles. "But like, since when are there twenty-one and older venues?"

I bite the inside of my cheek in hopes of keeping my smartassery at bay and gently reply, "Since...forever?"

Her eyelids fall closed, and a tear rolls down her cheek, slipping past her defenses. I'd tell her to stop crying, but Rory's Rory, and there's a reason the family calls her Squeaks. The girl's been a tear factory since birth. Puppy commercial? She cries. Old couple at a fast-food restaurant sharing French fries? Let me get her a tissue. Got a B on a test? Cue the waterworks, people.

Even though she hates that particular trait, I find it... endearing, almost. And reliable. I can always count on Rory Buchanan to *feel*. Meanwhile, people describe me as an ice queen most days. I'm not complaining. I'd rather keep my emotions in check than let them air out at the drop of a hat. But I digress. I should've expected this. Something messing up my birthday. The venue is for guests twenty-one and older. We're not allowed inside.

Of course, we aren't.

Grabbing her shoulders, I force her to face me. "Rory, I'm teasing. You're totally fine."

"No, I'm not," she squeaks. "I feel so stupid!"

"It could've happened to anyone."

Her bottom lip juts out even more, and she wipes at her cheeks. "I ruined your birthday."

"You didn't ruin anything," I argue. Determined to fix the situation just to stop my friend's tears from falling, I scan the venue in search of…I don't know. A solution, maybe? And then, it hits me.

I grin. "Come on. I think I have a plan."

Keeping myself in full-alert mode, I sneak around the edge of the massive building to a large metal door. If it's unlocked, we can sneak inside and no one will know. It'll be perfect.

"Tatum," Rory seethes behind me, realizing my intentions. "Tatum, this is a bad idea."

I keep my head down, scanning the small alleyway one more time. Reaching for the door handle, I confirm it's locked with a quick twist of my wrist. "Shit."

"Did you really think they'd leave it open?" Rory argues.

Peeking over my shoulder, I find Rory with her arms crossed and her head cocked in challenge.

Who's the smartass now?

Holding her gaze, I knock my knuckles against the thick steel.

She gasps. "You did not just knock."

"I think I did."

"What if someone answers?" she screeches while trying to keep her voice down as she glances over her shoulder toward the crowded front.

"Then someone answers." I turn back to the solid door and make a fist, preparing for another round of knocking when the door pulls open, and a blond guy appears with a cigarette dangling from his mouth.

Well, shit.

I jerk back, nearly running into a stunned Rory behind me. Not gonna lie. The guy's built like a god. Broad shoulders. Strong arms. A black shirt hugs his biceps, and light reflects off his warm, coffee-colored eyes and tan skin.

Did my tongue just grow three times its original size? I think—yup—it totally did. He's...well, he appears to be a surfer-boy with a side of bad decisions, and the tattoos etched onto his forearm are enough to make a girl like me fall to my knees and worship the bastard right here, right now. That is, if I didn't have my best friend three feet away from me, and I wasn't already on a mission to sneak into the place.

Catching the unlit cigarette in his hand, the stranger scans us up and down before his eyes cut to the front of the building, his brows pulled low in confusion. "What are you—"

"We're with the band," I rush out, snapping myself out of whatever daze his annoyingly gorgeous face put me in. But seriously. This guy is something else entirely.

"Uh, Tate?" Rory starts.

"I've got this," I promise her while holding the security guard's intimidating gaze. "Like I said, we're with the band, so..."

His brows lift. "The band."

"Yeah. We've actually been knocking for a solid fifteen minutes. I came out for a smoke, and the door locked behind us, and..." I paste on a syrupy sweet smile and hook my thumb toward the propped open door. "Do you mind?"

His eyes roll over my body again. "Which band?"

"Doomsday," I answer. "Obviously."

"Obviously." His mouth twitches, though I'm not sure why he's so amused by our conversation.

"Tate," Rory repeats from behind me.

Ignoring her, I say, "Are you security or something? Because we left our backstage passes inside, so..."

Now or never, Tatum, I silently remind myself. *Ask for forgiveness, not permission.*

"You'll have to excuse us," I continue. "We need to at least catch the second half of the set." Stepping forward, I start to scoot past him in an attempt to act like I own the place. Like I belong. Like I most definitely am not trespassing in hopes of easing my friend's guilt over not reading the fine print when she's the queen of following the rules.

The guy doesn't budge. His big, rock-hard body blocks the entrance, barely leaving any space for me to move past him. The problem is, I'm in too far to turn back now, so where does this leave me?

Keep going.

I continue my quest to enter, but the stranger grips the edge of the door, blocking my entry while somehow keeping us chest-to-chest.

All right, so he's not so easy to bulldoze. Good to know.

My gaze flicks up to him. "Is there a problem, Mr. Security?"

"You under eighteen?"

"Do I look under eighteen?"

He checks me out again and scratches his jaw with his free hand. When his gaze reaches my face, he shrugs. "Looks can be…deceiving."

I roll my eyes. "No, I'm not under eighteen."

His brow quirks. "Under twenty-one?"

"As of today, not anymore," Rory chimes in from behind me. "It's her birthday."

Keeping his focus on me, he murmurs, "Your birthday, huh?"

"Twenty-one years young," I answer.

"Happy birthday."

His coffee eyes swallow me whole, and my stomach flips. "Why, thank you."

"How long have you been with Doomsday?"

Doomsday. Right.

Sucking my lips between my teeth, I hold his gaze and mentally play out my options. Clearly, he's onto us. But I think he might have a thing for me—or at the very least, he's curious. Which swings the situation in our favor. However, I'd prefer it if he didn't escort us to Doomsday's dressing room, since I most definitely have never met anyone from the band. But getting inside the building is key if we want to actually watch Doomsday play tonight, so...

"Cat got your tongue, Birthday Girl?" he challenges.

"You know, usually, the security team isn't quite this chatty," I point out. "But if you don't let us in, Cooper will be sorely disappointed by our absence, especially when he's already on stage. I'm sure you don't want that, do you?"

"Cooper does love his toys," he agrees, repeating Doomsday's lead singer's name. His attention falls to my mouth as he lets the edge of the door go and pushes it open a little more, giving me space to slip beneath his toned bicep and forearm. As I move past him, my nipples brush against his chest. My lips part on instinct.

Well, shit. It's like my body registers the friction before my brain has a chance to catch up and shut down. Or at the very least, hide my response. But nope. This stranger gets to witness it first-freaking-hand.

Fantastic.

"Now, if you'll excuse me..." I wave behind my lower back, silently encouraging Rory to get her butt in gear. Like the obedient girl she is, she plays along without hesitation. As soon as I'm inside, Rory darts through the door, her fingers twisting in front of her. The question is…where do we go from here?

"You sure you know where you're going?" the security guard asks as if he's reading my thoughts.

"Yup." I peek toward both ends of the hallway, debating which way to go. It's a fifty-fifty chance. Left or right.

Come on, Tate. Pick one.

Left, it is.

I take a step toward the drum beat, praying it leads to where we're supposed to go.

"That's where the audience is," Mr. Security offers.

I freeze and peek back at him.

"Don't you want to be backstage with your boy toy?" he asks.

Yeah, that's probably where a groupie would be, isn't it?

Keeping my expression on lockdown, I counter, "I thought I was *his* toy, not the other way around. You know, since you said Coop likes his toys and all."

"Call it a hunch, but I have a feeling you're good at keeping boys like Coop wrapped around your finger."

He isn't wrong. I'm a sucker for leading guys on without giving in. Okay, sometimes I give in but not always. It depends on where my head is and how close I am to the anniversary of Archer's death. Call me a fickle bitch, but it is what it is.

"Cooper will find me after the set," I lie. "He likes the chase."

With a smirk, he folds his arms across his chest. "Don't we all."

My lips purse. "Have a good night, Mr. Security." Giving him my back again, I grab Rory's hand and start leading us a little further down the hall when a two-hundred pound linebacker in a black shirt rounds the corner.

Another one? Seriously? It's like we're trying to break into the Pentagon or something.

When he sees us, his gaze narrows, making my heart thrum faster as I weigh my options. Okay, we can run, or we can…continue lying out our asses and potentially be arrested for trespassing. Not the best way to celebrate my birthday, but hey. At least it'll be memorable, right? And I sure as shit am not backing down now, since we've made it this far.

"Hey!" the behemoth calls. "What are you—"

"They're with the band," Mr. Security announces from behind me.

The linebacker's attention snaps to him. "You sure they're legal?"

"Checked their IDs and everything," Mr. Security confirms. Listening to him lie through his teeth to protect me is kind of…hot. Or maybe I just haven't been laid recently.

"Of course." The linebacker's head dips. "Would you like me to escort them to—"

"I've got it," Mr. Security tells him.

"Sure thing, Pax."

Pax.

So he has a name. Interesting.

Part of me wants to face Mr. Security again, simply to taste his name while analyzing whether or not I find it fitting, but I don't want to push my luck. Not tonight, anyway.

"They're waiting for you," the linebacker adds.

"Just like always, am I right, Herb?" Mr. Security tosses back at him.

I can feel Mr. Security's footsteps over the thrumming music a few walls away. I shouldn't be able to, but I do.

Hell, maybe it's my imagination. But it doesn't change anything.

Step. Step. Step.

He's coming closer.

Before I can overthink it, I grab Rory's hand, then race along the corridor and past the linebacker. "Thank you!" I yell as our feet slap against the concrete floor. When we reach the arena, my heart is still racing. I slow to a walk and sneak us into the mosh pit near the front of the stage. All things considered, it's shockingly easy, especially compared to our efforts since I knocked on the metal side door.

Once we're past security, Rory announces, "You're insane."

I grin back at her. "You know you love me. And thank you for the tickets," I add, glancing at the now-empty stage, "even though we missed Doomsday. This is amazing."

"It's memorable, I'll give you that much," she grumbles.

She's not wrong.

And even if it was unintentional, sneaking into the concert and flirting with a cute security guard is giving me a high like no other. Basking in it, I listen to Rory chatter on about her plans this upcoming year and all the amazing things she's planning to do. I have no doubt she will. The girl has the power to do anything she wants in this world. She's smart. Beautiful. And has more connections than the Queen of England, thanks to her family's fortune.

I'm not sure how much time passes before I turn back to the stage just in time to watch IndieCent Vows take their places. Or at least, that's who I assume is up there. The only one I know is… There he is. Dodger Anders. We've never met. I've been cultivating distance from all things Lockwood Heights since long before Archer's death. But Rory, not so much. As long as no one brings up anything to do with Jaxon Thorne, she's an open book. This includes my family, her family, and all of their friends, including Dodger's parents.

I study the man standing in the middle of the stage. Curly, light brown hair cut close on the sides and longer on the top. Freshly-shaven face to show off his chiseled jaw. Strong biceps and veined forearms as he cradles the mic. And the voice of a fucking angel, though he isn't singing at the moment. Nope, he's making a smartass comment about their guitarist being MIA, when a man with sandy blond hair appears. His head is tilted down as he tinkers with his sleek black guitar. When he lifts his head and smiles at the crowd, my jaw drops.

Well, if it isn't Mr. fucking Security.

What are the odds?

Rory laughs beside me, clutching her stomach as her body threatens to topple over. Ripping my stare from the Adonis on stage, I glare at my best friend.

"You knew?" I screech.

"Of course, I knew! I tried to tell you when we were outside, but noooo," she drags out through bouts of laughter. "Someone had to be a know-it-all and fix things without my help, now, didn't you?"

Shaking my head, I turn back to the stage as Mr. Security's long fingers begin plucking at the strings.

Damn.

ALSO BY KELSIE RAE

Kelsie Rae tries to keep her books formatted with an updated list of her releases, but every once in a while she falls behind.

If you'd like to check out a complete list of her up-to-date published books, visit her website at www.shopauthorkelsierae.com/

Or you can join her newsletter to hear about her latest releases, get exclusive content, and participate in fun giveaways.

Interested in reading more by Kelsie Rae?

The Little Things Series

(Steamy Don't Let Me Next Generation Series)

(Steamy Contemporary Romance Standalone Series)

A Little Complicated - Maverick and Ophelia's Story

A Little Tempting - Reeves and Dylan's Story

A Little Jaded - Everett and Raine's Story

A Little Secret - Griffin's and Finley's Story

A Little Broken - Tatum and Paxton's Story

A Little Crush - Jaxon and Rory's Story

Harden Heights Series

(Steamy Contemporary Romance Standalone Series)

Coming Fall 2025

Jagger's Story

Ford's Story

Hawke's Story

Roman's Story

Don't Let Me Series

(Steamy Contemporary Romance Standalone Series)

Don't Let Me Fall - Colt and Ashlyn's Story

Don't Let Me Go - Blakely and Theo's Story

Don't Let Me Break - Kate and Macklin's Story

Let Me Love You - A Don't Let Me Sequel

Don't Let Me Down - Mia and Henry's Story

Wrecked Roommates Series

(Steamy Contemporary Romance Standalone Series)

Model Behavior - River and Reese's Story

Forbidden Lyrics - Gibson and Dove's Story

Messy Strokes - Milo and Maddie's Story

Risky Business - Jake and Evic's Story

Broken Instrument - Fender and Hadley's Story

Signature Sweethearts Series

(Sweet Contemporary Romance Standalone Series)

Taking the Chance

Taking the Backseat (novella)

Taking the Job

Taking the Leap

Get Baked Sweethearts Series

(Sweet Contemporary Romance Standalone Series)

Off Limits

Stand Off

Hands Off

Hired Hottie (A *Steamy* Get Baked Sweethearts Spin-Off)

Swenson Sweethearts Series

(Sweet Contemporary Romance Standalone Series)

Finding You

Fooling You

Hating You

Cruising with You (A *Steamy* Swenson Sweethearts Novella)

Crush (A *Steamy* Swenson Sweethearts Spin-Off)

Advantage Play Series

(Steamy Romantic Suspense/Mafia Series)

Wild Card

Little Bird

Bitter Queen

Black Jack

Royal Flush (novella)

Stand Alones

Fifty-Fifty

Sign up for Kelsie's newsletter to receive exclusive content, including the first two chapters of every new book two weeks before its release date!

Dear Reader,

I want to thank you guys from the bottom of my heart for taking a chance on A Little Secret, and for giving me the opportunity to share this story with you. I couldn't do this without you!

I would also be very grateful if you could take the time to leave a review. It's amazing how such a little thing like a review can be such a huge help to an author!

Thank you so much!!!

-Kelsie

ABOUT THE AUTHOR

Kelsie is a sucker for a love story with all the feels. When she's not chasing words for her next book, you will probably find her reading or, more likely, hanging out with her husband and playing with her three kiddos who love to drive her crazy.

She adores photography, baking, her two pups, and her cat who thinks she's a dog. Now that she's actively pursuing her writing dreams, she's set her sights on someday finding the self-discipline to not binge-watch an entire series on Netflix in one sitting.

If you'd like to connect with Kelsie, subscribe to her Patreon. Patrons receive a wide range of goodies including:

- Exclusive sneak peeks of works-in-progress
- ebook releases one week early
- Special edition signed paperbacks on all new releases
- So much more...

You can also sign up for her <u>newsletter</u>, or join <u>Kelsie Rae's Reader Group</u> to stay up to date on new releases and her crazy publishing journey.